Enid Blyton's

THE MYSTERY
OF HOLLY LANE

THE MYSTERY
OF HOLLY LANE

First published in Great Britain 1955
by Methuen & Co. Ltd
This edition first published 1991 by Dean
an imprint of the Hamlyn Publishing Group
Published 1996 by Mammoth
an imprint of Reed International Books Ltd
Michelin House, 81 Fulham Road, London SW3 6RB
and Auckland, Melbourne, Singapore and Toronto

Reprinted 1996, 1997

ISBN 0 7497 1978 8

A CIP catalogue record for this title
is available from the British Library

Printed and bound in Great Britain
by Cox & Wyman Ltd, Reading, Berkshire

CONTENTS

1   OFF TO MEET FATTY

'BETS—don't gobble your porridge like that!' said Mrs.Hilton. 'There's no hurry, surely!'

'Well, there is, Mother,' said Bets. 'I've got to go and meet Fatty's train this morning. Have you forgotten that he's coming home to-day?'

'But he's not arriving till the middle of the morning, is he?' said her mother. 'There's plenty of time. Please don't gobble like that.'

'I expect Bets wants to go and lay a red carpet down for Fatty, and get a band to play to welcome him,' said her brother Pip, with a grin. 'That's what you're in a hurry about, aren't you, Bets? Got to go and round up the band and see that all their instruments are polished!'

'Don't be so *silly*,' said Bets, crossly, and tried to kick him under the table. He dodged his legs out of the way and she kicked her father's ankle instead. He put down his paper and glared.

'Oh, Dad—I'm sorry!' said Bets. 'Please I'm very sorry. I meant to kick Pip. You see…'

'Any more of this kind of behaviour at breakfast time and you can both go out of the room,' said Mr.Hilton, and raised his paper again, leaning it against the big milk-jug. There was a dead silence for a minute or two except for the sound of spoons in the porridge bowls.

'Are you both going to meet Fatty?' asked Mrs.Hilton

at last.

'Yes,' said Bets, glad to have the silence broken. 'But I want to go round and collect Buster first. Fatty asked me to. That's why I'm in a hurry.'

'I suppose you're going to give old Buster a bath, and then dry him and then brush him, and then tie a red ribbon round his neck,' said Pip. 'Well, well—that will take half the morning, certainly. Are you going to wear your best dress to meet Fatty, Bets?'

'I think you're horrid this morning,' said Bets, almost in tears. 'I should have thought you'd be pleased to meet Fatty, too. It's maddening that his school should have broken up after Easter, instead of before, like ours did. It means we'll go back before he does.'

Pip stopped teasing Bets. 'Yes, it's a silly idea, some schools breaking up before Easter and some after. I'm coming to meet Fatty too, of course, and I'll go and collect Buster with you . I'll even help you to bath him.'

'I wasn't *going* to bath him,' said Bets. 'You know I wasn't. Pip—do you suppose Fatty will be in disguise— just to have a joke with us?'

'I hope to goodness you are not going to get mixed up in any nonsense again these holidays,' said her father, entering suddenly into the conversation again. 'I'm getting tired of having that fat policeman, Mr. Goon, round here complaining of this and that. As soon as that boy Frederick appears on the scene something always seems to happen.'

'Well, Fatty can't help it,' said Bets loyally. 'I mean— mysteries keep *on* happening, Dad, you can't stop them. The papers are full of them.'

'There's absolutely no need for you to be mixed up in

so many,' said her father. 'That boy Frederick—or Fatty as you so rightly call him—ought not to poke his nose into them. Leave them to the police!'

'Oh, but Fatty's *much* cleverer than our policeman, Mr.Goon,' said Bets. 'Anyway, I don't expect there will be time for anything exciting these hols.'

Pip changed the subject quickly. He didn't want his father suddenly to forbid him and Bets to have anything to do with any possible new mystery, as he had done once before. He had a kind of feeling that that was what would happen if he didn't hurriedly change the subject!

'Dad—the gardener is still away,' he said. 'Is there anything you want me to do in the garden, just to help out?'

Mr. Hilton looked pleased. 'Ah—I wondered if you were going to suggest giving a bit of help,' he said. 'Now, you come into my study before I go and I'll give you a list of jobs I'd like done. They'll keep you out of mischief anyway!'

Pip heaved a sigh of relief. He didn't particularly want to do any gardening, but at least he had headed his father off the subject of Mysteries. It would have been dreadful if he had been forbidden to take part in any during the three weeks that were left of the holidays. He gave Bets a frown to make her understand she was not to mention Fatty again.

After breakfast Pip disappeared into the study with his father. He came up to Bets later, as she was making her bed. He looked rather rueful.

'Look at this list! Whew! Dad must think I'm a super-gardener! I'll never do all this.'

Bets looked at the list. 'Please go and do some now,' she said. 'You don't want to spend all the afternoon doing it—Fatty might want us to go to tea, or something. I wish I could help you. I'll make your bed and tidy your room, anyway. Will you be ready to start at twenty to eleven, Pip! Fatty's train gets in just before eleven, and I must collect Buster'.

Pip heaved a mournful sigh as he looked at his list of jobs once more. 'All right. I'll go and start now. Thanks for saying you'll do my bed and tidy up. See you later!'

At twenty to eleven Bets went out into the garden to find Pip. He was just putting a rake away, and looked extremely hot. 'Is it time?' he called. 'Gosh, I've been working like ten gardeners rolled into one.'

'You look as if you're going to burst into flame at any minute,' said Bets, with a giggle. 'You'd better wash your hands, they're filthy. I'll go on ahead and collect Buster. Don't be long!'

She ran down the drive happily. She was tremendously glad that Fatty was coming back at last. Bets was very fond of him.She thought he must be the cleverest, most ingenious and certainly the kindest boy in the world . The things he could do!

'Those disguises of his! And the way he thinks out things—and the daring things he does!' she thought, as she turned out of the front gate and up the lane. 'Oh, I'm *glad* Fatty's coming back. Things are always dull without him. It's quite true what Dad said—things do begin to happen when Fatty is around!'

Somebody whistled loudly when she got into the main road and she turned quickly. It was Larry, with Daisy, his sister. They waved madly and began to run.

'Are you going to meet Fatty? So are we! Where is Pip? Isn't he coming?'

Bets explained. 'I'm on my way to collect Buster,' she said. 'Pip's just coming. Won't old Buster be pleased to see Fatty? I bet he knows it's the day he's arriving'.

'I bet he does,' agreed Larry, 'He'll be waiting for us, his tongue out, panting to go!'

But, oddly enough, Buster was not waiting. Mrs. Trotteville, Fatty's mother, was picking daffodils in the garden when the three children came up. She smiled at them.

'Going to meet Fatty? It will be nice to have him back, won't it?'

'Yes, very,' said Larry. 'Where's Buster, Mrs. Trotteville? We thought we'd take him along.'

'In the kitchen, I think,' said Mrs. Trotteville. 'I haven't seen him for a little while. He would keep treading all over the daffodils, so I sent him in.'

Larry, Daisy and Bets went to the kitchen door and called loudly. 'Buster! Hey, BUSTER! Come along, we're going to meet Fatty!'

But no Buster appeared. There was no scamper of short, eager legs, no welcoming volley of barks. The cook came to the door.

'He's not here,' she said. 'He did come in a minute or two ago, but off he went again. He's probably gone off with the baker's boy . He likes him, goodness knows why. He's a cheeky little monkey, that boy.'

'Well—we'll have to go without Buster,' said Larry, disappointed. 'How maddening of him to go off just at this time. Fatty will be disappointed.'

They set off to the station, joined by a breathless Pip. 'Where's Buster? Don't say he's gone off just when we want him! Not at all like Buster!'

They hurried on. 'Do you suppose Fatty will play a joke on us and turn up in disguise?' said Bets. 'I do hope he doesn't. I just want to see him nice and fat and grinning all over his face.'

'We shall be jolly late if we don't hurry,' said Larry, looking at his watch. 'Look—isn't that the train coming in now—and we're not nearly there. Buck up!'

They bucked up, and arrived at the station just as the train began to pull out again. The passengers had got out and were now walking down the platform. Two or three were waiting with their luggage for a porter.

'Look—there's old Buster!' said Pip, suddenly, 'Would you believe it! Sitting under that seat look—all by himself, watching.'

Sure enough, there was the little Scottie, patiently waiting there. 'How did he know that Fatty's train was due now?' said Bets, in wonder. 'However DID he know! So that's where he ran off to—the station! He was on time too, and we weren't. Clever old Buster!'

'Where's Fatty?' said Daisy, as the crowd of passengers came up to the door where the ticket collector stood. 'I can't see him yet.'

'He *may* be in disguise—just to test us and see how bright we are,' said Pip. 'Look at every one very carefully—especially people with glasses.'

They stood silently behind the collector as every one surged past, giving up tickets. A big, bustling woman—a pair of school girls—a man with a bag—two young soldiers in khaki, each with enormous kit-bags on their shoulders— two men bundled up in thick overcoats, both wearing glasses. Was one Fatty? They were both about his build. One said something in a foreign language as he passed by.

The four children stared after him doubtfully. He *could* be Fatty. They turned to watch the rest of the passengers, but there was no one who could possibly be Fatty.

At the end came Buster, all alone. Bets patted him, thinking that he looked sad. 'So you missed him too, did you?' she said. 'Buster, was he one of those bundled-up men?'

There was now no one left on the platform except a porter. 'Come on,' said Larry, making up his mind. 'Fatty *must* have been one of those men. We'll follow them. We can't have old Fatty tricking us as easily as this!'

2 A LITTLE BIT OF HELP!

THE four children went out of the station and looked up the road. Where had the men gone?

'There they are,' said Larry. 'Look—just at the corner!'

'But who's the man with Fatty?' said Pip, puzzled. 'He never said anything about coming back with somebody.'

'Look—they've shaken hands,' said Daisy. 'I expect old Fatty just fell into conversation with him to trick us a bit more. Come on—I'm sure the man who's gone off to the right is Fatty. He's got his walk, somehow.'

'And he's going in the right direction,' said Pip. 'It's Fatty all right.'

They hurried after him. When they got to the corner they paused. Now, where was he?

'There he is—talking to that woman,' said Larry. 'Hurry!'

They hurried. The man, his coat-collar turned up, wearing thick glasses over his eyes saying something very earnestly to a thin little woman with a shopping-basket.

The four came up behind him and listened with amusement. Oh Fatty, Fatty!

'I seek my sistair's house. You will tell me, pliss?

The house, it is called Grintriss.'

'Never heard of it,' said the woman, looking most suspiciously at the bundled-up man.

'Pardon? Where is zis house?' asked the man anxiously.

'I said, "NEVER HEARD OF IT," ' said the woman. 'There's no house called Grintriss that I know of. What's your sister's name?'

'Her name is Francoise Emile Harris,' said the man, going suddenly very French.

'Never heard of her either.' Said the thin little woman, looking more suspicious than ever. 'Why don't you ask at the post-office?'

'Pliss? What is zis postoffis?' began the man, but the woman walked off impatiently, leaving him standing there with his bag.

Pip nudged Larry. 'This is where we come in,' he said, in a low voice. 'We'll tell old Fatty we know where his sister lives, and that we'll take him there— and we'll lead him straight to his own house. That'll show him we've seen through him! Come on.'

'Where's his school trunk?' said Bets, pulling Pip back as he started off after the man. 'Are you *sure* it's Fatty?'

'He's sent his trunk carriage forward, of course,' said Pip. 'Come on—*look* at that walk—it's exactly like old Fatty's.'

They set off after the man. Daisy suddenly thought of something. Where was Buster? She looked round but he wasn't there.

'What happened to Buster?' she said. 'Surely

he didn't stay behind? I was just wondering why *he* didn't know it was Fatty, and dash round his legs.'

'He would have, if he'd been with us,' said Pip. 'He didn't recognize him in that crowd at the station and he's probably patiently sitting under the seat again, waiting!'

'Oh, poor Buster!' said Bets. 'Look—Fatty has stopped another woman. What a scream he is!'

The second woman had no patience. She just shook her head and hurried off. Larry put his fingers to his mouth and let off a piercing whistle, making the others jump.

'Don't,' said Daisy. 'You know you're not allowed to do that. It's a horrible noise and makes people awfully angry.'

'It's stopped old Fatty, anyway,' said Larry, pleased. 'Look, he's turned round.'

'He's gone on again,' said Bets, with a giggle. 'Let's catch him up. He's going the wrong way home now.'

They hurried after the man. 'We'll pretend we don't know it's Fatty,' said Pip. 'We'll make him think *he's* deceiving *us*—but we'll have the laugh all right, when we take him to his own house instead of to his mythical "sistair's" house.'

They caught up the man, and he stopped, peering at them through thick glasses. He had a small black moustache. His coat-collar was turned up, and not much could be seen of his face.

'Ah! Some children! You will help me, yes?' said the man. 'I look for my sistair's house.'

'Grintriss! Oh, yes, we know where that is,' said Larry

'Vous cherchez la maison de votre soeur?' said Pip, in his best French. The man beamed at him.

'Oui, oui! It is called Grintriss.'

'Grintriss! Oh, yes, we know where *that* is,' said Larry, most untruthfully, playing up to Fatty for all he was worth. 'This way, please. *Every*body knows Grintriss. A very nice house. Big one, too.'

'Beeg? No, my sistair's house is leetle,' said the man. 'Vairy, vairy leetle. Grintriss it is called.'

'Oh, yes. Grintriss. Vairy leetle,' said Pip. 'Er— do you feel the cold, Monsieur? You are well wrapped up.'

'I have had the bad cold,' said the man, and he sniffed, and gave a hollow cough. 'I come to my sistair for a leetle holyday.'

'Holiday, you mean?' said Daisy, and the four of them began to laugh. 'That's a nasty little cough you've got. Very nasty.'

The man coughed again, and Bets began to giggle. Didn't Fatty know they were pulling his leg? How often had she heard Fatty cough like that when he was disguised as some poor old man?

They all went up the road together, the man hunched up in his bulky coat. He pulled his scarf over his chin as they met the wind at a corner.

'We are soon at Grintriss?' he asked, anxiously. 'This wind is too—too—'

'Too windy?' said Pip, obligingly. 'That's the worst of winds. They're always so windy.'

The man gave him a sudden stare and said no more. Larry guided him round the next corner and over the road to Fatty's own house. Mrs. Trotteville was nowhere to be seen. Larry winked at Pip.

'We'll take him up to the front door and leave him there,' he said, falling behind to whisper, 'We'll just see what old Fatty says then!'

They marched him in firmly at gate and right up to the front door. 'Here you are,' said Pip. 'Grintriss! I expect your sistair will answer the door herself. I'll pull the bell for you.'

He pulled the bell and banged on the knocker too. Then the four of them retreated to the front gate to see what Fatty would do. Would he swing round, take off his glasses and grin at them? Would he say 'One up to you! You win!'

The door opened, and the house parlour-maid stood there. An argument seemed to arise, though the children couldn't hear all of it. The maid raised her voice.

'I said, "there's no one here of that name. And what's more I've never heard of a house called Grintriss, either."'

Bets suddenly heard quick footsteps coming up the road, and then a familiar bark. She ran through the gate, sure that it was Buster's bark.

She gave a shrill scream. 'Buster! FATTY! It's Fatty! Oh, Fatty, then that wasn't you after all! FATTY!'

She rushed down the road and flung her-self into Fatty's arms. There he has, as plump as ever, his eyes laughing, his mouth in a wide grin.

'Fatty! That wasn't you, then? Oh, dear!'

'What's all this about?' asked Fatty, swinging Bets into the air and down again. 'Gosh, Bets, you're getting heavy. I soon shan't be able to do that. Why weren't you at the station to meet me? Only Buster was there.'

Now all the others were round him too, astonished, Fatty! How had they missed him?

'You *are* a lot of donkeys,' said Fatty, in his cheerful voice. 'I bet you met the train that comes in four minutes before mine. Buster was *much* more sensible! He knew enough to wait for the right one—and there he was, prancing round the platform, barking like mad when he saw me. I looked for you, but you were nowhere to be seen.'

'Oh, Fatty—we must have met the wrong train—and, we've made an *awful* mistake,' said Daisy troubled. 'We thought you might be in disguise, just to play a joke on us—and when we couldn't see you anywhere, we followed a man we thought was you—and oh, Fatty, he asked us the way to some house or other—and we took him to yours!'

'*Well*!' said Fatty, and roared with laughter. 'You are a lot of mutts. Where's this poor fellow? We'd better put him right.'

The man was even now walking out of the gate, muttering and looking furious—as indeed he had every right to be. He stopped and looked at the name on the gate.

'Ha! You do not bring me to Grintriss. This is not Grintriss. You are wicket! You treat a sick man so!' He began to cough again.

The children were alarmed, and felt very sorry. However could they explain their mistake? He would never, never understand! He stalked up to them, blowing his nose with a trumpeting sound.

'Wicket! Wicket!' he repeated. 'Very bad. Wicket!'

He began to shout at them in French, waving his arms about. They listened in dismay. Suppose Mrs. Trotteville came out? It would be even worse to explain their silly mistake to her than to this man.

A bell rang loudly and a bicycle stopped suddenly at the kerb. A very familiar voice hailed them.

'Now, then! What's all this?

'Mr. Goon!' groaned Larry. 'Old Clear-Orf.' He *would* turn up, of course.'

Buster danced round Mr. Goon in delight, barking furiously. Mr. Goon kept a watchful eye on him, thankful that he had on his thickest trousers.

'Nasty little yapping dog,' he said. 'Call him off or I'll give him a kick.'

Fatty called Buster, and the Scottie came most reluctantly. Oh, for a bite at that big, loud-voiced policeman! Goon spoke to the bewildered Frenchman.

'What's all this? Have these children been annoying you? I'll report them, if so.'

The man went off into a long and angry speech, but as it was all in French Mr. Goon didn't understand a word. He debated whether he should ask Fatty to translate for him—but how was he to trust that fat boy's translation? Fatty looked at Goon with a gleam in his eye.

'Don't you want to know what he's saying, Mr.
Goon?' he said, politely. 'I can just catch a few
words now and again. Er—he doesn't seem to like
the look of you, I'm afraid. It sounds as if he's calling
you names.'

Mr. Goon felt out of his depth. These pests of
children again—and this foreigner who appeared to
be quite mad—and that nasty little dog longing to
get at his ankles! Mr. Goon felt that the best and
most dignified thing to do was to bicycle away
immediately.

So, with a snort that sounded like 'Gah' he pushed
off from the kerb and sailed away down the road,
followed by a fusillade of barks from the disappointed
Buster.

'Thank goodness!' said Daisy, fervently, and all
the five agreed.

3 IT'S NICE TO BE TOGETHER AGAIN!

THE Frenchman stared after the policeman in surprise. In France policemen did not behave like that. They were interested and excited when a complaint was made to them, they listened, they took notes—but this policeman had said 'Gah' and gone cycling away. Extraordinary!

He began to cough. Fatty felt sorry for him, and began to talk to him in perfect French. Trust old Fatty to know the right thing to do! The others stood round, listening in admiration. Really, Fatty might be French!

'How does he learn French like that?' wondered Daisy. 'Nobody at our school could even *begin* to talk like that. Really, Fatty is a most surprising person.'

The man began to calm down. He took a little notebook out of his pocket and opened it. 'I will show you the name,' he said. 'Grintriss. Why should nobody know this Grintriss house?'

He showed Fatty something written down on a page of the notebook. The others peeped over his arm to look.

'Oh! GREEN-TREES!' said Daisy. 'Why ever didn't you say so? You kept saying Grintriss.'

'Yes. Grintriss,' repeated the man, puzzled. 'All the time I say "Grintriss, pliss, where is zis house?" '

'It's Green-Trees,' said Daisy, pronouncing it slowly and carefully.

'Grintriss,' said the man, again. 'And now—where is zis house! I ask of you for the last time.'

He looked as if he were going to burst into tears. Fatty took his arm. 'Come on. I'll show you. No tricks this time, we'll take you there.'

And off they all went together, Fatty suddenly jabbering in French again. Down the road, round the corner, up the hill and into a quiet little lane. In the middle of it was a small and pretty house, smoke curling up from its chimneys.

'Green-Trees,' said Fatty, pointing to the name on the white gate.

'Ah—Grintriss,' said the man in delight and raised his hat to the two girls. 'Mesdemoiselles, adieu! I go to find my sistair!'

He disappeared up the little front path. Bets gave a sigh and slipped her arm through Fatty's. 'What a shame to welcome you home with a silly muddle like this, Fatty. We meant to be on the platform ready to give you a wonderful welcome—and only Buster was there—and we'd gone off after somebody who wasn't in the *least* like you.'

'Yes—but that's the worst of Fatty when he puts on a disguise,' grumbled Pip. 'He never does look in the least like himself. Come on, Fatty—let's take you back home now. Your mother will be wondering what's become of you.'

Mrs. Trotteville was quite relieved to see Fatty and the others trooping into the hall. She came out to greet them.

'Frederick! Did you miss your train? How late you

are! Welcome home again.'

'Hallo, Mother! What a nice smell from the kitchen! Smells like steak and onions. Buster, what do *you* think?'

'Wuff!' said Buster, ready to agree with every word that Fatty said. He dashed round Fatty's legs, galloped behind the couch, appeared again, and then, threaded his way at top speed between all the chairs.

'Jet-propelled obstacle race,' said Fatty. 'Hey, Buster, look where you're going, you'll knock me over.'

'He always behaves like that when you first come home,' said Mrs. Trotteville. 'I only hope he gets over the excitement soon. I simply daren't walk a step when he goes mad like this.'

'He's a darling,' said Bets. 'I know how he feels when Fatty comes home. I feel rather the same myself.'

Fatty gave her a sudden hug. 'Well, don't *you* start racing round the furniture on all-fours,' he said. 'Tell me—any mysterious mysteries or insoluble problems cropped up this last week? What a shame you all got home before I did!'

'Nothing's turned up yet,' said Pip. 'But I bet something will now you're here. Adventures go to the adventurous, you know.'

'I do hope nothing *does* turn up,' said Mrs. Trotteville. 'Or I shall have that silly Mr. Goon round here again. Now, the one *I* like is your friend, Superintendent Jenks!'

They all stared at her. '*Superintendent*! You don't mean that Chief-Inspector Jenks is superintendent now!' said Larry. 'My word—he's going up and up, isn't he?'

'We knew him first when he was an Inspector,' said Bets, remembering. 'And then he became a Chief-Inspector. Now he's a Superintendent. I'm glad. He's getting very very high-up, isn't he? I hope he'll still like to know us.'

'I expect he will,' said Mrs. Trotteville smiling. 'Oh, dear— I do wish Cook would keep the kitchen door shut when she is doing onions—what a smell came in here then.'

'Keep the door shut when it's steak and onions?' said Fatty, in horror. '*Shut*, did you say? Shut out a heavenly smell like that? Mother, don't you realize that I have, as usual, been half-starved all the term?'

'Well, it's a pity you weren't,' said his mother, looking at his tight overcoat. 'Those buttons look as if they are just about to burst off. Your trunk has come, Frederick. Do you want to unpack it, and get ready for lunch straight away? We're having it early as I thought you would be hungry.'

'Mother, I do love you when you think things like that,' said Fatty, in a sudden burst of affection. 'I'm starving!'

'Cupboard love!' said his mother, amused at Fatty's sudden hug.

'Can all the others stay to lunch as well?' asked Fatty, hopefully.

'Yes, if you'd like to share your bit of steak and onions round,' said his mother. But not even Fatty could rise to that, and so he said good-bye to the other four very reluctantly.

'They can all come to tea this afternoon, if you like,'

said Mrs. Trotteville. 'I'll get in plenty of cakes. Frederick, do control Buster. He's gone mad again. It really makes me giddy to watch him.'

'Buster! Behave yourself!' said Fatty, and the mad little Scottie turned himself miraculously into a quiet and peaceful little lamb, lying down on Fatty's feet and licking his shoes.

'Come back at three,' said Fatty, and took the others to the front gate. 'We'll have a good old talk and you can tell me all the news. So-long!' He went back to the house, sniffing for steak and onions again.

'I suppose, Frederick, you don't know anything about a bulky-looking foreigner who came to the front door this morning, and told Jane that this house was Grintriss, and wanted to force his way in and see some sister of his—do you?' said Mrs. Trotteville, when Fatty came back. 'He kept talking about some "wicket children" when Jane told him this wasn't the house. You hadn't anything to do with him. I suppose? You haven't been up to your tricks again already. I hope.'

'Of course not,' said Fatty, looking quite hurt. 'Poor fellow— I found him at the front gate, and we all took him to the place he wanted to go to. Green Trees, down Holly Lane. Oh, Mother, there's that heavenly smell again. Do you mind if I go and smell it even nearer? I haven't seen Cook or Jane yet.'

'Very well. But DON'T try lifting fried onions out of the pan,' said Mrs. Trotteville. 'Oh, Frederick—it's very nice to have you back—but I do wish I always knew what you were up to! Please don't get mixed up in anything alarming these holidays. Pip's mother was saying to me only yesterday that everything has been so *peaceful* this last week.'

There was no answer. Fatty was already in the kitchen sampling half-fried strips of onion, while Cook and Jane giggled at him, and promised to provide him with new gingerbread, hot scones and home-made raspberry jam when the others came to tea that afternoon. They loved Fatty.

'A caution, that's what he is,' Cook told her friends. 'Honestly, you just never know what's going to happen when Master Frederick is about.'

Fatty enjoyed his lunch thoroughly, and told his mother all about his last term. He appeared, as always, to have done extremely well.

'Though there *may* be something on my report about the—er—the advisability of sticking to my own voice,' he said , making his mother look up in surprise. 'It's all right, Mother. It just means that my ventriloquism has been rather successful this term.'

One of Fatty's talents was the ability to throw his voice, and he was now a very fine ventriloquist indeed— but unfortunately the masters at school did not approve of this as much as the boys did. Fatty's class had spent one whole morning searching for an apparently injured man somewhere up in the school attic. The groans had been tremendous and had caused a great sensation.

When it had been discovered that it was merely a ventriloquial stunt of Fatty's there had been another sensation—but not a very happy one for Fatty. In fact, he hadn't felt it wise to do any more ventriloquism that term, which was he thought, a great pity. He would get out of practice!

At three o'clock exactly there was the tramp of feet going down the garden to Fatty's shed. Fatty saw Larry, Daisy, Pip and Bets passing by under his window and hurriedly stopped his unpacking.

He shot downstairs with Buster, and went to join the others in his big shed at the bottom of the garden.

This was playroom, store-room, changing-room – anything that Fatty wanted. He had a key for it, and kept it well and truly locked. There were too many disguises and odd clothes there that he didn't want grown-ups to see. His mother would certainly have been astonished to see some of the old things he had picked up at jumble sales—dreadful old hats, ragged shawls, voluminous skirts, corduroy trousers, down-at-heel boots!

'Hallo!' said Fatty, appearing just as the others were looking in at the shed window to see if he was there. 'I'll unlock the door. I slipped down just after dinner to light the oil-stove. It should be nice and warm now.'

They all went in. It certainly was nice and warm. The sun slid in at one window and lighted up the inside of the shed. It looked dusty and untidy.

'I'll clean it up for you,' promised Daisy, looking round. 'I say—its nice to meet like this again isn't it— all the Five Find-Outers together!'

'With nothing to find out!' said Pip. 'I like it best when we've got something exciting on hand. And remember, Fatty, we go back to school a whole week before you do, so there isn't a great deal of time to get going on something.'

'We can always practise a bit,' suggested Larry. 'You know—go out in disguises—or do a spot of shadowing—or watching.'

'Yes. We could do that,' said Fatty. 'I want to practice my ventriloquism too—I've got out of practice this last term.'

'Oh, yes, *do* practise that!' begged Bets. 'Let's make some plans.'

'Right,' said Fatty, obligingly. 'We will!'

4 A FEW LITTLE PLANS

MANY ridiculous plans were discussed that afternoon over a really super-tea. Cook had kept her word, and there were lashings of hot scones and raspberry jam, new and very sticky gingerbread with raisins in, and a big round chocolate cake with a special filling made by Cook.

Buster had dog biscuits spread with potted meat, and approved of this very highly.

'It's three-treats-in-one for him,' explained Fatty. 'First he gets a fine sniff at the biscuits and potted meat. Then he gets a fine lick at them., Then he gets a wonderful cruch at them. Three-meals-in-one, so to speak.'

'Wuff,' said Buster, thumping his tail hard.

'And what is more,' said Fatty, cutting himself a huge slice of the chocolate cake, 'what is more, we can have every bit of this cake to ourselves. Potted-meat-biscuits take the *whole* of Buster's attention. He hasn't even *seen* this cake yet.'

'And when he does, it won't be there,' said Pip. 'Not if I can help it, anyway.'

They got back to their plans again. Fatty was in an uproarious mood, and made them all laugh till they choked.

'What about taking a clothes-horse with us, Larry, and going into the main street and pretending to be workmen chipping up the road?' suggested Fatty. 'Just you and I, Larry. Pip's not big enough yet to pass as a workman. We could put the clothes-horse round us, like workmen do, hang a red flag on it, and chip up the road!'

'Don't be an idiot,' said Larry. 'We'd get into an awful row.'

'I bet old Goon would let us sit there all morning chipping up the road,' said Fatty. 'He'd never dream of asking us what we were doing.'

'Fatty, I'm going to dare you to do something,' said Daisy, with a sudden giggle. 'Look—I'm trying to sell these tickets for our Church Sale. I dare you to try and sell one to old Goon.'

'Easy!' said Fatty. 'Very easy! Give me one, I'll sell it to-morrow. That shall be my little task.'

'What shall *I* do?' asked Larry.

'Er—let me see—yes, what about you putting on overalls, taking a pail and a leather and going to clean somebody's window?' said Fatty.

'Oh, no!' said Larry, in alarm. 'Nothing like that!'

'Yes, do, do!' begged Daisy and Bets.

'Only you'll have to choose a house that is all on one floor—a bungalow, for instance,' said Pip. 'You won't need a ladder then—and there wouldn't be so many windows to clean! Larry as window cleaner! That's good!'

'Do I have to *ask* if I can clean the windows?' said Larry, looking desperate. 'I mean—I can't just go to a house and start cleaning, can I? They might have their own regular window-cleaner.'

'Yes, that's true. You must ask first,' said Fatty, solemnly. 'And if you get any payment, you can buy one of Daisy's Sale tickets.'

'Oh, I say!' said Larry. 'That's a bit hard.' It occurred to him that these sudden plans were rather a mistake!

A FEW LITTLE PLANS

'What shall *I* do?' said Pip, with a giggle. They all looked at him. 'You can shadow Goon sometime to-morrow,' said Fatty firmly. 'Shadow him so that he doesn't know you're following him—do it really properly.'

'All right,' said Pip. 'I can do that, I think. What about the girls?'

'We'll think of something for them to do when we've done our tasks,' said Fatty. 'Now, any one want this last bit of gingerbread—or shall I cut it into five?'

It was duly cut into five. 'Any one seen Super-intendent Jenks these hols?' asked Fatty, handing round the gingerbread. 'Jolly good that he's promoted again, isn't it!'

'Super!' said Bets.

'Yes—super—intendent.' said Pip, and every one punched him. 'No—none of us has seen him—we're not likely to see him either, unless we have something in the mystery line to solve.'

'I wish he'd hand us over a few of his cases,' said Fatty, stacking the plates together. 'I'm sure we could help. I mean—we've had a good bit of experience now, haven't we?'

'The only thing is, Goon always knows about the cases, too, and he does get in our way when we're both working on the same mystery,' said Daisy. 'I wish we could work on some more clues—and suspects—and all the rest. It *is* such fun!'

They got out some cards and began to play a game. It was nice to be all together again. Things weren't the same somehow without Fatty. He said and did such ridiculous things, and nobody ever knew what he would do next.

Pip looked at his watch after a time and sighed. 'I must go,' he said. 'Come on, Bets. We shall only get into a row if we're late. Why does time always go so fast when you don't want it to?'

'Don't forget, Pip and Larry, you've got jobs to do to-morrow,' said Fatty, slipping the cards back into their case. 'Report here to-morrow after tea—and I'll have the money for Goon's ticket ready for you, Daisy!'

She laughed. 'It will be more difficult than you think!' she said. 'Come on, Larry.'

As Fatty cleared up the shed when the others had gone, he wondered how he could get Mr. Goon to buy the ticket. He ran his eye over the clothes hanging up at one side of the shed. He must certainly disguise himself, for Goon would never, never buy a ticket from him if he went as himself!

'I'll go as an old woman, and pretend to read his hand!' thought Fatty. 'He believes in that sort of nonsense. It should be fun!'

Pip was also planning his own task., When should he shadow Mr.Goon? Of course, it would be easiest to do it in the dark; but he didn't know what time Goon went out at night, and he couldn't very well hang about outside his house for hours. No, it would have to be in the morning, when Goon went out on his bicycle. Pip would take his and follow him. He would pretend that Goon was a suspect—a burglar or a thief—and track him wherever he went!

So, next morning, Pip got his bicycle and set out to the street where the policeman lived. There was his house, with POLICE above it in big letters.. Pip got off his bicycle, propped it against a big tree, and then quietly let all the air out of one tyre.

Now he could mess about with the wheel, pretending to pump up his tyre, and nobody would bother about why he was there, even if he had to wait for half an hour or more.

He did have to wait a good time, and got rather tired of pumping up his tyre and letting the air out again. But at last Mr. Goon appeared, wheeling his bicycle out, his trousers neatly clipped in at the ankles.

Pip was surprised to see a skinny little boy of about eleven following Goon to the door. Goon shouted a few words to him, mounted his bicycle ponderously and rode off up the street. Pip slid on to his saddle and rode of too.

Goon didn't seem to have the slightest idea that he was being followed. He sailed along, waving to this person and that in a very condescending manner. He got off at the front gate of a house, propped his bicycle up against the fence and went to the front door. Pip waited beside a hedge.

Out came Goon again, and rode down the road and into the main street. He got off at the post-office and went inside. Pip got tired of waiting for him and thought longingly of ice-creams. He was just near a shop that sold them. He suddenly decided to nip in and get one.

But, while he nipped in and got one, Mr. Goon came out and sailed away again on his bicycle. Pip only *just* managed to spot him, crammed his ice-cream down his throat so that he almost froze himself, and raced after Goon.

On the way he passed Mrs. Trotteville, Fatty's mother. She had Buster with her, and as soon as he saw Pip, and heard his voice calling out 'good morning,' he left Mrs. Trotteville and raced after Pip.

'No, Buster. Not this morning. Go back, there's a good dog!' shouted Pip. But Buster laboured after him, panting. Fatty had gone out without him—so he would go with Pip. But Buster couldn't keep up with Pip on his bicycle and was soon left behind. He followed at a distance, still panting.

Mr. Goon had gone down a lane that led nowhere except to a farm. Pip just managed to see him disappearing round the corner. He guessed what he had gone to the farm for. The farmer had been complaining bitterly that his sheep had been worried by dogs. Oh, well—Pip could sit under a hedge and wait for Goon to come out again. It was a bit dull shadowing him, really. He wondered how Larry was getting on with his window-cleaning.

Pip got off his bicycle, hid it in a ditch and then crept through a gap into the field. Sheep were there, with some fat woolly lambs about three months old. They were skipping about in a ridiculous fashion.

Pip sat with his back against a hawthorn tree and watched them. Suddenly he heard the scampering of feet and loud panting breath—and in another second Buster had flung himself on him through the gap in the hedge! He licked Pip's face and yelped for joy. 'Found you!' he semed to say. 'Found you!'

'Oh, Buster!' said Pip. 'Stop licking me!' He pushed Buster away, and the dog ran out into the field in a wide circle, barking. Some nearby lambs started away in alarm and ran to their mother-sheep.

And then a loud and familiar voice came through the hedge. 'Ho! So it's that fat boy's dog that chases Farmer

Meadows' sheep, it it? I might have guessed it. I'll catch
that dog and have him shot. I've just this minute been to
the farm to get particulars of sheep-chasing dogs—and
here I've got one caught in the act!'

Mr. Goon came crashing through the hedge, and Pip at
once sprang to his feet. 'Buster wasn't chasing the sheep!'
he cried, indignantly. 'He came to find *me*. He's only
arrived this very minute.'

'I'll catch that dog and take him off with me,' said Mr.
Goon simply delighted to think that he could find such a
good reason for catching Buster.

But it wasn't so easy to catch the Scottie. In fact, it
was far easier for Buster to catch Mr. Goon, as the
policeman soon realized when Buster kept running at him
and then backing away. In the end he had to shout to Pip
to call him off. Pip called him—and Goon just had time to
mount his bicycle and pedal away at top speed!

'I wonder where Fatty is,' groaned Pip. 'I must find
him and tell him about this. Blow you, Buster!—what did
you want to follow me for? NOW you're in for trouble!'

5 FATTY ENJOYS HIMSELF

PIP got on his bicycle and rode off. Buster ran beside him, keeping a good look-out for Mr. Goon. He would have very much liked another pounce at his ankles—but Goon was out of sight, on his way home. Visions of a nice hot cup of coffee, well-sugared, and a slice of home-made cake floated in his mind.

Pip rode to Fatty's house, but he wasn't there. 'Blow!' said Pip. 'I suppose he's gone off to sell his ticket to Goon. I wish I'd seen him. I bet he looks exactly like some old woman shopping in the town!'

Fatty had had a most enjoyable time in his shed choosing a disguise to wear when he went to sell the ticket to Mr. Goon. He had chosen a rather long black skirt, a black jumper, a shapeless dark-red coat and a hat he had bought at the last jumble sale.

It was black straw, and had a few dark-red roses in the front. Fatty put on a wig of dark hair, and made up his face, putting in a fews artful wrinkles here and there.

He looked at himself in the mirror and grinned. Then he frowned—and immediately the face of a cross old woman looked back at him out of the mirror!

'I wish the others could see me,' thought Fatty. 'They'd hoot with laughter. Now, where's my hand-bag?'

The hand-bag was a very old one of his mother's . In it was a powder-compact, a handkerchief and a few hair-pins, all of which Fatty kept there for use when he disguised himself as a woman. He delighted in taking out the powder case and dabbing powder on his nose, as he had so often seen women do! His mother would have been most astonished to see him.

He unlocked the door of his shed, and opened it a little, listening. Was any one about? Or could he slip safely out and into the road?

He could hear nothing, so he slipped out of the shed, locked the door and made his way up the side-path through the shrubbery.

As he went through the bushes, a voice hailed him, 'Hey, you! What you doing there?'

It was the gardener, looking with interest at the shabby old woman.

Fatty immediately went all foreign. He flapped about with his hands, moved his shoulders up and down and said 'Ackle-eeta-ommi-poggy-wo?'

'Can't you speak English?' said the gardener. 'See— there's the kitchen door if you want anything.'

'Tipply-opply-erica-coo,' said Fatty in a most grateful voice, and slid out of the gardener's sight. He grinned to himself. His disguise must be pretty good if the gardener didn't see through it!

He decided that it would be quite a good idea to go on being rather foreign. It was so easy to talk gibberish! Fatty could go on and on for a very long time, apparently speaking in a foreign language, shrugging his shoulders like his French master at school, and waggling his hands about.

He made his way down the road. Nobody took the

least notice of him, which was very good. Fatty decided that he looked rather like one of the faded old women who sometimes sat on committees with his mother.

He came to the road where Goon lived and went up to his house. Was Goon in? Fatty knocked at the door.

It opened, and a skinny little boy stood there, the same skinny little fellow who had followed Goon to the door when Pip had been waiting for him

The boy looked at him with sharp eyes. 'Mr. Goon's out,' he said. 'There's only my mum in. She's cleaning. If you want to leave a message I'll call her.'

'Ah—zat would be kind,' said Fatty, giving the boy a sudden beaming smile. 'I will come in.'

He pushed past the boy and went into Goon's office. He sat down, spreading out his skirts and patting the back of his hair with his hand.

'I'll fetch me Mum,' said the boy, who didn't quite know what to make of this visitor. Was she a friend of Mr. Goon?

' 'Ere, Mum—there's a funny old foreign lady come to see Mr.Goon,' Fatty heard the boy say. 'She's set herself down in the office.'

'All right. I'll see what she wants,' said mum's voice. Mum then appeared at the office-door, wiping her hands on an apron of sacking.

Fatty gave her a gracious smile and nodded her head. 'I come to see dear Mr. Goon,' he announced. 'He is expecting me—yes?'

'I don't rightly know,' said Mum. 'He's out just now. Will you wait? I'm just cleaning out for him—I come every morning. I have to bring Bert with me because it's holidays, but he's useful.'

Fatty beamed at the skinny little woman, who really looked very like Bert. 'Ikkle-dokka-runi-pie,' he said, in a very earnest voice.

'Pardon?' said Mum, startled. 'You're foreign, aren't you? I had a foreigner once who lodged with me. She was right down clever—read my hand like a book!'

'Ah—so!' said Fatty. 'I too read the hand. Like a book.'

'Do you really?' said Mum and came a little farther into the room. Fatty racked his brains to remember who she was. He knew he had seen her before. Then he remembered. Of course—she was a friend of Jane, the house parlour-maid, and sometimes came to help Cook when they had a party—he had heard them talking about her—what was her name now? Ah, yes—Mickle.

Mum wiped her hands again on her apron and held one out to Fatty. 'What's my hand tell you?' she asked, eagerly.

Fatty took it in his and frowned over it. 'Ah—your name it is Mickle! Mrs. Mickle. You live at—at—Shepherd's Crescent…'

'Coo!' said Mum, most impressed. 'Is that all written in my hand? Go on.'

'You have five sisters,' said Fatty, remembering the gossip he had heard, 'And er—er—you have brothers—how many? It is difficult to see in your hand.'

'I've got six,' said Mum, helpfully.'Perhaps they're hidden under that bit of dirt there. I'd have washed me hands if I'd known you were coming.'

'I see illnesses here,' went on Fatty, 'and children—

and cups and cups of tea—and…'

'That's right!' broke in Mum, quite excited. 'I've bin ill many a time—and I've got five children—Bert there is the youngest—and the cups of tea I've had—well, I must have had thousands in me life!'

'Millions,' said Fatty, still bent over her hand.

'Fancy you even seeing them cups of tea there,' said Mum. She raised her voice. 'Bert! This lady's a real wonder at reading hands. You come and listen.'

Bert was already listening just outside the door. He came right in when his mother called. He looked at Fatty disbelievingly.

'Where do you see them cups of tea?' he asked. 'How do you know they're not cups of coffee?'

Fatty decided that he didn't much like Bert. He thought it would be very nice indeed to read Bert's hand and see a great many spankings there. But Bert didn't ask to have his hand read. He kept them both firmly behind his back as if afraid that Fatty would start reading them at once. Young Bert already had quite a lot of things in his life that he didn't want any one to know about!

Some one rode up to the front gate and got off a bicycle. 'Coo—here's Mr. Goon back already and I haven't got the kettle on for his coffee!' said Mum, and disappeared at once. Mr. Goon opened the front door and came heavily into the hall. Mum called out to him.

'Mr. Goon, sir! There's a lady wanting to see you. I've put her in the office.'

Mr. Goon went into the kitchen. 'Who is she?' Fatty heard him say. 'What's she come for?'

'I didn't make so bold as to ask her *that*,' said Mum,

putting a kettle on the stove. 'She's a foreigner by the sound of her—funny-looking, you know, and speaks queer.'

'She read Mum's hand,' said Bert, slyly.

'You hold your tongue, young Bert,' said Mum, sharply. 'She read it like a book, sir—knew me name and everything. One of these clever ones. You ready for your cup of coffee, sir?'

'Yes. I could do with one,' said Goon. 'I've been attacked by a dog this morning.'

'You don't say!' said Mum. 'Did he bite you?'

Mr. Goon liked sympathy. He enlarged quite a bit on Buster's light-hearted game with him.

'It's a wonder my trousers aren't torn to bits,' he said. 'The dog came at me time and again. If I wasn't pretty nippy, I'd have been bitten more than I was. Good thing I had my thickest trousers on.'

'Well, there now! What a thing to happen to you, Mr. Goon!' said Mum. Bert stared down at Mr. Goon's trousers to see if they were torn. They didn't appear to be.

'You going to report the dog?' asked Bert.

'I caught it chasing sheep,' said Goon, taking off his helmet. 'Very serious crime, that, for a dog. I tried to catch it but I couldn't. I'd give anything to have that dog here under lock and key. I'd teach it a few things!'

'What would you give me if I got it for you?' asked Bert. Goon stared at him. Mum was taking no notice; she was busy at the cupboard with a cake-tin. Goon nodded his head towards the hall, and Bert followed him there.

Fatty had heard every word. He wondered whose dog this was that Goon was talking about. He knew that the farmer had been worried by sheep-chasing dogs. It never occurred to him that Goon was actually talking about Buster.

A whispered conversation followed. Fatty only caught a few words, but he guessed the rest. Goon was arranging with young Bert to catch the dog and bring it to him. The sum of half a crown was mentioned. Fatty frowned. How wrong of Goon to do a thing like that! He wished he knew whose dog it was—he would certainly warn the owner!

Goon appeared in the office, looking rather pleased with himself, and young Bert went back to the kitchen.

Fatty didn't get up. He held out a gracious hand and bowed in a very lady-like way. Goon was rather impressed with this behaviour, though not with Fatty's clothes. Still—foreigners did seem to wear peculiar things sometimes.

'What can I do for you, Madam?' said Goon.

'I am a friend of Mrs. Trotteville,' said Fatty, truthfully. 'A vairy GREAT friend.'

'Ah,' said Goon, impressed. He was in awe of Mrs. Trotteville. 'You staying with her, then?'

'I shall be wiz her for three wiks,' said Fatty, sticking to the truth. 'I sell tickets for the beeg Sale. You will buy one, yes?'

'Er—well—er—can I offer you a cup of coffee?' said Goon, seeing Mum coming in with a tray. 'I hear you can read hands. I suppose you'll be doing that at

Mr. Goon couldn't resist having his hand read

the Sale?'

'You would like me to read your beeg, beeg hand now—and you will buy a ticket?' offered Fatty.

Mr. Goon couldn't resist having his hand read. Mum fetched another cup of coffee—and Mr. Goon held out a large hand, palm upwards, to Fatty. How Fatty wished that Larry and the others could see him!

6   A FEW REPORTS

THAT evening, after tea, the Five Find-Outers met in Fatty's shed as arranged. Fatty was there first, grinning whenever he remembered how he had read Goon's hand. In his pocket were two half-crowns that Goon had given him for Daisy's ticket. Easy!

The others all arrived together. Fatty welcomed them. He had orangeade and biscuits, which every one was pleased to see, in spite of the fact that they had all made a very good tea not half an hour before.

'Now, are we all ready? We'll have our various reports,' said Fatty. 'You first, Pip—you seem to be bursting with news.'

'I am,' said Pip, and poured out the story of how he had shadowed Goon, seen him go to the farmhouse, and waited for him in the field. He told how Buster had also shadowed *him*, and burst on him as he sat watching the sheep and the lambs.

'Then old Buster got excited and some lambs were afraid and scampered away, making the sheep run,' said Pip. 'Up came old Goon and said that Buster ought to be shot for worrying sheep!'

'Good gracious!' said Daisy. 'Surely he didn't mean that? Buster has never, never chased a sheep, has he, Fatty?

'Never,' said Fatty, who was listening intently. 'Go on, Pip.'

'There's nothing much more to tell except that Goon was idiot enough to try and catch Buster,' said

Pip. 'And Buster had a fine old game with him, of course, trying to nip his ankles. It would have served Goon right if he *had* nipped them! The only reason that Goon said that Buster was chasing sheep was just so that he could report him—but, oh, Fatty, Buster *couldn't* be shot just on Goon's report, could he?'

'Don't worry. I'll see that he isn't,' said Fatty, grimly. 'We'd get on to Chief-Inspector— I mean, Superintendent—Jenks at once! It's funny, though, when I went to see Goon this morning, he came in talking all about some dog or other that he wanted brought in for sheep-chasing— I bet it was Buster, though he didn't say the name.'

'But—why did he tell you?' said Pip, surprised. 'He might have guessed you'd hear about it from me.'

'Oh, he didn't know *I* was sitting there in his office,' said Fatty. 'I was disguised, of course. I'll have to think about this story of yours, Pip. I have an idea that Goon has made some arrangement with a nasty, skinny little kid to catch Buster. Son of a woman who was cleaning the house for Goon.'

'I saw him at the door,' said Pip, remembering. 'Gosh, he'd never have the nerve to catch Buster, surely?'

'I don't know. We'll have to watch out,' said Fatty. 'Listen and I'll tell you how I sold the ticket to Goon.'

Daisy gave a shriek of delight. 'Oh, did you really manage to? Oh, Fatty, you *are* clever! You must have been jolly well disguised.'

'Well—I was,' said Fatty, trying to be modest, 'As a matter of fact, I don't believe even Bets here would have guessed it was me. I went as a friend of my mother, a foreign one, rather down-at-heel-you know, old lady-gone-to-seed-a-bit! Staying with dear Mrs. Trotteville for three weeks.'

Every one roared. 'Oh, Fatty!' said Bets. 'It's so true too—you are a friend of your mother—and you *are* here for three weeks. Marvellous!'

'I sold the ticket by reading Goon's hand,' went on Fatty, enjoying himself. 'He stuck his great fat paw on my knee, and I exclaimed over it, and said how extraordinary it was—and so it was, with its enormous fingers and great fat palm. I could hardly see the lines on it for fat.'

'What did you tell him?' asked Daisy.

'Oh—I told him his name was Theophilus, and that he had plenty of nephews—one very clever one called Ern,' said Fatty. Every one laughed. Mr. Goon disliked Ern intensely. 'I told him he would handle a lot of money,' went on Fatty.

'Yes! His wages every week!' grinned Pip.

'But the best bit was where I looked hard at his hand—like this,' said Fatty, clutching Daisy's hand suddenly and making her jump. He peered closely at it, then held it away, then peered at it again.

'Ha! Zis is a vairy pee-culiar thing I see!' said Fatty, sounding like the Frenchwoman again. 'I see— a fat boy—a beeg fat boy.'

There were roars of laughter at this. 'Oh Fatty!'

said Bets. 'You pretended you saw yourself in Goon's hand! What did he say?'

'He seemed very startled,' said Fatty, in his own voice. 'He said, "What! That toad! Tell me more."'

'So you told him more?' said Larry, grinning.

'Oh yes. I said "BEWAAAAARE of zis fat boy There is some mystery here. Ze fatboy and the mystery are togezzer!"' Fatty paused and twinkled round at the others.

'That made Goon sit up, I can tell you. He said, "What! A mystery! Go on—tell me about it. What mystery is it?"'

'What did you say?' said Bets, with a sudden giggle.

'I said, "I do not know zis mystery. It will come. But BEWAAAAARE of zis beeg, fat boy!"'

'Oh Fatty! I do do wish I'd been there,' said Bets, and the others all agreed fervently. Oh, to have sat and watched Fatty reading Mr. Goon's hand!

'Is that all?' asked Daisy. 'Tell us it all over again.'

'No. Now now,' said Fatty, reluctantly. 'We ought to hear Larry's story. Time's getting on. Anyway, the result of all this amazing hand-reading was that Goon handed over two half-crowns for Daisy's ticket like an absolute lamb. He even said that if I was going to be at the Sale he'd be along for another hand-reading to see if the mystery was any nearer. He simply BEAMED at me!'

'Oh, dear—what a wonderful morning you had,' said Larry, as Fatty handed over two half-crowns to the delighted Daisy. 'Now I'll tell my story.'

'Yes, tell yours,' said Daisy. 'You should have seen him dressed up as a window-cleaner, Fatty! He borrowed an old pair of dirty blue dungarees, put on a frightful old cloth cap that has hung in the shed for ages, and made himself filthy—hands, face, and neck! Honestly, I'd never employ him as a window-cleaner. He looked more like a sweep.'

Fatty grinned. 'Good work,' he said to Larry. 'Go on—tell us what you did.'

'Well,' said Larry, 'I dressed up, just as Daisy's told you. And I took an old pail and a leather, and off I went.'

'Where did you go?' asked Fatty.'

'Well, I remembered I'd better not choose a house that needed a ladder for upstairs windows,' said Larry. 'So I tried to think of a bungalow somewhere, with the windows all on one floor. And I remembered seeing one next to that house called Green-Trees—do you remember, the one that that foreigner went to—the man we mistook to be Fatty.'

'Oh, yes, I remember the bungalow too,' said Fatty. 'Good for you! In Holly Lane, wasn't it? A little place with an untidy garden, standing a bit back from the road.'

'That's right. What a memory you've got, Fatty! You never miss anything,' said Larry. 'Well, I took my pail and my leather and walked up the path to the bungalow. I knocked at the door.'

'Was any one in?' asked Bets.

'I didn't think so at first, because nobody answered,' said Larry. 'So I knocked again, very loudly. And a voice said "Come in." I opened the door and yelled inside. 'Window-cleaner! Is it all right to do the windows now?" And somebody shouted "Yes!" '

'Who was it? Did you see?' asked Fatty.

No, I didn't,' said Larry. 'Anyway, I got some water from a water-butt outside, and started on the back window—two of them. There wasn't any one in the room there; it was a bedroom with a single bed, a chair, and a table—rather poor. As I was doing those windows I heard the front door slam and somebody went up the path to the road. I didn't see him—or her, it might have been.'

'Was the house left empty then?' asked Fatty.

'I thought so, at first. But when I came round to the front to do the two front windows. I saw there was someone inside that room,' said Larry. 'And this is the queer part of my story.'

Every one sat up at once.

'Queer—how do you mean? asked Fatty.

'Well, at first I thought there wasn't any one in the room,' said Larry, 'and I thought I'd buck up and clean the windows and go, glad to have finished the job—actually, when I was doing it, I thought it was a bit silly! And then I suddenly saw some one on the floor.'

'On the *floor*! Hurt, do you mean?' asked Pip.

'No. He didn't seem to be hurt,' said Larry. 'He semed to be feeling the chairs—he felt first one, and then another, muttering to himself all the time.'

'But what for?' asked Fatty. 'And who was he,

anyway?'

'I don't know. He looked a very *old* man,' said Larry. 'He had a kind of night-cap on his head, and he wore pyjamas and a dressing-gown. He kept feeling one chair after another—under neath them— and then he came to a chair that seemed to satisfy him. He nodded and gave a kind of chuckle.'

'Extraordinary! What did he do next?' asked Fatty, most i rested.

'He crawl over the floor to a kind of wheelchair, and somehow got into it,' said Larry. 'His night-cap slipped off, and he was quite bald, poor old fellow. He sat in front of some kind of stove, and then he dropped off to sleep as I watched him.'

'Didn't he see you looking in?' asked Bets.

'No. I think he's almost blind,' said Larry. 'He had to *feel* for the chairs—as if he couldn't really see them. Funny, wasn't it?'

'Yes. Very queer,' said Pip. ' I wonder what he was feeling all over the chairs for. Do you suppose he had got something hidden in one of them? Money, perhaps?'

'Possibly. He might be afraid of robbers and have hidden his little hoard somewhere odd that he considered safe,' said Fatty. 'Well, it's a peculiar story, Larry, and it's a good thing you weren't a *real* window-cleaner—a dishonest one might easily have guessed what the old man was doing! Making sure his savings were still safe!'

'I stripped off my dungarees in the bushes, cleaned myself up a bit with the leather, and went home,' said Larry. 'I'd really rather work on a real mystery than do all this pretend shadowing and disguising and window-cleaning. It doesn't really *lead* to anything!'

But Larry was wrong. Quite wrong. It led to quite a lot of things. It led, in fact, to a really first-class Mystery!

7   WHERE IS BUSTER?

FOR the next day or two Fatty kept a sharp eye on Buster, wondering if the skinny little boy would really try to kidnap him. But there seemed to be no sign of Bert.

And then one evening Buster disappeared! Fatty had gone out on his bicycle with the others to the cinema, and had left Buster safely in the kitchen with the Cook, who was very fond of him. When he came back, he sat down and finished a book he was reading, and it wasn't until he had finished it that he realized that Buster had not come scampering to be with him as usual.

He went to the door and shouted. 'Buster! Where are you?'

It was half-past ten. Cook and Jane had gone to bed. His mother and father were out playing bridge and the house was very quiet.

'BUSTER! Where are you?' yelled Fatty again.

A voice came from upstairs. 'Oh, Master Frederick, is that you shouting? You did give me a start! Isn't Buster with you? He wanted to go out at half-past nine, and we thought he heard you coming in to put your bicycle away, so we let him out. Didn't you see him?'

'No, Jane! I haven't seen him since I've been in,' said Fatty. 'Where on earth can he be? I'll open the front door and yell.'

He stood at the front door and shouted. 'Buster

BUSTER!'

But no Buster came. Fatty was puzzled. Where could he have gone? Well, perhaps he would come in when his mother and father came back.

But Buster didn't. It was a very worried Fatty who greeted his parents when they came in at twelve o'clock.

'Frederick! Why aren't you in bed?' began his mother. 'It's midnight!'

'Have you seen Buster?' said Fatty... 'You haven't? Gosh, then, where can he be?'

'He's probably gone to visit one of his friends, and forgotten the time, like you do sometimes!' said his father. 'Get to bed now, Buster will be back in the morning, barking outside at six o'clock and waking us all.'

There was nothing for it but to go to bed. Fatty undressed and got between the sheets. But he couldn't help remembering the whispered conversation he had heard in Goon's little hall—and Bert's mean little face. Had Bert some how got hold of Buster?

Buster didn't come barking at the front door in the morning. He hadn't even appeared by breakfast-time! Fatty was by now quite certain that some how or other the skinny little boy had managed to get hold of the little Scottie. He went out into the garden to investigate. Perhaps he could find something to explain Buster's disappearance.

He did find something. He found a small bit of liver attached to a short piece of string. Fatty pounced on it, frowning fiercely.

'That's it! That little beast Bert must have come along with some liver, tied it on a bit of string and drawn it along for Buster to follow him. And old Buster leapt at it and got the liver and chewed the string in half. Then he must have followed Bert—and probably more liver—till Bert managed to slip a lead on him and take him off.'

He threw the bit of liver away and went indoors angrily. The telephone bell rang as he walked into the hall. His father was there and took up the receiver.

'Hallo! Yes, this is Mr. Trotteville speaking. Who's that? Mr. Goon? What's that? Do speak up, please, I can only hear a mumble.'

There was a short silence. Fatty stood near by, listening. Mr. Goon? Now what was this?

'I can't believe it!' said Mr. Trotteville into the telephone. 'Buster has never chased a thing in his life—except your ankles. All right—come and see me. I don't believe it!'

He put the receiver down and faced Fatty. 'That fellow Goon says your dog Buster was caught red-handed last night, chasing sheep.'

'It couldn't have been Buster,' said Fatty. 'It must be some other dog.'

'He says he's got Buster in his shed now,' said Mr. Trotteville. 'He'll be shot, you know, if this is true. Where was he last night?'

'Some one came and enticed him away,' said Fatty. 'Some one who's told a lie about Buster! Who says they saw him chasing sheep?'

'A boy called Bert Mickle,' said his father. 'Goon says this boy was out walking in the fields last night, and actually saw Buster worrying the sheep.

He managed to catch him, and slipped a rope under his collar. He took him to Mr. Goon's, but the policeman was out, so the boy locked the dog into the shed there— and he's there still. Now what are we to do?'

'It's an absolute untruth,' said Fatty, looking rather white. 'It's a plan laid between them. I'll pay Goon out for this. When's he coming, Dad?'

'In half an hour's time,' said Mr. Trotteville. 'I'll have to see him. I can't bear the sight of him.'

Fatty disappeared. He knew quite certainly that Buster had not been chasing sheep. He also knew that the horrid little Bert had told a lot of lies, and he was sure that Goon knew it. And Buster might be shot because of all that!

Fatty raced down to his shed. He put on a red wig, inserted some false plastic teeth in front of his own and dressed himself in an old suit, with a butcher-boy's blue-and-white apron in front. Then he jumped on his bicycle and rode off down to Goon's house. He stood whistling on the pavement opposite, apparently reading a comic with great interest—but all the time he was watching for Goon to come out.

Goon came at last and wheeled his bicycle out of the front gate. He looked exceedingly pleased with himself, and hummed a little tune as he rode off.

The butcher-boy opposite scowled and folded up his comic. Leaving his bicycle beside the kerb, he crossed the road and went round to the back of Goon's house.

He glanced at the shed in the garden. A subdued but angry barking came from it. Then a scraping at the door.

Fatty bit his lip. That was Buster all right!

He knocked at the back door. Mrs. Mickle came, wiping her hands on her apron as usual.

'You're wanted up at home, Mrs. Mickle,' said Fatty. 'Message to say you're to go at once.'

'Oh, dear! oh, dear! I hope my mother's not been taken ill again,' Mrs. Mickle. 'Bert! I'm wanted up at home. You'd better keep on here till I come back. Mr. Goon's out.'

'Bert had better go with you,' said Fatty, firmly. He wanted them both out of the way as quickly as possible.

'No. I'm staying here,' said Bert, thinking of the tarts and buns he could take out of the larder with both Mr. Goon and his mother out of the house.

That was that. Bert was not going to move, Fatty could see. All right—he would make him!

Mrs. Mickle took off her apron and fled up the street. Bert stood at the front door and watched her go. Fatty nipped in at the back door and hid himself in a cupboard outside the kitchen.

Bert came back, having shut the hall-door. He whistled. Ha, now for the larder! Fatty heard him go into the kitchen and open the larder door. It creaked. Fatty peeped out of the cupboard.

A hollow voice suddenly spoke behind Bert. 'Beware! Your sins will find you out. BEWARE!'

Bert turned round in a hurry. There was nobody in the kitchen at all. He stood there, trembling, a small jam-tart in one hand.

'Who took that dog away last night?' said another voice, which seemed to come from behind the kitchen door. 'Who took him away?'

'Don't, don't!' cried poor Bert, and the jam-tart fell from his hand. 'I took him, I took him! Who is it talking to me?'

A loud growling came from another corner and Bert yelled. He looked all round for the dog but couldn't see one. Then a loud me-owing began. 'MEEE-ow! MEEE-ow!'

But no cat was to be seen. Bert began to howl! and tears poured down his cheeks. 'Mum!' he cried. 'Mum!'

But Mum was far away up the street. Fatty began again. 'Who told a lie? Who took that dog away?'

'I'll tell the truth, I will, I will!' sobbed Bert. 'I'm a bad boy, I am.'

'BEWARE!' said the deep hollow voice again. It was too much for Bert. He fled into the hall and out of the front door, leaving it open as he went. Fatty heard the scampering of his feet, and grinned. So much for Bert. Served him right—trying to get an innocent dog shot!

Fatty went to the garden shed. He had with him a bunch of keys that he had seen hanging from a hook on the kitchen dresser. One of them unlocked the shed.

Buster flew at him, barking in delight. He careered round Fatty, and Fatty picked him up and squeezed him till the little Scottie had no breath left in his body. He licked Fatty's face vigorously.

Then Fatty suddenly caught sight of something— Mr. Goon's enormous black cat sitting high up on a wall, watching Buster out of sleepy insolent eyes. He knew he was too high up for any dog to catch. An idea came to Fatty.

'Just half a minute, Buster old fellow,' he said, and

put the Scottie inside the house, shutting the kitchen door on him.

Then he went to the great tom-cat. He stroked it and murmured flattering things into its pricked-up ear. It purred loudly. Most animals loved Fatty!

It allowed him to lift it off the wall and fondle it. He walked with it to the shed and took it inside. He set it down on a sack that had evidently been placed there for Buster, and stroked it.

Then he went swiftly to the door, shut it, locked it and took the keys back to the kitchen. Buster had been frantically scraping at the door, trying to get to Fatty. Fatty picked him up, and went out of Goon's house, across the road to his bicycle. He put Buster in the basket, and rode off whistling shrilly like an errand-boy, thinking happy thoughts!

'All right, Mr. Goon! You can take my father down to see Buster in the shed—threaten to have him shot! You'll find nothing there but your own black tom-cat!' Fatty grinned at his thoughts, and Buster yapped happily in the basket. Why had he been shut up like that? He didn't know. But nothing mattered now. He was with Fatty, and Buster's world was cheerful and happy once more.

Fatty shot in at his side-gate and cycled down to his shed. He tore off his errand-boy things. Then he shut Buster up in the shed, with many apologies, and went back to the house. Was Mr. Goon still there? Well, he could say what he liked! Buster was safe!

8 MR GOON GETS A SHOCK

MR. Goon had been at Fatty's house for about five minutes, and was thoroughly enjoying himself. He knew that neither Mr. nor Mrs. Trotteville liked him, and it was pleasant to Mr. Goon to bring them such bad news about Buster.

Fatty sauntered into the room, and Mr. Goon looked at him triumphantly. 'Morning, Mr. Goon,' said Fatty. 'Lovely April day, isn't it? Got any mystery in the offing yet?'

'I've come about that there dog of yours,' said Mr. Goon, almost joyfully. 'Been caught chasing sheep again.'

'Rubbish,' said Fatty, briskly. 'Never chased one in his life!'

'I've got evidence,' said Goon, going slightly purple. 'And I've got the dog too, see? Locked up in my shed.'

'I don't believe it,' said Fatty. 'I'll have to see the dog first, before I believe it's old Buster. He's not the dog in your shed, I'll be bound.'

Mr. Trotteville looked at Fatty in surprise. Fatty winked at him. His father heaved a sigh of relief. He had no idea what Fatty was up to; but he began to feel that somehow, somewhere, Goon was not going to get away with this tale about Buster.

Goon went very purple indeed. He turned to Mr. Trotteville. 'If you'll be so good, sir, as to come along with me and identify the dog. It would be a great help,' he said. 'Master Frederick had better come too. After all, it's his dog.'

'I'll come all right,' said Fatty. 'You coming too, Dad?'

'Yes. I'll get the car out,' said his father, still puzzled over Fatty's attitude. 'You can come with me, Frederick. You cycle off, Goon, and we'll be there as soon as you are.'

Mr. Trotteville went to get the car. Goon disappeared on his bicycle, purple but still triumphant. Fatty went to the telephone.

'Oh—is that Mrs. Hilton? Good morning. Please may I speak to Pip? Shan't keep him a minute.'

Pip was fetched. Fatty spoke to him urgently. 'Pip? Listen. No time for explanations. I want you to do something for me.'

'Right,' said Pip's voice, sounding excited. 'I say—is this a mystery starting up?'

'No. Nothing like that. Listen now. I want you to come up here quickly, unlock my shed, get old Buster out of it, and bring him down to Goon's house. Put him on a lead. Don't come into Goon's—just wait outside till I come out. Tell you everything then!'

Click. Fatty put down the receiver. He rubbed his hands and grinned. Ah, Mr. Goon, you are going to be very very surprised!

He got into the car beside his father, who glanced at him sideways. 'I gather, Frederick,' he said, 'that you are quite happy about this Buster affair now? But you possibly do not want to tell me why?'

'How right you are, Dad,' said Fatty, cheerfully. 'I'll just tell you this : Goon played a very dirty trick, but it's not going to come off!'

There was silence after that. Mr. Trotteville drove straight to Goon's house, and the two of them got out. Goon himself had just arrived, and was astonished to find the house completely empty. No Mrs. Mickle, no Bert!

Mr. Trotteville and Fatty went in at the front door, and at the very same moment Mrs. Mickle and Bert arrived at the back. Bert's eyes were red, and he looked frightened. Mrs. Mickle was in a rage.

She spoke to Mr. Goon. 'I'm sorry to have left the house so sudden-like, Mr. Goon—but that dratted boy of the butcher's come along and told me I was wanted at home—so I left Bert here in charge, and rushed home—and I wasn't wanted after all. Just wait till I get that butcher's boy!'

Bert gave a sudden sniff. Mrs. Mickle looked at him in disgust. 'And Bert—who I left here just to stay till you were back, sir—he come racing home, howling like I don't know what. Scared of being left in your place alone, and telling such tales as I never heard the like of in my life!'

'Mr. Trotteville, this is the boy who caught Buster chasing sheep last night,' said Goon.

'I never!' said Bert, suddenly, and burst into tears. 'I never, I never!'

'Bert! How can you tell stories like that?' said his mother. 'Why, you stood there and told Mr. Goon all about it this morning. I heard you!'

'He's a bit nervous, I expect,' said Goon, surprised

and most displeased. 'You caught the dog yourself, didn't you, Bert?'

'I never,' said Bert, who seemed quite incapable of saying anything else.

Goon gave it up. 'Well, the dog's in the shed, and it's the very dog Bert brought in and put there himself.'

'I never!' said Bert, making Mr. Goon long to box his ears. The big policeman strode out through the kitchen and into the garden, taking with him the keys of the shed. He inserted one into the lock, and flung the door open, expecting Buster to rush out and declare himself.

But no dog arrived. Instead, Mr. Goon's extremely large black cat strolled out haughtily, sat down outside the shed, and began to wash himself.

Goon's eyes nearly fell out of his head. Fatty gave a roar of laughter and Bert howled in fright. Bert *had* put Buster into the shed; and to see the black cat come out instead of the dog was quite terrifying to poor Bert.

'I never, I never, I never!' he sobbed, and hid his face in his mother's apron.

Goon's mouth opened and shut like a goldfish's, and he couldn't say a word. The cat went on washing itself, and Bert went on howling.

'Well, Mr. Goon, if it's a cat that was shut into this shed, and not Buster, I really don't think it's worth while our wasting our time with you any more,' said Mr. Trotteville, sounding quite disgusted. 'Did you say that you yourself saw the dog that was put into the shed?

Goon hadn't seen Buster. He had been out when Bert arrived with the dog and he had just taken Bert's word for it. Now he didn't know whether Bert had shut up a dog or the cat. He glared at the boy as if he could bite him.

Bert howled afresh. He put his hand in his pocket and took out half a crown. He held it out to Goon. 'Here you are. I've been wicked. Here's the half-crown you gave me, Mr.Goon. I'll never go after dogs again for you.'

'Well, I think we've heard enough,' said Mr. Trotteville, coldly. 'Goon, you deserve to be reported for all this. I've a good mind to do so. Come on, Frederick.'

'But—but I don't understand it,' said Goon, his eyes popping out of his head. 'Why, I *heard* that dog barking in the shed. I tell you! Hark! Isn't that him barking now?'

It was! Pip was walking up and down outside, with Buster on the lead, and Buster had recognized Mr. Trotteville's car parked nearby. He was barking his head off in delight.

They all went to the front door—and poor Goon nearly fainted when he saw Buster, Buster himself, pulling on Pip's lead and barking frantically.

'Hallo, Pip,' said Fatty, in a very ordinary voice. 'Thanks for taking Buster for a walk. Slip him off the lead, will you?'

'No. No don't,' said Goon finding his voice suddenly. 'Wait till I'm indoors.'

He shot into the house and slammed the door. Fatty grinned at his father. 'I *should* like to know how the cat took the place of the dog,' murmured Mr. Trotteville, getting into the car with Fatty and Buster. Pip got in too, puzzled, but grinning all over his face.

'Tell you when we get home,' said Fatty. 'My word— I wouldn't like to be young Bert right now!'

Mr. Goon's extremely large black cat strolled out haughtily

Young Bert was indeed having a bad time. Mrs. Mickle was crying, Bert was howling, and Goon felt rather like howling himself. He felt a fool, an idiot—to bring that high -and-mighty Mr. Trotteville down to show him a dog locked up his shed—and then his own black cat walked out! Gah!

Bert told a peculiar tale of voices in every corner, when he had been left alone in the house. Goon looked round uneasily. Voices? What did Bert mean? He suddenly remembered Fatty's ability to throw his voice, just like any ventriloquist. *Could* Fatty have been here? No, impossible!

The more poor Goon thought about it, the more impossible everything seemed. He looked at Bert with so much dislike that that skinny little boy decided he'd slip off home. What with his Mum cross with him, and Mr. Goon looking as if he'd like to eat him up, and those voices he had heard, life wasn't worth living! So Bert slipped off home.

'I think Pip and I will get out of the car, and have an ice-cream, Dad,' said Fatty to his father, as they drove down the main street. 'I somehow feel like one. You can have one too, Buster.'

'Right,' said his father and stopped. 'I'm glad Buster's all right, Frederick . I'll hear all about it later.'

Fatty and Pip got out with Buster. 'I say—do tell me what's been happening!' said Pip.

'Come in here and I'll tell you,' said Fatty. 'Goon tried to play a very dirty trick—and it didn't come off. Come along.'

And over three ice-creams Fatty told the horrified

Pip the dreadful story of how Buster had nearly been shot for doing something he hadn't done! Pip almost choked over his ice-cream!

'Look—there's Larry and Daisy and Bets,' said Pip, suddenly. 'Let's have them in and tell them too.'

But it turned out that the other three had already had ice-creams, and were now on their way to fetch something. 'Larry left the leather behind in the garden of that bungalow whose windows he cleaned the other day,' explained Daisy. 'And Mother's been hunting for it everywhere. So we thought we'd better go and find it in the bushes. It's sure to be there still.'

'We'll all come and then you can come back home with me and I'll tell you a most peculiar tale,' said Fatty. '*Most* peculiar—isn't it, Buster?'

'Not a mystery, is it?' asked Bets, hopefully, as they all went along together. Fatty shook his head.

'There's not even the smell of a one,' he said. 'Look—isn't this the place, Larry—that little bungalow there?'

'Yes,' said Larry, and went into the garden. He came back quite quickly, looking rather scared.

'I say—there's somebody shouting like anything in that bungalow. It sounds as if they're yelling "Police! Police! Police!"'

'*Really*? Come on, we'll see what's up,' said Fatty, and they all trooped in at the gate. Fatty went to the door. It was shut. From within came a curious croaking shout.

'Police! Police! Fetch the police!'

'Whatever can be the matter?' said Fatty. 'I'd better go in and see!'

9   THE OLD MAN IN THE BUNGALOW

THE five children and Buster went up the path. The front door was shut. Fatty went to look in at one of the windows, and the others followed.

Green curtains were drawn back to let the light into the room. In the middle of the room sat an old man in a small arm-chair. He was beating on the arms and shouting 'Police! Police! Fetch the police!'

'It's the old man I saw when I cleaned the windows,' said Larry. 'What's the matter with him? Why does he want the police?'

They all looked at the old fellow. He had on a dressing-gown over pyjamas, and a night-cap that had slipped to one side of his bald head. He had a small beard on his chin and a scarf tied loosely round his neck.

By the stove stood a wheel-chair with a rug half-falling off it, and on a shelf near by was a small portable radio, within reach of the old man's hand. The children could hear it playing loudly.

'Something's upset the old fellow,' said Fatty. 'Let's try the door and see if it's unlocked.'

They went back to the door, and Fatty turned the handle. The door opened at once.

They all went in, Buster too. The old man neither heard nor saw them. He still sat in the chair, beating its arms, and wailing for the police.

Fatty touched him on the arm, and the old fellow

jumped. He stopped shouting and blinked up at Fatty with watery eyes. He put out his hand and felt along Fatty's coat.

'Who is it? Is it the police? Who are you?'

'I'm some one who heard you shouting and came to see what was the matter,' said Fatty speaking loudly. 'Can we help you? What has happened?'

It was clear that the old man could hardly see. He peered round at the others and drew his dressing-gown round him. He began to shiver.

'Look—you get back to the fire,' said Fatty. 'I'll take one arm—Larry, you take the other. The old fellow has had a shock of some kind—he's trembling. Turn off that radio, Bets!'

The old man made no objection to being helped to his own chair. He sat down in it with a sigh, and let Daisy arrange his cushions and rug. He peered at them again.

'Who are you all? Fetch the police, I say,' he said, and his voice quavered as he spoke.

'Do tell us what's the matter,' said Daisy. But he couldn't hear her, and she repeated the question loudly.

'Matter? Matter enough. My money's gone!' he said, and his voice rose to a howl. ' All my money! Now what's to happen to me?'

'How do you know it's gone?' said Fatty, loudly. 'Didn't you keep it in the bank, or the post-office?'

'Banks! I don't trust banks!' wailed the old fellow. 'I hid it where nobody could find it. Now it's gone.'

'Where did you hide it?' asked Larry.

'What? What's that?' said the old man, cupping his

hand over his ear. 'Speak up.'

'I said, "WHERE DID YOU HIDE IT?"' repeated Larry. A sly look came over the old fellow's face. He shook his head.

'I shan't tell you. No, that's my secret. It was hidden where nobody could find it. But now it's gone.'

'Tell us where you hid it, and we'll have a good look for it ourselves,' said Daisy, loudly. But the old man shook his head more vigorously than ever.

'You get the police!' he said. 'I want the police!' Two hundred pounds that's what's gone—all my savings. The police will get it back for me. You get the police.'

Fatty didn't in the least want to go and find Mr.Goon. Goon would turn them all out and not let them help at all. He would be bossy and domineering and a perfect nuisance.

'When did you miss the money?' he asked the old man.

'Just now,' he said. 'About ten minutes ago. I looked for it—and it was gone! Oh, I'm a poor old man and people have robbed me! Get the police.'

'We will,' said Fatty, comfortingly. 'Just tell us when you *last* saw the money. Do you remember?'

'Course I remember,' said the old fellow, pulling his night-cap straight. 'But I didn't *see* it. I'm nearly blind. I *felt* it. It was there all right.'

'When was that?' asked Fatty, patiently.

'Last night,' said the old man. 'About mid-night I reckon. I was in bed, and I couldn't sleep, and I sat up and worried about my money. You see, I'm all alone here since my daughter's gone away. Well, I got out of bed and I came in here. And I felt for my money. It was there all right.'

'I see,' said Fatty. 'So somebody must have taken it between then and now. Has any one been to see you this morning?'

'Yes. Yes, of course,' he said. 'But I'm muddled now. I misremember who came—except my granddaughter, of course—she comes every day and cleans around. She's a good girl. And the grocer came. But I misremember. You get the police. They'll find my money for me!'

A big tear fell from one eye and rolled down his cheek. Bets felt very sorry for him. Poor old man—all alone, and worried about his money. Where could it be? Had it really been stolen—or had he just forgotten where he had put it? If only he would tell them!

'We'll have to tell Goon,' said Fatty to the others. 'It's a pity. We might have been able to clear this up ourselves if we'd had a chance.'

The five children suddenly heard footsteps coming up the path. Who was it? There was a loud knock at the door, then the handle turned, and a man walked in. He stared in surprise at the children. Buster barked loudly.

'Hallo!' said the man. He was young and smartly dressed. 'Who are you? Are you visiting my great-uncle? Hallo, Uncle! How are you?'

'Oh, Wilfrid—is it you?' said the old man, putting out a hand as if to find out where Wilfrid was. 'Wilfrid, my money's gone!'

'What! Gone? What do you mean?' asked Wilfrid.

'Didn't I tell you somebody would rob you if you didn't let me put it into the bank for you?'

'It's gone, it's gone,' said his uncle, rocking himself to and fro.

'Where did you keep it?' asked Wilfrid, looking all round. 'I bet it's not gone, Uncle! You've forgotten where you hid it! Maybe up the chimney—or under a floor-board?'

'I'm not telling any one,' said the old man. 'I want the police! I'm tired. I want my money and I want the police!'

'We'll go and telephone for the police, if you like,' Fatty offered. 'I see there are telephone wires leading next door. I expect they'd let me use the phone.'

'What are *you* doing here, anyway?' said Wilfrid, suddenly.

'Nothing. We just heard the old man calling,' said Fatty, thinking it better not to say that Larry had gone to find the leather he had left behind in the bushes, and had heard the old man shouting as he passed the bungalow. 'Anyway, we'll go and telephone now. The police will be up in a few minutes, I'm sure.'

'Good-bye,' said Bets to the old man, but he didn't hear her. He was moaning softly to himself. 'My money! Now what shall I do? All gone, all gone!'

The five of them went out with Buster. They went down the path and walked beside the fence till they came to Green-Trees. They went up the path to the blue front door. Fatty rang the bell.

A pleasant-faced woman answered it. She looked very French, and Fatty decided that she must be the sister whose house the bundled-up man had tried so hard to find.

'Excuse me,' said Fatty, politely. 'Do you think I might use your telephone? The old man in the bungalow next door has been robbed, and we want to tell the police.'

The woman looked startled. 'A robbery? Next door? Oh, the poor old man! Yes, come in and use my telephone! It is in this room here.'

She spoke English extremely well, but had a slight accent which was rather pleasant. She was very like her brother, dark and plump.

She took them into a room off the hall. A couch stood by the window, and a man lay on it coughing. He turned as they came in.

"Henri, these children want to use the telephone,' said the woman. 'You do not mind?'

'Enter, I pray you,' said the man, and then stared. 'Ah!' he said, 'zeese children I have seen before— n'est-ce-pas?'

'Yes,' said Fatty. 'We guided you to Green-Trees you remember?'

'Yes—Grintriss,' said the man with a smile. He looked quite different now, without his bulky overcoat, scarf and pulled-down hat—younger and pleasanter. He coughed. 'You will pardon me if I lie here? I am not so well.'

'Of course,' said Fatty. 'I hope you don't mind our coming in here like this—but the old fellow next door has been robbed of his money—or so he says—and we want to tell the police.'

Fatty took up the receiver of the telephone. 'Police Station,' he said.

A loud, sharp voice answered. 'P.C. Goon here. Who's calling?'

'Er—Frederick Trotteville,' said Fatty. 'I just wanted to tell you that...'

There was a loud snort from the other end and a crash. Goon had put down his receiver in a temper! Fatty was astonished.

'Gosh! I got Goon, and as soon as I began to speak to him he crashed back the receiver!' said Fatty. 'I suppose he's still furious about Buster. Well, I'll try again.'

He got the police station once more, and again Goon's voice answered.

'Look here, Mr. Goon,' said Fatty. 'Will you go to the bungalow called Hollies, in Holly Lane. There's been a robbery there.'

'Any more of your nonsense and I'll report you to Headquarters,' snapped Goon. 'I'm not going out on any wild-goose-chase, and have you come back here and shut my cat up in the shed again. Ho, yes,I...''

'MR. GOON! LISTEN!' shouted Fatty. 'This isn't a joke, it's...''

Crash! Goon had put down his receiver again. Fatty put down his and stared in comical dismay at the others. 'Goon's mad! He thinks I'm spoofing him. What shall we do?'

'Ring up Superintendent Jenks,' suggested Daisy. 'It's the only thing to do, Fatty!'

'I will!' said Fatty. 'It'll serve Goon right!'

10 GOON TAKES CHARGE

FATTY rang through to Police Headquarters in the next town, and asked for Superintendent Jenks.

'He's out,' said a voice. 'Who wants him?'

'Er—this is Frederick Trotteville,' said Fatty, wishing the Superintendent was in. 'I just wanted to say that a robbery has been committed at a bungalow called Hollies, in Holly Lane, Peterswood, and the old man who's been robbed asked me to tell the police.'

'You want to ring up *Peterswood* Police then,' said the voice.

'I have,' said Fatty. 'I—er—I can't seem to get hold of them. Perhaps you could ring through to tell them?'

'Right,' said the voice. 'Robbery—Hollies—Holly Lane—Peterswood. And your name is—?'

'Frederick Trotteville,' said Fatty.

'Ah, yes—I know! Friend of the Super, aren't you?' said the voice, in a more friendly tone. 'Right, sir—leave it to me.'

And so once more the telephone rang at Goon's house, and once more he answered it, snatching it up angrily, sure that it was Fatty again.

'Hallo, hallo! Who's that?' he barked.

A surprised voice answered. 'This is Head-quarters. Is that P.C. Goon?, A boy called Frederick Trotteville has just...'

'Pah!' said Goon, unable to help himself.

'What did you say?' said the voice, still more surprised.

'Nothing. Just coughed,' said Goon. 'What about this here boy?'

'He reports a robbery at the bungalow called Hollies, Holly Lane, in your area,' said the voice.

Goon's mouth fell open. So Fatty hadn't been trying to spoof him! There really had been a robbery. What a pest of a boy! Playing tricks on him and Bert—and the cat—and getting away with Buster—and now finding a robbery! What a Toad of a boy!

'Are you there?' said the voice, impatiently. 'Have you got what I said?'

'Er—yes—yes,' said Goon, scribbling down a few notes. 'Thanks. All right. I'll go right along.'

'You'd better!' said the voice, puzzled and annoyed. There was a click. Goon stared at the telephone and clicked back his receiver too. Now he'd get a rap on the knuckles for making Fatty ring Headquarters. Why hadn't he listened to him when he telephoned?

He got out his bicycle and yelled to Mrs. Mickle. 'Be back in half an hour, I expect. Have my dinner ready! This is an urgent job.'

The five children had not left Green-Trees by the time Goon cycled up. They were talking to the Frenchman, whose name turned out to be Henri Crozier. They told him all about the old fellow next door.

'I can see the front gate and front path of the bungalow from my couch,' said Henri. 'I got my sister to put the couch here because it's a pleasant view, and

I can see people who come and go down the road.'

They all looked out of the window.'You must have seen us going in, then,' said Fatty. 'Did you?'

'Oh, yes,' said Henri. 'First I saw zis boy—what does he call himself—Larry? He went in and up the path—and then he came running back to you, and you all went up the path and in at the front-door.'

Larry went red. He hoped to goodness that Henri wasn't going to ask him why he had first gone in at the gate. It wouldn't be at all easy to explain how it was that he had left a window-leather in the bushes!

Fortunately his sister came bustling in just then. Her name was Mrs. Harris and her husband, who was away, was English. She carried a box of French chocolates, very rich and creamy.

'Oh—thanks,' said Daisy, and took one. They all helped themselves, and then there came a sudden exclamation from Henri.

'See—the police have arrived!'

Sure enough, Mr. Goon was wheeling his bicycle up the front path next door. The door opened as he came and the young man, Wilfrid, appeared. He said something to Goon and they both disappeared into the bungalow.

'Well, now, perhaps the old man will be happy,' said Fatty. 'My word—what a super chocolate! We don't get chocolates like that here, Mrs. Harris.'

'We'd better go,' said Pip, looking at his watch. 'Do you know it's almost one o'clock? Good gracious! Mother said we must be back by five to. Buck up, Bets.'

The five said good-bye to Henri and his sister. 'You

will come again?' said the sister. 'Henri is so bored. He has been very ill and now he comes to me to—how do you call it?—to convalesce. Come and see him again.'

'Thank you. We will,' said Fatty, hoping fervently that Mr Goon would not also take it into his head to go and see Henri and his sister, and ask them if they had noticed visitors at the bungalow that morning! It might be very awkward to explain Larry's visit there an hour or so before. Blow that window-leather! And yet, if Larry hadn't gone to find it, he wouldn't have heard the old man shouting.

'Gosh—I never got Mother's window-leather after all!' said Larry. 'What an idiot I am . I'll slip in and get it now.'

'No, you won't,' said Fatty, firmly. 'You'll leave it there. We don't want Goon to come rushing out and asking you what you're doing. You can get it when Goon's not there.'

They all went home. Fatty was thinking hard. Why wouldn't the old man say where he had hidden his money? It was silly of him, because he might have made a mistake when he hunted for it—it might quite well still be in the bungalow in some place he had forgotten.

'Larry said that the old fellow was crawling about, feeling under the furniture, the day he went to clean the windows,' thought Fatty. 'Why feel so *much* of the furniture? Did he sometimes put the money in one place and sometimes in another? Or perhaps he divided it up— it might be in notes—and put it in several places. That's quite likely. Well, it's not a *real* mystery—only an ordinary robbery. Goon will soon find the robber. He's

The young man, Wilfrid, appeared

only got to get a list of the people who visited the bungalow this morning, and weed them out.'

That afternoon Goon arrived at Fatty's house. He asked for Fatty—and Jane showed him into the study.

'That fat policeman wants you, Master Frederick,' said Jane, when she found Fatty. 'I hope Buster hasn't got into trouble again!'

'Wuff,' said Buster, and danced round Jane. Fatty debated whether to take the little Scottie into the study with him or not. He thought he would. It might keep Goon in his place!

So in marched Fatty, with Buster at his heels. Goon was standing at the window, frowning. He was feeling angry about a lot of things. He was angrier still when he felt Buster sniffing at his heels.

'Come here, Buster,' said Fatty.'Oh, won't you sit down, Mr. Goon? Anything I can do for you?'

Goon swung round, eyeing Buster balefully. That dog! Had that tiresome Bert locked him up in the shed the night before, or hadn't he? He couldn't get a word out of Bert now.

Goon sat down heavily and took out his bulky notebook. 'I've come about the robbery,' he said.

'Well, I'm not guilty,' said Fatty, smoothly. 'I do assure you I...'

'I know you're not guilty,' said Goon, looking as if he wished Fatty were. 'What I want to know is—how did you come to be around there just when the old man was yelling blue murder?'

'He wasn't,' corrected Fatty. 'He was yelling for the police.'

'Pah!' said Goon. 'You know what I mean. Seems a funny thing to me the way you kids are always about when anything happens. Snooping round. Prying. Interfering with the Law.'

'If that's all you've come to tell me you might as well say good-bye,' said Fatty, getting up. 'I mean, I can easily bike over to the Superintendent this afternoon and tell *him* everything. I don't want to interfere with the Law. I want to help it. We couldn't help being there just at that moment. Well, good morning, Mr. Goon.'

Goon looked extremely startled. 'Now, you sit down,' he said, trying to speak pleasantly. 'I'm only just saying what a remarkable thing it is that you always seem to be around when things happen. Nothing wrong in saying that, is there?'

'You mentioned something about snooping. And prying,' said Fatty.

'Ah, well, I'm a bit upset-like,' said Mr. Goon, taking out an enormous handkerchief and wiping his forehead with it. 'Let's forget it. I don't want to interview you, but the law's the law. It's the last thing I wanted to do to-day—see you again. But I've got to ask you a few questions seeing as you and the others were the first on the spot, so to speak.'

'Ask away,' said Fatty, 'but don't be too verbose— I've got plenty to do.'

Goon wondered what 'verbose' meant—some thing rude, he'd be bound! He determined to look it up in the dictionary when he got back. Verbose!

He began to ask Fatty a few routine questions.

'What time had Fatty and the others been there?

Any one about? Anything disarranged in the living-room? What had the old man said?'

Fatty answered shortly and truthfully, thankful that Goon had no suspicion that they had actually gone to the bungalow garden to fetch something.

Goon imagined that they had been out for a walk, and had heard the old man's yells as they passed.

'That's all,' said Goon, at last. Fatty thought that he had asked the questions very well. He had left nothing out that might be useful.

Goon looked at Fatty. 'Er—I suppose you've got your own ideas about this already?' he said.

'Oh, yes,' said Fatty. 'I've no doubt it will be quite easy to find the robber. Didn't the old man give you a list of the people who had been to visit him this morning?'

'Well, he seemed so muddled,' said Goon. 'He might have been remembering *yesterday's* visitors. He's old and forgetful. I wouldn't be surprised if that money isn't still there somewhere. Er—hm—what do you think about it all?'

Fatty wasn't going to give Goon any help at all. He remembered how Goon had given Bert half a crown to catch Buster. He got up suddenly, not wanting to look at the fat policeman any more.

'Good morning,' he said to Goon, and showed him out very firmly. Let Goon find out what he could—Fatty didn't mean to help him!

11   TEA AT PIP'S

THE Five met that day in Pip's playroom at half-past three. Mrs. Hilton had said they might all go to tea, and had sent Pip and Bets out to buy cakes from the baker's.

They had staggered in with baskets full, and had arranged all the goodies themselves on big dishes. They were set on the table, ready for tea.

'Why do you put them under our noses like this?' groaned Daisy. '*Look* at those macaroons—all gooey and luscious. What a frightful temptation.'

'And look at that gingerbread cake—and that fruit cake,' said Larry. 'We never seem to have such nice teas as you do, Pip.'

'Oh, it's only when people come to tea that Mother goes a splash like this,' said Pip. 'Buster, you've got your favourite tit-bit—dog-biscuits spread with potted meat. Sniff!'

Buster sniffed, shot out a pink tongue—and the biscuit disappeared with one crunch!

'Oh, Buster! Manners, manners!' said Fatty. 'You don't see your master doing things like that, do you?'

Every one laughed. Pip got out some cards and shuffled them. Fatty told them of Goon's visit to him that afternoon.

'How you could bear to be polite to him when you knew he had planned to have Buster shot. I *don't* know!' said Pip.

'Well, I *wasn't* awfully polite, actually,' admitted Fatty. 'Also I was a bit afraid he'd ask why we were there. I wish to goodness you'd taken away that window-leather, Larry. I wouldn't put it past old Goon to snoop round the garden and find it.'

'Blow!' said Larry. 'Mother keeps on asking about it. I really must get it soon. I would have bought a new one, but when Daisy and I looked in the ironmonger's shop this afternoon, the big ones were about fifteen shillings. Fifteen shillings! I call that wicked.'

'I'll get it from the bungalow garden for you,' said Fatty. 'You mustn't go bursting in at the garden gate in full daylight, and come out waving a window-leather! I'll go to-night and get it, when it's dark.'

'I shouldn't have gone in daylight anyhow,' said Larry, a little offended. 'I'm not *quite* an idiot. But I'd be glad if you got it for me, actually, because it's difficult for me to slip out at night. It's easy for you—you can always say you're taking Buster for a walk.'

'I usually do take him for a run last thing at night,' said Fatty. 'I'll go to-night, and I'll bring the leather here to you to-morrow.'

'Are we going to go and see that old man again?' asked Daisy. 'Are we going to treat this as a mystery—a rather small one. I know—and try to find out who the robber is, or are we going to let Goon get on with it, and not bother about it at all ourselves?'

'Well, I don't actually think there's much mystery,'

said Fatty. 'Either the money is still there, hidden, and the old fellow has forgotten where, or some one's taken it who knew it was hidden. If so, it can only be one of his relatives, I should think. Quite a straightforward case. Anyway I somehow don't want to have anything more to do with Goon, after this Buster business. I just can't bear the sight of him.'

'Right. Then we don't count this as a mystery,' said Daisy. 'We'll just go on hoping. What I *was* going to say was that the person who would *really* know who visited the old man this morning would be that Frenchman—Mr. Henri. He lies on that couch and watches every one who passes—and he has a jolly good view of the bungalow's front door.'

'Yes. You're right,' said Fatty. 'He would be the first one we'd ask for a bit of information. But I think we'll leave this to Goon. To tell you the truth, I'm a bit afraid of somebody asking about a window-cleaner! Somebody may have spotted Larry—and we'd look rather foolish if it came out about his cleaning the windows.'

'I always thought it was rather a silly thing to ask me to do,' said Larry. 'I said so at the time.'

'Well, maybe it was a bit mad,' said Fatty. 'We'll forget it. Come on—whose deal is it? We'll just have time for a game before tea.'

They had a hilarious game, and an even more hilarious tea. During the game, Buster discovered that by sitting on a chair, he could reach his plate of potted-meat biscuits, and he devoured every one of them without being noticed. He then quietly jumped down and went and lay by Bets.

'Isn't he good and quiet to-day?' said Bets, patting him. 'He's usually too silly for words when we play cards and don't take any notice of him. Last time he smacked all my cards out of my hand, I remember. Didn't you, Buster?'

'Wuff,' said Buster, in a quiet voice. He was beginning to feel very guilty.

Larry tickled him. Buster didn't jump up and caper round as he usually did. He just let Larry tickle him. Larry looked at him closely.

'Why don't you you wag your tail?' he said. 'I say—don't you think Buster's gone rather quiet? Buster, old fellow, what's up?'

Buster's tail remained quite still, without a wag. Bets looked at him in alarm. 'He can't be feeling well! Buster! Good dog! Stand up, Buster, and wag your tail!'

Buster stood up, looking the picture of misery, head down and tail down. What a fuss the children made of him! He was patted and petted, stroked and fondled.

'Ought we to take him to the vet?' said Bets. 'Fatty, do you think anything's wrong?'

'We'll try him with one of his favourite potted-meat biscuits,' said Fatty, getting up. He saw the empty plate at once.

'BUSTER! You greedy pig! How dare you show such bad manners when I take you out to tea! I'm ashamed of you. Go to the corner!'

'Oh, what's he done?' cried Bets, as poor Buster

walked to the nearest corner, and sat there, face to the wall.

'Eaten every single one of his biscuits whilst we weren't looking,' said Fatty. 'I never heard a single crunch, did you? Bad dog, Buster! No. Bets, you're not to go to him. Look at the plate next to his biscuits, too. It looks as if Buster has been taking a few licks at that macaroon!'

'Well, I'd rather he was naughty than ill,' said Bets, making up her mind to slip Buster a bit of macaroon at tea-time. 'Oh Buster! What a thing to do!'

Buster made a moaning sound, and hung his head still more. 'Take no notice of him,' said Fatty, 'Another word from us and he'll burst into tears.'

'It wouldn't matter. He'd lick them all up,' said Bets. 'That's the best of being a dog—if you upset a dish you can always lick up the mess.'

'Now don't even mention Buster's name,' said Fatty, firmly. 'He's in disgrace. Come on—it's my turn to play.'

Buster had to remain in the corner while the five children had their own tea. Bets spilt some runny strawberry jam on the clean table cloth.

'Get something to wipe it,' said Pip. 'You really are a messer, Bets.'

'I'm a dog. I'm going to lick it up,' said Bets, and she did, which made them all laugh. Tea became more and more hilarious until Pip laughed so much that he fell off his chair and pulled a plate of cake-slices on top of him.

The door opened and Mrs. Hilton looked in. 'What was that crash?' she said. 'Is anybody hurt? Oh, *Pip*! What *are* you doing on the floor with cakes all over you? Please get up. Remember you are the host.'

'Be hostly, Pip,' said Bets, and Pip began to laugh again. Buster came out of his corner hopefully when he saw the pieces of cake on the floor.

'No, Buster, the floor is perfectly clean and we can eat the slices ourselves, thank you,' said Pip. 'Has Mother gone? Oh, dear, I really must be hostly. Shall we let Buster stay out of his corner? I'm sure he must be very sorry now.'

So, much to Buster's joy, he was allowed to join the others again, and was so pleased to be in favour that he went round licking every one in all the bare places he could find.

'Really, we need a towel!' said Daisy. 'That's the third time you've licked my knees, Buster—they're dripping with lick!'

The evening went too quickly. Fatty exclaimed when he looked at the playroom clock. 'Whew! Almost seven o'clock. You have your supper at seven, don't you, Pip?'

'Gosh, yes. And we've got to go and wash and get tidy,' said Pip, scrambling up. 'Sorry to rush you off; but you know what our household's like—everything on the dot. The gong will go in a minute. See yourselves out, will you!'

Fatty, Larry, Daisy and Buster went down-stairs quietly and out of the garden door. It was getting dark. 'It's a pity we haven't a mystery on hand,' said Larry, lighting his bicycle lamp. 'I feel like one, somehow. It's nice when we've got our teeth into a good, juicy mystery!'

'Well, one may turn up at any time,' said Fatty. 'Your lamp all right, Daisy? Good-bye, then. We'll see each other sometime to-morrow.'

They all cycled off, parting at the corner. Fatty yawned. He had slept very little the night before because he had been so worried about Buster. He felt very sleepy now.

'I'll go to bed early,' he thought. 'I'll take a book and read. I'll soon be asleep.'

So, much to his parents' surprise—for Fatty was usually rather a late bird—he went up to bed about a quarter to nine, with Buster at his heels.

He had a bath, and was soon settled into bed. He opened his book and read a page or two—and then, before he had even turned out his light, he was fast asleep! Half-past nine struck. Ten o'clock. Half-past ten. Eleven. Every one in the house was now in bed, and Fatty's light was the only one left on.

Buster lay quiet for some time. Then he stirred. Why hadn't Fatty taken him out for a run? He leapt on the bed and woke Fatty up with a jump.

'Gosh, it's you, you little wretch!' said Fatty, sitting up suddenly. 'I thought you were a burglar or something. What's the time—almost half-past eleven! Now don't say you want a walk at this hour, because you won't get one. I'm going to turn out the light, see?'

It was just as he switched off his lamp that Fatty remembered something. 'Blow, blow, blow! I never went to get that horrible window-leather. BLOW!'

He thought about it. Well, he *must* go and get it. He had promised Larry—and, anyway, it was important. He swung his feet out of the bed and dressed hurriedly. 'We'll be back soon,' he said to Buster. 'We'll only be a few minutes!'

But he wasn't back soon. Fatty had a most peculiar midnight adventure!

12 STRANGE HAPPENINGS

FATTY went cautiously down the stairs with Buster.
Buster always knew when he had to be quiet. He almost
held his breath as he padded downstairs at Fatty's
heels!

'Out of the garden door, Buster,' whispered Fatty,
and Buster led the way down the side-passage. Fatty
unlocked and unbolted the door quietly, and closed it
again. He locked it behind him.

Then he and Buster made their way to the back-
gate and slipped out into the road.

Buster liked this. It was exciting to be all alone
with Fatty late at night. Smells seemed much stronger
than in the day-time. Shadows were more exciting.
Buster jumped up and gave Fatty's hand a small lick.

'We're going to that bungalow called Hollies,'
Fatty told him. 'Got to collect something for Larry. If
I can't find it, *you'll* have to sniff about for it, Buster.'

'Wuff,' said Buster, happily, and ran on ahead. Up
this way—down that—round a corner—and by a
lamp-post. The street—lights went off at twelve. Soon
it would be midnight, and then there would be not be
even a lamp to break the darkness.

It was a very cloudy night, and the clouds were
low and thick. Fatty felt a spot of rain. He put his
hand in his pocket to make sure he had his torch.
Between the lamp-posts the way was very dark. Yes,

his torch was there—good.

'I'll need it when I creep into the bungalow garden,' thought Fatty. 'I'll never find Larry's leather without a light.'

He came to the turning into Holly Lane. The street lamps suddenly went out—twelve o'clock! Fatty got out his torch. He simply couldn't see a step in front of him without it on this dark night.

He came to the front gate of the little bungalow. It was all in darkness. Fatty stood and listened. Not a sound could be heard. He could go and search in safety.

He opened the front gate, shut it softly, and went up the path with Buster. He turned off to the side of the bungalow and went into the little thicket of bushes there. He switched on his torch and began to hunt around.

He couldn't see the window-leather anywhere. Blow Larry! He came up against a fence—the fence that separated the bungalow garden from the one belonging to Mr. Henri's sister. He stood and considered the matter.

'Could the wind possibly have blown the leather over the fence?' he wondered. 'No. Leathers are such heavy things when wet, as Larry's was. On the other hand, the wind might have dried it, and it would then become dry and light. The wind *might* take it then—there has been quite a breeze.'

Fatty climbed over the fence, torch in hand. He hunted all about the garden there. It was very much tidier than the garden of Hollies. He began to get into a panic. Where was this tiresome leather? Surely Goon hadn't found it?

He heard a noise and switched off his torch. It was the sound of a car-engine coming up the road. Fatty thought he would wait for the car to pass, and then have one more look.

But the car didn't pass. It semed to stop quite near by. Fatty frowned. Why didn't the car go through some gateway, and on into its own garage, so late at night?

Then he remembered that there was a doctor's house opposite. Possibly the doctor had come home for something, and gone into his house for it. He would come back in a few munutes and drive off again to a patient.

So Fatty crouched under a bush and waited, with Buster by his side. The car's engine had been turned off. Fatty could hear no footsteps at all. But he suddenly thought he could hear a bump or two— and surely that was somebody panting?

He was puzzled. It all sounded rather nearer than the doctor's house. Surely the car wasn't outside *Hollies*? If so—what was going on?

Fatty crept back to the fence that separated the two gardens. He climbed over it cautiously, lifting Buster up too, and putting him down in the bungalow garden.

'Ssh, Buster!' he whispered. 'Quiet now!'

Buster froze still. He gave a tiny growl as if to say 'Funny goings-on somewhere!' then was quite quiet. Fatty crept between the bushes, and stopped suddenly.

He could see a torch bobbing along about two feet above the front path. Somebody was there, carrying it—somebody who was panting hard. Somebody who wore rubber-soled shoes too, for not a footstep could be heard!

Fatty suddenly heard a whisper. So there were *two* people then? Who were they? And what in the world were they doing? Surely they weren't kidnapping the old man?

Fatty frowned. He had better find out about that poor old fellow. He slept in the back room of the bungalow. That was where Larry had seen his bed.

'If I slip round to the back, and shine my torch in at the window, I could perhaps see if the old man is there or not,' he thought. So he crept round the bushes once more and came to the back of the little bungalow.

The window was open. Fatty was just about to shine his torch through the opening when he heard a noise.

Some one was snoring! Snoring very loudly indeed! The old man was safe then. Fatty stood and listened for a while, and then made his way back into the bushes. He really *must* see what was up!

He heard the sound of the front door closing very quietly. He heard a tiny little cough, but he caught no sound of footsteps going down to the gate. He stood and listened, his ears straining for the slightest noise.

He heard another door being shut—the door of the car, perhaps. Yes, that was it. Then the car-engine started up suddenly, and began to throb. Almost at once the car moved off down the road. Fatty leapt to the front fence and shone his torch on it. He saw only a dark shadow as the car drove away. His torch could not even pick out the number.

'What a peculiar business,' thought Fatty. 'What did those fellows come to fetch—or perhaps they *brought* something? I'll go and peep in at the front windows.'

But thick curtains of some green material stretched across the front windows, with not a crack between them to shine his light through. Fatty went to the front door and tried it.

No, that was now locked. It was all most mysterious. What were the midnight visitors doing in the bungalow?

Fatty went to the back and took another look through the window. This time he shone his torch on the old man. Yes, there he was on his bed, fast asleep, his night-cap all crooked. Beside him was a plain chair, and a small table. There didn't seem to be anything else in the room at all.

Fatty switched off his torch, and went round to the front. He was puzzled to know what to do for the best. He didn't like to wake the old man; he would be sure to be in a terrible fright if Fatty awoke him suddenly—and how was Fatty to explain to him about the midnight visitors? The old man would be so terrified that he wouldn't go to sleep again!

'It wil have to wait till morning,' said Fatty to himself. 'I'm not going to ring up Goon. For one thing he wouldn't believe me—for another thing there may be a simple explanation—and for a third thing I can't see that it will matter waiting till morning.'

So he went off with Buster at his heels, puzzled, and half-doubtful about leaving the old man all by himself, with midnight visitors coming and going!

He let himself in at the garden-door, and he and Buster went upstairs very quietly. They disturbed nobody. Buster curled up at once in his basket and went to sleep.

Fatty lay awake thinking over everything for a few minutes, and then fell off to sleep as suddenly as Buster. He didn't awake till full daylight. The breakfast gong was sounding through the house. Fatty leapt out of bed in a hurry!

'Gosh, I must have been sleepy!' he said. He stirred Buster with a bare foot. 'Wake up, sleepy-head! You're as bad as I am!'

He didn't remember about his midnight adventure for a minute or two, he was so much engrossed in dressing as quickly as he could. Then he suddenly remembered and stopped tying his tie. 'Whew! Was it a dream, or real? Buster, do you remember our midnight walk, too? If you do, it was real.'

Buster did remember. He gave a small wuff, and leapt on Fatty's warm bed.

'Get down,' said Fatty. 'Well, I'm glad you remember our walk last night, too. Funny business, wasn't it, Buster? Shall we pop round to that bungalow immediately after breakfast, just to see what's happened—if anything?'

STRANGE HAPPENINGS

So, after breakfast, Fatty got his bicycle and set off slowly with Buster running beside him, panting. 'This will do you good, Tubby-One,' said Fatty, severely. 'Why is it that you always get so fat when I'm away at school? Can't you possibly go for walks by yourself?'

Buster was too much out of breath even to bark. Fatty turned into Holly Lane, and rode up to the bungalow. The door was shut, but the green curtains were now pulled back from the windows. Fatty peeped in to see if things were all right.

He got a terrible shock! Mr. Goon was there—a most important Mr. Goon—and with him was Mr. Henri from next door! The old man was nowhere to be seen.

But what startled Fatty most was that there was not a stick of furniture in the front room! It was completely empty—not even a carpet on the floor!

He stood gaping in at the window. Mr. Goon swung round and saw him. He stepped to the window and flung it open, scowling.

'You here again! What have you come for? Nobody knows about this yet!'

'What's happened?' said Fatty.

Mr. Henri began to explain. 'About seven o'clock zis morning,' he said, but Mr. Goon interrupted him. He didn't want Fatty to know more than could be helped. Interfering Toad!

Fatty wasn't going to be put off, however. He had to know about this. He spoke rapidly to Mr. Henri in French, asking him to reply in French and tell him everything.

So, to the accompaniment of Mr. Goon's scowls and snorts, Mr. Henri explained everything in French. He had awakened at seven o'clock that morning and had heard somebody yelling. His bedroom faced towards the bungalow. At first he hadn't taken much notice and fell asleep again.

'Then,' he said, in his rapid French, 'then I awoke later and the noise was still there—shouting, shouting, always. So I dressed and came to the bungalow to see what was the matter.'

'Go on,' said Fatty.

'It was the old man shouting,' said Mr. Henri, still in French. 'The door was locked so I got him to unlock it—and when I came inside, I saw that this room was quite empty—except for the curtains, which had been drawn across the windows so that nobody might see into the empty room. The old man had awakened this morning, and staggered out to this room—and when he found everything gone, he yelled the place down!'

'It's a mystery!' said Fatty, amazed, and Goon swung round sharply. 'Mr. Goon—we're in the middle of a mystery again! Got any clues?'

13   SUSPECTS – AND CLUES!

MR GOON didn't feel that he could possibly stand any cheek from Fatty at that moment. He was completely mystified, he had no clues at all, and he simply couldn't *imagine* when, how or why all the front-room furniture had been removed.

'You clear orf,' he said to Fatty. 'This has got nothing to do with you. It's a job for the police.'

'I must just go and see how the poor old man is,' said Fatty, and brushed past Goon to go to the back bedroom. Goon scowled. He looked round the room helplessly. Except for the stove, which kept alight all night, the fender, one lamp, and the green curtains, there was nothing left in the room. What was the point of taking all the furniture away? It wasn't worth much anyway!

Fatty was talking to the old man, who was almost weeping with shock. 'My money first—then my furniture!' he moaned. 'All my money—then my furniture!' What's to become of me?'

'Didn't you hear anybody?' asked Fatty.

'No, no! Not a thing did I hear,' he said. Fatty stopped questioning him. It was plain that he was too upset to say anything sensible.

Mr. Goon made a few notes in his black book. 'I must know the granddaughter's address,' he said. 'She'll have to come along here and take this old fellow to her home. He can't stay here alone, with no furniture. Hey, Dad! What's your grandaughter's address?'

'It be 5, Marlins Grove, Marlow,' said the old man. 'But you won't get me there, that you won't. It's full of pesky old women, always grumbling and nagging. I'm not going there.'

'But you can't stay here all alone with no furniture!' shouted Mr. Goon, half because the old man was deaf, and half because he was angry.

'Don't yell at him like that,' said Fatty, seeing the poor old fellow cower back. Mr. Henri touched Goon on the shoulder.

'My sistair, she is vairy kind,' he said in his broken English. 'She has a small bedroom. Zis old man can stay there till his grand daughter arrives.'

'Well, that would help a bit,' said Goon, putting his notebook away. 'Will you lock up after you? I must go back to my house and telephone all this to my chief. It's a funny business—can't make it out—first the money, then the furniture!'

He turned to Fatty. 'And you'd better go home,' he said. 'There's no call for you to meddle in this. Always snooping round. What made you come up here this morning I just can't think. Wherever I find trouble I find you.'

It took quite a time to explain to the trembling old man that the people next door would help him. But when he understood he seemed to think he would like to go there. Mr. Henri went to tell his 'sistair' everything, and sent a gardener to help Fatty to take

'You can't stay here all alone with no furniture!'

the old fellow to his house. Between them they carried him there, and kind Mrs. Harris soon got him into a warm bed.

'I'll just keep him warm here, till his people come,' she said. 'I don't mind driving him over to Marlow if it will help. What an extraordinary thing to happen— taking away his furniture in the middle of the night. I never heard even the smallest noise!'

Fatty went back to the bungalow. He had a good look round. He was just as puzzled as Mr. Goon. There was no doubt that the old man had hidden his money somewhere in his furniture—perhaps in several places—but the money had gone.

'So WHY take the furniture!' wondered Fatty. 'We'll have to get busy on this—there should be at least a few clues—and every one who visited the old man yesterday morning up to the time he discovered that his money was gone is on the list of suspects.'

Fatty examined the bedroom. The bed was a plain iron one with an ordinary wire spring. Nobody could ever hide money in that. The mattress was thin and poor. Money might have been hidden in that—but no, it would have to be sewn up again each time the old took it out. He was too blind to do that. Anyway it was clear that nobody had unsewn and then re-sewn the mattress. All the threads were dirty, and had obviously been untouched for years.

The pillow was thin and hard. Fatty took of the slip and looked at it. No—nobody had ripped the pillow up and re-sewn it.

He looked at the floor-boards. There were no marks anywhere to show that any had been taken up. All were nailed down fast. The chimney place was no good for hiding anything either. The stove fitted too closely.

'Well, it beats me. WHY did somebody take the risk of coming at midnight and carrying out all the furniture, when the money had obviously been stolen?' said Fatty. 'Unless—unless—they were sure it was still there, somewhere in the furniture! They didn't like to risk coming and making a really good search, so they took *all* the furniture, meaning to search it at leisure.'

He thought about that. 'No, that seems silly. But then everything seems a bit silly. Buster, don't you think this is rather a *silly* mystery?'

'Wuff-wuff,' said Buster, quite agreeing. He wasn't very interested in this little house. Not even the smell of a mouse! He pawed at Fatty's leg.

'All right, I'm coming,' said Fatty. 'I'll just lock the door. I'd better leave the key with Mr. Henri.'

He locked the door, and then went to have one more look for Larry's leather in the daylight. No, it was gone. He hoped that Larry wouldn't get into trouble over it.

Fatty made his way to the house next door, after fixing a bit of paper to the front door of Hollies. On it he had written 'KEY NEXT DOOR' just in case the granddaughter should come back.

Mrs, Harris answered the door and told him to come in. 'We are having a cup of coffee,' she said.

'You must join us. My brother would like a word with you too.'

Fatty also wanted a word with Mr. Henri. He thought it would be distinctly useful to have a list of all the people that Mr. Henri had seen going to the Hollies the morning before. One of those people must have been the thief who took the money.

Mr. Henri was ready to tell all he knew. He was just as much interested in the matter as Fatty was. He had already made a neat list, and he showed it to Fatty.

Fatty ran his eyes down it. There were six people on the list.

1. Lady with papers or magazines
2. Window-Cleaner
3. Grocer's Boy
4. Man in car, number ERT too. Carried bag.
5. Man, well-dressed, young, stayed for only a minute
6. Young woman, stayed a long time.

Fatty read the list again. 'Quite a long list,' he said. 'It will be a bit of a business checking all these. I wonder if the old man could help a bit with some of them.'

'He said his granddaughter came to do some cleaning,' said Mr. Henri, 'so that must be the "young woman." And he says he thinks his nephew came— but he's so muddled. He doesn't seem to remember any of the others. I can give you more details, of course. For instance, the woman with the magazines or papers wore a red coat and had a hat with red roses in.'

'Yes—all the details would be a help,' said Fatty. 'What about the grocer's boy?'

'He came on a bicycle with the name of "WELBURN" on the front of the basket,' said Mr. Henri, who seemed a remarkably observant fellow. 'A red-haired boy.'

'Did you notice if the window-cleaner had a name on his pail or bicycle?' asked Fatty, wondering if the cleaner had noticed how remarkably clean the windows of Hollies had been! After all, Larry had cleaned them only a day or two before!

No. Mr. Henri hadn't seen the window cleaner's name. But he thought it must be the same that his sister had. They could ask her.

'Well, we can go through all these, and see if any of them are *likely* to have taken the money,' said Fatty. 'But I think we can cross out the grocer's boy, for instance.'

'Ah, no,' said Mr. Henri. 'He was in Hollies for quite a long time. It might well be he.'

'Oh! Yes, you're right. We must go into every one of these names,' said Fatty. 'Well, I'll get the others to help. They'll have to do some real detective work, I can see!'

He drank his coffee and talked a little longer. Mr. Henrri was now back on the couch, coughing rather a lot. 'It is the excitement,' said his sister. 'He is really much better. Come and see him whenever you like, and ask him what you like. It is a puzzle he would like to solve!'

Fatty said good-bye and went. He was just walking home when he suddenly remembered that he had come on this bicycle. Where had he left it? Oh, yes, by Hollies. He went back to get it and wheeled it to the road.

A thought flashed into his head. The car that had taken away the furniture last night! It must have stood just here. In the road outside Hollies' front gate. But now he was sure that it couldn't have been a car. It must have been a small van of some kind—perhaps a small removal van.

He looked down on the road. It was not a good road, and was muddy and soft just there. The marks of wheels were plainly to be seen.

'Ah!' said Fatty, pleased. 'I'm a jolly bad detective lately! I nearly forgot to check up for wheel-marks! And here they are, under my nose.'

The tyre-marks were big and wide—too wide for an ordinary car. Fatty decided. Much more like those of a small removal van. He got out his notebook and sketched the pattern left in the mud by the tyres. Then he measured them across and entered the figures down in his notebook. The tyre patterns were so plain that Fatty thought the tyres must be quite new. That might be a help.

Near by was a lamp-post , and a mark on it caught Fatty's eye. It was a straight brown mark almost a cut in the white lamp-post. Fatty looked at it.

'That van might quite well have run too close to it,' he thought. Anyway, it's worth nothing down.

"Van may be painted a chocolate-brown, and may have a scratch on wing about two feet from ground." Well, we're getting on—I hope!'

He shut his book, put it into his pocket and rode off with Buster in the front basket. He wanted to call a meeting of the Five Find-Outers that afternoon. This *was* a mystery, after all. And it needed getting down to, because there were quite a lot of suspects.

'What a bit of luck that I went to look for Larry's window-leather last night!' he said to himself, as he cycled home. 'If I hadn't gone and heard all that noise last night and hadn't gone again to explore this morning, old Goon would have had the field to himself. He wouldn't have told us a thing. Now, as it happens, I know more than he does!'

'Wuff,' said Buster, agreeing thoroughly. 'Wuff-wuff-wuff!'

14   FATTY TELLS QUITE A STORY

AT three o'clock that afternoon Larry, Daisy, Pip and Bets came along to Fatty's shed. He was already there, and on the bench at one side were two or three sheets of neatly written notes. Fatty was just reading them over.

'Come in!' he called, and the four trooped in. They looked excited. Fatty had already telephoned to them to say that there really *was* a mystery now, and they wanted to know all about it.

'All sorts of rumours are flying round, Fatty,' said Larry. 'Is it true that somebody took away all the furniture in the middle of the night from Hollies Cottage—and the old man was found lying on the floor because the thieves even took his bed?'

Fatty laughed. 'How do people get hold of these things? It's true that the furniture went—but the old man slept peacefully all through the robbery, on his own bed. They didn't touch that. They did the job so quietly that he never heard a thing—snored all through it.'

'How do you know that,' said Pip, a little scornfully. 'You weren't there!'

'Well, it so happens that I was,' said Fatty, surprising the others very much. They stared at him.

'You were *there*—last night—when the furniture was all taken away?' said Larry at last. 'Well, why didn't you stop them, then?'

'Because I had no idea what was being taken,'

said Fatty. 'It was pitch dark, and they did the whole thing so quietly. But look—let me tell you everything in its right order—quite a lot has happened actually—and we've got to get right down to this and really find out what's going on.'

'Yes—but just let me interrupt for a minute,' said Larry. 'Did you find my window-leather? Mother was on and on about it this morning.'

'No, I didn't,' said Fatty. 'I'm sorry about that, but honestly it wasn't anywhere to be found. All I hope is that Goon didn't find it.'

'Well, he'd think it belonged to the woman who cleans out Hollies Cottage,' said Daisy. 'We'll just have to buy Mother another one, Larry.'

'Blow!' said Larry. 'That really was a silly idea of yours, Fatty—making me go and clean those windows.'

'Yes, but remember that it was all because of that that we're in on this mystery,' said Fatty. 'It really began with your seeing that old man crawling about jabbing at all his furniture—and then us going back to collect your leather and hearing him yelling for the police.'

'That's true,' said Larrry. 'Well, all right, I'll say that a very silly idea happened to turn out well—but that's as far as I'll go.'

Fatty changed the subject. He picked up his notes. 'Now, listen,' he said. 'I've written out a short summary of what's happened so far—just to get our minds clear, so to speak—and I'll read it. Then we'll discuss any clues, and all the suspects, and make plans Ready?'

'Yes! This sounds good!' said Pip, settling himself comfortably on a box.

'Well, get ready to use your brains,' said Fatty. 'Buster, sit still and listen, too. It disturbs me if you keep snuffling for mice in that corner. Sit, Buster.'

Buster sat, his ears pricked as if he were quite ready to listen. Fatty went quickly through his notes.

'The mystery begins when Larry goes to Hollies to clean the windows. He saw the old man there, crawling about, poking at his furniture. We know now that he was looking to make sure that his savings were safely where he had hidden them—either the whole two hundred pounds in some particular chair or sofa, or divided up and put into different places. Possibly in some carefully prepared, hidden pocket under a chair or chairs.'

'Oh, that reminds me!' said Daisy, suddenly 'Excuse my interrupting, Fatty, but our charwoman told me she knew the old man when he was younger—and he was an upholsterer, so he'd know very well how to make some kind of hidden pockets in furniture, wouldn't he?'

'What's an upholsterer?' asked Bets.

'Bets! You're a baby!' said Pip at once. 'It's some one who makes chair covers and curtains, and stuffs couches and chairs and things—isn't it, Fatty?'

'Yes,' said Fatty. 'That's an interesting bit of information of yours, Daisy. Very interesting. The old man probably made himself quite a lot of hiding-places here and there in the upholstery of his chairs or sofas. I'll just add a note about it.'

Daisy looked pleased. 'It's a sort of a clue isn't it?' she said. 'A very small one, I know.'

'It all helps to fill in the mystery,' said Fatty. 'I always think of our mysteries as jigsaws. We've got a great many bits and pieces—but not until we fit them together properly do we see the whole picture. Now, then, I'll go on.'

'We're listening,' said Bets, happily.

'Well, we come next to when we all of us went with Larry to find the leather he had left behind,' said Fatty. 'And we heard the old man yelling for the police. He is certain that his money was in its usual place—or places—about midnight the night before, but in the morning it is gone. He doesn't discover that it's gone, however, until six people, at least, have been to Hollies Cottage for some reason or other.'

'And all those six are Suspects, then, till we prove them otherwise,' said Larry. 'Good! Who are they, Fatty?'

'All in good time,' said Fatty. 'Don't keep interrupting. Buster, sit! There is NO mouse in that corner!'

Buster sat, looking as if he knew better than Fatty where mice were concerned. Fatty went on.

'We decided at this point that it was only a question of straightforward robbery, and that Goon would be able to deal with it,' he said, 'But last night I went to get Larry's leather, and as I told you, I arrived just about the time the car, or lorry, or van came to remove the furniture out of that front room.'

'Extraordinary!' said Larry, unable to stop himself from interrupting.

Fatty went on to describe what he had heard. 'Actually I *saw* nothing,' he said. 'And I didn't even know till this morning that the midnight visitors were taking away all the furniture. I didn't know that they might have a van or a lorry—I thought it was a car. I imagined they might be kidnapping the old man, but I both saw and heard him, fast asleep, on his bed in the back room.'

'What did you *think* was happening?' asked Pip.

'I simply couldn't imagine!' said Fatty. 'All I heard were a few thuds and bumps and pants and a whisper-and it was all over quite quickly, really. Well , I thought I'd better go back to Hollies early this morning, just to see if I could find out anything, and when I got there, I had quite a shock.'

'Why?' asked Bets, hugging her knees. 'This is awfully exciting, Fatty!'

'Well, I found Goon there, and the old fellow, of course, and Mr. Henri, that Frenchman you all thought was me in disguise. He is staying with his sister next door, as you know, and he heard the old man yelling for help again early this morning. So he went to see what the matter was and then called the police.'

'Oh, so Goon was in on this pretty quickly!' said Larry, disappointed.

'Yes, But I wasn't much later in arriving,' said Fatty, 'and wasn't I amazed to find no furniture in that front room! Of course I knew at once what had happened, because I'd actually heard the men removing it last night—though I didn't tell Goon that, of course!'

'What happened next?' asked Bets

'Nothing much. Goon went off, leaving Mr. Henri and me with the old man—and Mr. Henri's sister said she'd give him a room till one of his relations came along. So he's there now. I had a good look round Hollies, but couldn't see anything to help me. Then I went back to Mr. Henri, and got a proper list of the people he had seen going to the bungalow yesterday morning. They're the Suspects, of course.'

'Let's have a good look,' said Larry; but Fatty hadn't quite finished.

'I've only got one clue,' he said, 'but it *might* be an important one.' He told them about the well-marked prints of the tyres in the mud outside Hollies, and showed them the pattern in his note-book.

'I *think* it must have been a small removal van,' he said, ' because the distance between the front and back wheels was rather more than there would be in even a big car. Oh!—and the car or van may be a chocolate-brown. There was a new brown mark on a near-by lamp-post, as if the van's wings had scraped it.'

'Well, it seems as if we have got to tackle the Suspects,' said Larry, 'and look out for a chocolate-brown van which probably has new tyres of a certain pattern. We'd better all copy out that pattern, Fatty. It would be maddening to see a chocolate-brown removal van with new tyres—and not be able to check the pattern!'

'Yes, Well, will you make four tracings of the diagram in my notebook?' said Fatty. 'I'll go on with the list of Suspects and we can discuss them. You can trace the markings while you're listening.'

Fatty turned to his list of six Suspects. He read them out. 'One—Lady with papers or magazines, dressed in red coat, and black hat with roses. Two—Window-Cleaner. Three—Grocer's boy, from Welburn the grocer's, red-haired, and was in the bungalow quite a time. Four—man with bag, came in car with number ERT 100. Five—well-dressed young man, who stayed for only a minute. And six—a young woman who stayed a long time.'

'Quite a list,' said Larry. 'A window-cleaner, too! I wonder if he noticed how clean the windows were!'

'That's what *I* wondered,' said Fatty, with a laugh. 'I'm going to have a word with the old man about these Suspects; he may be able to give me a few more clues about them. Then we must tackle each one.'

'I never much like that,' said Bets. 'I'm no good at it.'

'Yes, you are,' said Fatty. 'Anyway, doesn't your mother have Welburn's for her grocer? You could hang about for the grocer's boy, and have a word with him when he brings your groceries. You and Pip could do that.'

'Oh, yes!' said Bets, glad that Pip was to help her. 'What about the lady with the magazines? Would she be the vicar's sister? It sounds rather as if it was somebody delivering the Parish magazine.'

'Yes. I can easily find that out,' said Fatty. 'Mother knows her. I'll go and see if she was delivering at Hollies that morning. If so, she's not a Suspect, of course. But we can't afford to rule any one out till we've proved they're all right.'

'And we can look out for car ERT 100,' said Pip. 'I wonder who the young man is—and that young woman who stayed such a long time.'

'Probably the old man's granddaughter,' said Fatty,' shutting up his notebook. 'She comes to clean for him. Pip, you and Bets get on with the grocer-boy Suspect. Larry, you finish these tracings, will you, and let us each have one. I'll go and find out a bit more about these six people if I can. Daisy, will you wander about with Buster, and see if you can spot that car—ERT 100 remember.'

'Right!' said every one and got up. This was exciting. A mystery they could really work on! Now who, of all those six, was the thief?

15   FATTY GETS GOING

FATTY went straight off to Mr. Henri. His sister, Mrs. Harris, was quite pleased to see him. Fatty had excellent manners, and the Frenchwoman liked a boy who knew how to behave.

Soon he was sitting beside Mr. Henri's couch. 'Well, have you come to ask me more questions?' said the man, in French. 'We will speak in French, will we not?' It is so much easier for me—and you, you talk French like a native! You are a most accomplished boy!'

Fatty coughed modestly, and restrained himself from agreeing whole-heartedly with Mr. Henri. 'I just wanted to ask you a few things about our six Suspects,' he began.

'Ha! Mr. Goon also asked me many questions,' said Mr. Henri. 'He is a stupid fellow; but he asks good questions. They are well-trained in this, your police.'

'Oh,' said Fatty, disappointed to hear that Goon had had the bright idea of questioning Mr. Henri too. 'Blow Goon! Well, it can't be helped. Mr. Henri, who, of all these six people on our list, went into the bungalow—right inside, I mean?'

'All of them,' said Mr. Henri. 'The door could not have been locked. Every one turned the handle and walked in.'

'What! The window-cleaner too?' said Fatty.

'Yes, he too,' said Mr. Henri. 'By the way, my sister says that he is the same one she has. He came to do her windows first, and then went to Hollies.'

'Does she think he's honest?' asked Fatty.

'Perfectly,' said Mr. Henri. 'And a good cleaner. But you should see him and question him, Frederick.'

'Oh, I will,' said Fatty. 'Decidedly. You told me too about the lady with the papers or magazines. I think she may have been the vicar's sister, delivering Parish magazines.'

'So? I do not know what they are,' said Mr. Henri. 'But yes, the lady may have been of that type—she too went in, but she did not stay long.'

'What about the well-dressed young man you said went in for a short time?' asked Fatty.

'Well, he came again, when you were there,' said Mr. Henri. 'You saw him—quite well-dressed. Did he not say who he was?'

'Gosh, that was the old man's great-nephew!' said Fatty. 'He called him uncle, I remember. So he came during the morning, *too*, did he—before we got there—and afterwards as well. Very interesting! I'll find out where he lives and do a spot of interviewing.'

'The young woman must have been the granddaughter who cleans and cooks for the old fellow,' said Mr. Henri. 'There was also the man who came in a car—that is all, is it not? Well, which do you suspect the most?'

'I don't know,' said Fatty. 'I really don't. The one I suspect *least* is the lady with magazines—but even so I'll have to check up. The worst of it is Goon has probably checked up too. That makes it more difficult for me. I mean—a policeman has the right to interview people. I haven't!'

Mrs. Harris came in. 'You will stay to tea, won't you?' she said. 'We are just going to have it.'

Fatty shook his head most regretfully. 'I'm awfully sorry. Nothing I'd like better. But I must go and do a spot of interviewing before Mr. Goon gets too far ahead of me.'

He shook hands politely, thanked Mr. Henri, and let himself out. It was about a quarter to five. He was quite near the Vicarage. Should he chance his luck and go and see if the Vicar's sister was in?

Fatty decided that he would. So he cycled away quickly and was soon riding up the Vicarage drive. He saw somebody just by the house, kneeling on a mat, weeding. The Vicar's sister! What a bit of luck!

Fatty got off his bicycle and said good afternoon. The Vicar's sister looked up. She was a small, kindly faced woman, who knew Fatty's mother well.

'Ah, Frederick!' she said. 'Do you want to see the Vicar?'

'Well, no, I really wanted to see *you*,' said Fatty. ' I won't keep you a minute. It's about that poor old man whose money has been stolen. I and my friends happened to be the first ones to help him when he discovered his loss. And...'

'Yes, I was *so* sorry to hear about that,' said the Vicar's sister. 'I had been to see him myself only that morning, left him the Parish magazine, you know—his granddaughter reads it to him—and he was sitting in his chair, quite happy, listening to the radio. It was going so loudly that I could hardly hear myself speak!'

'Did you see anything suspicious at all?' asked Fatty. 'We couldn't see anything out of the way when we arrived there.'

'No. Everything seemed just as usual,' said the kindly-faced woman. 'I just left the magazine, had a few friendly words and went. Such a pity to hide money in one's house—a real temptation to thieves.'

'Yes,' said Fatty. 'Well, thanks very much. I didn't think you could help me really—but you never know.'

'How did you know I called there yesterday?' asked the Vicar's sister, looking suddenly puzzled.

'Oh, I just heard that you did,' said Fatty, turning his bicycle round. 'Thank you very much. My kind regards to the Vicar and his wife!'

'*One* off the list of Suspects,' said Fatty to himself as he rode away. 'I felt sure that "woman with magazines" sounded like the Vicar's sister. Anyway, it's quite, quite obvious she had nothing to do with the money. She didn't say if Goon had gone to see her—I suppose he hasn't, or she would have told me. Well, I should have thought he would have shot along to interview her, even though he knew she wasn't really a Suspect.'

But Goon had not thought of the Vicar's sister. The description of the woman with the magazines had rung a different bell in Goon's mind. Aha! A red coat—and a black hat with roses! Didn't that sound like the woman who had sold him that ticket and read his hand? The woman who had actually seen that fat boy Frederick in his hand—and a Mystery also!

'There's more in this hand-reading business than any one would guess,' said Goon to himself. 'Much more. I don't reckon that woman who read my hand has got anything to do with the theft of the money, but I'm pretty certain she's the woman with the papers who visited Hollies yesterday morning, so I'll go and interview her—and may be she'll read my hand a bit more. May be she could tell me more about this Mystery she saw in my hand.'

Poor Goon! He had no idea that his visitor, the woman in the red coat, who had sold him the Sale ticket, had been Fatty in disguise! He cycled hopefully up to Fatty's house, and rang the bell. The woman had told him she was staying for three weeks with Fatty's mother, so she should still be there.

Fatty had just arrived back himself, and was washing his hands in the bathroom. He saw Goon cycling up the drive and was puzzled. *Now* what did Goon want? He dried his hands and slipped downstairs, going into the lounge, where his mother was sewing.

Jane came into the room almost at once. 'Mr. Goon, the policeman, would like a word with you, Madam,' she said.

Mrs. Trotteville frowned. She was not fond of Mr. Goon. 'Show him in here,' she said. 'Don't go, Frederick. It may be something to do with you.'

Mr. Goon came in, his helmet in his hand. He was

always on his best behaviour with Mrs. Trotteville.
'Er—good evening, Madam,' he said. 'I wondered
if I could have a word with the lady who is staying
with you.'

Mrs. Trotteville looked surprised. 'There is no
one staying with me at present,' she said. ' Why do
you think there is?'

'But—but there must be!' said Mr. Goon, startled.
'Why—this lady—she came to see me the other
morning and sold me a ticket for a Sale of Work—
five bob—er, five shillings I paid for it. She said she
was a friend of yours and was staying with you for
three weeks. I wanted to see her to ask her a few
questions. I have reason to believe that she was one
of the people who went to Hollies—where the
robbery was, you know—on the morning that the
old man discovered that his money was gone.'

Fatty turned round and poked the fire vigorously.
How marvellous! How super! Goon really and truly
thought that one of the Suspects was the woman in
the red coat who had visited him and read his hand—
Fatty himself in disguise!

'Really, Mr. Goon, I can't think why in the world
this woman said she was staying with me,' said Mrs.
Trotteville, very much on her dignity. 'I have never
heard of her in my life!'

'But—but she sold me this ticket for five bob!'
said poor Mr. Goon, in anguish. 'Five bob! Is it a
dud, then?' He pushed the ticket at Mrs. Trotteville.

'No. It is not a dud,' she said. 'I also have those
tickets for sale.'

'She read my hand too,' wailed Goon. 'And the things she said were true.' He stopped suddenly. No, it wouldn't do to tell Mrs. Trotteville what the woman had said about a fat boy.

Fatty was having a violent coughing fit, his handkerchief to his face. His mother looked at him, annoyed. 'Frederick, go and get a drink of water. Mr. Goon, I'm sorry not to be able to help you; but I do assure you that I have no friend who goes about reading people's hands. Some one has—er—deceived you. Still, you've got the ticket. You can always go to the Sale. There will be plenty of good things for you to buy.'

Mr. Goon made a peculiar noise—half snort and half groan. He got up, said good evening, and stumbled to the door. That woman in the red coat! Who could she have been? Telling him fairy tales like that—making him stump up for a silly Sale of Work ticket! What a waste of money. All the same, she did warn him against that fat boy, and she did know that a Mystery was near. Strange. Most peculiar.

Fatty appeared in the hall. 'Oh, are you going, Mr. Goon?' he said. 'Do let me see you out. Very strange that that woman should have said she was staying here, isn't it? By the way, how are you getting on with this new Mystery? For Mystery it is! You no doubt have plenty of clues?'

Goon looked at him with a surly face. 'Yes, I have,' he said. 'And one or two of them you won't like—Mister Clever! I told you you'd poke your nose into things once too often!'

'What exactly do you mean by that?' said Fatty.

'Wait and see,' said Goon, rudely. Fatty opened the door and Goon marched out. Fatty called after him politely.

'Oh —er, Mr. Goon! Did that woman who read your hand warn you against a fat boy, by any chance? She did, did she? Well, take her advice. Beware of him!'

And Fatty gently shut the door on a most bewildered Mr. Goon. Now—HOW did Fatty know what that woman had read in his hand? Goon puzzled over that for a very long time indeed!

16 MOSTLY ABOUT
WINDOW-CLEANERS

IT was too late to do anything else that evening. Fatty decided that he would go and see the window-cleaner first thing the next morning, then he would go to Pip's at ten o'clock for the next meeting of the Five. By that time the others might have something to report, too.

'After the meeting I'll see if I can find that young man—the great-nephew,' said Fatty. 'And have a word with the granddaughter too. By then we might be able to see daylight a little. My word—fancy Goon going right off the track, and coming up here to trace a woman who doesn't exist—the woman who read his hand. Poor old Goon. He's got hold of a bit of jigsaw that doesn't fit!'

Fatty decided that he would dress up in old clothes the next day, find the window-cleaner, and pretend that he wanted some advice about going in for window-cleaning himself. He might get the man to talk more freely if he thought he was not being interviewed.

'I'd better go early, or he'll be off to work,' thought Fatty, and arranged with Cook to have breakfast at an earlier hour than usual. He was up in good time and came down just as Jane brought a tray of breakfast for him into the dining-room. She looked in surprise at Fatty.

'My word! Are you going in for chimney-sweeping

or something?' she said. 'Where *did* you get those dirty old clothes? Don't you let your father see you!'

'I won't,' said Fatty, and began on his breakfast. He propped his notebook in front of him as he ate, considering all the facts of the robbery and the removal of the furniture. Pity they couldn't find out where the furniture was—it would help matters a good deal!

He had the address of the window-cleaner. Mr. Henri's sister had given it to him. 'Sixty-two, North Street, Peterswood. The other end of the town. Well, I'll be off.'

Fatty didn't cycle. His bicycle was too expensive-looking to be owned by a young man who wanted a job at window-cleaning. He set off at a good pace, with Buster at his heels.

It took him about twenty minutes to get to the address. No. 62 was a smart little house, with a television aerial on the roof. Evidently window-cleaning was quite a well-paid occupation. Fatty walked round to the back door.

A man sat there, cleaning some boots. He looked up at Fatty and Fatty grinned.

'Hallo, mate! What do you want?' said the man, liking the look of this cheerful-faced fat boy.

'Just wanted to ask you if you could give me a few hints about your job,' said Fatty. 'I might like to take it up—if any one would teach me!'

He spoke in a rough kind of voice, so that the man would not suspect him to be any other than he seemed.

The window-cleaner looked him up and down.

'You seem a likely sort of lad,' he said. 'I might do

with a mate meself. When are you free?'

'Oh, not for some time,' said Fatty, hastily, marveling at the ease with which one could get a job. He then began to ask the window-cleaner a few questions: how much did a ladder cost? Could one be bought second-hand? Were leathers expensive?

'Look here, if you want a job at window-cleaning, you come and be my mate,' said the man, at last. 'You and I would get on fine. Don't you worry about ladders and leathers—I'll supply those if you like to come in with me. You go home and think about it, and let me know.'

'Right,' said Fatty. 'That's kind of you. I say, did you hear about that robbery at Hollies?'

'I should think I did!' said the man, taking up another boot to clean. 'Why, I was cleaning the windows that very morning! Funny thing was, though I hadn't cleaned them for a month they were as clean as could be! I told the old man that when I went in for my money. His granddaughter was there, ironing the curtains, and she seemed surprised to see me—said another window-cleaner had been along a day or two before, and hadn't asked for any money at all.'

Fatty listened to this with great interest, hoping that Goon wouldn't get suspicious if he heard about the other window-cleaner!

'Have the police asked you if you saw anything when you cleaned the windows that morning—anything unusual, I mean?' asked Fatty.

'No. I haven't seen the police,' said the man. 'I've got nothing to fear. I've been a window-cleaner for years

'You seem a likely sort of lad,' he said

and every one knows me. Anyway, I couldn't have taken the money—the granddaughter was there all the time, ironing away!'

'Yes. That certainly rules you out,' said Fatty, thinking that the window-cleaner was another Suspect to cross off. 'Well, I must go. Thanks very much for your help. If I decide to be your mate I'll come right along and tell you.'

The window-cleaner waved a shoe-brush at Fatty, and the boy went round to the front, untied Buster from the fence and walked back home. He was thinking hard.

Why hadn't Goon interviewed the window-cleaner? He had had time. Didn't he know who the man was? Well, he was one up on Goon over that. Another Suspect gone!

Fatty arrived at Pip's just after ten o'clock. The other four were sitting waiting for him in Pip's playroom. Fatty was surprised to see such long faces.

'What's up?' he said. 'Bets, you look as if you're going to burst into tears!'

'Fatty, something awful's happened,' said Daisy. 'Simply AWFUL! Goon found that window-leather Larry used, and it had our name on it—Daykin! Mother always marks all her household cloths.'

'Good gracious!' said Fatty. 'If only I'd known that! I'd never have let that leather lie there so long.'

'Well, we're in an awful fix now,' said Larry, 'and really I can't help saying again, Fatty, that it was a most idiotic idea of yours to tell me to go and clean windows. You see, Goon saw the name "Daykin" on the leather, and he knows that my name is Larry Daykin, and he immediately leapt to the conclusion that one or other of us five had played the fool, and was the window-cleaner on the morning of the robbery!'

'Whew!' said Fatty, and sat down suddenly. 'This is a blow!' He sat and stared at the serious faces of the others.

'Did he come up to your house with the leather?' asked Fatty.

'Of course he did,' said Larry. 'And what's more he took the leather away again, saying something about its being a "piece of evidence"—whatever that may be. So Mother hasn't got it back yet!'

'And he had us in, Larry and me, and asked us outright if we had cleaned the window of Hollies two mornings ago,' said Daisy. 'But fortunately we were able to say we hadn't, because, as you know, it was a day or two *before* that that Larry cleaned them—not the morning of the robbery. But we felt AWFUL! We *had* to say it was Mother's leather, of course, but we didn't dare to say that Larry had cleaned the windows with it two days before the robbery—we just kept on saying that we didn't clean the windows on the *robbery* morning.'

'And *he* kept on saying "Then how did this leather get into those bushes?" said Larry. 'He's most awfully suspicious about it. It's dreadful. I don't know what will happen when Dad comes home and hears about it. I bet he'll get it out of Daisy or me that I was idiot enough to clean the windows two or three days before that robbery! He'll think I'm stark staring mad!'

'I'll go and see Goon, said Fatty, getting up. 'I can

put things right, I think.'

'How?' asked Larry.

'Well, it so happens that I've been to see the actual window-cleaner who *did* clean the windows on the robbery morning,' said Fatty. 'Man called Glass—good name for a window-cleaner!'

Nobody could raise even a smile.

'Well, anyway, this fellow says he did clean the windows that morning, and when he'd finished he went into the bungalow, and the granddaughter was there— ironing curtains or something, he said—and she paid him his money.'

'Oh, what a relief!' said Larry, looking more cheerful. 'If Goon knows *that*, may be he won't keep on trying to make me say I was there cleaning windows that morning too. Honestly, Fatty, I began to feel that he thought I'd stolen the money!'

'I'm sorry about this, Larry,' said Fatty. 'I'll go and see Goon now.'

He went off with Buster, leaving four slightly more cheerful children in Pip's playroom. Daisy got up.

'Come on, let's go out. I feel quite depressed. Let's have some ice-creams—always a good cure for things that make us feel miserable!'

Fatty went straight to Mr. Goon's. He saw the policemen's bicycle outside and was thankful. Mrs. Mickle answered the door.

'Mr. Goon in?' asked Fatty. She nodded and showed him into the office. The skinny little Bert stood slyly in the hall. Fatty gave him a look.

'Hallo, Skinny! BEWAAAAAAARE!'

The 'beware' seemed to come from behind Bert, and reminded him of those awful voices he had heard a day or two ago. He looked behind him, gave a yelp and disappeared.

No one was in the office—but, draped over a chair-seat, was Larry's window-leather! Fatty's eyes gleamed. He spoke softly to Buster.

'Buster! Look—what's that? Fight it, then, fight it!' And Buster leapt on the leather in delight, caught it in his teeth and dragged it round the room, shaking it and worrying it exactly as if it were a rat.

'Take it outside, Buster,' said Fatty, and Buster obediently ran into the front garden with it, growling most ferociously.

Mr. Goon walked into the room thirty seconds later, looking quite jubilant. Ha! He had got Larry and Daisy into a fine old fix. Larry was the window-cleaner, was he? Then he was one of the Suspects on the morning of the robbery. What would his father have to say to *that*?

But Fatty soon made him look a little less jubilant. 'Oh, Mr. Goon,' he began, 'I thought it might interest you to know that I have this morning interviewed the window-cleaner who cleaned the windows of Hollies on the morning of the robbery—a man called Glass, living at 62, North Street, Peterswood.'

'What?' said Goon, startled.

'He told me he cleaned the windows, then went into the bungalow for his money. The granddaughter of the old man was there, ironing, and she paid him. He couldn't have stolen anything under the very eyes of the young woman, so I should think we needn't consider the window-cleaner any further. What do you feel about it Mr. Goon?'

Mr. Goon felt furious. He cast his eyes round for the window-leather—he would face Fatty with that and see what he would say! But where WAS the leather? He couldn't see it anywhere.

'Are you looking for something, Mr. Goon?' asked Fatty, politely.

'That leather,' said Mr. Goon, beginning to be agitated. 'Where's it gone?'

'Oh, dear, I do hope Buster hasn't got it,' said Fatty. 'He's out there growling like anything, Mr. Goon. Would you like to see what he's got?'

Mr. Goon looked out of the window. Buster had torn the leather to pieces! Nobody would ever have known that it had once been a most respectable window-leather.

'That dog!' said Mr. Goon, in a tone of such fury that even Fatty was surprised.

'I'll go and scold him,' said Fatty, and went out. 'By the way, you didn't thank me for coming to give you information about Mr. Glass the window-cleaner, Mr. Goon!'

Mr. Goon said the only thing he felt able to say— 'Gah!'

17   A TALK IN THE ICE-CREAM SHOP

FATTY went straight back to Pip's house, but the others were not there. 'I should *think* they've gone to have ice-creams,' said Mrs. Hilton. 'I believe I heard somebody mention the word!'

'Right. Thank you,' said Fatty, wishing he had his bicycle. All this rushing about on foot would make him quite thin! 'I'll go and find them, Mrs. Hilton.'

He went off with Buster, who still proudly carried a small bit of the window-leather in his mouth. Fatty stopped at an inronmonger's in the main street, and bought a magnificent leather. It cost him sixteen shillings. He stuffed it into his pocket, and went on to the dairy.

The other four were there, eating ice-creams. They were very pleased indeed to see Fatty's cheerful face.

'Is it all right?' asked Bets, eagerly, and Fatty nodded. He ordered a round of ice-creams for every one, and two for himself, as he was one behind the others.

'I went to see Goon,' he said, 'and I told him how I'd gone to see the real window-cleaner this morning. He was most annoyed.'

'I bet he was!' said Larry. 'He was just too pleased for anything to think he'd got *me* pinned down as one of the Suspects. But what about the leather? He's still got that. He'll come and flourish it at Daddy to-night, and make an awful scene.'

'Buster, come here, sir,' said Fatty, and Buster came. From his mouth hung the last bit of the window-leather. He wagged his tail.

'Well, well, well, if Buster hasn't taken it upon himself to remove that leather from Goon's office, fight it and chew it to bits!' said Fatty, solemnly. 'Is that the very last bit, Buster?'

'Wuff,' said Buster, and dropped it. Larry picked it up. 'Yes,' he said, 'look! There's a bit of the name-marking on this corner—Dayk? Oh, Buster, you're the cleverest, cheekiest, best dog in all the world!'

'And he deserves a double ice-cream!' said Daisy, thankfully. 'Oh, Fatty, I don't know *how* you do these things, but there's simply nobody like you for putting things right—going straight for them...'

'Taking the bull by the horns, tackling the fury of the storm, putting the enemy to flight, and all the rest of it,' said Fatty, grinning. 'No, but honestly, I was really upset. Goon had something on us there; and you and Daisy could have got into a fearful row, Larry, all through my fault.'

'But now Mr. Goon can't do anything, can he?' said Bets, happily. 'He knows who the real window-cleaner was—you've told him—and he hasn't got the leather any more.'

'And Mother's the only one who has suffered,' said Larry. 'She's lost her window-leather for good now!'

'Oh, I forgot,' said Fatty, and pulled the brand-new leather from his pocket. He tossed it across to Larry. 'A present for your mother,' he said.

'Oh, *thanks*,' said Larry, delighted. 'Mother will be so thrilled that she won't say another word about Mr. Goon's accusations.'

'Tell her he made a mistake,' said Fatty. 'And a bad mistake it was for him!'

'Fatty! Pip and I saw the grocer's boy when he came with the groceries last night,' said Bets, remembering.

'Good for you!' said Fatty. 'What happened?'

'Well, Pip and I kept biking up and down the drive, waiting for him,' said Bets. 'And he came at last, on his bicycle. Pip had let down his tyre so that it was a bit flat and he yelled out to the boy to ask if he'd lend him his pump.'

'Good idea,' said Fatty. 'So, of course, you just fell into conversation. What did the boy say?'

'Not much,' said Bets. 'Your turn now, Pip, you tell.'

'I asked him if he ever went to Hollies, where the robbery had been,' said Pip, 'and he was simply thrilled to tell us all he knew. But it wasn't much.'

'Tell me,' said Fatty. 'Just in *case* there's something.'

'Well, he went to the front door as usual,' said Pip. 'He knocked, and shouted "Grocer." Some one called "Bring the things in," and in he went.'

'Who was there?' asked Fatty.

'The old man was there, with the radio on full

strength,' said Pip, 'and a young woman, the old man's granddaughter. He said she called the old fellow "Grandad." She was very busy sewing something green. She told him to take all the things out of the basket and put them in the little larder. So he did.'

'And that was all,' said Bets. 'He just stayed and listened to the wireless for a bit, and then went.'

'Yes. Mr. Henri said the boy was in the bungalow for quite a time,' said Fatty. 'That explains it. Well, *he* couldn't have taken the money either. The granddaughter was there all the time.'

'Perhaps *she* took it,' said Larry. 'She had plenty of chance!'

'Yes. But why take it that morning when so many people seemed to be in and out?' said Fatty. 'Anyway, we'll know better when we see her. She *sounds* a good sort, I must say, going up and looking after old Grandad like that. Still, you never know!'

Fatty took out his notebook, and opened it at his page of Suspects. 'We can cross quite a few off,' he said. He drew his pencil through 'Grocer Boy.' Then he crossed out 'Window-Cleaner.' He also crossed out 'Lady with magazines.'

'Oh, have you found out about her too?' asked Pip, interested.

'Yes,' said Fatty, and told them. He also related how Goon had gone wrong, and had imagined that the lady with the papers, 'in red coat, black hat with roses' must have been the funny old thing who had sold him Daisy's ticket for the Sale, and had read his hand—and how Goon had gone to Fatty's house to ask his mother if he might interview her!

Every one roared. 'Oh! You had told him that you were staying with Mrs. Trotteville for three weeks, so he thought the woman must still be there!' giggled Bets. 'Whatever did your mother say?'

'Oh, she soon put Goon in his place,' said Fatty. 'Poor old Goon—he's getting a bit muddled over all this! No, Buster, you can NOT have another ice-cream. That was a double one, in case you didn't notice!'

'Good old Buster—eating up that leather!' said Larry, patting him. 'I must say it was a very fine way of getting rid of—of—*what* is it I want to say, Fatty?'

'A fine way of getting rid of a bit of incriminating evidence,' said Fatty, promptly. 'No, I'm not going to explain that, Bets. Use your brains.'

'Who have we got left on the list of Suspects now?' asked Daisy, craning over Fatty's arm to see. 'Oh, man in car, with bag—ERT 100. Fatty, I looked all over the place but I couldn't see any ERTs and I didn't see 100 either. Shall we stroll round again and look? I feel it must be a local person.'

'Right. And then I think I'll go and interview the smartly dressed great-nephew, and find out what he wanted Great-Uncle for that morning,' said Fatty. 'He apparently went in for a very short while, and then came out, and, if you remember, he turned up again when we were there listening to Granpa's laments about his money having been stolen.'

'Yes. The granddaughter had left by that time,' said Pip. 'Where does this fellow live?'

'Mr. Henri told me,' said Fatty, turning over the pages of his notebook. 'Here we are—the old man told him the address, because Mr. Henri wanted to get in touch with his relatives—No. 82, Spike Street, Marlow. Apparently both he and the granddaughter live at Marlow—though at different addresses.'

'When will you go and see them? To-day?' asked Daisy. 'Shall we come too?'

Fatty considered this. 'Yes. On the whole I think it would be a good idea,' he said. 'Goon has probably interviewed them both by this time, and if they see me coming along full of questions, too, they may resent it. But if we all blow along, full of innocent curiosity, so to speak, we might do better.'

'I can't go before lunch,' said Daisy. 'Nor can Larry. We've got an aunt coming . We could meet you about three though, outside your house, on bicycles. We'll have tea at that nice little café in Marlow High Street.'

'Yes. That's settled then,' said Fatty, putting his notebook away. 'Come on out, and we'll look for ERT 100.'

They paid the bill and went out, Buster still with his tiny bit of leather. He growled at every dog he met.

'Don't be an idiot, Buster,' said Fatty. 'You don't really suppose any other dog wants your smelly bit of leather, do you?'

They looked at every single car they met, or that

passed them. Not an ERT anywhere! They went to the car-park and examined every car there, which made the attendant extremely suspicious of them.

'What are you looking for?' he called.

'An ERT,' said Fatty.

'What's that?' asked the attendant. 'Never heard of it. There aren't no erts here, so you can go away.'

'You're right,' said Fatty, sadly. 'There isn't a single ERT to be seen.'

'There's Mr. Goon,' said Bets, suddenly, as they walked out of the car-park. 'Perhaps he's looking for ERTs too.'

'No. He has other ways of finding out who owns any car,' said Fatty. 'The police can always trace any car by its number—and Mr. Henri is sure to have given Goon the number. Old Goon will be one up on us over the man with the bag and car ERT 100.'

Buster ran out into the road, barking, when he saw Mr. Goon riding by. Goon kicked out at him, and nearly fell off. 'That pesky dog!' he shouted, and rode on at full speed.

'Buster! You've dropped your bit of incriminating evidence,' said Fatty, disapprovingly, pointing to the rag of leather that had fallen from Buster's mouth when he barked at Goon. Buster picked it up meekly.

They all went to Larry's house first. In the drive stood a car. 'Hallo! —who's this?' said Larry. 'Not our Aunt Elsie already, surely? No, it isn't her car.'

A man came down the front steps of the house carrying a neat brown case. 'It's the doctor!' said

Daisy. 'Hallo, Doctor Holroyd! How's Cook?'

'Much better,' said the doctor, smiling round at the five children. 'Well, there doesn't look to be anything wrong with *you*!' He got into his car, started the engine, and put in the gear-lever. He went off down the drive.

Bets gave a loud yell, and pointed. 'ERT! ERT 100 Look, do look! ERT 100!'

So it was. 'Gosh, to think we all stood here with it staring us in the face,' said Fatty, 'after hunting for it all the morning! Man with a bag too—why EVER didn't any of us think of a doctor?'

'We're not nearly as bright as we imagine,' said Daisy. 'Good old Bets! She spotted it.'

'Shall you go and interview him?' asked Pip.

'No. I'm sure he couldn't help us at all,' said Fatty. 'He couldn't *possibly* have stolen the money—every one knows Doctor Holroyd! I expect he just went to have a look at the old man, and then shot away again in his car. All the same, we ought to feel jolly ashamed of ourselves not to have spotted the number, when it was right in front of our noses!'

'There's Aunt Elsie! Quick, Larry, come and wash!' said Daisy, suddenly, as a small car crept in at one of the gates. 'Good-bye, you others!'

They fled, and the other four walked sedately down the drive. 'See you at three outside your house!' called Bets. 'Good-bye, Fatty. Good-bye, Buster! Hang on to your bit of—of—discriminating evidence!'

18 A CHAT WITH WILFRID—
AND A SURPRISE

EVERY ONE was outside Fatty's gate at three o'clock,
Buster included. 'I'll have to put him into my bicycle
basket,' said Fatty. 'Marlow's too far for him to go
on his four short legs. Up with you Buster!'

Buster liked the bicycle basket. He sat there
happily, bumping up and down when Fatty went over
ruts. He looked down on other dogs with scorn as
he passed them.

It was about three miles to Marlow, and a very
pleasant ride on that fine April day. They asked for
Spike Street when they got there. It was a pretty
street leading down to the river. No.82 was the last
house, and its lawn sloped down to the water.

The five got off their bicycles. 'Put them by this
wall,' said Fatty. 'Then we'll snoop round a bit to
see if we can find the great-nephew—Wilfrid King
is his name. We've all seen him, so we know what
he is like.'

They sauntered alongside the wall that ran round
the little front garden of No.82. They came to a path
that led to the river. They went down it, looking
across to the lawn that led down to the water.

They could see no one. They came to the water's
edge and stood there Then Fatty gave Daisy a nudge.
A boat lay bobbing not far off, and in it a young man

lay reading, a rather surly-looking fellow, in smartly creased grey-flannel trousers and a yellow jersey.

'There's Wilfrid,' said Fatty, in a low voice. 'Let's call out to him and pretend to be very surprised to see him. Then we'll fall into conversation. Remember we've just ridden over here to see the river—it's such a lovely day!'

Wilfrid, however, saw them before they could hail him. He sat up and stared. 'Aren't you the kids who heard my great-uncle shouting for help the other morning?' he said.

'Oh, yes! Why, you're Wilfrid, aren't you?' shouted back Fatty, appearing to be most surprised. 'Fancy seeing you here! We've just ridden over, it's such a heavenly day.'

'Did you meet that fat-headed policeman?' asked Wilfrid. 'He's been over here to-day asking umpteen questions. Any one would think I'd robbed the poor old fellow myself!'

'Oh, has Mr. Goon been over?' said Fatty. 'Do come and tell us. *We* think he's a bit of a fat-head too. But, really, fancy thinking *you* would rob your great-uncle. Poor old man!—I wonder who did.'

'Ah!' said Wilfrid, and looked knowing.

'What do you mean—AH!' said Larry.

'Oh, nothing. That policeman wouldn't see a thing even if it was right under his nose,' said Wilfrid. 'I told him that it was I who kept on and on at my uncle, begging him to put the money into a bank. It's most dangerous to keep it in the house. Anyway, it appears that a lot of people visited Hollies that morning—

there are quite a few persons who *might* have stolen the money!'

'Yes, that's true,' said Fatty. 'It's funny how many people went in and out all the time. Still, the old man's granddaughter was there most of the time, cleaning or something. She can probably clear most of the ones who came.'

'Yes. She can clear me, for instance,' said Wilfrid. 'She was there when I went in. Marian's my cousin, and she and I don't get on, so I didn't stay long. She actually wanted me to help her with the work! Me! She said if I was going to stay long, I could jolly well put up the curtains for her, so I just walked out.'

'Well, anyway, she can clear you, as you say,' said Fatty. 'It's a funny thing—she can clear most of the people who went in and out, except perhaps the doctor and he doesn't really need to be cleared.'

'Oh, is that so?' said Wilfrid. 'Have you got a list of the suspected persons? I'm there, too, I suppose.'

'You can be crossed off if Marian, the grand-daughter, can clear you,' said Fatty, handing him the list.

'My word!' said Wilfrid, looking at it. 'Six of us, and all crossed off except for Marian and myself.'

'Yes. And you say that Marian can clear you, so you'll be crossed off too, soon,' said Fatty. 'Perhaps Marian has already seen Mr. Goon, and he's crossed you off.'

'She's out for the day,' said Wilfrid. 'I told him

that, so I don't expect he's seen her yet. I say, all of us will be crossed off—except one.'

'Except one,' said Fatty, watching Wilfrid as he bent his head thoughtfully over the list. 'Did you know where the old man hid his money, by any chance?'

An angry look came over Wilfrid's face. 'No, I didn't. He would never tell me. I thought that if only he would, I would take it and put it into the bank, but now it's too late. Somebody else has got it.'

'And you think you know who?' said Fatty quietly.

Wilfrid hesitated. 'Not for certain. I'd better not say any more. You're only kids, but you might go and say something silly.'

'Yes. We might,' said Pip, who had begun to dislike Wilfrid. It was quite apparent to them all that Wilfrid thought his cousin Marian had taken the money—but they couldn't help thinking that *he* would have had it, too, if he could!

'We must go,' said Fatty, looking at his watch. 'Well, I hope that Marian clears you, Wilfrid—it's rather important that she should!'

They went back to their bicycles and rode off to the little café they liked. Not a word was said till they got there.

They were early, so there was no one else in the room. They began to talk in low voices.

'It can't have been Wilfrid who took the money. If he and his cousin disike each other, she certainly wouldn't have sheltered him if he *had* taken the money right in front of her eyes.'

'So he can't be the thief,' said Pip. 'Well, then,

who is?'

'It looks like Marian,' said Fatty. 'We'll go and see her after tea. What beats me is why some-body took all that *furniture* away the next night. I keep going round and round that, but I just can't see where that bit of the jigsaw fits into the picture.'

'I can't either,' said Daisy. 'The furniture was cheap stuff—worth very little. *Could* the thief have imagined that the money was still there? No, I give up. It's a puzzle!'

They had a good tea and then went to call at Marian's house, hoping that she would be in.

'Here we are,' said Fatty. "No.5, Marlins Street. Why, it's a little hotel!'

So it was—a small boarding-house, beautifully kept. The children rang the bell, and a neat, middle-aged woman came to the door.

'Is Miss Marian King in?' asked Fatty. 'If so, may we see her?'

'I don't think she's in yet,' said the woman. 'I'll go and find out. Come into the drawing-room will you?'

They all trooped in. An old lady was there reading. She smiled at the children and nodded.

'Do you want to see some one?' she asked.

'Yes,' said Fatty. 'We'd like to see Marian King, if she's in.'

'Ah, Marian!' said the old lady. 'She's a sweet girl! Good to her mother, good to her old grandad—and good to tiresome old ladies like me. She's a dear.'

'We know she used to go and do all kinds of things for her grandfather,' said Fatty, glad to have some information about Marian.

'Oh, yes! That girl was always thinking of him!' said the old lady. 'Taking him up tidbits she had cooked. Doing his washing and ironing. As particular as could be, she was. She told me she was going to take down, wash and iron his curtains last time she went—quite a job—and kind of her too, because the old man wouldn't be able to see them!'

'Yes, she did do the curtains,' said Daisy, remembering what had been seen by the grocer's boy. 'She must have been very fond of her grandfather.'

'Oh, she was!' said the old lady. 'She thought the world of him and couldn't bear him to live alone. And now I hear that the poor old man has been robbed of his money—dear, dear, Marian will be so upset!'

Fatty wondered why the woman who had opened the door had not come back. Had she forgotten they were waiting? He decided to go and find out. He slipped out of the room and into the passage. He heard voices at the end and walked down the carpeted hall-way.

Some one was crying. 'I don't know *what* to say about Marian. First, that policeman comes to see her and I say she's out—now these children. Where *is* she? She's been gone for two days now! People will say she took the money! It isn't like Marian to do this. Oh, dear, oh, dear, I do so hope she's not come to any harm!'

Another voice comforted her. 'Well, you do as you think best. Marian's a good girl, that I will say, and as for stealing money from her old Grandad— and she so fond of him, too—why, that's nonsense. I do think you should let the police know to-morrow that she's missing. I do indeed.'

'But they'll think she's run off with the money; it'll be in all the papers,' said the first voice, sobbing. 'My girl Marian, my only daughter, as good as gold!'

Fatty went back quietly to the drawing-room. He was worried—and very puzzled. This was something he hadn't expected. Where had Marian gone? *Could* she have taken the money? Every one seemed to speak well of her—and yet—and yet—why had she gone away?

Fatty entered the drawing-room and spoke quietly to the others. 'I don't think we'll wait.' He turned to the old lady and spoke politely.

'If the maid comes back, will you please say we're sorry we couldn't wait? Thank you!'

The old lady nodded, thinking what well-behaved children these were. The five went out, and collected Buster from the post to which he had been tied. He was delighted to see them.

'Don't say anything now,' said Fatty, in a low voice. 'I've got some news.'

They mounted their bicycles, and waited until they were beyond Marlow in a deserted country road. Fatty jumped off his bicycle. The others did the same. They went to a gate, leaned their bicycles there and gathered round Fatty, puzzled at his serious face.

'Marian has disappeared,' he said. 'I over heard her mother say so. They're terribly upset—half afraid she's gone off with the money, and worried about what the papers will say if they get to hear of her disappearance! What do you think of that?'

'Gosh!' said Larry. 'It really does look as if she's the thief. After all, she's the one most likely to have wormed herself into the old man's confidence and got his secrets out of him—where the money was kept, for instance.'

'Yes. There doesn't seem any other reason why she's gone,' said Fatty. 'Well, until she comes back, we can't get much further in this mystery. We don't know two important things—where or why Marain has gone, and where or why the furniture has gone. This is one of the most puzzling mysteries we've tackled.'

'Yes. And I'm sure that NOBODY could solve it, even if they knew all we know,' said Pip. 'Well, let's get back. There's not much more we can do now.'

So they rode back to Peterswood, disappointed and puzzled. Well, perhaps the simplest explanation was the right one: Marian had taken the money and gone off with it!

And yet —what about that stolen furniture! Could that have been Marian too? They gave it up!

'It's too mysterious a mystery!' said Bets. 'Mr. Goon CERTAINLY won't solve it!'

19 AN EXTRAORDINARY FIND

FATTY was unusually quiet that evening. The five of them, with Buster, were down in Fatty's shed. Bets slipped her hand through his arm.

'What's the matter, Fatty? Are you worried?'

'I'm puzzled more than worried,' said Fatty. 'I really am. I CAN'T believe that the grand daughter Marian would rob an old man she had been looking after so lovingly. And yet I feel certain that Wilfrid hasn't got the money, and what's more doesn't know where it is.'

'Then is there somebody else—a seventh person—that we don't know about?' asked Larry.

'I did wonder if there could be,' said Fatty. 'Some one who perhaps went round the *back* of the bungalow that morning of the robbery, and got in without being seen. Mr. Henri could see every one going in at the front, but not at the back.'

'Yes. That's true', said Daisy. 'Also, I suppose it *is* possible that he wasn't looking out of his window every minute of the time.'

'That's so,' said Fatty. 'But I think the old man would have mentioned any one else. Mr. Henri had a good talk with him, and is pretty certain there was no one else.'

'Let's have a game,' said Pip, who was getting

just a bit tired of all this talky-talk.

'No. You have one, and let me think,' said Fatty. 'I'm at my wits' end—and yet I feel as if there's some clue that would give me the key to the whole mystery!'

'Well, anyway, the money's gone,' said Pip. 'So has Marian. It's a bit fishy.'

'Perhaps it's still at Hollies,' suggested Bets. 'In a place where nobody has looked.'

'I hunted everywhere,' said Fatty. 'It's such a *small* place —there really is nowhere to hide anything, once you rule out the chimney and the floorboards. There's no furniture now to speak of—just the old man's bed, a chair, and a little table in that back room. And a lamp, a stove..."

'That old fender,' put in Daisy.

'And the curtains,' said Bets 'They had to leave those, I suppose, in case old Goon came by at night and shone his torch in at the window. He'd have discovered the bare room then, of course.'

'Oh, come on, do let's have a game,' said Pip. 'I know when I'm beaten. There's something peculiar about all this, something we don't know about.'

Fatty grinned suddenly. 'All right!' said. "I'm inclined to think you're right. There are some bits of this jigsaw that we haven't got—it isn't that we can't fit them into the picture. We just haven't got them. Hand over the cards, Pip. You never shuffle properly.'

When the others went, Fatty walked part of the way with them, Buster at his heels. It was a lovely evening, and looked like being a glorious day tomorrow.

They went round a corner in a bunch, and bumped into a burly form. 'Hey!' said a familiar voice. 'Can't you look where you're going?'

'Oh, good evening, Mr. Goon,' said Fatty. Out for a little stroll? Solved the mystery yet?'

'Oh, yes!' said Goon. 'No mystery in it at all—if you're talking about the Hollies affair, that is. Plain as the nose on your face. It's that girl Marian.'

Fatty was thunderstruck. 'What do you mean? Surely she didn't take the money?'

'You wait and see the papers to-morrow morning,' said Mr. Goon, enjoying himself. 'Thought yourself so clever, didn't you? Well, you're not.'

'Has the money been found?' asked Fatty.

'You wait and see,' said Mr. Goon again. 'And look here—I bin thinking—do you know anything about that lady that read my hand?'

Mr. Goon looked extremely threatening and Bets prompty went behind Larry.

'Let me see now, which lady do you mean?' asked Fatty, as if plenty of people read Goon's hand.

Goon gave one of his snorts. 'You're a pest!' he said. 'But this time I'm on top see? You watch the papers to-morrow morning!'

He went on down the road, loking very pleased with himself. Fatty gave a hollow groan.

'I do believe that fat policeman knows something we don't. Blow him! I'll never forgive myself if we've let him get the better of us. It rather looks as if Marian is the black sheep.'

'I thought she was,' said Pip. 'Going off like that. Perhaps they've found her, money and all.'

'We'll have to wait for the morning papers,' said Fatty. 'Well, good-bye. It's sad to think this mystery is coming to an end while we're still in the middle of it, so to speak.'

Bets squeezed Fatty's arm. 'Perhaps something else will happen,' she comforted him. 'You never know!'

'It's not very likely,' said Fatty, and gave her a hug. 'Good-bye—see you to-morrow, all of you.'

Fatty was down early the next morning to see the papers. There was nothing on the front page, but inside was a whole column. It was headed :

MISSING GIRL
AND
MISSING MONEY

It then went on to describe Hollies, the old man, the missing money, the sudden disappearance of the furniture, and now the disappearance of Marian! It didn't say that Marian had taken the money—but any one reading the news about the Hollies affair would immediately gather that Marian had taken both money and furniture!

'Now I suppose the hunt is on,' Fatty thought.

'Every one will be looking out for Marian. I suppose her mother told the police the girl was missing—or more probably Goon wormed it out of her and reported it. Gosh, I wish I could have been a bit cleverer over this mystery! I do feel that I've missed something, some clue, that might have been the key to the whole affair.'

Fatty put down the paper and thought. 'I'll go round to Hollies once more,' he decided. 'For the last time. Just to see if any bright idea comes to me. I'll go by myself without any of the others. I'll just take Buster with me.'

He fetched his bicycle and rode off. He soon came to Holly Lane and went into Green-Treees to get the key. Mr. Henri still had it.

'The old man has gone to Marlow,' he said. 'They came to fetch him last night.'

'Oh, and so I suppose when he asked for Marian and was told she was missing he made a fuss!' said Fatty.

'I'll tell you something he told me,' said Mr. Henri. 'He said that Marian knew where his money was. He had actually told her, and made her promise she would never, never tell anyone.'

Fatty groaned. 'So it looks as if she was the only one who knew—and I must say things look bad for her now. Well, if she took it, she deserves what's coming to her! May I have the key, Mr. Henri? I know I'm beaten, but I just want to have a last look round.'

Mr. Henri gave it to him, and Fatty went off next door. He let himself in. The curtains were drawn across the windows, and the room was dark. He switched on the light, but it was very dim. He drew the curtains away from the windows and the sun streamed in.

Fatty remembered how Marian had washed and ironed the curtains on the morning of the robbery. 'Surely she wouldn't have done that if she had been going to steal the money and clear out!' thought Fatty. 'It doesn't make sense. In fact nothing makes sense!'

He stood there, looking at the fresh, green curtains. He had his hand on the side-hem that ran from the top of the window almost down to the floor. It felt stiff and he rubbed it between finger and thumb.

'Funny,' said Fatty, and felt the hem a bit higher up. Then he felt it round the bottom of the curtains. He held it to his ear and rubbed and squeezed. A faint crackle came to him.

Fatty suddenly grew excited—tremendously excited. He was filled with sudden exultation.

'I've found the money! I believe I've FOUND THE MONEY! Gosh, what a bit of luck!'

He took out his pocket-knife and ripped up the bottom hem of the curtain, cutting the stitches. The hem was now loose enough for him to insert finger and thumb.

He felt about, and came across something papery. He pulled it out gently and stared at it, whistling softly. It was a pound note, rather dirty—a pound

He held it to his ear and rubbed and squeezed

note!

'So that's where she hid the money—to keep it from Wilfrid who had begun to suspect that it was somewhere in the furniture! He must have come and threatened her that he would search for it after she had gone that morning! And so she ripped open the hems of the curtains she was ironing, and sewed the money into them. What an idea!'

The curtain hems were packed with the pound notes. Fatty could feel them all the away round. He debated what to do about it. Should he take the money out? No, he might get into trouble. It would be perfectly safe to leave it there—nobody had guessed so far, and not a soul was likely to guess now.

'Anyway, no one will come here,' said Fatty. 'And what's more, I'll make certain they don't!'

He went out of the bungalow and locked the door. He put the key into his pocket. 'I shan't take it back to Hollies. I'll just tell Mr. Henri I'll keep it—and ask him to keep an eye on anyone who comes up to the front door. Wilfrid's got a key, that's certain, but I don't think he'll come again—and Marian certainly won't.'

Fatty was so excited that he found it difficult to keep his news to himself. Finding the money had suddenly shed light on all kinds of things.

Marian hadn't taken it. She had hidden it in the curtains to make sure that Wilfrid didn't find it if he hunted for hiding-places in the furniture. She hadn't even told the old man where she had put it, in case Wilfrid wormed it out of him—and the old fellow, looking for it after Marian had gone that morning, had thought it was stolen.

Why had Marian disappeared? Not because she had taken the money.She hadn't! Had Wilfrid anything to do with her disappearance? It was almost certainly Wilfrid who had come with some kind of van or lorry that night and removed all the furniture. Why? Probably because Marian vowed that she hadn't got it, but that it was still hidden at Hollies.

'The pieces are fitting again,' said Fatty to himself jubilantly. 'If only I could find Marian—or the furniture. Would the furniture still be in the van? It would obviously be dangerous for Wilfrid and his helper to unload it anywhere. His people would be very suspicious to see furniture suddenly appearing in the house or in the yard. He probably had to leave it in the van.'

Another thought struck him. 'Perhaps Wilfrid's family are in the House Removal business! May be they have big vans, and it might be in one of those. Gosh, I'll have to find out quickly!

Fatty could hardly get home fast enough. Quick, quick! He might defeat Goon yet, and solve the whole thing before Marian was arrested!

20 NIGHT ADVENTURE

FATTY rushed to the telephone directories in the hall as soon as he got home. He wanted to look up King's of Marlow. Were they Furniture Removers? They must be! He was certain they would be. Quick—he must find King's in the directory.

There were a good many Kings — A. King, Alec King, Bertram King, Claude King, Mrs. D. King.....all the way down the list of Kings went Fatty's eager finger. At last he came to the end of them.

He was bitterly disappointed. Not one of the Kings was a Furniture Remover. There was a butcher and a baker ; but the Kings apparently did not go in for House Removals. Fatty stared at the list in despair.

'I'll go down it again, very, very carefully,' he thought. 'Now, then—A. King, Alec King, Bertram King, Butcher, Claude King, Dentist Mrs. D. King, Edward King, the King Stables, Henry King.....wait now—stables! STABLES! That's it! That's it! Stables mean horses—and horses mean horse-boxes—horse-boxes mean vans capable of removing furniture! I've got it, I've got it!'

Fatty threw the directory on the floor and did a most complicated jig up and down the hall with

Buster flying after him, barking. He knew that Fatty was excited, so he was excited too.

Mrs.Trotteville suddenly came out from the lounge into the hall. 'Frederick! What on earth are you thinking of? I have a meeting in the lounge, and you choose just this minute to act like a Red Indian.'

'Oh, Mother! I'm so sorry,' said Fatty, and in his excitement and jubilance he went up and hugged her. 'But I've just made a great discovery, and I was celebrating it. *So* sorry, Mother.'

'Well, go and celebrate down in your shed,' said his mother. 'And, by the way please don't forget that your grandfather will be here by the eleven o'clock train. I want you to meet him.'

Fatty stared at his mother in the utmost dismay. 'Gosh, I'd forgotten every word about it! Oh, Mother—I *can't* meet Grandad! I'm so sorry.'

'But you must, Frederick,' said his mother, shocked. 'I have this Committee meeting—and besides, you always do meet your grandfather. He is only coming for the day and would think it very rude of you if you go off somewhere. You *knew* he was coming.'

Fatty groaned. 'Yes, but I tell you I forgot every word about it. I promise you I did, Mother. It isn't that I don't *want* to meet him or be with him—I do; but it just happens that I've got something, very, very important to do, and it can't wait.'

'Well, either it must wait, or you must get Larry or Pip to do it for you,' said Mrs. Trotteville, in an icy voice. She went back to her meeting and shut the door.

Fatty stared at Buster, who had put his tail down at Mrs. Trotteville's annoyed voice. 'That's done it!' said Fatty. 'JUST when I'm really on to something. Edward King, the King Stables, Marlow—another bit of the jigsaw that was missing, and now I can't fit it into the picture because Grandad's coming. Why, oh why, did he have to come to-day?'

Fatty was very fond of his grandfather, but it really was most unfortunate that he should have to meet him and entertain him on this day of all days.

'The old man's furniture will be in a horse-box,' he told Buster. 'It might be discovered at any moment—but *I* want to find it, Buster. What a shock for old Goon if I produce both the money *and* the furniture!'

He debated whether to telephone Larry or Pip and tell them his ideas. 'No,' he decided. 'If I get them to go over to Marlow and snoop about for a horse-box with furniture inside, they may make some kind of silly move and spoil everything. I'll have to put it off till to-night.'

So Fatty went to meet his grandfather, and entertained him well the whole day.

'Any more mysteries?' asked the twinkling-eyed old man. 'In the middle of one, I suppose? Well, mind you don't let that fat policeman—what's his name? —Goop—Goon—get the better of you!'

'I won't,' grinned Fatty. 'I'll tell you all about it next time you come Grandad.'

He saw his grandfather off at six o'clock that evening, and then dashed round to Pips. Fortunately Larry and Daisy were there too. Bets was delighted to see Fatty.

'Oh, Fatty! You do look excited. Has anything happened?' she asked.

'Plenty,' said Fatty and poured out everything— the finding of the notes in the hem of the curtains— his idea about Removal Vans which now might be Horse-Boxes, or so he hoped—and his determination to go to Marlow that night and hunt for a horse-box full of furniture!

'I'll come with you,' said Larry at once.

'You and Pip can both come,' said Fatty. 'We'll go and see the film called *Ivanhoe* at the cinema first—and then, when it's quite dark, we'll go hunting for horse-boxes!'

'Can't Daisy and I come?' asked Bets

'No. This isn't a job for girls,' said Fatty. 'Sorry, Bets, old thing. You can't come to the cinema with us either, because *Ivanhoe* won't be over till late — and you two girls can't wait about afterwards for us. We may be ages.'

'All right,' said Bets. 'Oh, my goodness!—isn't it exciting? Fatty, you really are very, very clever. Fancy thinking of the curtain hems!'

'I didn't really,' said Fatty, honestly. 'I just happened to be holding a hem, and it felt—well, rather stiff. But it does clear Marian, doesn't it? She didn't take the money—she merely hid it from Wilfrid! Jolly good show!'

'Why did she disappear then, I wonder?' said Daisy.

'I don't know. That's a bit of the jigsaw I just simply can't fit in anywhere,' said Fatty. 'Still we're getting on!'

The three boys cycled off to Marlow, after an early supper. Buster unfortunately was not allowed to go with them, as cinemas do not welcome dogs. He howled dismally when Fatty left.

Ivanhoe was exciting and the three boys enjoyed it. Along with the excitement of the film was an added feeling of delicious suspense—the thought of the 'snooping' they meant to do afterwards! They didn't even wait to see the short second film, but came out into the clear night at the end of *Ivanhoe*.

'I've found out where the stables are,' said Fatty. 'I rang up and inquired. King's thought I wanted to hire a horse—but I don't! The stables aren't by the river : they are away up on the hill.'

They lighted their lamps and cycled quietly along a country road. Soon Fatty turned to the right, up a steep hill. 'This is the way,' he said. 'Good—here comes the moon! We shan't be in the pitch-dark tonight.'

They had to get off their cycles because the hill was so steep. A private road branched off to the left and the boys walked up it. They left their cycles in the shelter of a hedge.

Buildings loomed up near by. A horse coughed. 'These must be the stables,' said Fatty, in a low voice. 'Keep quiet and walk in the shadows.'

Nobody appeared to be about. The stable-doors were all shut. A horse stamped occasionally, and one whinnied a little.

'Where do they keep the horse-boxes?' whispered Fatty. 'I can't see any here.'

'Look—there's another path up there, quite a wide one,' said Pip. 'Perhaps they're along there.'

They went up the broad path, The moon suddenly shone out brilliantly and lighted every rut in front of them. Fatty stopped suddenly.

'Look—see those tyre-marks? Aren't they the same pattern as the one in my notebook, the one you copied Larry? You ought to know—you made four copies!'

'Yes, they *are* the same pattern,' said Larry and got out his copy. He shone a torch on it, though the moonlight was almost brilliant enough for him to read by. 'Yes, it's the same. Goody! We're on the right track. Wilfrid must have taken a horse-box to remove all the furniture, and brought it away up here.'

The path went on for quite a way and at last came out into a field. No horses were there just then, but the boys could see half a dozen in a field a good way down.

'Look—horse-boxes, and lorries, and carts!' said Pip, pointing. Sure enough, neatly arranged in a big corner of the field was a fine collection of horse-boxes. The boys went over to them.

'Look inside each one,' said Fatty. There were four, and none of them was locked. The boys shone their torches inside; but to their great disappointment each horse-box was empty, save for a few bits of straw. Fatty was puzzled.

'Let's look at the tyres,' he said. 'Find a horse-box with newish tyres, the pattern clearly marked.'

But none of the horse-boxes had four new tyres, and the patterns on them were not a bit the same as the one Fatty had seen outside Hollies.

The boys looked at one another. 'Now, what?' said Pip. 'Dead end, again!'

'Better look round a bit,' said Fatty. 'It is possible that Wilfrid hid away the horse-box with the furniture.'

So they hunted round. They walked across the big field—and at the other side was a copse. Fatty saw a bridle-path leading into the bushes. He followed it, and suddenly came to a muddy piece where, plainly to be seen, were tyre-marks and each of the three saw at once that they were the ones they were seeking!

Out came Fatty's notebook. 'Yes! These are the ones! Come on, we're on the trail now!'

They followed the bridle-path, and then, neatly pushed into a clearing, they saw a small horse-box!

'Brown!' said Fatty. 'And look—here's a scratch on the back wing where it scraped that lamp-post. *Now* we're on the track!'

The boys tried the door. It was locked. 'I thought it would be,' said Fatty. 'Here, give me a shove-up, and I'll look in at the window. Half a mo—I've dropped my torch!'

He picked it up and flashed it on. Then Pip and Larry hoisted him up to look into the window of the horse-box. He saw that it was badly broken. He flashed his torch inside.

'Yes, the furniture is here!' he called, softly. 'All of it! Hallo—wait—what's this!'

Before he could say any more to the others, a loud scream came from inside the horse-box. It so startled Pip and Larry that they let go of Fatty. He fell to the ground with a bump.

The scream rang out again. Then came an anguished voice. 'Help! Oh, help! Help me!'

'Who is it?' whispered Pip, scared. 'We've frightened somebody. Let's go.'

'No,' said Fatty. 'I know who it is. It's Marian! Gosh, she has been locked up with the furniture!'

21 MARIAN

FATTY rapped on the locked door. 'I say! Don't be scared. Can we help you?'

There was a silence, and then a trembling voice came from the horse-box. 'Who are you?'

'Just three boys,' said Fatty. 'Are you Marian?'

'Yes. Oh, yes—but how do you know?' said the voice. 'I've been locked up here for ages. Wilfrid locked me in—the beast!'

'Whew!' said Fatty. 'How long have you been there?'

'It seems as if I've been here for days,' said Marian. 'I don't know. Can you let me out?'

'I think I can force the door,' said Fatty. 'What a pity the window's so tiny, Marian—you could have got out of it.'

'I smashed it, hoping some one would hear the noise,' said poor Marian. 'And I yelled till I couldn't yell any more. That beast of a Wilfrid got a horse and dragged the box into some safe place, where nobody could hear me.'

'I'll soon have you out,' said Fatty, and took out a leather case of finely made tools, small but very strong. He chose one and began to work at the door with it.

Something snapped. Fatty tried the handle and the door opened! A white-faced girl stood there, smiling

'Oh, thank you!' she said. 'I've been so miserable'

through her tears.

'Oh, thank you!' she said. 'I've been so miserable. What made you come here to-night?'

'It's a long tale,' said Fatty. 'Would you like us to take you back to your mother? She's frantic about you. And what about food? I hope you've had something to eat and drink while you've been kept prisoner.'

'Yes. Wilfrid put plenty of stuff in the box,' said Marian. 'Not that I could eat much. He's a beast.'

'I agree,' said Fatty. 'I suppose he kept on worrying you to tell him where your grandfather kept his money?'

'How do you know about all this?' said the girl, in wonder. "Yes, Wilfrid got into debt, and he asked my Grandad—his great-uncle—to give him some money and Grandad wouldn't. Wilfrid was very angry. He knew Grandad kept his money hidden somewhere, and he asked me where it was.'

'And did you know?' said Fatty.

'Yes, I did,' said Marian. 'Grandad told me a little while ago; but often enough I've seen the old man grope about under this chair and that, when he thought I wasn't there, to feel if his money was safe. But I never told a soul.'

'You remember that morning you washed the curtains?' said Fatty. 'Did Wilfrid ask you again for the money then—to tell him where it was?'

'Yes, and I told him I knew, but that I wouldn't ever tell a mean thing like him!' said Marian. 'He said he only wanted to borrow some and he'd put it back later; but I knew him better! He would never repay it!'

'Go on,' said Fatty.

'Well, that morning he said, 'All right, Marian. When you've gone I shall come back and hunt everywhere— and I'll find it, you see if I don't!' And I was dreadfully afraid that he would.'

'So you were very, very clever and sewed the pound notes into the hem of the curtains!' said Fatty.

Marian gave a little scream. 'Oh! *How* do you know all this? Surely Wilfrid hasn't found them? Oh, I've worried and worried since I've been shut up here. I wanted to tell Grandpa not to be upset if he couldn't find his money—I'd got it safe for him—but I didn't have a chance.'

'It's all right. The notes are still inside the hems,' said Fatty. 'It was a brilliant hiding-place. Tell me, what made Wilfrid come and take away the furniture?'

'Well, that afternoon Wilfrid came to see me at my home,' said Marian. 'He said he'd been to Hollies and Grandad was moaning and crying because his money had gone—and Wilfrid accused me of taking it. He said he'd get the police if I didn't share it with him!'

'Well, well, what a pleasant person our Wilfrid is!' said Fatty.

'I swore I hadn't got the money. I said it was still at Hollies, in the living-room, in a place he'd never find,' said Marian. 'And I told him I'd get it myself the next day and take it to a bank, where Wilfrid couldn't possibly get his hands on it.'

'I see. So he took a horse-box in the middle of the night, and went and quietly collected every bit of furniture from the living-room,' said Fatty. 'He meant to go through every stick of it at his leisure and find that money before you took it to the bank.'

'Yes, but he couldn't find it because it was in the curtains, and he didn't think of taking those down,' said Marian. 'And oh, dear, when he went through the furniture and ripped it to pieces, he still couldn't find the money, of course, so he got me up here by a trick, pushed me into the van and locked the door.'

'But why?' said Fatty, puzzled.

'Oh, he was quite mad, quite beside himself,' said Marian, trembling as she remembered. 'He said I could either find the money myself in the furniture, or, if I was lying, I could tell him where I'd hidden the money in my own home! And here I've been ever since, shouting and yelling, but nobody heard me. And each day Wilfrid comes to ask me if I've got the money, or will tell him where it is. He's mad!'

'He must be,' said Fatty. 'Cheer up, Marian, 'everything's all right. We'll take you back home, and to-morrow we'll deal with dear Wilfrid. Will you come up to Hollies at half-past ten? We'll be there, and you can take the money out of the curtains yourself.'

'Oh, yes, I *must* do that,' said Marian. 'How do you know all these things? It's queer to find you three boys here, in the middle of the night, telling me all kinds of things!'

'You walk along with us to where we've left our bikes,' said Fatty, taking Marian's arm. 'I'll tell you how we know—as much as I can, anyhow. Larry, take the number of this horse-box, will you?'

The boys took Marian back to where they had left their bicycles, passing the quiet stables as they went.

Fatty told Marian a good deal of his tale, and she listened in amazement.

'Poor Grandad!' she said. 'He must have been so upset. Never mind, he'll be all right when he gets his precious money back. How marvellous you three boys are—finding out everything like that. You're better than the police!'

Fatty took Marian back to her own home. 'It's not so late as you think,' he told her. 'It's not eleven o'clock yet. Look—there's still a light in that side-window. Shall I ring the bell for you?'

'No. I'll slip in at the side-door and surprise my mother,' said Marian. She gave Fatty a sudden hug. 'I think you're a marvel! I'll be up at Hollies at half-past ten to-morrow morning without fail, with some scissors to undo the hems!'

She disappeared. Fatty waited till he heard the side-door open and shut softly. Then he and the others went to get their bicycles from the front hedge.

'Good work, wasn't it?' he said, with much satisfaction.

'My word, yes!' said Larry. 'Gosh, I was so scared when I heard Marian screaming in the van that I let go of you, Fatty; you came down an awful bump.'

'That's all right,' said Fatty, in great good humour. 'My word, what an evening! Who would have thought that Wilfrid would shut Marian up like that! He must be in great need of money to do such a thing. I have an idea that that smartly dressed young man is going to get into considerable trouble.'

'Serve him right,' said Pip. 'He deserves it. I think

Marian is a jolly nice girl. I *thought* she couldn't have stolen that money!'

They were now cycling quickly home. Pip began to feel uncomfortable. 'I say!' he said. '*I'm* going to get into trouble too—being out late like this.'

'I would, as well, if my people didn't happen to be out,' said Larry. 'You're lucky, Fatty, your people never seem to mind.'

'I'm older than you are,' said Fatty, 'and wiser! If you get into trouble to-night, Pip, just say that something unexpected happened that you can't yet tell about, but that everything will be explained to-morrow morning.'

'Right', said Pip. 'What are you going to do now, Fatty? I bet I know! You're going to ring up Superintendent Jenks!'

'Quite right. Go to the top of the class!' said Fatty. 'Well, we part here. See you to-morrow morning, half-past ten, at Hollies. Bring the girls too.'

Fatty put away his bicycle when he got home and let himself in at the side-door. His parents were playing bridge in the lounge. Good, he wouldn't disturb them. He would telephone Superintendent Jenks from his mother's bedroom—where there was an extension—not from the hall. He could say what he liked there.

He tiptoed into his mother's room and shut the door. He went to the telephone and gave Police Headquarters number. A voice answered almost immediately.

'Police station here.'

'Is Superintendent Jenks in?' asked Fatty. 'If not, I'll ring his private number. It's important.'

'He's not here. I'll give you his private number,' said

the voice. 'Banks, 00165.'

'Thank you,' said Fatty and rang off. He telephoned again and got the private number. He heard the Superintendent's voice almost at once.

'Yes. What is it?'

'Frederick Trotteville here,' said Fatty. 'First of all, my hearty congratulations, sir, on your promotion!'

'Thanks, Frederick,' said the Superintendent, 'but I don't imagine that you're ringing me up at almost midnight just to tell me that.'

'No, sir,' said Fatty. 'The fact is, we've done a bit of work on that Hollies affair.'

'Hollies affair? Oh, yes, the old man whose money was stolen, whose furniture disappeared, and then the granddaughter vanished—am I right?' said the Super.

'Quite right, sir,' said Fatty. 'Er...'

'Wait now,' came the Super's voice, 'let me hazard a guess, Frederick. You've found the money, you've located the furniture, and you've got the girl! Am I right?'

'Well, yes, sir,' said Fatty, with a laugh. 'How did you know?'

'Oh, I had a report in two days ago from Goon, in the course of which he complained that Master Frederick Trotteville was greatly hampering the course of justice,' chuckled the Superintendent. 'I imagined that meant you were getting on with the case a lot better than he was. Actually he said that it was pretty certain the girl had gone off with the money, and should be arrested as soon as found.'

'Did he? Well, he's not quite right,' said Fatty.

'Would you care to come along to Hollies, the bungalow where all this happened, at half-past ten to-morrow morning, sir, and I'll have the whole affair neatly tied up for you.'

'Right, I'll be there,' said the Super. 'I was coming over anyhow to see what was happening. I didn't like the disappearance of the girl—from all accounts she's a good girl. I hope you will produce her, Frederick.'

'I hope to, sir,' said Fatty, trying to sound modest. 'And—er—will Mr. Goon be there?'

'Of course! I'll have a message sent to him,' said the Super. 'Well, well, I don't know why we don't leave all our local affairs to you, Frederick. How's little Bets? Is she in on this too?'

'Oh, yes. We all are,' said Fatty. 'Right, sir. We'll all be up at Hollies at half-past ten. Good-night!'

Fatty put down the telephone, and rubbed his hands gleefully. Good, good, good! He was about to do a delighted jig round the room when he stopped. No — his mothers' bedroom was just over the lounge—it would cause quite a lot of trouble for Fatty if some one came up to hunt for the elephant stamping round the room above!

'I'll go and find old Buster,' he thought. 'I can hear him scraping at my bedroom door now. I'm coming, Buster. Good news, old thing! Get ready to bark your head off, Buster. Hurrah!'

22 QUITE A PANTOMIME!

QUITE a lot of people walked up Holly Lane the next morning. Fatty, Larry, Daisy, Pip and Bets went first, talking excitedly. Bets and Daisy had been tremendously thrilled the night before when Pip and Larry had crept in to tell them the news of the Marlow adventure.

Fatty went up the front path, took the key from his pocket and unlocked the door. Mr. Henri, at the window next door, saw them, and left his couch. In a minute or two he was walking up the path.

'Good morning!' he said. 'You did not leave me the key, Frederick, and that young man—what is his name?—ah, yes, Wilfrid—he was annoyed to find I did not have it. He said he had forgotten his own key, and wished to enter Hollies to see that all was right.'

'Oh, he did, did he?' said Fatty. 'Thought he'd have one more hunt round, I suppose. Good thing he didn't.'

'He is coming back again soon,' said Mr. Henri.

'Good! Couldn't be better,' said Fatty. 'The more the merrier. Would you like to stay, Mr. Henri? There is going to be a bit of a do here soon—you might enjoy it. After all, you've been in this affair almost from the beginning.'

'I stay with pleasure,' said Mr. Henri, beaming, 'Ah, who comes now?'

'It's Marian!' said Fatty. He darted to the door to

meet her. She looked much better now. She smiled round at the others. Then she saw the empty room.

'Oh, how queer it looks without the furniture!' she said. Her eyes went to the curtains. She put out a hand and felt one of the hems. Fatty smiled at her.

'Jolly good hems, aren't they?' he said. 'Marian, I wonder if you'd be sweet enough to go and sit in the back bedroom till we call you. I want to produce you as a sort of—well, sort of surprise.'

'Yes. I'll go.' said Marian. 'But let me leave the door open. I want to hear everything.'

'You're setting the scene as if a play was going to be acted!' said Bets, giggling.

'Well, a play *is* about to be acted,' said Fatty. 'Now, who's this?'

It was Mr. Goon. He looked a bit puzzled as he rode up to the gate. He got off his bicycle, wheeled it up to the front door and put it against the wall.

Fatty opened the door for him. 'Welcome!' he said. Mr. Goon scowled.

'What you doing here?' he said. 'You'd better clear orf. The Superintendent's coming. He wants particularly to talk to me about this case here. I've got all my notes with me, so just you clear orf. And keep that dog away from my ankles, or I'll report him to the Super.'

'Sit, Buster,' said Fatty. 'My word, Mr. Goon, what a sheaf of notes you've got! Wonderful work! Have you solved the mystery?'

'No mystery about it,' said Goon, scornfully. 'That girl went off with the money—*and* the furniture. I'll soon have my hands on her. I've had information where she is.'

'Really?' said Fatty. 'Anywhere in this district?'

Goon snorted. 'No! Miles away! Anyway, I'm not saying anymore. You're not going to pick my brains. Me and the Superintendent are going to have a good talk, and you'd better clear out before he comes. Get along, now!'

'Here he is,' said Fatty, as a sleek, black police-car drew up at the gate, and the Superintendent got out with a plain-clothes man behind him. Bets tore out to meet him. He swung her up into the air.

'If it isn't young Bets! Well, well, how nice to see you again! Well, Daisy, how are you? Larry, Pip, Frederick, you all look very merry and bright.'

'I told them you were coming, sir, but they wouldn't buzz off,' said Goon, hoping that the Superintendent would take the hint and send the five away. But he didn't. He asked who Mr. Henri was, and Fatty explained.

Goon rustled his sheaf of notes and coughed. The Superintendent turned and looked at him sharply.

'Got something to say, Goon?' he inquired.

'Well, sir, yes, of course, sir,' said Goon, looking hurt. 'I supposed you wanted to see me about this Hollies case, sir. If you could just send these kids away...'

'Oh, no. They may have something to say that would help us, Goon,' said his chief. 'They may even know a few things that we don't know!'

Goon looked most disbelieving. 'There's really not much to this case, sir,' he said. 'Just a bad girl who robs her old grandfather of his money, gets away with his furniture, too, and does a disappearing act.'

'But I thought she was a girl of very good character, Goon,' said the Super. 'Girls like that don't suddenly do wicked things. How do we know she stole the money, anyway?'

'She didn't,' said Fatty, to Goon's surprise. 'Nobody stole it.'

'You're potty,' said Goon, quite forgetting himself. 'Where's this money then, if nobody stole it?'

'The girl hid it,' said Fatty. 'She was afraid her cousin Wilfrid would get it if she didn't put it somewhere safe.'

'Pah!' said Goon. 'What a tale! I'll believe that if you show me where she hid the money!'

'Right,' said Fatty, and stepped to the curtains. He put his finger and thumb into the hem whose stitches he had snipped the day before, and pulled out a pound note. He displayed it to Goon, Mr. Henri and Superintendent Jenks. They all stared in surprise, and Goon gaped, his mouth open in amazement.

'See—a pound note!' said Fatty, and took another from the hem, rather as if he were doing a conjuring trick. 'The hems of the curtains are full of these notes— a first-class hiding-place. You remember that Marian, the girl, was washing and ironing curtains, don't you, on the morning of the supposed robbery Mr. Goon? Well, Wilfrid came and threatened to look for the money when she had gone, if she didn't give it to him then and there...'

'And she was scared he'd find it, so she took it from its hiding-place—wherever that was—and undid the curtain-hems to make a new hiding-place!' said the Superintendent. 'Sewed them all up again too. A most ingenious girl, this Marian.

Mr. Goon swallowed two or three times. He could find nothing at all to say. Mr. Henri laughed in delight.

'Very neat,' he said. 'And now you will tell us where the lost furniture is, yes?'

'Pah!' said Goon, unable to stop himself.

'What did you say, Goon?' asked his chief. 'Can *you* tell us where the furniture is?'

'No. And nobody can!' said Goon. 'Nobody saw it go, nobody knows who took it, nobody knows where it is. I've had it searched for everywhere!'

'Frederick, can you throw any light on this subject?' asked the Superintendent.

'Yes,' said Fatty. 'Wilfrid and another man came at midnight and carried it out piece by piece.'

'Gah!' said Goon. 'Anybody would think you were there!'

'Well, as it happened, I was,' said Fatty. 'It was taken away in a horse-box—got the number, Larry? Yes, OKX 143—and it is now in that same horse-box, rather the worse for wear, in a copse near the stables belonging to King's, in Marlow. I can take you there any time you like, Mr. Goon.'

'You've got the money, you've got the furniture, but you haven't got the girl!' said Goon. 'And I've had information where she is!'

'That's clever of you, Mr. Goon,' said Fatty. 'You tell me where *you* think she is—and I'll tell you where *I* think she is!'

'I have information here that she's gone across to Ireland,' said Mr. Goon.

'And I have information that she's in the next room,' said Fatty, with a grin. 'Marian! Are you there!'

And to Mr. Goon's undying amazement Marian walked shyly into the room! Mr. Henri gave an exclamation. He had wondered who Marian was. The Superintendent glanced at his amazed plain-clothes officer and winked.

'Quite a pantomime!' he said, and the plain-clothes man grinned and nodded. He moved forward and asked Marian a few questions. Where had she been since she disappeared? Why had she gone away? He wrote down her answers rapidly, while Goon listened in the utmost astonishment.

'I understand, then, that these three boys found you locked up in the horse-box last night?' he said. 'And that your cousin Wilfrid was responsible for detaining you there?'

"Here, wait a minute!' said Goon, unable to believe his ears. 'You say these kids found her in that horse-box. How did *they* know about it? Why wasn't *I* told?'

'Frederick telephoned me last night,' said his chief. 'Quite rightly, too. It is possible that you might not have believed him, Goon.'

Goon collapsed. His face went slowly purple and he turned and looked out of the window. That boy! That Toad of a boy!

'And now all we want to complete the merry little company is our friend Wilfrid,' said the Superintendent. 'I imagine that even *you* can't supply him, Frederick?'

Fatty was about to say sorrowfully that no, he was afraid he couldn't , when he heard the front-gate click.

He looked out of the window and saw—Wilfrid!

Yes, Wilfrid had chosen that moment to come back and hunt round once again for the money. He saw that the door was now open and hurried to go inside. He stepped over the threshold—and stopped abruptly. The plain-clothes man moved casually beside him.

'Oh!' said Wilfrid. 'What's all this? Something happened?' Then he saw his cousin, and went very white.

'Marian! What are you doing here?'

'You thought I was still in the horse-box, didn't you?' said Marian. 'Well, I'm not. I'm here. I've come to get the money of Grandad's I hid away—see, in the hem of the curtains! You won't get it, Wilfrid! You won't have it to pay your bills!'

Wilfrid stared at the notes that Marian was pulling out of the curtain-hem. He ran his hand over his forehead. Then he made a sudden backward dart for the door.

But the plain-clothes man was there, and a hand with fingers of steel gripped Wilfrid's arm and held him fast.

'Don't go yet, Wilfrid,' said the Superintendent. 'There are quite a lot of questions we want to ask you.'

His voice was suddenly very different from the merry, kindly voice that the children were used to. Bets shivered a little. The Super was their friend, their very good friend, but to people like Wilfrid he was an implacable enemy, stern and unyielding. Wilfrid stood before him, as white as a sheet, trembling from head to foot.

'Johns—you and Goon stay here and let him tell you about the midnight move,' said the Superintendent.

'Where he parked the van and everything. Then take him along to the police station. I'll be there in an hour.'

'Right, Sir,' said Johns, the plain-clothes man. Goon muttered something, but nobody could catch what he said. Still, as nobody listened, it didn't matter! Poor Goon, he looked very downcast as the five children and Marian went away with the Superindent.

Mr. Henri went with them and said good-bye at the gate. 'I have such a story to tell to my sistair,' he said. 'Please to come and see us soon! Au revoir!'

'Where are we going?' asked Bets, hanging on to the burly Superintendent's arm.

'Well, isn't there some place here that sells ice-creams and macaroons?' said the big man. 'I had an early breakfast—and I don't often see you. I'd like to stand you all a treat this morning—Marian too! She looks as if she wants feeding up a bit! Been starved in that horse-box, I expect, Marian!'

'I couldn't eat very much,' she said. 'But I'm quite all right now, thank you. So is my mother. She was *so* thankful to see me. I'd still be a prisoner if it wasn't for these three boys!'

'Ah, here is the place I mean,' said the Superintendent, stopping outside the spotlessly clean dairy. 'Yes. Best macaroons I ever had in my life came from here. In we go!'

And in they went, Buster too, much to the surprise of the little dairy-woman, who didn't expect quite so many customers all at once—seven—and a dog who was as good as a customer any day, because he was just as fond of macaroons and ice-creams as the children were!

'Er—twenty-one macaroons,' please. Oh, I beg your pardon, Buster—twenty-four. I mean,' said the Superintendent. 'And a first round of eight ice-creams—and orangeade for every one but the dog.'

'Yes, sir,' said the dairy-woman, and hurried away. She brought the oragngeade at once. 'The other things are just coming,' she said.

The Superintendent lifted his glass. 'Let us drink to the day when Frederick Trotteville becomes my right-hand man!' he said. Fatty blushed with pride, and they all drank heartily.

Then Fatty lifted his glass. 'To my future chief, Superintendent Jenks!' he said, and every one again drank heartily. Now, only the Superintendent had any orangeade left.

'Ah, can't waste it!' he said. 'To the Five Find-Outers—and Dog. Many more mysteries!'

Yes, we all wish them that. Many more mysteries—and may each one be more mysterious than the last!

Enid Blyton

THE MYSTERY OF THE BURNT COTTAGE

This is the first of Enid Blyton's thrilling mystery books. Fatty, Larry, Daisy, Pip, Bets—and Buster the dog – turn detectives when a mysterious fire destroys a thatched cottage in their village. Calling themselves the 'Five Find-Outers and Dog' they set out to solve the mystery and discover the culprit. The final solution, however, surprises the Five Find-Outers almost as much as Mr. Goon, the village policeman. They can hardly wait for the next mystery to come along!

Enid Blyton

THE MYSTERY OF THE DISAPPEARING CAT

The second book in the popular *Mystery* series in which the Find-Outers – Larry, Fatty, Daisy, Pip, Bets and Buster the dog-turn detectives again to solve a very puzzling mystery.

A valuable Siamese cat is stolen from next door and suspicion falls on the children's friend, Luke the gardener's boy. How can they find the real thief and clear Luke of blame, especially with Mr. Goon the policeman interfering as usual? The Find-Outers are plunged into the middle of a first class mystery with only the strangest of clues to work on.

Enid Blyton

THE MYSTERY OF THE SECRET ROOM

This is the third book in the *Mystery* series.

It is the Christmas holidays, and the Five are looking for mysteries. Then out of the blue Pip discovers a room, fully furnished, at the top of an empty house. Whose room is it? What is it used for? This is the problem that must be solved in *The Mystery of the Secret Room*. With the help of their friend Inspector Jenks, the Five Find-Outers eventually reach a solution in this most entertaining book.

Enid Blyton

THE MYSTERY OF THE SPITEFUL LETTERS

This is the fourth in the amusing adventures of the Five Find-Outers, and Dog. Fatty, Larry, Daisy, Pip and Bets are together once more for the Easter Holidays and quickly become involved in a very peculiar situation, trying to solve the mystery of the spiteful letters that arrive unsigned, for various people in Peterswood.

Mr. Goon, the policeman, tries to solve the mystery too, and comes up against Fatty, who in various disguises, manages to mystify the poor old policeman completely.

Enid Blyton

THE MYSTERY OF THE MISSING NECKLACE

The fifth book of the popular *Mystery* series, in which Fatty, Larry, Daisy, Pip, Bets – and Buster the dog, all play their parts as Find-Outers.

There are a great many clever burglaries going on and it is suspected that members of the gang have their meeting place somewhere in Peterswood. The children naturally determine to solve the mystery and they tumble into other mysteries, too, in the process. Who is the old man on the seat? Who is Number Three? Where is the missing necklace? For once Mr. Goon, the policeman defeats Fatty one strange night at the Waxworks Hall! But it all ends up most unexpectedly and amusingly with the children finally triumphant.

Enid Blyton's

THE MYSTERY

OF TALLY-HO COTTAGE

Enid Blyton's

THE MYSTERY

OF TALLY-HO COTTAGE

Mammoth

CONTENTS

1   AT PETERSWOOD STATION

ONE afternoon four children and a dog walked into the little railway station at Peterswood. The dog ran about happily, his tail wagging all the time.

'Better put Buster on the lead,' said Pip. 'We're early, and two or three trains may come through. Here, Buster––come to heel, old boy!'

The little Scottie trotted up, his tail wagging nineteen to the dozen. He gave a few short barks.

'Yes, I know you're longing to see Fatty,' said Pip, bending over him to clip on his lead. 'So are we all! Hey, keep still!'

'Hang on to him—here comes a train!' said Larry. It's going right through'

Buster stood his ground bravely until the train gave a piercing whistle as it tore through the station—then he tried to scuttle under a wooden seat and dragged Pip after him. He sat down with his back to the train and trembled. That awful whistle!

'It made *me* jump!' said Bets. 'Cheer up, Buster-Fatty will soon he here. We've loved having you while Fatty's been away, and you've been Very Very Good!'

'Even Mother likes you!' said Pip, patting him. 'Though she didn't a bit want us to keep you while Fatty was in Switzerland!'

'I can't think WHY Fatty had to go off to Switzer-land for a whole fortnight, and be away all Christmas time,' complained Bets.

'Well, he had to go with his parents,' said Daisy. 'I expect he had a jolly good time in all that snow.'

'Yes. And he wouldn't mind falling down a bit, he's so plump!' said Larry, with a laugh. What's the time? Gosh, we're early! What shall we do?'

'It's cold on the platform. Let's go into the waiting-room,' said Daisy. 'Come on, Buster.'

Buster sat firm. Pip pulled on the lead. 'Come on, idiot. We're only going into the waiting-room. Fatty's train isn't due yet.'

Buster refused to move. Fatty was coming on one of the trains that clattered into the station, and would alight on this platform—and therefore Buster wished to wait there and nowhere else.

'Tie him up to the seat,' said Larry. 'He'll be miserable if we make him go into the waiting-room. Buster, you're an ass. *I* wouldn't sit down on that icy-cold stone platform for anything.'

They tied Buster to the seat and left him there. They went into the waiting-room, which had a very minute fire, but was at least sheltered from the cold wind that blew through the station.

'There's one thing,' said Daisy, sitting down on a hard wooden bench, 'Fatty won't be in disguise, so he can't trick us this time! He'll be arriving with his father and mother, and will have to be himself.'

'I'm glad,' said Bets. 'I want to see him just as he really is, fat and jolly and grinning all over his face! We haven't seen him for months! Three months at school —and then he rushes off to Switzerland!'

'I bet I know what he'll say as soon as he sees us,' said Pip, grinning. 'He'll say, "Well—got any mystery on hand?"'

'And we haven't,' said Larry. 'Peterswood has been as good as gold. Goon can't have had anything to do at all!'

Goon, the village policeman, had indeed had a peaceful fortnight. Not even a dog had chased a sheep, and nothing as exciting as even a small burglary had happened. Goon had had plenty of time for snoozing in his big armchair!

A taxi drove up to the station, followed by a second one. A man leaned out of the window of the first one and beckoned to the one and only porter.

'Hey, porter! Come and take these cases. Look slippy, we've not got much time!'

The voice was loud and clear. The porter ran up at once, and took two small cases. A man got out of the taxi and helped out a woman. Both were middle-aged, well dressed and cheerful-looking. The woman carried a tiny white poodle.

'Darling Poppet' she said. 'Don't get a cold in this icy wind!' She tucked the little thing under her fur coat and only its quaint little pointed nose looked out. The four children, watching from the window of the waiting-room, thought it was a little dear!

Four or five people got out of the second taxi, all rather hilarious. They had evidently come to see off the first two.

'Buck up, Bill—you've not got much time to get the tickets!' said the woman with the dog.

'Plenty of time,' said Bill, and strode into the station. 'Hallo—is that a train in the distance? My word, we'll have to hurry after all!'

The woman rushed on to the platform with the little dog. "Oh, it isn't our train after all!' she said. 'It's going the other way. Oh, Poppet, what a shock I got!'

The new-comers made such a stir and commotion

that the four children came out of the waiting-room to watch. Everyone was very hilarious.

'Well, be sure to have a good time!' said a red- haired fellow and thumped the man called Bill on his back, so that he had a coughing-fit.

'Send us a telegram when you get there. We'll miss you and your parties!' said a woman.

The woman with the dog sat down on the seat to which Buster was tied, and set the little poodle down on the platform. At once Buster began to sniff at her woolly fur, and the little poodle yelped in sudden fright. Buster ran round to the front of the seat, twisting his lead across the woman's legs. She screamed and snatched Poppet up at once, afraid that Buster was going to snap at the poodle.

To make matters worse another train thundered into the station at that moment and Poppet nearly went mad with fright. She leapt out of her mistress's arms and tore off at top speed. Buster tried to race after her, forgetting all about his lead, and nearly strangled himself! He got caught up in the woman's legs, and she fell over, squealing loudly.

'Oh! Catch Poppet, someone! Oh, what's this dog doing? Get away, you brute!'

There was a terrific commotion. All four children tried to catch Poppet, and then Pip went to rescue poor Buster who was being well and truly kicked by the scared woman. She was very angry indeed.

'Whose dog in this? What do you want to tie him up under a seat for? Where's a policeman? Where's my dog?'

'Now now, Gloria, don't get upset,' said the man called Bill. Nobody took any notice of the train that had just come in, not even the four children. They were so concerned about Buster, and poor frightened Poppet!

So they didn't even notice Fatty stepping from the train with his father and mother—an extremely sun-burnt Fatty, looking plump and the picture of health. He soon saw the others, and was rather astonished to find them so engrossed that they weren't even looking out for him!

'You get a taxi, Mother,' said Fatty. 'I'll walk back with the others. I see they're here.'

Fatty walked over to where Pip was trying to apologize to the angry woman and her husband. He now had his hand firmly on Buster's collar, and Buster was trying his hardest to squirm away. He began to bark loudly-and then suddenly wrenched himself from Pip's hand.

'Well!' said a familiar voice, 'at least SOMEbody recognizes me! Hallo, Buster!'

All the four swung round at once. Bets ran at Fatty, almost knocking him over. 'Fatty! You're here!'

'It looks like it!' said Fatty, and then there was a general clapping-of-backs and friendly punches. Buster nearly barked the station down, he was so excited. He pawed so hard at Fatty's legs that Fatty had to lift him up, and carry him!

'Whose dog is that?' demanded the man called Bill. 'I never saw such a badly behaved one in my life. Knocked my wife over, and made her coat all dusty! Ah —there's a policeman—come over here, my good man. I want to report this dog. It's been out of control, attacked my wife's poodle, and caused my wife to fall down!'

To the children's horror, there was Mr. Goon! He had come to buy a paper at the station, had heard the commotion, and walked on to the platform to see what it was. He still had his bicycle clips on his legs, and his bulging eyes gleamed with pleasure.

'Sir! This dog made a savage attack, you say! Just let me take down a note. Ah—this dog's been a pest for a long time—a very—long—time!'

Goon took out his notebook and licked his pencil. What a bit of luck to have a real complaint about that horrible dog!

The train pulled out of the station, but nobody noticed. Everyone was looking at the little group of children surrounded by grown-ups. Buster leapt out of Fatty's arms as soon as he saw Goon and danced joyfully round his ankles. Goon flapped at him with his notebook.

'Call this dog off! Here, you, call this dog off. I'll report him all right. I'll...'

Suddenly the woman gave a squeal of joy. 'Oh—here's Poppet back again—with Larkin. I thought you weren't going to come in time to take Poppet back home with you, Larkin!'

Larkin was a queer-looking fellow, who stooped as he walked, and dragged one leg behind him in a limp. He looked fat and shapeless in an old and voluminous overcoat, and had a scarf round the bottom part of his face and an old cap over his eyes. He carried Poppet in his arms.

'Who's this?' demanded Goon, looking with surprise at the queer fellow who suddenly appeared with Poppet.

'Oh, it's only Larkin, who lives in the cottage in the grounds of Tally-Ho, the house we rent,' said the woman. 'He was told to come to the station in time to collect Poppet and take her back again with him. He's going to look after her—but I *did* want to have my darling Poppet till the very last minute—didn't I, Poppet?'

She took Poppet into her arms and fondled her. She spoke to Larkin again. 'You'll look after her well, won't you? And remember all I told you to do. I'll soon be back to see to her. Take her now, before our train comes in and scares her.'

Larkin shuffled off, limping as he went. He hadn't said a word. Poppet had been handed back to him as if she were a doll, and was now snuggled into his coat again.

Goon was growing impatient. He still had his note-book in his hand. The children were wondering whether they could make a dash and go, but Goon had his eye on them.

'Now, Madam,' said Goon, 'about this dog here. Can I have your name and address, please and ...'

'Oh! Here's our train!' squealed the woman, and immediately everyone elbowed poor Goon aside and began to kiss and shake hands and shout out farewell messages. The man and woman climbed into a carriage and off went the train, with everyone waving madly.

'Gah!' said Goon, in disgust, and shut his note-book. He looked round for Buster and the others— but they were gone!

2   IT'S FUN TO BE TOGETHER AGAIN

THE five children and Buster were halfway down the road, running at top speed!

'Good thing that train came in when it did!' panted Pip.

'Horrid old Goon! He *would* turn up just then!' said Bets. It' wasn't Buster's fault. He wasn't doing any harm.'

'Let's hide somewhere till Goon's gone by,' said Daisy. 'He's got his bike, I expect, and he'll have a few nasty things to say to us if he sees us.'

'Oh yes, *do* let's hide,' said Bets, who really was very scared of the big policeman.

'Right. Here's an empty watchman's hut!' said Fatty, spotting it standing beside a place where the road was being repaired. 'Hop in. It will just about take us all. The back is towards where Goon will come from. He'll sail right by!'

They crowded into the little hut—only just in time! Goon turned the corner on his bicycle and came sailing down the road at top speed, on the look-out for the Five—and especially for that Pest of a Dog!

They all watched him sail past, his feet going rapidly up and down on the pedals. They caught sight of his grim face as he went by. Fatty grinned.

'There he goes. Well, we'd better keep out of his way for a day or two,' he said. 'I expect he'll be after us about old Buster. What *did* happen? Tell me. I was jolly surprised to find you all on the platform with your backs to me, not caring tuppence whether I arrived or not!'

'Oh, Fatty-everything happened so quickly!' said Bets, as they walked home with him. She told him all about tying Buster up to the seat, and how the man and woman had arrived with their friends, and how Poppet had got mixed up with Buster.

'It was such a to-do!' said Pip. 'I'm awfully sorry about it, Fatty—just as your train arrived too!'

'That's all right!' said Fatty, 'I was only pulling your leg about it. Has Buster been good with you and Bets while I've been away?'

'He's been angelic!' said Bets. 'I *shall* miss him. Mother wouldn't let him sleep in my room or Pip's, as he does in yours, Fatty—but he was *most* obedient, and only came scratching at my door once in the middle of the night.'

'You're a very well-brought-up dog, aren't you, Buster?' said Fatty, and the little Scottie danced in delight round his ankles. 'Blow Goon! It was bad luck that he came up at that minute. I bet he'll be after us for details of "Savage Behaviour of Dog out of Control". I expect that's what he wrote down in his note-book. We'll have to think what to say to him.'

'Here we are,' said Pip, stopping by Fatty's gate. 'When shall we see you again, Fatty? You'll have to go in and unpack now, I suppose?'

'Yes,' said Fatty. 'Come round tomorrow to the shed at the bottom of my garden. And if you see Goon just say that as I own Buster, I'm the one for him to see. Well, so long! All news tomorrow!'

He went through the gate and round to the garden-door of his house. Bets sighed. 'Oh, I do wish we could all have had tea together or something. I'm just longing for a good talk with Fatty. Isn't he *brown*?'

Much to Bets' relief, Mr. Goon didn't appear at her home that day. When she and Pip set out the next morning to go to Fatty's shed, they both kept a good look-out for the fat policeman, but he didn't appear either on foot or on his bicycle.

Larry and Daisy were already down in the shed with Fatty. It was warm and cosy, for the oil-lamp was lighted and burning well. Fatty was just the same old Fatty, handing out bars of chocolate, and opening bottles of ginger-beer and lemonade. He grinned at Pip and Bets.

'Come on in. Seen old Goon?'

'No. Has anybody seen him?' asked Bets.

Nobody had. Buster went over to Bets and lay down beside her. 'He feels as if he belongs to you as well as to me, now,' said Fatty, smiling at Bets. He was very fond of little Bets, and she thought the world of Fatty.

'You *are* brown, Fatty!' said Bets, looking at his sunburnt face. 'If you wanted to disguise yourself as an Indian or some other foreigner you'd easily pass for one.'

'Good idea!' said Fatty. 'I might try it on old Goon! I'm longing to get back to some real detective work again, and try out a few disguises. I don't get much chance at school—I only dressed up once last term. '

'What as?' asked Daisy, with a giggle. 'Go on—tell us. I know you want to!'

'It wasn't anything much,' said Fatty airily. 'Our French master fell ill and the Head had to send for a new one—and he—er—arrived early, and made a bit of a fool of himself.'

'Oh—did *you* pretend to be him?' said Pip. 'What did

you do, Fatty? You really are a caution!'

'Well, I togged myself up, put on a moustache and those false teeth of mine,' said Fatty, 'and a wig of curly black hair, and a smile you could see a mile off because of the teeth...'

The others laughed. They knew Fatty's frightful false front teeth!

'Did you ask for the Head?' asked Bets.

'Gosh no—I'm not as fat-headed as all that!' said Fatty. 'I knew I'd find three or four of the masters watching the football that afternoon, so I made my way to them and talked to very *earnestly* about the school. 'And ze dear boys—zey await my coming, is it not? And ze—how you call him—ze Head—he awaits me also? Zis is ze football, is it not? Boom—boom-how zat boy kicked ze ball!'

Fatty acted a Frenchman to the life, and the others roared at him. 'I don't think they liked me very much,' said Fatty. 'They all muttered something about classes and wandered off one by one. My teeth put them off, I suppose. They were jolly surprised when the *real* French master turned up!'

'What was he like? Anything like you pretended to be?' asked Larry.

'Not a bit. He was little and rather bald, and had a beard and teeth you'd hardly notice!' said Fatty. 'It all caused quite a commotion. A scare went round that the first man must have been someone who wanted to get in and rob the Head's safe—and the poor new man couldn't *think* why people were so surprised to see him.'

'I don't know how you dare to do such things,' said Pip. ' I'd *never* dare—and if I did I'd be found out at once. I can't think why you're hardly ever spotted, Fatty. There must be something about you—you do carry things off so well!'

Fatty looked pleased. 'Oh well—I've got to practise a bit if I'm going to be a real detective some day. Have some more ginger-beer? Now—have you found any mystery? A mystery would be just about the best news I could hear.'

'There's not been a sniff of one,' said Larry, drinking his ginger-beer. 'Goon must have been thoroughly bored this Christmas—I don't believe anything's happened at all.'

'Sad,' said Fatty. 'After two weeks of doing nothing but fall about in snow I did hope I could exercise my brains as soon as I got home.'

'Tell us about Switzerland,' said Bets. 'Did you really fall down much?'

It appeared that, far from falling down even once, Fatty had done extremely well in all forms of winter sport, and had carried off quite a few prizes. He tried to talk about them modestly, but, being Fatty, this was very difficult.

'Still the same old Fatty,' said Larry, after about twenty minutes of listening to Fatty's exploits. 'The Wonder Boy! Can't put a foot wrong even on skis!'

'Didn't stand on his head once!' said Pip, grinning. 'My cousin Ronald said he was more often upside-down than the right way up, when *he* went to the winter sports. But not our Fatty!'

'Don't tease him!' said Daisy. 'You'll stop his traveller's tales. He's got plenty more, haven't you Fatty?'

'Well, *I* want to hear them, even if nobody else does!' said Bets who never minded Fatty's boasting.

Fatty sighed heavily. 'Ah well—I don't want to bore

you!' You tell me *your* news. How many Christmas cards did you have? Was your turkey done to a turn? Did the fairy doll look nice at the top of your Christmas tree?'

'Shut up, Fatty,' said Pip and gave him a punch. That was the signal for a general scrimmage in which Buster joined in delight. They were all shrieking so loudly that nobody heard a knock at the shed door. Buster was almost barking his head off, and he didn't hear it either.

The shed door opened and Fatty's mother, Mrs. Trotteville, looked in. 'Frederick!' she called, in amazement. 'FREDERICK! Whatever is going on here? You'll have the oil-stove over. FREDERICK!'

Buster heard her first, and stopped barking. He stood and stared at her, and then gave a yelp as if to say 'Stop this fooling, everybody! Beware!'

Pip suddenly caught sight of Mrs. Trotteville and extricated himself from the heap of bodies on the floor. Fatty's was underneath, having been well and truly pummeled.

'Fatty!' said Pip, in Fatty's ear. 'Look out—danger!' With a great heave Fatty sat up and looked round. He saw the open door and his mother standing in astonishment there. He smoothed back his hair and grinned.

'Oh—Mother! I didn't hear you, I can't think why!' said Fatty, politely. 'Do come in. Have a chocolate — or some lemonade? I think there's a drop left.'

'Don't be foolish Frederick,' said his mother. 'Really, to see you behaving like this—you must all have gone mad! You'll certainly have that oil-stove over, and then the whole place will go up in flames.'

'I've got a bucket of water ready over there, Mother,' said Fatty. 'Honestly, you don't need to worry. We were only—well, actually we were so *pleased* to be together again that we—er—we...'

'I can't wait while you think up some silly explanation,' said Mrs. Trotteville impatiently. 'I just came to say that policeman, Mr. Goon, is on the tele-phone and wants to speak to you. I do hope, Frederick, that you haven't upset him *already*. You only came back yesterday.'

Goon on the telephone! The Five looked at one another in dismay. That meant he was going to get after old Buster all. Blow!

'All right. I'll go and speak to him,' said Fatty, getting up and brushing the dust off various parts of himself. 'Blow Goon! It's all right, Mother—don't look at me like that, there's a dear. I HAVEN'T DONE ANYTHING WRONG, truly I haven't.'

And off he went up the garden path and into the house, Mrs. Trotteville behind him, and Buster scampering along too.

The others looked at one another. NOW what horrid things had Goon to say?

3   POPPET THE POODLE

MR. GOON was getting impatient. Why didn't that Toad of a Boy come to the telephone? He began to bellow into it at his end.

'Hallo! HALLO! Are you there? HALLO!'

When Fatty picked up the receiver he was almost deafened by Mr. Goon's yells. He shouted back.

'HALLO, HALLO, GOOD MORNING, HALLO, HALLO, HAL...'

This time it was Goon that was almost deafened. 'Ho—you've come at last, have you? he said. 'What you yelling at me like that for?'

'Nothing. I just thought we were having a kind of shouting-match,' said Fatty, in a most polite voice.

Goon began to boil. Fatty always had a very bad effect on him. He spluttered into the telephone.

'Now then, you look here, and don't you ...'

'Can't hear you properly,' said Fatty, in a most concerned voice. 'Mr. Goon, can you speak a little closer to the mouth-piece?'

'No!' roared the angry policeman, 'and just you look here, I ...'

'Look where? Down the telephone, do you mean?' said Fatty inquiringly.

Poor Mr. Goon nearly flung down the telephone. He roared again. 'I want you to come down here to my house tomorrow morning at ten o'clock sharp,' he shouted. 'About that complaint, see? That dog's out of control, and well you know it.'

'There wasn't time for you to get a proper com-plaint,' said Fatty.

'Ho, I got enough to go on,' said Goon.

'Ho, you didn't,' said Fatty, exasperated.

'What's that you say?' bellowed Goon.

'Nothing of any importance,' said Fatty. 'Right—I'll be along tomorrow—with my witnesses—including Buster.'

'No—don't you bring that there pest of a dog!' cried Mr. Goon. But it was too late—Fatty had put down the receiver with a bang. Blow Goon!

He went to tell the others, and they listened gloomily.

'We'll all come with you,' said Bets loyally. 'And of course we'll take Buster. He's the defendant, isn't he? —is that what you call it?—and he ought to speak up for himself!'

'He'll speak all right!' said Pip. 'What a nuisance Goon is! We haven't got a *great* deal of the holiday left, and we don't want it messed up by Goon.'

'Let's go for a walk,' said Fatty. 'The sun's out now, and I want to get the taste of Goon out of my mouth!'

They all laughed. 'You say such silly things!' said Daisy. 'Come on—let's go down to the river. There are some baby swans there, and the parents bring them to be fed. We'll take some bread.'

They put on hats and coats and went up the garden path to the kitchen door to ask for bread. The cook put it into a basket for them and they set off for the river.

They fed the swans and then wandered up the river-path, enjoying the pale January sun. The swans swam with them for some way, the little cygnets following behind. They came to a small gate that gave on to the river-path, and Bets looked over it idly.

Then she pulled at Fatty's arm. 'Look—isn't that

exactly like the dear little poodle we saw yesterday at the station-the one whose mistress made all the fuss about Buster?'

They all looked over the gate. 'No-I don't think it's the poodle,' said Pip, adding, in his usual brotherly way, 'you *always* jump to conclusions, Bets. Now I come to look more closely, it's not a *bit* like the poodle we saw. It's too big.'

An argument began. 'It's not too big—it's about the right size,' said Daisy.

'You girls have no idea of size,' said Larry loftily.

'I'll soon prove it, anyway,' said Bets suddenly, and she began to call loudly. 'Poppet! Poppet, are you Poppet? Here, Poppet!'

And the poodle straightway ran over to the gate, its stiff little tail wagging like a pendulum!

'There you are!' said Bets triumphantly. 'What did I tell you? Poppet, you're a darling! Fatty, isn't she sweet? She trots about as if she learns ballet-dancing!'

'So she does,' said Fatty, seeing exactly what Bets meant. 'At any moment now Poppet will rise on her toes and pirouette! Poppet, why did you cause all that upset with Buster?'

Poppet put her little pointed nose through the gate and sniffed at Buster, who sniffed back. He licked the tip of Poppet's nose, and Bets laughed.

'He likes her! I wonder if she's lonely without her mistress? I didn't much like the look of that man who took her back home, did you?'

'Well, I didn't like what I could *see* of him, which wasn't' much,' said Fatty. 'I wonder where they live—in that cottage there, I suppose.'

THE MYSTERY OF TALLY-HO COTTAGE

A small, not very well-kept cottage stood at the side of the garden. Much further away rose a big house, probably the one that Poppet's master and mistress had left the day before. No smoke rose from its chimney, so presumably it was now empty. But smoke rose up from the chimneys of the little cottage steadily and thickly, and the five children immediately pictured the muffled-up man sitting hunched over a roaring fire.

Poppet wanted Buster to play with her. She pranced away from the gate, came back, and pranced away again, looking over her shoulder as if to say, 'Do come! I'd like a game with you!'

Buster scraped at the gate and whined. 'No, no, Buster,' said Fatty. 'You're already in enough trouble with Mr. Goon without getting into any more! We'd better go.'

They were just turning away when a voice came from the cottage. 'Poppet! 'Ere, Poppet. Where are you? You come along in!'

Poppet immediately disappeared into a bush to hide, and lay there quietly. The children watched in amusement.

'Where's that dog gone?' said the voice, and foot-steps came down a path—limping, shuffling steps—and into view came the same man they had seen the day before, dressed in much the same way, except that now he had no scarf round his neck.

The children saw that he had a dirty-looking, unkempt beard and moustache, shaggy eyebrows and bits of grey-black hair sticking out from under his cap. He wore glasses with thick lenses, and seemed to be short-sighted as he peered here and there for the hidden dog.

'I bet you could dress up EXACTLY like that awful man,' whispered Bets in Fatty's ear. He turned and nodded, amused.

'Just what *I* was thinking!' he said. 'He'd be very easy to copy, shuffle and all! Look at Poppet—she's not going to give herself away—she's lying as still as a mouse.'

'Poppet! Poppet! Where is that wretched dog!' said the man in an exasperated voice. 'Wait till I get you, I'll show you I mean what I ses! Slipping out like that! I won't, half thrash you!,

Bets and Daisy looked horrified. What, thrash a little thing like Poppet? Surely the man couldn't mean it!

Another voice came on the clear wintry air. 'Bob Larkin! Didn't I tell you to help me with them pota—toes? You come in and do them!'

The man scowled. 'I'm just coming!' he said. 'I'm after this dratted dog! It's got out.'

'Oh my word—I hope as how that gate's shut!' cried the second voice. 'We'll get into trouble all right if anything happens to that precious dog!'

A woman now came into sight, very thin, wearing a draggled skirt and a dull red shawl wrapped tightly round her. Her hair was so extraordinary that the children gaped to see it. It was obviously a wig, mouse-colour and much too curly-and much too crooked!

'That's a wig,' muttered Daisy to Bets. 'Poor thing, I expect she's bald.'

The woman was not a very attractive sight. For, besides the wig, she wore dark glasses. She coughed now and again, and pulled a thick green scarf round her throat and chin. Then she sniffed loudly.

'Bob Larkin! You come on in. I'm not going to make my cold worse coming out here and yelling for you. You come on in!'

The man suddenly saw the little dog hiding in the bushes. He pounced on her and gripped her. She whined in sudden fear. The man shook her angrily.

'I'll teach you to slip out like this! I'll give you a real good lamming!'

'Here, hold on,' said Fatty, at once. 'She's only a little thing.'

The man swung round and peered short-sightedly at the watching children. He hadn't noticed them before. Buster gave a sudden growl.

The man looked hard at the little Scottie, then at the children again. 'Why—you're the kids whose dog caused all that rumpus yesterday!' he said. 'Mr. Goon's been round to see me about that. That dog of yours is going to get into trouble, see? Now you get off that gate and go away—and don't you start telling me what I'm to do! I'm in charge here, and I'll complain to that bobby if you make any trouble!'

This wasn't pleasant hearing. Bets felt frightened, and took hold of Buster's collar. Buster's nose was still sticking through the bars of the gate, and he growled when Bob Larkin took hold of Poppet's collar very roughly and dragged her up the garden.

'Yes—you'd like to go to Poppet's help as much as we would, Buster, old fellow,' said Fatty, frowning after the man. 'But you've got into enough trouble for the time being. I'm sorry that fellow recognized us.'

'I suppose he and Goon have cooked up a whole lot of complaints between them,' said Larry. 'Well, at least you know that Goon's been to see this Bob Larkin, and you won't be surprised when he tells you tomorrow!'

'What an unpleasant pair,' said Fatty, as they walked on. They suddenly heard dismal howls coming from the cottage and looked miserably at one another. Poppet must be getting her 'lamming'. Horrid old man!

Buster growled and ran back to the gate, pawing at it. 'Good old Buster!' said Pip. 'Sorry we can't let you do a bit of rescue work!'

They went back feeling rather subdued. An interview with Goon tomorrow—and upset over a dear little dog like Poppet. Things didn't look too good! Even Fatty couldn't think of any jokes, and they parted with hardly a smile.

'Tomorrow at Goon's, at ten o'clock,' said Fatty, when they said good bye.

'Right,' said the others, and went off looking extremely gloomy!

4 A SLIGHT VICTORY

FATTY's mother had already inquired why Mr. Goon had wanted him on the telephone. When he told her she looked vexed.

'How unfortunate! Who is this woman that Buster tripped up?'

'I don't know,' said Fatty. 'She and her husband appeared to be going off on some trip or other, and four or five of their friends came to see them off. They were pretty noisy. I think they live at that house called Tally-Ho down by the river—next to the Daniels. I don't know what their name is.'

'Oh—*those* people!' said his mother.

'Yes sound as if you know them, but don't want to!' said Fatty, amused.

'I know which people you mean, but I certainly don't have anything to do with them,' said Mrs. Trotteville. 'They have behaved very badly since they took Mrs. Peters' house while she went to America-giving silly parties, going out in boats at all hours of the night—and, so I hear, not paying their bills! Let me see—what is their name? Oh yes-Lorenzo, I think!'

'Well, it was they who complained to Goon about Buster,' said Fatty.

'I see,' said his mother. 'I heard they were rather fourth-rate film-actors, both the man *and* the woman —but haven't had any film-work to do for some time. Anyway, my dear boy, if they have gone away, Goon can't make much of a complaint. He's just being unpleasant, I expect.'

A SLIGHT VICTORY

'Well, I'm going now, Mother,' said Fatty. 'I hope I come home all in one piece—and I hope Buster leaves Goon all in one piece, too!'

'You do exaggerate so, Frederick!' said Mrs. Trotteville. 'Just be firm with that tiresome policeman, and don't take too much notice of what he says!'

'I won't,' said Fatty, feeling suddenly quite cheerful. 'Good-bye, Mother—I'll tell you what happens as soon as I get back.'

He set off on his bicycle, Buster in the basket. The others were already waiting for him outside Goon's house. Bets looked rather pale and Fatty squeezed her arm.

'Cheer up! We're going to have some fun. I've got a lot saved up to say to Goon!'

They went to Goon's front door and knocked on it. Rat-a-tatta-tat-tat-TAT!

There came the sound of slippered feet and the door opened. It was the woman who came to clean the house for Mr. Goon. She stared at them in surprise.

'We've come to see Mr. Goon,' said Fatty. 'He told us to be here at ten o'clock.'

'Did he now?' said the woman, looking as if she didn't quite know what to do. 'Well, he didn't say anything to me about that. He went out in a hurry like, about half an hour ago—maybe he'll be back soon.'

'We'll come in and wait, then,' said Fatty firmly. 'He said ten o'clock, and it's exactly ten now.'

A clock in Goon's office began to strike just as if it had heard what Fatty said. The woman motioned them into the hall.

'I'd better not put you into Mr. Goon's office,' she said. 'He's got private things in there—important things. I don't have to move so much as a sheet of paper if I dust in there.'

'We'll wait in the parlour then,' said Fatty, and they all marched into a musty fusty little room full of the smell of pipe-smoke. 'Pooh-let's leave the door open. What a smell!'

'I'll be out in the garden hanging up the washing,' said the woman,' but I'll hear Mr. Goon when he comes and tell him you're here.'

'Pa Goon looks as fat as Goon is now,' said Larry. 'And oh *look*—this podge of a boy with eyes sticking out of his head must be Goon!'

They all chuckled at the sight of Goon as a boy. 'He's very like Ern,' said Bets, and, indeed, he was! Ern was one of Goon's nephews, who had once been to stay with him and had a most unpleasant time!

'I wonder what Ern's doing,' said Bet's remembering the admiration he had had for Fatty. 'He came to see you just before Christmas, Fatty, to give you a Christmas present he'd made you—and he almost burst into tears when he heard you were in Switzerland.'

'Poor Ern,' said Fatty. 'I've no doubt he'll turn up again with whatever it is. Hallo—is that Goon?'

It was—and judging by the heavy tramp of feet in the hall, there were two others with him. Fatty debated what to do. Should he go and announce himself? But if Goon had visitors, he wouldn't be too pleased to be interrupted.

'We'd better wait a bit,' he said to the others. 'Perhaps that woman will hear him and go and tell him we are waiting.'

'She's busy talking to the woman next door,' said Bets, looking out of the window. 'How they can understand what the other is saying, I really don't know—they're both talking at once!'

Voices came from the office next to the room the children were sitting in. First they were fairly quiet, and then they became loud. The children heard various words, and at first took no notice.

Then a word came that made Fatty sit up. 'Lorenzo!' Now, where had he just recently heard that name? It certainly rang a bell!

'They've *got* to be traced!' said a voice that was not Goon's. 'These Lorenzos are the ones we want, I'm sure. Get hold of anyone who knows anything about them. Get hold of their best friends here and ask questions and...'

The voice fell and the next words could not be heard. Fatty listened in wonder. He remembered now where he had heard the name Lorenzo—his mother has said it was the name of the people who owned Poppet the little poodle.

'Funny!' thought Fatty, 'it sounds as if they've run into trouble. I hope they have—if so, old Goon won't bother about Buster!'

There was the sound of movement in the little office, and then footsteps. The visitors must be going!

'Well, good-bye, Goon,' said a voice. 'You'll have to get going on this—it's a big thing. Pity we've just missed those rascals! Find out what you can from the Larkins—they may be able to tell you something. If we can't get our hands on the Lorenzos, we might at least be able to get hold of that picture. So long!'

There was the tramp of feet to the front gate. Fatty sat still, feeling startled. Why—what was this going on?

Something had unexpectedly cropped up, that was certain. A sudden feeling of excitement surged up in him—it might be a Mystery! Something was Up! Something had to be Found Out! He'd tackle Goon about it and get the Five Find-Outers on the job at once!

Bets was surprised to see Fatty's face suddenly go red with excitement. She thought he was feeling nervous at having to meet Goon and she slipped her hand through his arm. Fatty never even noticed it! He was thinking so very hard. What *could* the Lorenzos have done? What was this 'picture'? He must find out, he must!

Goon came back from the front gate humming a tuneless song. He was evidently feeling pleased with life. He didn't go back into the office but walked straight into the parlour, not knowing that anyone was in it.

He stopped dead when he saw the five children there, Buster safely on Fatty's knee. Buster gave tongue at once and tried to leap off, but Fatty held on to his collar.

'What's all this?' thundered Mr. Goon. 'What are you here for?'

Fatty stood up. 'Well, you said ten o'clock, and it's now twenty past,' he said. 'Perhaps you're too busy with the Lorenzo case to see us now?'

Mr. Goon looked extremely startled. 'The—the Lorenzo case?' he said. 'What do you know about *that?*'

'Not much,' said Fatty honestly. 'We couldn't help overhearing a few things just now, that's all.'

Mr. Goon lost his temper. 'Oho! Listening with your ear to the keyhole, I suppose? Eavesdropping on the Law! There's a penalty for that kind of thing, Mister Snoopy, let me tell you that! How *dare* you listen to private matters?'

'I didn't. I couldn't help hearing,' said Fatty. 'We all heard

'What's all this?' thundered Mr. Goon

a few things. Short of stopping up our ears we couldn't help but hear. As for listening at the key-hole that's nonsense. Your door was wide open and you know it.'

'Now, none of your cheek,' said Goon, beginning to go purple. 'I remember now—I told you to come about this here Pest of a Dog of course. Yes—a serious complaint has been made, very serious.'

He took out his notebook and looked through it, while the Five gazed at him. Larry, Daisy, Pip and Bets hadn't the remotest idea what Fatty had been talking about, of course, because they didn't know who or what these mysterious 'Lorenzos' were.

'I know that the Lorenzos made a kind of complaint yesterday,' said Fatty, 'and I know that you've been to see the Larkins, who are in charge of Poppet... and...'

'How do you know that?' almost shouted Mr. Goon. 'Snooping round—interfering—I can't get rid of you. You're a Toad of a Boy. I always said so! Now about this here dog of yours...'

'If the Lorenzos have gone off and nobody knows where, any complaint they made is not likely to be of any use to you,' said Fatty scornfully. 'Hadn't you better forget about Buster, and concentrate on finding the Lorenzos—or the picture, whatever it is, Mr. Goon?'

Mr. Goon knew when he was beaten. He shut his notebook and began to bluster. 'Well, if any-body else makes a single complaint about that dog—a *single* complaint, I say—he'll soon learn what happens to dogs that are Out of Control. Time he did too. If ever there was a more aggravating dog—yes, and a more aggravating set of children, I' d like to hear of them.'

'I'll be sure to let you know if ever we do hear of

any,' said Fatty, in his most courteous voice, the one that always drove poor Goon to fury. 'Well, I take it you don't need us any more—unless you'd like to tell us a bit about this new case, so that we might help you?'

'GAH!' said Mr. Goon furiously, and drove the Five out before him, Buster barking madly. They all went out of the front gate and Mr. Goon bellowed over it, almost shaking his fist at them.

'And if you try Interfering with the Law, and messing about in this case, and telling me Clues that aren't Clues, I'll come and tell your parents!' he shouted.

'Mr. Goon, Mr. Goon, you'll be had up for a Breach of the Peace,' said Fatty solemnly. 'You're making everyone look out of their windows.'

Mr. Goon retreated hurriedly into his house, muttering fiercely. The children got on their bicycles and rode off.

'A slight victory to us, I think,' said Fatty happily. 'Buster, you can breathe again!'

5   NOT SO GOOD!

THE chief topic of conversation that day was the five children's interview with Goon. Larry, Pip, Daisy and Bets could hardly wait till they got to Fatty's shed to ask him what he meant about the Lorenzos.

'Who are they? How did you know about them?' demanded Larry.

'I didn't. But my mother happened to mention this morning that the people who owned Poppet were called the Lorenzos,' said Fatty. 'So when I heard the name spoken by that other policeman—or perhaps he was a sergeant by his manner to Goon—well, it just rang a bell, and I knew they were all talking about the people who made a complaint about Buster!'

'But what have they done—the Lorenzos. I mean?' asked Bets.

'I don't know any more than you do,' said Fatty. 'Except that they seem to have gone away just when the police wanted them for something. And there's something about a picture too. My mother told me that they didn't pay their bills, so perhaps the trouble is about *that*!'

'Is it going to be a mystery?' asked Pip.

'I hope so, said Fatty cheerfully. 'And if it is, old Buster here led us to it-didn't you, Buster? You've got a nose for mysteries now, haven't you?'

'Wuff,' said Buster, thumping his tail on the floor of the shed. Fatty gave him a biscuit.

'Well, there you are—a small reward for leading us to a probable mystery,' he said. 'The trouble is, we don't know enough about it to set about solving it. I mean–

—we don't *really* know what the mystery *is*!'

'Ring up Superintendent Jenks and ask him,' suggested Larry.

'Fatty shook his head. 'No. I don't somehow think he'd like it—and I'd have to tell him I overheard talk about it in Goon's house—and Goon would get into trouble for discussing things like that without first finding out if anyone was about. After all, for all he knew, that woman in the kitchen might have over-heard every word!'

'Well—I don't see how we're to find out *any*thing,' said Larry. 'Goon certainly won't let us in on it.'

They discussed the matter over and over again. Should they go and interview the old fellow called Bob Larkin and see if they could get anything out of him? No, because he was already annoyed with them, and anyway Goon had got to interview him—and anyway again they didn't know what to ask the old fellow!

'We're being silly,' said Fatty, at the end of the long discussion. 'We're trying to run before we can walk. Let's forget it now—and sleep on it tonight. Things may be clearer tomorrow morning.'

Fatty spoke the truth! Things were indeed much clearer the next morning! The Five Find-Outers knew as much about the Mystery as Goon did!

It was in all the papers, splashed across the headlines.

'*Priceless old picture stolen from famous gallery. Thieves just escape the net of the police, leaving their dog behind. Police looking everywhere for the Lorenzos.*'

Mrs. Trotteville was down to breakfast first, and saw the paper. She gave an exclamation. 'Why—the thieves are those Lorenzos! The ones that live next door to the Daniels. No wonder all Peterswood disliked them!'

Fatty came in at that moment, and his mother told him

the news. "The thieves were the people you told me about yesterday, Fatty—the Lorenzos. I told you how badly they behaved, and what wild parties they gave. They upset their neighbours the Daniels very much. See—they're in the news this morning-the police are after them. My goodness me—our Mr. Goon will be puffed up with importance over this. It's right under his nose!'

Fatty slid into his seat and took the paper, his eyes gleaming. Aha! If it was all in papers it didn't matter about Goon not telling him anything. The Five Find-Outers could make their own plans, and get going themselves. What a thrill!

Fatty read and read! He forgot all about his breakfast, and never even saw his father come into the room.

'Good morning, Frederick,' said his father, and neatly took the paper from Fatty's hands. 'What about eating your bacon and egg? By the look of it, it's almost congealed on the plate!'

'So it is!' said Fatty, surprised. 'Well, it isn't often I don't get on with a meal. My word, Mother this is a bit of excitement for dull old Peterswood, isn't it?'

'I hope it doesn't mean you're going to get mixed up with that aggravating policeman again,' said his father, pouring milk over his porridge. 'Actually, I should imagine that your friend, Superintendent Jenks, will send a good man down here to deal with anything that arises. I can't imagine that Moon—Coon—what's his name now-Goon—could tackle a big thing like this. That picture was priceless-worth at least fifty thousand pounds!'

'I shan't get mixed up with Goon,' said Fatty. 'It's much more likely he'll get mixed up with *me!* Anyway, I think I'll ring up Superintendent Jenks and ask if can do anything to help.'

'Well, he seems to think a lot of you, goodness knows why,' said Mr. Trotteville, 'and it does seem as if you have a few brains sometimes, Frederick. Now, for pity's sake eat up that horrible-looking mess on your plate.'

Fatty swallowed his breakfast, thinking hard. The telephone went just as he had finished it, and he rushed to answer it, quite sure it must be the Superintendent ringing up to ask his help!

But it wasn't. It was Larry, very excited.

'I say! Did you see the news in the paper? It *is* a mystery after all! Right under our noses. When are we going to get on to it?'

'I'm going to ring the Super,' said Fatty. 'We'll get on to it all right. I'll telephone you later. Ring Pip and Bets for me, will you?'

'Right, Chief!' said Larry, with a chuckle, and hung up. Peterswood was in the news! And he and the rest of the Find-Outers would soon be Right in the Middle of Something!

Fatty sat down and thought for a while. What should he tell the Superintendent? That he had seen the two Lorenzos on the station yesterday—but then many people had. Should he ask if he could go and see the Larkins? He might be able to get something out of them that Goon couldn't. Anyway he was certain that he could do *some*thing.

He went to the telephone and asked for the number. It was engaged. He tried again in ten minutes. It was still engaged. The police wires were humming today in that district!

At last he got the number and asked for the

Superintendent. 'It's Frederick Trotteville here,' said Fatty. 'He knows me.'

His name was passed through to the Chief's office and Fatty heard that Superintendent's voice, sharp and impatient.

'Yes. Frederick? What is it?'

'Sir, it's about the Lorenzos,' said Fatty. 'As it's right where I live, can I do anything?'

'I fear not,' said the Chief. 'The Lorenzos are not there—and I doubt if the missing picture is, either. If they could be found, they would be found together!'

'Oh,' said Fatty, in disappointment. 'Then—isn't there *anything* I can do, sir?'

'Nothing—except keep your eyes and ears open as usual,' said the Chief. 'I'm sending a man down to go over the house with a tooth-comb, just in *case* the picture's there—but I've no real hope of it.'

'Will Mr. Goon be working on the case, sir?' Asked Fatty, rather forlornly.

'Yes—but there isn't much case at Peterswood to work on,' said the Superintendent. 'I wish Goon had kept his eye on the Lorenzos more—they've a shocking reputation, as everyone now knows!'

'I suppose I couldn't go and talk to the Larkins, sir. Could I?' asked Fatty, feeling that this mystery was slipping out of his hands altogether!

'No. Certainly not,' said the Chief at once. 'My man is doing that, with Goon. No sense in your butting in there—you'll do more harm than good. I don't mean that you mustn't pass the time of day with them if you meet them—but you must remember that this case has really left Peterswood now—and gone goodness knows where! I don't for one moment think that the Larkins can possibly know anything that will be of the slightest help to us.'

'I expect you're right, sir,' said Fatty, feeling very down in the dumps indeed. 'Well, I won't keep you, sir. Good luck!'

He put down the receiver and looked gloomily at Buster, who was sitting nearby, with cocked ears.

'No go, Buster,' he said dolefully. 'It's all come to nothing. The mystery has fled from Peterswood and disappeared. Now I must telephone to the others.'

The other four were most disappointed. 'Oh, Fatty!' said Daisy, 'there must be *some*thing we can do! There really must. Come along up here to us, and we'll get Pip and Bets too, and talk about it. You do sound miserable!'

So they all met at Larry's at half-past eleven and sat down to a mid-morning snack of hot buns from the oven and cups of cocoa. They felt more cheerful after a couple of buns each.

'The Chief really did seem to think we can't do a thing this time,' said Fatty. 'Apparently the two main things are—*one*, to find the Lorenzos, who are probably out of the country by now—and *two*, to find the picture. And the Chief thinks that where one is, the other will be there also.

'Well, we can't possibly go gallivanting all over the country looking for them ourselves,' said Daisy. 'So we must just be content to do nothing.'

'I think we might keep a watch on the house, perhaps?' said Larry. 'Just in *case* the Lorenzos come back to it.'

'They won't,' said Fatty.

'But what about their little dog?' said Bets. 'Mrs. Lorenzo really did seem attached to it—she might send for that, mightn't she? If it suddenly disappears we'd know that the Lorenzos had sent a messenger of some sort for it.'

"That certainly is a point,' said Fatty. 'Yes—perhaps on the whole, we won't give this up straightaway . But the thing is—how on earth are we to keep a watch on the Larkins to *see* if any messenger is ever sent? I mean— the house is some way from where we live, and we can't spend all our days—or nights—there!'

'Hopeless,' said Pip, who didn't particularly want to spend any part of a cold day or night watching people like the Larkins. 'We can't do it. If we knew somebody who lived next door, it would be easy—but we don't, so...'

'Hallo!' said a voice, suddenly interrupting, and a tousled head peeped round the door. 'I've been to your house, Fatty, and your mother sent me here. I've brought the Christmas present I made you!'

'ERN!' cried everyone. And sure enough it *was* Ern, plump as ever and red in the face. Good old Ern!

6 THE SAME OLD ERN!

ERN came right into the room, beaming, and holding rather a large parcel.

'Still the same old Ern!' said Fatty, and solemnly shook hands with him. Ern thereupon felt that he must shake hands with everyone, even Buster. Buster was very pleased indeed to see Ern, and leapt on him as if he were a long-lost friend.

'This is an unexpected pleasure,' said Fatty. 'How are your twin brothers, Sid and Perce? We haven't seen them since we all solved the Mystery of the Vanished Prince—do you remember?'

'Coo, yes,' said Ern. 'That wasn't half a do! I enjoyed that, I did. Perce is all right, as far as I know. I don't seem to notice him much. Sid's all right too.'

Sid had been a great toffee-sucker, unable to speak at all at one time because of the toffee glueing up his mouth! Bets remembered and giggled.

'Does he still suck toffee?' she asked.

'Well, he rationed himself up to Christmas, because he wanted to save money to buy presents,' said Ern. 'But then everyone went and gave him gave him tins of toffee, of course, and he's off again. Can't get a word out of him now.'

'Except "Ar", I suppose?' said Pip. He used to say "Ar" quite a lot, I remember.'

'Yes. Well, he still says it,' said Ern. 'He isn't much of a talker, old Sid.'

'Sit down and have a bun,' said Daisy. 'What's in that parcel?'

'Coo, I was almost forgetting ,' said Ern, beaming round again. 'It's something I made for you, Fatty. We did carpentry at school last term, and I said to myself— "Ah, Ern—this is where we do something for Fatty!" And I made *this!*'

He pulled off the paper and showed Fatty a small table, plain and simple. He had polished it till it shone.

Everyone exclaimed in surprise. 'Why, *Ern!*' said Bets, amazed, 'did you really make it all yourself?'

'Never let anyone touch it but meself!' said Ern proudly.

Fatty examined it from every side. 'It's a masterpiece,' he said. 'A beautiful piece of work. Thanks, Ern. I like it very much.'

Ern was bright red with delight. 'No kidding?' he said. 'You *do* like it?'

'I tell you, it's a masterpiece, said Fatty. 'First-rate! We'll have it in my shed at home so that we can all see it and use it as much as possible.'

Ern was quite overcome. He swallowed once or twice, rubbed his sleeve over the table-top to make quite sure it was perfect, and then beamed at every—one again.

'Nice to see you all again,' he announced, sitting down. 'Anything on? Any mysteries going? I heard about them people called Lorenzos. Proper set-up that was! I bet my uncle Goon's excited!'

'Have you seen him yet?' asked Daisy.

'Oooh no!' said Ern, in horror. 'I' d run a mile if I saw him—he'd box my ears as soon as look at me! I kept a good look-out for him this morning, I can tell you.'

They discussed the Lorenzo case, and how maddening it was that the most important things concerned—the Lorenzos themselves and the picture—had

'Why, Ern, did you really make it all yourself ?'

both gone.

'So, you see, there's nothing much we can do Ern,' said Fatty. 'I can't see anything we can get hold of—no clues or suspects, like we usually do.'

'Yes, it's bad luck,' said Ern sympathetically. 'I was hoping I might be able to help a bit, if you really wanted me. I'm coming to stay in Peterswood. My Mum's got to go to hospital for a bit—she's got a bad leg, poor Mum—so us kids are going to relations and friends for a week.'

'Good gracious—you're not staying with Mr. Goon again, are you?' said Bets.

'You bet I'm not!' said Ern. 'When my Mum suggested it, I fell off my chair in fright. Straight I did. I got this bruise, see?'

Ern proudly displayed a large bruise just on the point of going yellow and green.

'What did your Mum say then?' asked Pip. The Five were always interested in the doings of Ern's large family.

'She said, "All right, Ducks, I'll think of someone else,"' said Ern. 'And she did,'

'Who was it she thought of?' asked Bets. 'Anyone we know?'

'I don't reckon so,' said Ern. 'It's my father's cousin—a Mrs. Woosh.'

'What a wonderful name!' said Daisy.

They all tried it over. 'Wooshl! Mrs. Woosh Whoooooosh!'

'Sounds as if her husband ought to make rockets,' said Larry, and everyone laughed.

'Where does you Auntie Woosh live?' asked Bets.

'She's in the cottage belonging to Mrs. Daniels, who

lives at High Chimneys,' said Ern. 'Her husband is the gardener, and she helps in the house. She's got twins—girls they are, about the same age as Sid and Perce.'

Ern stopped when he saw the sudden, intense interest on Fatty's face, at the mention of the Daniels. He looked at Fatty in surprise.

'What's up?' he said. 'You look all sort of worked up, Fatty.'

'I am,' said Fatty. 'I'm all of a dither as our cook says when she falls over Buster. The Daniels! Did I *really* hear you say the Daniels, Ern?'

'Yes,' said Ern, puzzled. 'What's wrong with that?'

'Nothing,' said Fatty. 'Is's perfect. It's too good to be true! Don't you know that the Daniels live next to the house that the Lorenzos rented, Ern? And we wanted to keep a watch on it, but it's a good way from our own homes-and...'

'COO!' said Ern, light dawning on him suddenly. 'You mean—I say, do you mean I can come into this because I'll be able to pop my head over the hedge and watch any goings-on at the house next door?'

'You've got it, Ern!' said Fatty, and clapped him on the back. 'We were almost on the point of giving up the mystery when you came in—now we'll be on it full-speed! WHAT a bit of luck that you'll be staying with the Wooshes!'

Ern was so overcome that he was speechless for a moment. He stared round with bright eyes, and opened and shut his mouth like a goldfish.

He suddenly found his voice. 'I'll do my bit,' he said, in a suddenly solemn voice, just as if he were going off to war. 'You just give me my orders, Fatty—and I'll obey!'

There upon a most animated conversation began.

The newspapers were fetched from downstairs, and everyone pored over the reports of the Lorenzo case. The Five Find-Outers meant to get every single bit of information they could find.

'It even says here that they left Poppet the poodle behind,' said Bets. 'And here's a picture of her in Mrs. Lorenzo's arms. And listen, it says: "Gloria Lorenzo is passionately attached to her little poodle, whom she has had for seven years. It is the first time she has ever left the little dog behind—and therefore it seems that the Lorenzos meant to flee the country."'

'Ern could keep an eye on those awful Larkins too,' said Daisy, 'and see that they don't ill-treat dear little Poppet.'

'I'll keep an eye on them ,'promised Ern. 'You just give me my orders!'

'He could keep an eye on Tally-Ho the house, as well' said Larry. 'Just in *case* the picture has been left behind, hidden there somewhere after all. If he sees any suspicious strangers about, he'd have to report to us at once.

'Yes, I will,' said the excited Ern. 'I'll have my bike, see—and I'll keep it all pumped up and ready to fly off to Fatty's if I've anything to report.'

They talked and talked. It was most exciting. Ern's face grew redder and redder and his hair became more and more tousled. He had never had such a thrilling morning in his life!

'I expect old Goon will be round there quite a bit,' said Fatty. 'He'll keep an eye on the Larkins, and on the house too. So look out for him.'

'Lovaduck!' said Ern, suddenly doleful. 'I forgot about my uncle. I'd better keep out of his sight. He'll go mad if he sees me snooping around.'

'He certainly will,' agreed Fatty. 'Don't let him know you're staying at the Wooshes if you can help it. Don't let him see you at all, in fact!'

'Oh, I won't,' said Ern fervently. 'I'm scared of my uncle, I really am, sure as my name's Ern Goon.'

Buster gave a sudden growl when he heard the name of Goon. 'There!' said Ern, 'he thinks the same as me. Good old Buster. I know how you feel about biting his ankles. I'd like to bite him too.'

Buster thumped his tail on the floor, and looked at Ern with approval.

'I say,' said Pip, 'how old are these twins of your aunt's? About Sid and Perce's age did you say? You could have a game of ball with them, perhaps—and let the ball go into Tally—Ho gardens-and slip over and look for it—or...'

'Coo yes—I'll be able to think of plenty of excuses for slipping into next door,' said Ern. 'I'll pry into every corner—you never know where that picture might be hid, do you!'

'Well, it probably wouldn't be in the rubbish-heap or in the coal-cellar,' said Fatty gravely. 'I wouldn't bother about the picture, Ern—just keep your eyes and ears open and report anything unusual to us-strangers about, or noises in the night, or lights.'

'Yes—and report to us if the Larkins are cruel to little Poppet!' said Bets. 'If they are I'll get the R.S.P.C.A. to report them. I will. I really will!'

'Good old Bets,' said Fatty. 'Don't worry—the dog is a valuable one and the Larkins won't dare to starve it or hurt it badly.'

'I say—just *look* at the time!' said Pip, in horror. 'We'll be late for our dinner again—and Mother will blame *you*, Fatty, as well as us! Come on, Bets, for goodness' sake!'

Larry and Daisy came to the front gate to see them off. They all rode away on their bicycles, Ern too.

'So long!' he said, with his usual beaming smile. 'I'm off to the Wooshes now. They're expecting me for dinner. I've got all my things in my bike-basket!'

'So long!' said Fatty, amused at the tiny bundle in Ern's basket. Ern obviously didn't think he needed much luggage for a week's stay at the Wooshes! 'And thanks most awfully for the splendid table, Ern.'

Ern rode off, pleased at the sight of Fatty riding away on his bicycle with the table under one arm. He'd be able to tell those twins something, when he got to his aunt's!

7   ERN HAS AN IDEA

ERN arrived late at his aunt's, having quite forgotten that his uncle, the Daniels' gardener, knocked off work at half-past twelve and went in for his dinner.

Mrs. Woosh was not too pleased with him. 'Oh—here you are at last, Ern!' she said. 'Well, we've almost finished dinner—and thinking you weren't coming, Liz and Glad have eaten your share of the stew.'

'Oh! said Ern, dismayed, for he was very hungry indeed. 'Sorry I'm late, aunt. I've been with my friends and forgot the time.'

'What friends?' asked his aunt, in surprise.

'Well, there's Frederick Trotteville, and the Hiltons and...' began Ern proudly.

Liz and Glad tittered. 'Oooh, isn't he *grand*!' said Liz. 'Those aren't his friends, are they Mum?'

'You hold your tongue, Liz,' said Mrs. Woosh. Liz nudged Glad and they both went off into giggles that made Ern long to slap them.

'If you were my sisters,' he began, glaring at them, but Mrs. Woosh stopped him.

'Now, Ern, don't start throwing your weight about as soon as you come. There's some cheese over there that your uncle left, and some bread. Help yourself. We've got plenty of pudding left.'

Ern sighed in relief and began on the bread and cheese. The twins sat and stared steadily at Ern for a few minutes, nudging each other every time he put a huge bit of bread and cheese into his mouth. He decided that they required a firm hand. They needed a brother, that's what they needed—someone like Ern himself, Ern decided. *He* would Keep Them in Their Place all right!

At last Glad and Liz slipped away from the table and went out into the garden to play. Mrs. Woosh heaved a sigh of relief.

'I'll be glad when the holidays are over' she said. 'Always under my feet, those twins are. I don't know how you manage with Sid and Perce, Ern—but twins are a handful, my word they are! If one isn't in mischief, the other is.'

'Mum's always saying the same about Sid and Perce,' said Ern. 'I'll take the twins off your hands for you a bit, Auntie—play ball with them, and such-like.'

'That's right, Ern,' said Mrs. Woosh. 'I expect you know about the happenings next door, don't you? The Lorenzos, I mean, who were in the papers today. My word—I could tell you of some going-on there, I could!'

Ern Felt excited. He might hear Something Important-something he could report back to Fatty He wondered If he ought to write anything down in his notebook. Yes, Perhaps he'd better—his aunt might let a few clues drop! That would be fine.

So Ern pulled a notebook out of his pocket, licked his pencil, and glued his eyes on his aunt.

'You tell me everything!' he said. 'And don't leave NOTHING out Auntie!'

His aunt was pleasantly surprised to find Ern so interested in her chatter. Neither her husband nor the twins ever listened to her for more than a few seconds, and she was a born talker. She leaned her elbows on the table and began.

'Well, the Lorenzos came about six months back. They took the house, furnished, from the Peters' who are in America. They brought their own servants with them, and...'

'What about the Larkins?' said Ern, remembering what the Five had said about them. He'd better ask for news of them too!

'Oh, the Larkins—they've been in that cottage for donkeys' years,' said Mrs. Woosh. 'Don't interrupt me, Ern. I don't hold with them Larkins-dirty, untidy couple they are, shuffling and sniffing about. I just pass the time of day and that's all. He's supposed to look after the boilers, and go up to the house for the boots to clean and things like that. Dirty old man!'

'They've got the little poodle, Poppet, haven't they?' said Ern, trying to scribble fast enough to keep up with Mrs. Woosh's chatter.

'Yes—and why the Lorenzos left it with them, goodness knows!' said Mrs. Woosh. 'We once had a cat, and it wandered into their garden—and will you believe it, they stoned the poor creature, and almost broke one of its legs.'

Ern was horrified, and wrote down 'legs' and underlined it. On and on went his aunt, telling him about the extraordinary parties that the Lorenzos gave; 'midnight bathing in the river and hide-and-seek in the garden afterwards,' she said. 'And once they all dressed up as animals and I wasn't half startled to meet a giraffe and a bear going along the lane that night!'

Ern was soon so fascinated that he forgot write in his notebook. He began to wish that he too lived next door to people like the Lorenzos—there would always be plenty of excitement!

'The house is shut up now,' said Mrs. Woosh, 'no lights, no smoke from the chimneys. I passed the time of day with Mr. Larkin yesterday, and he said that even he and his wife can't get in. Not even to air the house. He says the police have got the keys.'

Ern decided this might be important, so he wrote down 'Shut house. Keys.' His aunt frowned.

'Why do you keep scribbling in that notebook of yours, Ern, when I'm talking to you? That's rude. Any-one would think you were your uncle, P. C. Goon—he's always got a notebook he's scribbling in. My word, I've just thought of an idea!'

'What?' said Ern, his pencil poised over notebook at once. 'Quick, Aunt!'

'I'll ask Mr. Goon in to tea while you're here—I'll tell him it's just so he can see his nephew. But really it'll be because I want to hear what he's got to say on this Lorenzo business!' Mrs. Woosh looked delighted at her idea. 'He's a wonderful man, your Uncle Theophilus Goon—always on to something. Yes, I'll ask him to tea.'

Ern stared at her in the utmost horror. He could think of nothing worse than having his uncle to tea, and be-ing made to sit opposite his big, angry face. Why, he didn't even want his uncle to *know* he was in Peterswood.

'Please, Auntie, don't ask him,' begged Ern. 'He—well, he isn't very fond of me. I'm right down scared of him.'

'Oh, go on with you!' said Mrs. Woosh. 'He's not a bad fellow. I always say it's useful to have a policeman in the family.'

Ern didn't think so. He could have done without Mr. Goon in his own family, that was certain! He put away his notebook gloomily. What a pity it had reminded Mrs. Woosh of his uncle!

'Well, I'd better wash up, I suppose,' said Mrs. Woosh. 'You go on out and play with Glad and Liz, Ern. You'll get on with them fine!'

Ern wasn't so sure that he would. He put on his coat and went out. He was immediately pelted with bits of earth, and greeted with squeals of laughter. He looked round to see where the twins were. Up in that tree!

Ern was about to shout at them, when he stopped. The tree was a tall one. It stood by the hedge, and overlooked the Larkins' cottage and garden. It would, in fact, be a perfectly splendid spying-place!

Ern decided not to be angry about the clod throwing. He called up the tree. 'Hey, you kids! Like me to show you how to build a house in a tree?'

There was a moment's silence. Then Glad looked down cautiously. 'Yes. But don't you try lamming us when you come up. We'll push you down, if you do.'

Ern immediately felt like 'lamming' them. But he must keep guard on his temper. The twins might come in very useful!

The tree was some kind of evergreen fir, very tall and broad. Its branches were admirable for climbing. Ern went up to where the twins sat. They grinned at him.

'Did we hit you with the clods of earth? We waited and waited for you. Did Mum talk to you all that time?'

As the twins never really expected any answers to their questions they didn't at all mind when Ern ignored them, and began to make a peep-hole through the thick branches, so that he might look down on the Larkins' cottage over the hedge.

'What are you doing? Are you going to make a house

up here? Can we live in it? Will it have a chimney?'

Ern found that he could see right down into the Larkins' garden—in fact, the cottage was so near that he could smell the smoke from the chimney. He took out his knife and began to cut away some of the greenery, so that he could have a kind of window through the branches to peep from. The twins watched him with interest.

'What are you doing? Is that a spy-hole? Can we spy on the Larkins? We don't like them. Let's throw a stone down their chimney!'

The last idea appealed to Ern very much. He had never tried throwing stones down a chimney, but it certainly looked quite easy from where he sat. Then he reluctantly dismissed the idea from his mind. No—he might be lucky enough to get one stone down the chimney, but there would be a dozen stones that missed—and they would rattle on the tiles and bring out the Larkins in fury. That would never do!

'Now you listen to me,' said Ern, taking command firmly. 'We'll play that the Larkins are our enemies, see? And we'll play that we've got to keep a watch on them and all they do. So we'll build a little house up here, and I'll keep watch.'

'Us too!' said the twins, both together. Ern nodded.

'All of us—when I'm not up here, you two can take a turn—and you'll have to report to me, see, because I'm your chief. This is our hidey-hole!'

The twins were thrilled. They gazed at Ern in admiration. He was clearly much, much cleverer than he looked.

'I'll go down and see if there's any bits of wood and stuff to bring up here,' said Ern, and disappeared rapidly. He stood at the bottom and called up cautiously. 'Now, keep watch while I'm gone, you two!'

He met his uncle as he walked back to the cottage. Uncle Woosh was a tall, silent man who only came into the house for meals and for very little else. Ern was rather afraid of him, but decided that his uncle was the man to ask about planks and nails.

'Yes. Get what you want out of my shed,' said his uncle. 'Plenty there.' He took himself off, and Ern ran to the shed, pleased.

Now to build a little place up in that tree—what a fine spy-hole! What would Fatty say to *that!*

ERN KEEPS WATCH

TWO days went by. Fatty and the others pored over the papers each day, but there was no more news of the Lorenzos, except that the police seemed more or less certain that they were hiding somewhere in the country, waiting to fly out as soon as things had quietened down a little.

'I should have thought that it would be very difficult to hide *anywhere*, with everyone on the lookout for you,' said Daisy. 'I mean—the Lorenzos would be very easy to recognize—their photographs have been in every single paper!'

'You forget that they have been actors,' said Fatty. 'It would be easy for them to disguise themselves so that nobody would know them.'

'Yes. I forgot that,' said Daisy. 'After all—if anyone was after *you*, Fatty, you'd be able to disguise yourself so that nobody in the world would recognize you!'

'Like you do sometimes now,' said Bets. 'Oh, Fatty—things are a bit dull at present—can't you disguise yourself? You know-dress up as an Indian or something. You do look so very very brown with all that dazzling Swiss sun——you'd pass anywhere for a foreigner. Go on—just for a bit of fun!'

'I'll think about it,' said Fatty, making up his mind that he would certainly do a bit of disguising, as Bets suggested, and have a little fun. 'By the way—I wonder how Ern is getting on. We haven't seen anything of him for two days.'

Ern had been getting on well. He now had the twins

almost eating out of his hands—in fact, they were quite embarrassing in their hero-worship, and followed Ern about whenever they could.

He had made the house in the tree. Ern was very good with his hands, and thoroughly enjoyed taking charge of the proceedings, ordering the twins about, and showing off his clever carpentering.

Even his Uncle Woosh had taken an interest, and had helped Ern considerably. His aunt thought it was a lot of silly nonsense.

'Messing about up trees!' she said. 'Getting filthy dirty. Just look at the state the twins are in, after being up there all the morning!'

Their father looked at them and made one of his rare remarks. 'Can't see a mite of difference in them,' he said. 'They're always dirty.'

He walked out, followed by a string of exasperated remarks from his wife. Ern followed him.

'Women!' said Mr. Woosh, with a backward jerk of his head towards the cottage. 'Women!'

Ern nodded understandingly. Once his uncle had discovered that Ern, like himself, was interested in carpentry, he had been very friendly. Ern was quite enjoying his stay, especially now that the twins were so completely under his thumb.

The house in the tree was finished. It was quite an elaborate affair, and made of good strong planks securely fastened down. There were three walls and a very peculiar roof, that had to fit under some rather awkward branches. The missing wall, of course, was the 'spy-hole' that looked through the branches down on to the Larkins.

The twins' mother gave them some cups and plates,

and allowed them to have snacks up in the tree. The twins were too thrilled for words, and were ready to do anything in the world that Ern told them.

Ern felt as excited as his two cousins. He had never imagined that it would be so easy to build a house up a tree. Of course, his uncle had helped a lot. Ern had to admit that.

He and the twins sat up there continually—but Ern preferred it when he was quite alone. There was something very thrilling indeed about sitting up in the thickly-leafed evergreen, in his own little tree-house, peering quietly through the opening he had cut in the greenery.

The Larkins had no idea that they were being spied on by three children. To the twins, of course, it was merely a game, like Red Indians—but to Ern it was serious. He was helping Fatty. He might be able to gather a few clues for him. He might see something suspicious—he might even help to solve the Lorenzo mystery! Though Ern had to admit to himself that that wasn't *very* likely!

He peered down at the Larkins' cottage whenever he could, watching for any sign of movement. He had supplied himself with a tin of bull's-eye peppermints, enormous things that bulged out his cheek, but lasted for a very long time. He also had a comic that he read at intervals, and he really thoroughly enjoyed himself, sucking away at his bull's eye, hidden in the little tree-house he had built.

'Old Man Larkin doesn't do much!' Ern thought. 'Just goes out and picks some sprouts—and does some shopping —and lets the dog out and yells for it to come back. Poor little dog-it looks down in the dumps all right, and I'm not surprised!'

Certainly Mr. Larkin didn't appear to do very much work. As for Mrs. Larkin, she hardly appeared at all. Apparently she had a bad cold, and Ern could often hear her coughing. Once when she ventured out for a minute or two, to hang up some washing, Ern could hear her sniffing all the time. Sniff, sniff! Cough! Sniff, sniff!

She groaned as she bent down to pick up her washing-basket. Ern watched her, thinking she was a very ugly woman with her extraordinary wig of hair, and her very white face and red nose.

Poppet came out with her, her stiff little tail down. She kept well out of Mrs. Larkin's reach. The woman spoke to her in a hoarse voice. 'Don't you dare run off, or I'll lam you again, nuisance that you are!'

Poppet slunk into the house, and Mrs. Larkin followed, sniffing. Ern scribbled down a few notes about her in his notebook. He had torn out the notes he had made when his aunt had chattered to him, because when he examined them afterwards, such words as 'Donkeys' years', 'legs', 'midnight bathing' didn't make any sense to him.

But, siting in peace up the tree, he could write quite sensibly. 'She sniffs and coughs,' he had written down. 'She wears a wig. Her voice is hoarse and croaky. Poppet is afraid of her. She groans when she picks things up.'

After two days had gone by, Ern decided that it would be a good idea to go and see Fatty and the others again, so off he went, notebook in pocket.

He found all the Five, with Buster, down in Fatty's shed, playing a game of cards. They were very pleased to see him.

Buster welcomed him at the top of his bark. Ern felt

pleased to see that the table he had made for Fatty was standing in the middle of the shed, with a plate of chocolate biscuits on its polished top. He stood and grinned.

'Come in, Ern. Make yourself at home,' said Fatty, gathering up the cards. 'We've just finished our game. What's your news?'

'Well, I haven't much,' said Ern. 'Except that I've got a house up in a tree that looks right down on the Larkins' cottage, and into the grounds of Tally-Ho. I sit there and watch like anything.'

'Is it *really* a house in a tree?' said Bets, thrilled. 'Oh, I *would* like to see it! Ern, you *are* clever!'

Ern blushed. He drew out his notebook, and gave it to Fatty. 'I've made a few notes,' he said. 'Not that they're worth anything—but you never know!'

Fatty glanced through them rapidly, and handed back the notebook. 'Very good,' he said. 'You're doing well, Ern. Yes, those might come in useful sometime—if only we could get going!'

Ern was pleased. 'You got anything interesting to tell me?' he asked.

'Nothing,' said Fatty dismally. 'It's too maddening to have something like this under our noses, so to speak, and not to be able to get even a bite at it!'

'The only thing that's new was in the paper this morning,' said Larry.

'What?' asked Ern, who hadn't seen a paper.

'Well, the Lorenzos were spotted somewhere up north,' said Larry. 'Near an airfield, in a small hotel. And what is more they had a crate with them this time, as well as two small suitcases.'

'Coo—the picture!' said Ern. 'Weren't they caught then?

Did they get away?'

'Yes—fled in the night—took someone else's car out of the garage and went,' said Fatty. 'Complete with suitcases and crate. I don't somehow think they will try to get out of the country at present. They'll hide somewhere safe and wait.'

'Would they come back to Peterswood?' asked Ern, thrilled. 'I'd better keep a strict watch from my tree-house.'

'They might,' said Fatty. 'And. as we said before, they might send someone to fetch Poppet, so keep a watch for any stranger at the Larkins' cottage, Ern, and keep a watch too to see that the poodle is always there.'

'Oh, I will' said Ern.

He spent a pleasant morning with the others, and then, remembering that his dinner was at half-past twelve, not one o'clock, he rose to go.

'I'll be along again sometime,' he said. 'Good-bye, all. Thanks for the biscuits. Good-bye, Buster!'

Buster came with him as far as the gate, and saw him off politely, his tail wagging fast. He liked Ern. Ern mounted his bicycle and rode off at top speed. He rang his bell going round the corner just at the same moment as somebody else rang theirs. Ern swung round the corner, pedalling furiously—to meet his uncle, Mr. Goon, also pedalling furiously on his bicycle! Mr. Goon, unfortunately, had cut the corner and was on his wrong side. The bicycles were about to crash together, when Ern quickly swerved. His pedal caught Mr. Goon's, and over they both went.

'Oooh! Oh!' groaned Mr. Goon, as he landed very heavily indeed. His bicycle fell on top of him.

'Oooh!' yelled Ern, and he too fell to the ground He

sent a terrified glance at Mr. Goon and got up. Mr. Goon groaned again. Then he saw who the other cyclist was, and stared open-mouthed.

'What! *You*, Ern! How dare you ride at sixty miles an hour round a corner! How...'

'It wasn't my fault, Uncle,' said poor Ern, scared stiff. 'You were on your wrong side.'

'I was not!' said Mr. Goon, most untruthfully. 'Do you mean to say you're accusing me of causing this here accident? You just wait, young Ern! What you doing in Peterswood, anyhow?'

Ern was not prepared to tell him that. He put his foot on the left-hand pedal, and was about to swing his leg over to sit on the saddle, when his uncle gave a really most alarming groan.

'Oh, my back! It's broken! Here, young Ern, you help me up, come on, now!' He held out an enormous hand to Ern. 'Come on—give me a pull!'

Ern put out his hand too—but saw the gleam in Goon's eye just in time. He snatched back his hand and jumped on his bicycle, panting hard. Coo—his uncle had *almost* got him!

ERN cycled back to his aunt's at top speed, turning round every now and again to see if Goon was after him. But mercifully there was no sign of his uncle.

It took Goon quite a minute to heave himself to his feet, and examine his bicycle to see if it could be ridden in safety. It appeared to be all right. Goon knew that it was no good trying to chase Ern. Indeed, if he did, Ern would certainly win!

Goon said a lot of things under his breath. 'That Ern! Wait till I get him! I'll pull all his hair out! I'll box every ear he's got! Why, he might have killed me. Speed fiend, that's what he is! What's he doing in Peterswood, I'd like to know!'

Goon had no idea that Ern was staying in Peters-wood––and certainly none at all that he was living next door to the Lorenzos' house. He got on his bicycle very very carefully, fearful that something might be broken and give way beneath his weight.

He wondered what Fatty was doing. He hadn't seen or heard of him since the morning that all the Five had visited him. He began to scowl.

That fat boy was too cunning for words. Was he hoping to do something about the Lorenzo Mystery? Had he gone to see the Larkins and got out of them more than he, Goon, had managed to get? Was he working out something? Mr. Goon began to worry. He pedalled back to his house, still frowning.

' I think I'll go up to the cottage at Tally-Ho House and pop in to see the Larkins again,' he thought. 'I'll ask Bob Larkin if that fat boy has been snooping round—and if he has I'll have Something to Say about it.'

But Fatty had not been to see the Larkins because the Superintendent had said that he did not wish him to. Fatty was still rather down in the dumps, though he kept a cheerful face with the others.

He thought about Ern's rough notes, and wondered how little Poppet was getting on. In his notes Ern had put that she was afraid of Mrs. Larkin. She was terrified of Mr. Larkin too, so her life couldn't be a very happy one. After seven years of love and fuss and petting, life must seem very grim to little Poppet these days!

'I'm sure Mrs. Lorenzo will try to get her dog back, if she can't get out of the country,' said Fatty to himself. Or she will send someone to fetch her, and put her in a home with kindly people. I think it wouldn't be a bad idea if I went to see Ern's tree-house this afternoon; and did a bit of snooping round myself.'

He sat and thought a little more. 'Better not go as myself in case I bump into Goon. I'll disguise myself—I'll be an Indian, as Bets suggested!'

He looked at himself in the mirror, and twisted a face-towel over his head like a turban. Bets was right—he looked exactly like a brown-faced Indian! Fatty grinned and felt much more cheerful.

'It doesn't suit me to sit and do nothing when there's something on,' he said. 'That's not the way to make anything happen! Come on, Fatty—stir yourself. Get out your fancy clothes and dress up!'

Immediately after he had had lunch, Fatty set to work down in his shed. He found a fine strip of gay cloth that would do for a turban, and looked up 'Turbans—how to wear,' in a very useful little book called *Dress up Properly*. He practised turban-tying for some time and at last produced a most satisfactory one, wound correctly round his head.

He pencilled a faint black moustache, rather thin, on his upper lip, and darkened his chin to make it seem as if he had a shaved beard. He put cheek-pads in to alter the shape of his face, and at once looked older, and fatter in the cheeks. He darkened his eye-brows and made them thicker, then gazed at himself in the glass, putting on a sinister, rather mysterious expression.

'That's all right,' he thought. 'Gosh, it's queer looking at myself in the mirror and seeing somebody quite different! Now, what else shall I wear?'

He decided that the Eastern clothes he had were a bit too gay for January weather. He didn't want a crowd of kids following him around! He suddenly thought of some Eastern students he had seen in London.

'They wore turbans, and rather tightish, but ordinary black trousers, and an overcoat,' he remembered. 'Didn't want to shiver in our cold climate, I suppose! Perhaps it would be best if I just wore a turban, and ordinary clothes. My face is so very sunburnt that just wearing a turban makes me look Eastern!'

He found a pair of rather dirty, very tight black trousers, which he couldn't do up at the waist. He had a brain-wave and tied a sash round his middle instead. Then he put on an old overcoat.

'A foreign student from somewhere out east!' he said to himself. 'Yes—that's what I am! Come on, Fatty—off to Tally-Ho!'

He left Buster behind, much to the little Scottie's dismay, and set off, passing rapidly by the kitchen window, hoping that the maids would not see him.

But his mother saw him, and gazed after him in surprise.

'Who's that?' she wondered. 'A friend of Fred-erick's, I suppose. What a peculiar-looking fellow in that gay turban!'

Fatty went off down to the river, and made his way along the river-path. He only met an old lady with a dog, and she gazed at him uneasily. Was he going to snatch her handbag? But he passed quickly, and she heaved a sigh of relief.

Fatty came to the river-gate leading into the grounds of Tally-Ho. It was only a small wicket-gate, quite unlike the two imposing drive-gates at the front of the big house, through which so many cars had driven in and out that summer.

Nobody was about at all. Fatty went a little way along and climbed over the fence into the grounds. He made his way cautiously to the big house, standing, desolate and empty, with no smoke coming from its many chimneys.

He peeped into a window. Inside was a big room, with dust-sheets over the chairs. A large, polished table stood in the middle. On it was a great bowl full of dead flowers.

Fatty's gaze slid round the room. Chairs. Little tables. A stool—and lying on the floor beside the stool was a curious little object, grey, solid, and rubbery.

Fatty wondered what it was. And why was it on the floor? He stared at it curiously. Then he suddenly knew what it was. Of course! It was a little rubber bone, the kind given to dogs to play with and chew!

'Must be Poppet's,' said Fatty. 'One of her playthings that she left behind on the floor.'

He left the window and went along a path under a

Mr. Larkin jumped violently and dropped his wood

rose pergola—and suddenly, just at the end of it, he came face to face with Mr. Larkin, who was trudging round the corner with some firewood.

Mr. Larkin jumped violently and dropped all his wood. Fatty stepped forward at once and picked it up. Then he addressed the scared Mr. Larkin in a very foreign-sounding voice indeed!

'Excuse, please! I come here to see my old friends, the Lorenzos—ah, such old friends they are! And I find the house shut tight—nowhere is there anybody. Please, good sir, you can tell me of my friends?'

'They've gorn,' said Mr. Larkin. 'Ain't you seen the papers? Bad lot, they are.'

'Gorn?' echoed Fatty, in a very puzzled voice. 'I do not understand.'

'Well—they've gorn—just *gorn*,' said Mr. Larkin impatiently. Fatty stared at him. He looked just the same miserable fellow as before—plumpish under his untidy old overcoat, a scarf round his chin and throat, and a cap pulled down over his eyes. He peered at Fatty suspiciously through his thick glasses.

'We don't allow no strangers here,' said Mr. Larkin, backing away from Fatty's stare. Fatty was taking him all in, suddenly filled with a longing to disguise himself like this old fellow. If he disguised himself as Bob Larkin he could go all round the house and peep into every window without anyone being surprised. He might even get into the house if he could find the keys. Possibly Larking had some. Yes—he would do it one night —it would be fun.

'You'll have to give me your name,' said Mr. Larkin, suddenly remembering that the police had asked him to take the name of anyone coming to the house. 'Foreigner, aren't you?' He took out a dirty little note-book and sucked a pencil.

'You can write down my name as Mr. Hoho-Ha,' said Fatty politely, and spelt it out carefully for Mr. Larkin. 'And my address is Bong Castle, India.'

Mr. Larking laboriously wrote it all down, placing his notebook on a window-ledge to write legibly. When he looked up again, Mr. Hoho-Ha had gone.

Larking grunted and picked up his firewood. All this silly police business annoyed him. Why couldn't he be left in peace to do his job? But he didn't seem to have much of a job now! All those boilers raked out—nothing to light or keep going. No nice warm boiler-house to sit in and read his paper. Nothing to do but look after a silly little poodle!

Fatty was behind a bush, watching Larkin going down the path. He noted every action-the shuffling limp, the stoop, the way the cap was pulled half-side-ways over the man's face. Yes—he could disguise himself well enough as Larkin to deceive even his old wife!

Fatty had a good look round while he was about it. He looked into shed and greenhouses. Boiler-house and summer-house, keeping a sharp look-out for any-one else. But he saw nobody.

He would, however, have seen somebody if he had been near the Larkins' cottage! He would have seen Mr. Goon! Mr. Goon had ridden up to have another talk to the Larkins, and he was at that moment trying his hardest to get something out of Mrs. Larkin besides coughs, groans and sniffles.

Fatty would also have seen two other people if he had looked up into the tall fir-tree that grew beside the hedge which separated Tally-Ho grounds from the grounds of High Chimneys next door. He would have seen Glad and Liz!

They, faithful to their trust, had been on guard in the tree for two hours, while Ern was mending his bike. Ern's brakes had gone wrong, owing to his crash with Mr.Goon, and he wanted to put them right.

'Glad and Liz, you sit up there and keep your eyes open,' he said. 'And here's two bull's-eyes each to keep you going.'

Glad spotted the strange foreigner as soon as he climbed over the fence. She was so surprised that she swallowed the bull's-eye she was sucking and choked so violently that she nearly fell out of the tree-house.

When at last she recovered, the foreigner had disappeared. She found that Liz had spotted him too, and the twins gazed at each other in excitement.

'He must still be there!' said Glad. 'Come on, Liz— let's climb down and tell Ern. He'll go after him all right. Won't he be pleased with us!'

GLAD and Liz almost fell down the tree in their hurry. They went into the little shed where Ern was busy with his bicycle.

'Ern! We've seen somebody,' said Glad, in a penetrating whisper that could be heard all over the garden. Ern looked up, startled.

'Where? Who?' he asked, getting up at once.

Glad and Liz told him, and Ern straightway made for the hedge, and disappeared through it. He went cautiously round the Larkins' cottage––and then stopped in horror. Mr. Goon was standing at the door talking to Mrs. Larkin! The twins had not seen him because he had arrived after they had climbed down the tree.

Mr. Goon caught sight of Ern at the same moment that Ern caught sight of him. He couldn't believe his eyes. Ern again! Ern here in the Larkins' garden!

Mr. Goon gave such a roar that Mrs. Larkin disappeared indoors immediately and shut the door with a slam. Ern was too petrified to move. Mr. Goon advanced on him majestically.

'*You* here!' said Mr. Goon. 'Now you just come-alonga me, Ern. I've a few things to say to you, I have.'

Ern fled just in time. He ran blindly down the path and charged full-tilt into Mr. Larkin, who was shuffling along still carrying his firewood. He dropped it for the second time as Ern ran straight into him and almost knocked him over. He caught hold of the boy and held on—and was then almost sent flying by the burly form of Mr. Goon chasing after Ern.

'Ere! What's all this!' said Mr. Larkin, startled and annoyed.

'Hold that boy!' commanded Mr. Goon breathlessly. 'Hold him!' Mr. Larkin tried to hold the wriggling Ern, but had to let him go—and Mr. Goon just pounced in time to stop poor Ern from escaping. He shook him so hard that Ern didn't quite know what was happening.

'What you doing here?' demanded Mr. Goon angrily. 'Is that fat boy here too, snooping round?'

'No,' said Ern, feeling certain that Fatty and the others were playing some nice, friendly game far away in Fatty's shed.

'Mr. Goon, sir,' said Mr. Larkin, 'there's bin a furriner wandering round Tally-Ho grounds just now. Name of Hoho-Ha.'

'Why didn't you tell me?' said Mr. Goon unfairly. 'Standing there saying nothing. Where is the fellow?'

He hung on to Ern so tightly that the boy groaned. 'Uncle, let me go. I'm after him too. I'll look for him, if you'll let me go.'

'What do you mean, you're after him too?' said Mr. Goon, looking all round as if he thought he would be able to see plenty of 'furriners'.

'You let that boy look for him, sir,' suggested Mr. Larkin from under his old cap. 'A kid can snoop round quietly and not be seen. You're too big for that. You let this boy loose and tell him to find that furriner—yes, and follow him for you till you can catch up and nab him!'

Goon gave Ern a shake. 'If I let you go will you do that?' he said. 'Mind you, Ern, I've a good mind to put you across my knee here and now and give you the finest spanking you've ever had in your life!'

'No, Uncle!' said Ern, almost in tears. 'You let me find that fellow for you, and I'll shadow him wherever he goes. I promise you, Uncle!'

'He wears a turban,' said Mr. Larkin. 'Sort of towel round his head' he added, as Goon looked mystified. 'Can't mistake him. He can't be far off, so let this kid go now or you'll lose the furriner.'

Goon let go Ern's arm and the boy darted off thankfully. Oh, what bad luck to run into Goon again —just as he was hoping to get some news for Fatty too! Now he had got to find and shadow someone for his uncle —someone who might have been of great use to old Fatty!

Ern remembered the lessons in shadowing that he had had from Fatty, and went silently from bush to bush, watching and listening—and soon he heard the crack of a twig on a path. Ah—the 'furnier' must be there!

Ern peeped round the bush. It was getting rather dark now but he could see a man—and he was wearing a turban!

'Nasty-looking chap,' thought Ern. 'Proper foreigner. Up to no good. Might have a knife on him somewhere so I'd better be careful'

Ern felt very thrilled. 'Almost as if I was in a film!' he thought, remembering the dramatic moments in some of the cowboy films he had seen lately. 'Coo! What will Fatty and the others say when they hear about this!'

The man in the turban moved down the path to the little wicket-gate. Ern followed cautiously some way behind. Goon caught sight of both of them and followed cautiously too. Ern was after the man, so if he kept the boy in sight Ern would lead him to wherever the man was going!

Fatty had absolutely no idea that he was being shadowed by Ern, with Goon some distance behind. He sauntered along, thinking of Larkin, and what fun it would be to disguise himself as the old fellow, and meet him some morning down the street! What *would* Larkin say if he came face to face with himself?

Ern followed carefully, holding his breath. Fatty went along the river-path and turned up into Peters—wood village. Ern stalked him, keeping in the shadows.

Goon followed, wishing he hadn't left his bicycle behind at the Larkins. Now he would have to walk all the way back to get it that night!

Fatty suddenly felt that he was being followed, and looked round. Was he or wasn't he? Was that a figure hiding beside that bush? Well, never mind, he was nearly home!

Fatty suddenly took to his heels and ran for home, thinking that it wouldn't do to be stopped by Goon, if it *was* Goon. He had no idea it was Ern. He came to his gate and slipped through it, ran to the garden door and into the house. Up the stairs he went, two at a time, and into his bedroom. Buster welcomed him with a volley of delighted barks.

It didn't matter what disguise Fatty put on, Buster was never deceived. Fatty always smelt like Fatty, no matter what he looked like—a 'furriner' an old man, a gypsy woman, a butcher's boy. One sniff and Buster knew him!

'Coo,' said Ern, stepping out of the shadows as Fatty went in at his gate. 'Look at that! He ran off all of a sudden, and I'm blessed if he didn't go in at Fatty's gate. Perhaps he's a friend of Fatty's. Gosh—here's

Uncle!'

'Where'd that man go?' demanded Mr. Goon, holding Ern's shoulder in a vice-like grip.

'Into Fatty's gate,' said Ern. 'I say, Uncle—perhaps he's a friend of Fatty's. You'd better not go after him.'

'Ho! I'd just like to know who Master Frederick Trotteville is sending to snoop round Tally-Ho grounds,' said Goon. And in at the gate he went, leaving Ern miserably outside. Had he got Fatty into trouble?

Mr. Goon knocked loudly at the door and the maid answered promptly.

'Is Master Frederick in?' asked Goon, in his most pompous voice. Before the maid could answer Mrs. Trotteville came into the hall.

'What do you want, Mr. Goon?' she inquired. 'Was it you who knocked so loudly?'

'Er—well, yes I suppose it was,' said Goon, forgetting to be pompous. He was rather afraid of Mrs. Trotteville. 'I came about a foreigner.'

'A foreigner?' said Mrs. Trotteville. 'But there is no foreigner here. What makes you think there is?

'Well, he came in at your gate,' said Goon. 'Man in a turban.'

'Oh—dear me, I remember seeing a man in a turban going past the windows this afternoon,' said Mrs. Trotteville. 'I'll call Frederick. He may have seen him too.'

'Frederick!' she called up the stairs. 'Are you in?'

'Yes, Mother,' said Fatty, appearing suddenly at the top of the stairs, dressed in his ordinary clothes, and looking very clean and tidy. 'I was just reading. Do you want me?'

'Mr. Goon has come about some foreigner he thinks is

here,' said Mrs. Trotteville. 'He says he came in at our gate a little while ago.'

'I think Goon must be seeing things,' said Fatty, in a concerned voice. 'Do you feel quite well, Mr. Goon? What was this fellow like?'

'He wore a turban,' said Goon, beginning to feel annoyed.

'Well, I really haven't seen anyone walking about just wearing a turban,' said Fatty. 'I think I'd have remembered if I had.'

'Don't be stupid, Frederick,' said his mother. 'I saw somebody wearing a turban this afternoon, but as far as I could see his other clothes were ordinary ones. Who can this fellow be, Frederick?'

'A new paper-boy perhaps,' suggested Fatty. 'Or some friend of the maids? Or just somebody taking a short cut through our garden? People do, you know.'

'Well—this man is obviously not here, Goon,' said Mrs. Trotteville. 'I don't imagine you want to search the house?'

Goon would dearly have liked to, but Mrs. Trotteville looked so forbidding that he said a hasty good night and went off to the front gate. Fatty ushered him politely all the way and watched him stride away in the twilight.

'He was just going in when a low whistle reached his ears. He swung round. Ern's voice came urgently from a bush nearby. 'Fatty! I've some news for you!'

'Ern! What in the world are you doing there?' said Fatty, startled. Out came Ern, very cautiously.

'There was a strange man snooping about in Tally-Ho grounds this afternoon,' he began. 'And I followed him to your house. He wore a turban.'

Fatty groaned. 'Fathead, Ern! That was ME! I disguised myself as a foreigner and went up and had a snoop round and a few words with our friend, Mr. Larkin! How on earth did Goon come into this?'

Ern explained sadly, feeling that he had not been at all clever. He had even taken Goon to Fatty's house! Golly, Fatty might have been caught in his disguise! What an upset that would have been. Poor Ern was really very miserable.

'Cheer up, Ern,' said Fatty, patting him on the shoulder. 'It just shows two things-one, that my disguise was really jolly good—and two, that you're certainly quick off the mark!'

Ern felt more cheerful. Good old Fatty-he always took things the right way, thought Ern. He determined to be even more on the look-out than ever. Next time he would track a *real* suspect—not just Fatty!

Fatty went up into his bedroom again, rather depressed after his interesting afternoon. This wasn't a real mystery—it was just a stupid, idiotic newspaper case!

FATTY was tremendously surprised to see the papers the next morning. Somehow they had got hold of the fact that a foreigner of some kind had been seen wandering about the grounds of Tally-Ho House.

'Mystery of the Lorenzos and Stolen Picture Flares up Again,' said one headline. 'An Old Friend found in the Grounds.'

'Indian chased by Brave Constable,' said another paper.

'Stolen Picture Probably hidden in Tally-Ho House,' said a third. 'Foreigner Found Breaking in.'

Fatty stared at these headlines in the utmost dismay. Goodness—what in the would had Goon been saying? Some reporter must have got hold of him last night and had asked if there were any news about the Lorenzos—and Goon hadn't been able to stop himself from enlarging on his encounter with the disguised Fatty.

Fatty heart sank down into his boots. Why, Goon hadn't set even a finger on him! He had only followed Ern, who had been following him. Suppose Superintendent Jenks got to hear of this?

Fatty went round to see the others as soon as he could. They hadn't known, of course, that he was going to disguise himself as an Indian, and had been most astonished to see the papers. Larry and Daisy had gone to call for Pip and Bets, on their way down to Fatty's, and they were very pleased to see him.

'Seen the papers?' said Pip, as soon as Fatty came

in at the playroom door, with Buster at his heels. Fatty nodded. The others stared at him in surprise.

'What's up? What are you looking like that for?' asked Larry. 'We were jolly pleased about it—it looks as if something might happen here after all!'

Fatty sat down and groaned in such a desperate manner that Bets ran to him at once. 'What is it? Are you ill, Fatty?'

'I feel ill,' said Fatty. '*I* was the Indian—didn't you guess? I thought I'd disguise myself as a foreign student, and just go for a little snoop—and of course first I bumped into old Larkin and gave him a shock—and then *Ern* discovers me and tells old Goon, who happens to be interviewing Mr. Larkin—and then Ern is told to shadow me so that Goon can see where I go.'

The others listened in horror. 'Fatty! And now you're in all the papers!'

'Yes—but mercifully nobody knows *I* was the Indian–
–except Ern. I told him. Wish I hadn't now. He'll never be able to keep his mouth shut. And oh—I've just thought of something else. Oh, my word!'

'What? What is it?' said Bets, quite overcome with all this. All kinds of dreadful ideas filled her mind.

'Old Larkin met me—and I asked him where my old friends the Lorenzos had gone,' said poor Fatty. 'And when he asked me for my name I told him an idiotic one–
–and he *wrote it down*! If Goon gets it out of him, and realizes the Indian was spoof—in other words, me—there'll be an awful lot of fat in the fire!'

'What name did you give?' asked Larry.

'Mr. Hoho-Ha of Bong Castle, India,' said Fatty with another groan.

There was a moment's silence—and then a squeal of

laughter from Daisy. 'Oh, Fatty! Oh Mr. Hoho-Ha! Do you mean to say old Larkin *really* wrote that down?'

'Rather,' said Fatty, still unable to raise even a smile. 'It's no laughing matter, Daisy. If Ern splits on me, I'm in the soup—jolly hot soup too. We're sure to get the reporters down here then, interviewing me as the Boy who Deceived the Police. Frightful! Why did I do it?'

'Ern won't give you away,' said Bets.

'I think he would,' said Pip. 'He's not very brave and he's so scared of Goon that he'd say anything to get away from him.'

There came a knock at the door. Everyone turned their heads, expecting they hardly knew what. Goon perhaps—except that he wouldn't knock. He'd walk straight in!

The door opened. It was Ern! Ern, looking very flushed and rather fearful.

'Ern! We were just talking about you,' said Bets. 'Have you split on Fatty? You haven't told Goon that Fatty was the Indian, have you?'

'Coo, no,' said Ern, much to everyone's relief. 'Uncle's been at me like anything this morning—but I never said a word about Fatty. What do you take me for?'

'I knew you wouldn't Ern,' said Bets.

'I just came to tell you something,' said Ern. 'My uncle's gone all funny—like this morning. Don't know what to make of him.'

'Exactly what do you mean?' asked Fatty, interested. 'Well—he came up to my Aunt Woosh's place this morning, though goodness knows how he found out I was staying there,' said Ern. 'And he took me into the wood-shed and shut the door. I was that scared I could hardly stand! I thought he was going to take a stick to me.'

'Poor Ern!' said Daisy.

'Well, he didn't,' said Ern. 'He was as sweet as sugar. Kept patting me on the shoulder, and telling me I wasn't such a bad kid after all—and then he said he wanted to keep me out of any unpleasantness, so he wanted me to promise I'd not say a word about how I discovered the Indian yesterday, nor a word about me shadowing him...'

Fatty laughed suddenly. 'Gosh! He's so proud of this Indian business that he wants everyone to think *he* discovered him, tackled him and shadowed him! He doesn't want *you* to figure in this show at all, Ern.'

'Oh—so that's it, is it?' said Ern. 'Well, my Aunt Woosh got a paper this morning, and when I saw all about you in it, Fatty—well, about the foreigner, I mean—I got the shock of my life. I was all of a tremble when my Uncle Goon came in—and I was worse when I saw him. I'm all of a tremble now, even when I think of it.'

'Have a sweet?' said Pip. 'It's good for trembles.'

Ern took one. 'Phew!' he said. 'I wasn't half glad when my uncle let me go. I promised I wouldn't say a word to anyone—and I was never so glad to promise anything in my life! Never!'

Fatty heaved a sigh of relief. 'Good old Ern,' he said, with much feeling. 'You've taken a load off my mind. If Goon goes about saying *he* discovered the Indian, and tackled him, and then shadowed him, I'm all right. Though he shouldn't really say anything, if he's on a case.'

'Suppose one of the reporters from the papers finds out from Larkin that the Indian gave him the name of Mr. Hoho-Ha of Bong Castle,' said Pip. 'Won't he smell a rat?'

'No. I don't think so,' said Fatty, considering the

matter. 'He'll probably think the Indian was just spoofing the old fellow. I hope Superintendent Jenks doesn't hear that, though—he'll know it's the sort of idiotic name I'd think up myself.'

'You are a one!' said Ern, round-eyed. 'How you dare! Coo, Fatty, *I* never knew it was you! You don't even *walk* like yourself when you're in disguise. You ought to be on the stage!'

'Good gracious, no!' said Fatty. 'Be on the stage when I could be a detective? Not on your life!'

'We'd better lie low for a day or two, hadn't we?' said Daisy. 'Not go anywhere near Tally-Ho House. Once this new excitement has died down, things will be all right––but Fatty oughtn't to risk anything at the moment.'

'You're right, Daisy,' said Fatty. 'But personally I'm beginning to think that the next thing we'll hear is that the Lorenzos have managed to get out of the country—with the picture—and that will be that.'

'Oh, I hope not!' said Pip. 'This is a most *annoying* mystery—there's nothing to get hold of—no clues, no suspects——'

'Except the Indian,' said Larry, with a grin.

'Well—let's drop the whole thing for a couple of days,' said Fatty. 'Then we'll see if anything further has happened. We'll know by the papers.'

'Shan't I keep watch from my tree-house?' said Ern, disappointed.

'Oh yes—no harm in that,' said Fatty. 'Do those twin cousins of yours still enjoy themselves up there?'

'Oooh yes—they've got all their dolls up there now,' said Ern, sounding rather disgusted. ''There's nowhere to sit except on dolls—and one squeaks like anything if you tread on it. Gave me—real fright, I can tell you!'

They all laughed. 'Well, you let the twins sit up there as much as they like, and report to you *if* they see anything,' said Fatty. 'I wish I'd known I could be so easily seen from that tree when I wandered in yesterday. I forgot all about it! Those cousins of yours must have been keeping a pretty sharp look-out.'

'They're not bad,' said Ern. 'I've got them properly under my thumb now. They think I'm the cat's whiskers and the dog's tail and the kangaroo's jump, and...'

'Oh, Ern!' said Bets, and joined in the laughter. Ern beamed. He did so love the Five to laugh at any of his jokes.

'Ern, have you written any more poems?' asked Bets. Ern was very fond of writing what he called 'pomes' but as he rarely got beyond the first three or four lines, they were not very successful.

Ern pulled out a notebook, looking pleased. 'Fancy you remembering my pomes,' he said. 'Well, I began one last week. It might be a good one—but I got stuck again.'

'What is it?' said Fatty, grinning. 'Let me help you.'

Ern read out his 'pome,' putting on a very solemn voice.

> 'A pore old woman had a dog,
> And it was always barkin,
> Its name was...'

'Well, that's as far as I've got,' said Ern. 'There's all sorts of ideas swarming round in my head, but they just sort of won't come out.'

'My dear Ern, it's a fine poem,' said Fatty earnestly. 'Don't you really know how it goes on? Listen!'

Fatty stood in the middle of the room and recited in a voice exactly like Ern's.

> 'A pore old woman had a dog,
> And it was always barkin,
> Its name was Poppet, and of course
> The woman's name was Larkin.
>
> She sniffed and coughed the whole day long,
> And said the wind was nippin,
> And when the dog got in her way
> She handed out a whippin.
>
> Her husband shuffled in an out,
> He wasn't very supple,
> They weren't at all what you might call
> A really pleasant couple!'

Fatty stopped to take breath. Ern had listened in the greatest awe. The others laughed in delight. Fatty could go on like this for ages, without stopping. It was one of the many extraordinary things he could do.

'Cool!' said Ern. 'How do you it, Fatty? Why, that's *just* what I wanted to say in my pome but I got stuck. You're a wonder, Fatty!'

'Oh, that was just a lot of nonsense,' said Fatty, feeling much better.

'It wasn't. It was simply marvellous,' said Ern. 'I must write it all down—but it's really *your* pome now, not mine, Fatty.'

'No, it's yours,' said Fatty generously. 'I don't want it. I'd never have thought of it if you hadn't told me the first three lines. You can have it for your very own, Ern.'

Ern was delighted—and, for the next twenty minutes

Fatty recited in a voice exactly like Ern's

he didn't join in any of the fun. He was most laboriously writing out his new 'pome'.

THERE was nothing more in the papers about the 'strange foreigner'. In fact, as far, as Fatty could see, there was no mention of the Lorenzo case at all. He was rather relieved.

For two days the Five led perfectly normal lives, with Ern and Buster following them around. The Lorenzo mystery wasn't even mentioned, except that Ern volunteered the information that the twins were getting rather tired of the tree-house.

'You see, it's been windy, and their things keep falling out of the tree when the wind shakes it,' explained Ern. 'And they got annoyed because I wouldn't let them blow bubbles over the Larkins' cottage.'

'Blow bubbles over the cottage?' said Fatty, in surprise. 'But why should they want to? The bubbles would burst at once, anyhow.'

'Not the kind they've got,' said Ern. 'They aren't ordinary soap-bubbles—you make the mixture, and blow the bubbles—and they come out very big and strong— they can bump into things without breaking, so they go on flying about for ages.'

'I see,' said Fatty, having a sudden vision of Mr. and Mrs. Larkin being surrounded by big, bouncing bubbles every time they put their noses out of doors. 'Well—it does sound a most tempting thing to do, I must say—but you'd better restrain the twins at present, anyway. The tree-house spy-hole would certainly be discovered if they start anything like that.'

'I've told them not to do it,' said Ern. 'But they're not all *that* obedient, Fatty. They keep on and on about it. When they first thought of it they almost fell out of the tree with laughing.'

'Yes. Well it's quite a bright idea,' said Fatty. 'One we might use sometime, but not just now. Come on—we are all going to the cake-shop for coffee and hot buttered scones.'

They cycled off to cake-shop. Ern thought that this custom of the Five of popping out to eat and drink in between meals was a Very Very Good One. His aunt didn't feed him as well as his mother did, and poor Ern was in a constant state of hunger.

The cake-shop woman was very pleased to see them. Six children and hungry dog were better than twelve grown-ups, because they seemed to eat three times as much! She brought out a plate heaped with hot, buttery scones.

'Curranty ones!' said Pip. 'Just what I like. It's decent of you to keep standing us this kind of thing, Fatty. You always seem to have a lot of money.'

'Well, this is my Christmas money,' said Fatty, who had a good supply of generous aunts and uncles and grandparents. 'Sit, Buster. Well-mannered dogs do NOT put their paws on the table, and count the number of scones.'

'They'd take some counting!' said Ern eyeing the plate with much approval. Then he jumped violently, as a large burly figure suddenly appeared at the door.

'Oh—good morning, Mr.Goon,' said Fatty. 'Do come and join us. Do you like hot, buttery scones?'

Mr. Goon stalked in , his lips pursed up as if he was afraid he might say something he didn't mean to. He eyed all the children, and Ern squirmed.

'I've bin looking for you,' he said to Fatty. 'Mr.

Hoho-Ha! Ho yes, I've read it in Larkin's notebook. Think you've made a fool of me, don't you? Do you want me to tell the Superintendent?'

'What do you mean?' said Fatty. 'I read in the papers that you tackled a strange man very bravely the other day in the grounds of Tally-Ho House. Congratulations, Mr. Goon. I wish I'd been there.'

Ern disappeared under the table, and Buster welcomed him heartily, licking his face all over. Goon didn't even see him go.

'What do you mean—you wish you'd been there?' demanded Mr. Goon. 'You were there all right, Mr. Hoho-Ha! Just let me say this, Master Frederick Algernon Trotteville—you'd better go back to BONG CASTLE, see? Else you'll get into Very Serious Trouble.

Having made this extraordinary fierce joke Mr. Goon marched out again. The cake-shop woman stared after him in amazement. Whatever was he talking about?

'Poor man. Mad as a hatter,' said Fatty sympathetically, reaching for another scone. 'Come out, Ern. You're safe now. Buck up, or all the scones will be gone.'

Ern came out from under the table in a hurry, still looking rather pale. He opened his mouth to ask a question.

'We're not talking about certain things just, now Ern,' said Fatty warningly and Ern's mouth shut, only to open again for a bite at a scone.

'I suppose Goon saw all our bikes outside, and couldn't resist coming in to say a few words to you,' said Daisy in a low voice. 'I thought he was going to burst!'

The rest of the day passed very pleasantly, as Pip's mother had asked all the Find-Outers to tea and games.

'Mother says she will be out from three o'clock till seven,' said Pip. 'So if we want to make a noise or do anything silly, she says now's our chance!'

'Very thoughtful of her,' said Fatty approvingly. 'Your mother is strict, Pip, but always fair. I hope your cook is in?'

Pip grinned. 'Oh yes—and she says if you go down to the kitchen and do your imitation of the gardener when she's been and picked some parsley without asking him, she'll make you your favourite ginger-bread.'

'A very reasonable bargain,' said Fatty. He had once been at Pip's when the hot-tempered gardener had discovered the cook picking his parsley, 'without so much as a by-your-leaf'. Fatty had thoroughly enjoyed his remarks, and the cook had been delighted to hear Fatty acting the whole thing to the others afterwards. She had even lent him her cooking apron for an imitation gardening apron.

Fatty was amused to see the apron waiting on a chair for him. Pip chuckled. 'It must be nice to be you, Fatty,' he said. 'Getting your favourite cake because you can imitate our hot-tempered old gardener—getting the finest oranges at the green-grocer's because you do a bit of ventriloquism there, and make a cow moo at the back of the shop just to please the shop-boy-and getting...'

'That's enough,' said Fatty. 'You make it sound like bribery but it's merely good bargaining! Now, let's go down and do the Parsley Act straightaway, so that your cook has got plenty of time to make a smashing plate of gingerbread!'

They all went down, Ern following behind. Ern was like Bets—he thought Fatty was a wonder—there couldn't be anyone like him. He considered that he was very very lucky to be made welcome by every one of the Five. For the hundredth time he made up his mind to serve Fatty faithfully. 'Or die!' thought Ern dramatically, as he watched Fatty doing his ridiculous Parsley Act, croaking in the old gardener's voice, and flapping his apron at the enraptured cook, who was almost dying with laughter.

'Oh bless us all!' she said, wiping her eyes. 'I never saw such a thing in my life. You're old Herbert to the life. He flapped at me just like that! Stop now, I can't bear any more!'

They had their gingerbread—a magnificent pile—and old Herbert, the gardener, was immensely surprised to see Pip coming out with a very large piece for him. He took it in astonished silence.

'As a mark of gratitude from us all,' said Pip solemnly and Herbert was even more mystified.

The evening paper came just as they were all in the hall, saying good-bye to Pip and Bets. It was pushed through the letter-box and fell on to the mat. It lay there, folded in half, with the top half showing clearly. Fatty gave an exclamation as he picked it up.

'Look here! See what it says! "The Lorenzos reported in Maidenhead!" Why, that's quite near here!' He read the paragraph quickly. 'Oh well—apparently it's only just a guess by someone. Anyway surely the Lorenzos wouldn't be foolish enough to travel about undisguised. I expect we'll keep on getting these reports from all over the country, just to keep interest alive.'

'Coo,' said Ern. 'Maidenhead! If it *was* them, they might visit Tall-Ho House—or the Larkins' cottage to get Poppet.'

'Will Goon be watching the place tonight, do you think?'

asked Larry.

'I don't know. Possibly, if there *is* anything in the report,' said Fatty. 'Ern, keep your eyes skinned tonight, will you?'

'Oooh, I will,' promised Ern, thrilled. 'I wouldn't mind scouting round a bit myself-but Uncle may be about, and I wouldn't dare. I'd sure to bump into him.'

'I'll be along before midnight,' said Fatty, making up his mind. 'Just in case.'

'Right,' said Ern, more and more thrilled. 'I'll hoot like an owl to let you know I'm there.'

He put his shut hands to his mouth, with the thumbs on his lips and blew softly. Immediately the hall was filled with the sound of quavering owl hoots.

'Jolly good,' said Larry admiringly. 'It's all right, cookie--we haven't got an owl in the hall!'

The cook, who had run out in surprise, went back into her kitchen. 'Master Frederick again I expect.' she said to her friend sitting there. 'What a one!'

But it was Ern this time, and he hooted again, Pleased to have such an admiring audience.

'Right,' said Fatty, 'You be up in the tree-house—and I'll be scouting around till midnight. I don't really expect anything to happen, but I won't leave anything to chance. I'll look out for Goon, of course.'

'Good-bye!' said Larry, hearing seven o'clock strike. 'Thank you for a lovely time. Buck up, Daisy!'

They all went off, and Pip shut the door. Ern left the others at the corner and rode back to his aunt's, full of excitement over his night's plan. The tree-house at night! He'd take a rug and some cushions, and make himself comfortable. And a bag of bull's-eyes to suck.

So, at nine o'clock, when his aunt and uncle had gone

early to bed, and the twins were sound asleep in their small room, Ern sat bolt upright and listened to hear if his uncle and aunt were asleep. Yes—as usual they were both snoring-his uncle with great big long-drawn-out snores and his aunt with little polite ones.

Ern dressed warmly, because the night was cold. He decided to take both the blanket *and* the rug off his bed. He had already put a couple of old cushions up in the tree-house, and in his coat-pocket he had the bag of bull's-eyes and a torch. Now for it!

He crept out of bed, and down the little stairway, carrying the blanket and rug. He opened the kitchen door and went out into the garden. In a minute he was at the tree. He climbed up carefully, the rugs round his neck.

He was soon in the little tree-house, peering through the peep-hole in the branches. The moon was coming up and the night was quite light. Ern popped a bull's-eye in his mouth and prepared to keep watch. He had never in his life felt so happy!

FATTY did not arrive at Tally-Ho grounds till much later. His parents did not go to bed until ten past eleven that night, and Fatty waited and waited, fully dressed. He was not in disguise, because he did not intend to meet anyone if he could help it!

He had on his very thickest overcoat and a cap pulled over his thick hair. He whispered to Buster to keep quiet. The little Scottie watched him sorrow—fully. He knew that Fatty meant to go out without him, and he was grieved. He wouldn't even wag his tail when Fatty gave him one last pat.

The night was light and dark alternately. When the moon sailed out from behind a big cloud the road was as bright as day. When it sailed behind a cloud, it was difficult to see without a torch. Fatty kept in the shadow of the trees, and walked softly, listening for any footsteps.

He met no one at all. Peterswood had certainly gone to bed early that night!

He went down to the river and walked along the river-path to the wicket-gate leading into Tally-Ho grounds. He felt that to go in at the front gates would certainly attract attention—and, indeed, it was possible that Goon might be there, keeping watch also. 'Though I don't really believe that Maidenhead report,' thought Fatty. 'For one thing it would be silly of the Lorenzos to try and come back so soon—and for another, if they *were* going to, they would disguise themselves too thoroughly to be easily recognized!'

He let himself in at the gate. The Larkins' cottage was in

darkness, and there was not a sound. Fatty remembered that Ern would be watching from the tree-house, and he stopped under a bush to send out a hoot.

'Hoo!' called Fatty, on exactly the right note. 'Hoo-hoo-Hoo!'

And back came the answer from Ern in the tree. 'Hoo! Hoo-hoo-hoo-Hoo!' It was so exactly like an owl that Fatty nodded his head approvingly. Ern was good!

He began to make his way to the big house. It was in utter darkness. Fatty wished he could suddenly see a flicker or flash there, to tell him that somebody was about—that would be exciting. But everything was silence and darkness in the deserted house.

Ern hooted again. Then, before Fatty could answer, there came another hoot, and then another.

Whatever was Ern doing? Then Fatty laughed. Of course! If was real owls this time. They liked hunting on a moonlight night like this.

He thought he would send back a hoot, however, in case it *was* Ern. So he put his thumbs to his mouth and sent out a long and quavering hoot.

Immediately an answering hoot came, one that sounded quite urgent! *Was* it Ern? It was impossible to sense exactly the right direction of the hoot. Could Ern be trying to give him a message—was he warning him?

Fatty decided to stand under a thick dark bush for a while and wait quietly. The night was so silent that he might be able to pick up any any noise if someone was about.

So Fatty stood absolutely still and listened. He heard nothing at all for about five minutes. Not even a hoot!

Then he was sure he heard a soft crunch as if

someone was walking carefully on frosty grass. Oh, very carefully!

Fatty held his breath. Could it be one of the Lorenzos? Had he—or she—come back to get something from the house? They would be sure to have keys. He stood still again. The moon swung out from behind a cloud and everything was suddenly lighted up. Fatty crouched back into the bush, looking round to see if he could spy anyone.

Not a sound! Not a sign of anything at all suspicious. The moon went behind a cloud again—a big cloud, this time, likely to last for some minutes.

The sound came again—a little crunch of frosted grass. Fatty stiffened. Yes—it came from round the corner of the house, he was sure of it. Someone was there—standing there––or moving very cautiously bit by bit.

A loud hoot sounded so near Fatty's head that he jumped violently. This time it really *was* an owl, for he saw the dark shadow of its wings, though he could not hear the slightest sound of the bird's flight.

The tiny crunch came again. Fatty decided that it was someone waiting there—standing on the frosty grass, and occasionally moving his feet. Who was it?

'I really must see,' thought Fatty. If it *is* Lorenzo I'd better scoot off and telephone Superintendent Jenks. It can't be Goon—I should hear his heavy breathing. This fellow doesn't make any sound at all, except the tiny crunching noise.'

As the moon was still behind the cloud Fatty decided he had better try and have a look at the man, whoever he was, straightaway. He made his way very very carefully from the bush, glad that the grass was not so frosty on his side of the house.

He trod unexpectedly on some dead leaves and

He slid his head carefully round the corner

they rustled. Fatty stopped. Had the noise been heard? He was nearly at the corner of the house now. He went forward again, and then nerved himself to peer round.

He slid his head carefully round the corner—and very dimly, he saw a figure standing by the windows of Tally-Ho House. The figure was absolutely still. Fatty could not see any details at all, except that it seemed to be a fairly tall man. It was certainly not the short, burly Goon.

Fatty's heart began to beat fast. Who was this? He fumbled for his torch, meaning to flash it suddenly on the man's face, and then run off at top speed to telephone a warning.

He forgot about the moon! Just as he was about to switch on his torch, the moon shot out from behind the cloud, and immediately the place was flooded with light!

Fatty found himself gazing at a tall policeman in a helmet—and the policeman was also gazing at Fatty, looking most astonished! He put a whistle to his mouth and whistled shrilly, taking a step towards Fatty at the same time.

'It's all right,' began Fatty, 'I...'—and then, up galloped Goon from his hiding-place behind the nearby summer-house. His mouth fell open when he saw Fatty.

Then he advanced on him in rage. 'You! You again! Don't I ever get rid of you, Toad of a Boy! You were all them owls, I suppose, hooting like mad! What you doing here? I'll tell the Chief of this. Obstructing the Course of Duty-Interfering with the Law—messing up things when we're on watch!'

'I didn't know you were watching, Goon,' said Fatty. 'I'm sorry to have disturbed you. This is honestly a mistake.'

The other policeman stood gaping in surprise. Who was this boy?

'What's your name?' he said, taking out a notebook.

'I know his name!' said Goon angrily. 'I've heard it too often, I can tell you that! This is Frederick Trotteville, and this time he's going to get into trouble. Arrest him as an Intruder on Private Property, Constable!'

'Wait a minute—is this really Frederick Trotteville?' said the other policeman. 'He's a friend of the Chief's isn't he? I'm not arresting *him*, Goon. You can do that if you want to!'

'You do as I tell you,' said Goon, losing his temper. 'Who do you think you are, giving me my orders? You're under *my* orders tonight, P.C. Johns, as well you know.'

The moon went most coveniently behind a thick cloud at this point, and Fatty thought it would be just as well if he slipped away. The really didn't want to be arrested—and he was sorry that he had barged into Goon's little spot of night-duty. No wonder Ern had done such a lot of urgent hooting—he must have seen Goon and the other policeman wandering about in the bright moonlight!

Fatty slipped out of the wicket-gate and trotted swiftly home pondering over what was the best thing to do. Should he ring up the Superintendent and tell him of his unfortunate meeting with Goon and his companion? Surely the Chief would know that Fatty was only trying to help?

Perhaps on the whole it would be best to leave it till the morning, and then telephone. Goon would have simmered down by then. Fatty would go and see him and apologize for barging in. Goon loved an apology!

So Fatty did not telephone, but went soberly to bed hushing

Buster's ecstatic but silent welcome. He heard an owl hooting nearby and grinned as he pulled the sheet up to his chin. Poor Goon! He must have been quite. bewildered by all the owl-hoots sent out by the terrified Ern!

Ern was still up in the tree. He had an extremely good view of the grounds when the moon was out, for everything was then as distinct as in the daytime, though the shadows were very black.

Ern was shivering, not so much with cold as with excitement and panic. He had spotted Goon and his companion about eleven o'clock, before Fatty had appeared, when the moonlight had suddenly glittered on their helmets. There was no mistaking his uncle, of course—plump and stocky. The other policeman Ern didn't know.

Ern watched them walking round the big house peeping into all the windows and trying the doors. Then they disappeared. Were they expecting the Lorenzos after all? Were they hiding and lying in wait?

Old Fatty wouldn't know that! He might walk straight into them. Ern fell into a panic and shivered so much that he shook the little tree-house from end to end.

He wondered what to do. Should he slip down the tree and go and see if he could meet Fatty and warn him? No—he didn't know which way Fatty would be coming—by the river-gate or the front gates. He might miss him!

Well, should he stay in the tree and wait for Fatty to come, and then try to warn him by hooting and hooting? But would he *see* Fatty? The moon might be in behind a cloud, and then he couldn't possibly see anyone!

Ern decided, shivering, that the best thing to do would be to wait and hope to see Fatty—and then hoot for all he was worth.

He spotted Fatty easily as the boy trod stealthily up the

garden. Ern's spy-hole was indeed a good one! He hooted—
and Fatty answered him. And then poor Ern spied Goon and
the other policeman, standing behind the corner of the house—
—and now, where had Goon gone? Oh, yes, behind the
summer-house! Ern hooted urgently—and to his utter disgust,
an owl flew over in surprise, hooting too. Ern shook his fist at
it—spoiling all his plans! Now Fatty wouldn't know one hoot
from another!

Ern then saw the encounter between Fatty and Goon
and the other policeman, though he could hear nothing
except a murmur of voices. His eyes nearly fell out of his
head with trying to see what was happening. Oh, Fatty,
make a run for it! Ern found himself saying the words
over and over again.

Then the moon went behind a cloud—and when it came
out again, oh joy! Ern saw a running figure on the river-path
—and the two policeman hunting here and there for the
vanished Fatty!

Ern heaved an enormous sigh of relief. He slumped
back into the tree-house, feeling quite tired after all the
suspense.

Stir yourself, Ern! The night isn't finished yet!

ERN gave a few more sighs, each one less enormous than the last. By now Fatty would be well on the way home. Had Goon recognized him? Ern was afraid that he had. He sat up again and peered out.

Ah—there were Goon and the other constable walking side by side, arguing. Then Goon stood and began to swing his great arms to and fro across his chest.

'He's cold,' said Ern to himself. 'Serve him right! I hope he freezes! I hope he's got to stay and watch Tally-Ho House all night long. Grrrrr!'

It was a most blood-curdling growl that Ern gave, and he even scared himself. He realized that his hands and feet were remarkably cold, and he thought longingly of his warm bed.

'I can't do anything more tonight,' he thought, beginning to climb down the tree, with the rug and blanket draped round his neck. 'I'll go back to the house.'

He climbed right down and went to the cottage. To his horror the kitchen door was now locked! He shook it quietly, filled with dismay. Who had locked it? He supposed that his uncle must have awakened at some noise—and have got up to investigate, and found the door unlocked. Blow, blow, blow!

'Well—I'm not going to knock at the door and give everybody a fright,' thought Ern. 'I'll just go back to the tree now, and explain tomorrow morning that I thought I'd like a night-out up there, and that's where I was. They'll think I'm potty, but I can't help that!'

Ern debated with himself. He would have liked another blanket. He remembered that there were piles of old newspapers in his Uncle Woosh's shed. He had heard that newspaper was very, very warm covering, so he decided to take a few dozen papers up the tree with him.

Armed with these, he went back to the tree-house. It really seemed very cosy and comfortable after the cold air down in the yard. Ern spread out the newspaper and made himself a kind a bed. Then he wrapped a few papers round him, pulled the blanket and the rug over him, and put his head on the cushion. He had to lie curled up, because the tree-house was really very small. On the other hand Ern was not really very big!

He began to get warm. He felt quite comfortable. He yawned a huge yawn. At the same moment an owl passed by the tree and hooted.

'Hoo! Hoo-hoo-hoo-Hoo!'

Ern was up like a shot. Was that old Fatty back again? He peered out of the tree but could see nothing— not even a sign of Goon and his companion. The gardens lay bathed in the brilliant moonlight, undisturbed and peaceful. The owl flew by again, and this time Ern saw it.

'Hoo!' began the owl, 'hoo, hoo...'

Ern put his hands to his mouth in the proper position for hooting, and joined in loudly. 'Hoo-HOO-HOO-HOO-HOO!'

The owl gave a frightened 'tvit' and swerved off at once. Ern watched it go. 'Now don't you come hooting round me again!' he said. 'I've had enough of you tonight!'

And once more Ern cuddled down in his newspapers and blankets and shut his eyes! This time he fell fast asleep, and slept for about two hours.

Then a noise awakened him. At first he couldn't think where he was. He sat up in a fright. Then he saw the moonlight outside the tree and remembered. What had awakened him?

He heard a noise. It was a quiet, humming kind of noise, some way away. Was it an aeroplane? Perhaps. Was it a car far away on a road? Yes—it sounded more like that.

Ern lay down again. He shut his eyes. Then he heard another noise and sat up.

Splash! Splash-splash! Ern looked out of the tree again. Was somebody swimming in the river at this time of night? No—not on a frosty night in January! Still—there was that soft splash-splash again! Ern strained his eyes over towards the river.

He saw something white sailing on it—two white things—and one or two shadowy ones behind. He laughed.

'It's the swans—and their babies! I'm daft! Imagining all kinds of things when it's only a couple of swans and their family. Well, fancy them keeping awake all night! I thought they put their heads under their wings and slept.'

Ern lay down again, determined that he wouldn't he disturbed by any more noises. There was no sign of Goon now, or of his companion. The owl had stopped hooting. The swans had stopped splashing. He didn't mean to let himself be disturbed by ANYTHING else!

He was soon half-asleep. Small noises came to him on the night-wind, and once he thought he heard voices, but was sure he was dreaming. He imagined he heard a dog barking and half-opened his eyes. Yes, it was. Probably Poppet—it sounded exactly like her high little bark.

She'd get slapped for waking the couple up in the middle of the night!

Ern fell into such a sound sleep that not even the owl awoke him when it came and sat on his very tree, and gave a sudden mournful hoot. Ern slept on. Dawn came slowly, and the sun sent golden fingers into the sky. Soon it would be light.

Ern awoke. He sat up, bewildered, but then remembered everything. He'd better get up and climb down the tree. His aunt would wonder where he was—she must be up and about.

Ern was just about to climb down the tree when he heard shouting. Loud, angry shouts—and then he heard bangs—bang-bang-bang! BANG, BANG, BANG! Gracious goodness, what was all that? Ern slithered down the tree and went to the hedge and listened. The noise came from somewhere in the grounds of Tally-Ho House. Ern wondered what it was. It couldn't be Fatty back again, and in trouble, surely!'

He slipped through the hedge and went by the Larkins cottage. The door opened and the old man came out, plump in his old overcoat, his scarf and cap on as usual. He limped over to Ern.

'What's that noise?' he said, in his hoarse voice. 'You go and see. My wife's ill today and I don't want to leave her.'

Ern nodded at the dirty old man and went cautiously in the direction of the noise. It grew louder. BANG-BANG! HELP! LET US OUT! BANG-BANG!

Ern was mystified. Who was locked in and where—and why? It wasn't Fatty's voice, thank goodness.

Ern went in the direction of the noise. It sounded round the further corner of the house, where the boiler-house was. Ern turned the corner and saw the small boiler-house not far off.

Yes—the noise was coming from there. Ern looked at the little place fearfully. He wasn't letting anyone out till he knew who they were!

He went cautiously up to the boiler-house and stood on a box outside to look in at the small window. He was so astounded at what he saw that he fell off the box.

Inside the boiler-house, furiously angry, were Mr. Goon and the other policeman! Their helmets were hanging on a nail. Ern saw two hot, furious faces up-turned to him as he appeared at the window, and heard more loud shouts.

'Open the door! ERN! What you doing here? OPEN THE DOOR AND LET US OUT!'

Goon had been most astonished to see Ern's scared face at the tiny little window, but very thankful. Now perhaps they could get out of this stifling boiler-house and get something to eat and drink.

'Why did we ever come in here?' groaned Goon, as he heard Ern struggling with the large, stiff key in the outer side of the door. 'It was so cold, and it seemed such a good idea to light up the boiler and shut the door and have a little warm!'

'Must have been the fumes that sent us off to sleep so sudden-like,' said his companion dolefully. 'I feel as if my head's bursting. Drat that boy—why can't he unlock the door?'

'Buck up, Ern, you dolt!' roared Mr. Goon. 'We're cooking-hot in here.'

'Who locked us in?' said the other man. 'That's what *I* want to know. It wouldn't be the Lorenzos, would it now?

They couldn't have come after all, could they?'

'No! I've told you—it was that boy Frederick Trotteville—the one we found here last night,' said Goon crossly. 'One of his funny tricks—ho, he'll laugh on the other side of his face this time. I go straight to the Chief about this—dead straight! Locking us into a boiler-house —why we might have been dead with the fumes this morning! ERN—what you doing out there? You've only got to turn the key. Are you asleep, boy?'

'No, Uncle. And don't you talk to me like that when I'm doing my best to help you,' panted Ern. 'It's a whopping big key and very rusty. I've a good mind to leave you here if you don't talk proper to me when I'm trying hard.'

Mr. Goon was amazed to hear his cheek from Ern. But he had to swallow his wrath and speak in honey-like tones, afraid that Ern really would go off and leave them.

'Now, Ern—it's only because we're almost cooked,' he said. 'I know you're doing your best. Ah—there's a good lad—the key's turned!'

Ern fled as his uncle and the second policeman walked out of the boiler-house. One look at their beetroot-like faces and protruding eyes was enough for him. Goon and his companion walked with as much dignity as they could muster past the Larkins' cottage on their way to the river.

The old fellow came out of his door, shuffling as usual. 'What was the matter?' he said, in his hoarse voice.

'Tell you later,' said Goon, who was not particularly anxious that the tale of the boiler-house should go all round Peterswood. 'Nothing much. We just kept watch last night, that's all. You didn't hear anything, did you? We never heard a sound—so we're going off-duty now.'

Mr. Goon went back to his house and took up the telephone, a grim look on his face. He made a brief report, which caused quite a stir at the other end. It even made the Chief himself come to the telephone.

'Goon? What's this story about Frederick Trotteville? I don't believe it.'

'Sir, I wouldn't tell you such a story if it wasn't true,' said Goon earnestly. 'And P.C. Johns, who was with me, will tell you that this boy was in the grounds last night, snooping round after us—one of his little jokes, sir, this was. He thought it would be funny to lock us in.'

'But what were you doing in the boiler-house, Goon, when you should have been outside on duty?' said the Chief's sharp voice.

'Just looking round, sir,' said Goon, and then let his imagination get the better of him. 'We heard footsteps outside, sir, then the door banged and the key turned in the lock, and we heard Master Frederick's laugh, sir—a most horrible laugh, sir, and...'

'That's enough, Goon,' said the Chief's voice. 'All right. I'll see to this. Did you hear or see anything at all last night?'

'Nothing at all, sir,' said Goon, and then the telephone was clicked off at the Chief's end. Goon stood quite still his face red with delight.

'Ho, you Toad of a Boy,' he said. 'Now you've gone too far at last. You're finished!'

FATTY was just down to breakfast when a big black police car swept up the drive to the front door, and out got Superintendent Jenks, looking rather grim. Fatty was thrilled.

'He's got some news! And he wants me to help in some way!' thought Fatty joyfully. He went to open the door himself.

'I want a word with you, Frederick,' said the Chief, and Fatty led him into the study, struck with the Superintendent's sharp voice.

Once the door was shut, the Chief looked straight at Fatty.

'What possessed you to lock Goon and the other fellow up last night?' he demanded grimly.

Fatty stared in surprise. 'I don't know what you mean, sir,' he said at last. 'I really don't. Where am I supposed to have locked them up? In the cells?'

'Don't play the fool,' said the Chief, his eyes like gimlets, boring into poor Fatty. 'Don't you realize that you can go a bit too far with your jokes on Goon?'

'Sir,' said Fatty earnestly, 'do believe me when I say I haven't the remotest idea what you are talking about. I saw Goon last night, in the grounds of Tally-Ho House, where I was keeping watch in case the Lorenzos turned up—I had seen a report that they had been spotted at Maidenhead. Goon had another policeman with him. I left the grounds a few minutes after I had see them and said a few words to them, and went straight home to bed. They were not locked up when I left them. I must ask you to believe me, sir. I never tell lies.'

The Chief relaxed, and sat down. 'Right, I believe you, of course, Frederick,' he said. 'But I must say it's queer how you always turn up in the middle of things. Goon and Johns were locked up all night in the boiler-house at Tally-Ho, and Ern let them out this morning.'

'Ern!' said Fatty, startled.

'Yes, *he* seemed to be about too,' said the Chief. 'Goon and Johns were apparently half-cooked, the boiler-house was so hot.'

'The boiler wasn't going when I left them, sir,' said Fatty. 'I'd have noticed if it was—I'd have seen the glow when I went near it.'

'Oh. Then who lit it?' said the Chief.

'Goon and Johns, I suppose,' said Fatty. 'It was a cold night, and they might have thought it a good idea to light up the boiler and have a warm, sir. And possibly they—er—well, quite possibly they fell asleep.'

'Yes. That thought also occurred to me,' said the Chief.

'It might have been the fumes that sent them off, of course,' said Fatty generously. 'They might not have meant to sleep there—only get warm.'

'Yes. Quite so,' said the Superintendent. 'Still, the fact remains that SOMEBODY locked them in.'

'Yes. WHO?' said Fatty. 'Do you think the Lorenzos *could* have slipped back, sir—for some reason or other perhaps to fetch the little poodle Mrs. Lorenzo is so fond of—or even to get something from the house?'

'It's possible,' said the Chief. 'Yes quite possible. They've a reputation for being dare-devils. We'll find out if the dog is gone—or if the house has been entered and anything personal taken—something that they had left behind and wanted. What a fathead that fellow Goon is, isn't he? Still, I'm glad I came over here. I'd like you to take a hand now, in this mystery, Frederick.'

'Oh—thank you very much, sir,' said Fatty, thrilled.

'I'm not telling Goon this, because he's such a blunderer,' said the Chief, 'but I have a distinct feeling that the Lorenzos are back in Peterswood for some reason or other—perhaps as you say, to get back the dog. Mrs. Lorenzo is quite mad about it—idolizes it—and I think it possible that they will try to get it. Or again, it's just possible that they didn't take the picture with them, but have left it behind in case they were caught-for some accomplice to fetch.'

'But what about the crate they were said to have been seen with up north?' asked Fatty.

'That might have been a blind to put us off,' said the Chief. 'They're clever, these Lorenzos. You wouldn't believe the things they've done—and got away with too. They are about the cleverest tricksters I've had to deal with.'

'Well, I'll be proud to help,' said Fatty, as the Chief got up to go. 'Is there any particular thing you'd like me to do?'

'No. Go your own way. Do what you like,' said the Chief. 'Short of locking Goon in a boiler-house, of course! Though I feel very like doing that myself this morning!'

Fatty saw him off and went into the breakfast room feeling most elated. So Goon had told the Chief a thumping big lie about him, had he? Well, it hadn't done him any good. He, Fatty, was now more or less in charge of something that was turning out to be jolly interesting—in fact, a very promising mystery!

Ern came to see Fatty immediately after his breakfast. He had had to do a lot of explaining to his aunt about his night in the tree-house, but it was over at last. Now all he wanted to do was to tell Fatty about Goon and his companion in the boiler-house—and how they had said that it was Fatty who locked them in.

'*Did* you Fatty?' said Ern, looking at him in awe. He was half-disappointed when Fatty shook his head.

'No, Ern. Much as I wish I could have done it, I didn't. Ern, you were up in that tree all night you say. Did you hear' or see anything at all?'

'Well, owls, of course,' said Ern. 'What with you and me and the owls *all* hooting...'

'I don't mean owls,' said Fatty. 'Think hard, Ern—did you hear any out-of-the-way sounds at all?'

Ern thought back to night in the tree. 'Well, I heard a kind of humming noise,' he said. 'I thought at first it was an aeroplane. But it might have been a car.'

'Ah,' said Fatty. 'Go on. Anything else?'

'I heard splashing, and saw the swans swimming in the moonlight,' said Ern. 'They looked as white as snow. And I *thought* I heard voices once, and a dog barking.'

Fatty was alert at once. 'Voices? A dog barking? Would that be Poppet?'

'Yes, I think it was,' said Ern. 'Her bark is sort of high, isn't it?—more like a yelp.'

'You're sure about the voices?' said Fatty. 'And the barking? You see, *somebody* besides me and Goon and Johns must have been there last night—and locked them up!'

'Coo yes,' said Ern. 'Lot of people about last night, it seems! Well, these voices and barking were some time after you'd left. I tell you, I was half-asleep by then.'

'You couldn't have heard voices unless they had been fairly *near*,' said Fatty, frowning and thinking hard. 'Would they have been in or near the Larkins' cottage, do you think?'

'Well—I don't reckon I'd have heard them if they'd been *inside* the cottage,' said Ern. 'I'd have heard them *outside* all right.'

'Did Poppet's bark sound pleased or frightened?' asked Fatty.

'Pleased,' said Ern, at once.

'Oh, That's interesting,' said Fatty. 'Very interesting. Ern, I think the Lorenzos came to get their dog from the Larkins last night—and perhaps to get a few things from the big house as well. They saw Goon and Johns asleep as they passed the boiler-house and neatly locked them in.'

'You're right, Fatty,' said Ern, in great admiration. 'It's wonderful to see how you work these things out. Well, if the dog's gone, we'll *know* it was the Lorenzos who were there last night.'

'Yes. But it doesn't *really* get us any further forward,' said Fatty. 'I mean—we still shan't know where the Lorenzos are—or where the picture is either.'

'You'll find all that out too, Fatty, straight you will,' said Ern solemnly. 'You and your brains!'

'You go and tell the others to meet down in my shed at half-past nine,' said Fatty. 'We'll all have a talk together.

So, at half-past nine, the whole company was gathered together in the little shed, and heard the grand tale of the night in the grounds of Tally-Ho, and all that had happened there. Pip was so tickled to hear about Goon and Johns being locked in the boiler-house that he laughed till he ached.

'Now the first thing we must do is to go up to the Larkins and find out about Poppet,' said Fatty. 'If she's gone, it proves that the Lorenzos were there last night. 'We'll then put the Larkins through a lot of questions, and try to get out of them what really did happen last night.'

'Right,' said Larry. 'Let's go now.'

'We shan't be able to see *Mrs.* Larkins,' said Ern. 'She's ill. I saw old Bob Larkin this morning when I went to set Mr. Goon free. He heard the shouting and banging too.'

'Well—we can perhaps get something out of Larkin,' said Fatty. 'Everyone got their bikes?'

Everyone had. Buster was put into Fatty's basket, and off they all went. They chose the river-path again because the Larkins cottage was so near it.

They leaned their bikes against the railings, and marched up the path to the cottage. Fatty knocked on the door.

It opened—and out came Mr. Larkin, still with his cap and scarf on, thought he had discarded his overcoat and now wore a shapeless, baggy old tweed jacket.

'Oh—what do you want?' he said in his hoarse voice, peering through the thick lenses of his glasses at the six silent children. When he saw Buster he shut the door behind him, and stood just outside it.

'Er—Mr. Larkin—could we have a word with you?' asked Fatty.

'I don't charge nuffin' for that,' said the man. 'What's up?'

'Er—could we come inside?' It's a bit cold out here,' said Fatty, feeling certain that Mr. Larkin had carefully shut the door behind him so that they couldn't see that the little dog was no longer running about inside.

'You can come in if you leave your dog outside,' said the man. 'I don't want the little poodle upset. She's over-excited today.'

Fatty stared. It sounded as if the poodle was still there! 'She's in her basket, beside my wife,' said Larkin hoarsely. He coughed.

'Oho!' thought Fatty, 'so *that's* going to be the tale! His wife's not well—keeps to her bed—and the poodle keeps her company—though really it has been taken away in the night. Very clever. The Lorenzos must have thought that out!'

'I'd like to see the poodle,' said Bets suddenly, seeing that Fatty was now in difficulty. 'Can I go into your wife's room and stroke her?'

'No,' said the man. The children looked at one another. Very, very suspicious!

And then something surprising happened. A loud excited barking came from the little cottage—then a patter of feet could be heard—and then the little white poodle appeared at the kitchen window, her nose pressed against the pane as if she was looking for Buster! *How* all the children stared!

ALL the six stared at Poppet as if they couldn't believe their eyes! As for Buster, he nearly went mad with excitement to see the dear little poodle with her nose at the window, looking down at him.

Poppet wagged her tail hard and barked loudly. She seemed full of life and happiness—quite different from when they had seen her before.

'I suppose she's so pleased because she saw her beloved mistress last night—but did she, after all? We just thought it must be the *Lorenzos* who had come and gone—and fetched Poppet. But it might have been anyone, because Poppet is still here! Gosh —I've got to work things out all over again! Fatty frowned as he stood looking at the dog.

Mr. Larkin stood blinking at the children through his thick glasses. He wiped his sleeve across his nose and began to shuffle away, half limping as he went.

'Mr. Larkin!' called Fatty. 'Just half a minute— did you hear much disturbance last night? Did you see anyone—or do you know who locked up the two policemen?'

Larkin shook his head. 'I heard noises,' he said. 'But I didn't stir from out my bed.'

He shuffled off towards the boiler-house, and the children watched him go.

Fatty looked back at the little cottage. Somebody *had* come there last night-Ern had heard voices and that meant that people were talking outside the cottage.

He went to the window where Poppet was still barking

Larkin was not telling the truth when he said he had not stirred from his bed. He *had* left his bed to open his door and talk to someone. Had he taken a message? Had he––ah yes—had he perhaps taken in a parcel-a *crate*? It would surely be an ingenious idea to bring the picture back and store it in the little cottage!

He went to the window where Poppet was still barking, pawing at the pane excitedly. He looked in cautiously, trying to see what was in the small room. It was a poor, dirty place, with makeshift furniture. There was certainly no crate there, or large, wrapped-up parcel.

There was no sign of Mrs. Larkin. Larkin had told Ern she was ill, so presumably she was in bed in the back room.

A thought suddenly struck him. Could the Larkins *possibly* be hiding the Lorenzos? The couple were apparently unable to get out of the country, and must be on the run, hiding here and there—running the risk of being spotted. It would be a clever thing to do to come hide in the very place where no one would think they would dare to be!

There didn't seem anything else to do now but walk away. Now that Poppet was still there, after all, new plans would have to be made, and new ideas thought of. Especially some plan that would bring in the possibility of searching the cottage in case the Lorenzos *were* hiding there!

'Larry! Pip! Let's go!' called Fatty. 'Hey, Buster, stop trying to paw down the wall under Poppet's window. Come on, Bets and Daisy—you coming too, Ern? Let's go back to my shed and talk.'

They left Poppet still barking happily at the window, her stiff tail wagging hard. There was no sign of Larkin.

He was presumably raking out the boiler-fire, still warm from the night before.

They all rode off together, Fatty thinking hard. They piled their bicycles against Fatty's shed, and went in. Fatty lighted the little oil-stove.

'Biscuits on that shelf, Larry,' he said. 'Lemonade below—or shall we have cocoa? I feel cold.'

Everyone voted for cocoa, and Pip was sent up to the kitchen to ask for milk.

'We can boil it on the oil-stove as usual,' said Fatty. Daisy will you see to it?

It was soon cosy and warm in the shed, and the milk boiled quickly on the top of the stove. Everyone sat down on boxes or rugs, Ern too. He loved times like this. He gazed round the shed in awe—coo, the things that old fatty had there!

Fatty's shed was indeed a medley of all kinds of things— —old clothes of every kind for disguises—a few wigs hanging on nails—boxes of make-up, with many kinds of moustaches inside, as well as grease-paint and powder. There was no end to the fascinating array. There was even a postman's hat and uniform! Now how in the world did Fatty get that, Ern wondered.

Once they were all supplied with biscuits and hot cocoa, Fatty began to talk.

'I think the time has come for a recap,' he said. 'We...'

'What's a recap?' said Bets, much to Ern's relief. He too had no idea what Fatty meant by a 'recap' but did not dare to ask.

'Oh—recap is short for recapitulation,' said Fatty. 'I...'

'Yes, but I don't know what recapit—pit—what-ever you said, is either,' said Bets.

'Dunce!' said Pip, in his brotherly way.

'All right—you tell her what it is, Pip,' said Fatty, at once.

'Well, it's—it's—well, I don't exactly, know how to explain it, but I know what it means,' said Pip.

'Dunce! said Fatty, and turned to Bets. 'A recap just means I'll go quickly over all that has happened, so as to give us a clear picture—and then it makes future planning easier. Got it, Bets?'

'Oh yes,' said Bets gratefully, 'Go ahead, Fatty.'

Fatty began. 'Well, the tale begins when we all saw the Lorenzos that day at the station, being seen off by their friends. Poppet was with them—but was given to old Larkin who had apparently been told to fetch her and take her home when the Lorenzos had departed in the train. He went off with her under his coat. Correct?'

'Correct,' said everyone.

'Right. The next thing we heard was that the police were after the Lorenzos because they had apparently been clever enough to steal a very valuable picture from some picture gallery. They probably meant to leave this country with it and sell it abroad somewhere. Correct?'

'Correct,' chorused everyone.

'They were then spotted here and there, and apparently gave up the idea of trying to get out of the country for the time being. A crate was seen in a car which they stole to get away from one of their hiding-places—presumably containing the picture.'

'But, Fatty, they only had two little suitcases with them when *we* saw them,' said Daisy. 'No crate at all.'

'Well, they wouldn't go off on a journey with an enormous crate!' said Fatty. 'I imagine that after they had stolen the picture, frame and all, they got some friend of theirs, someone as dishonest as themselves, to hide the picture for them—and have it crated and put ready for them at some place where they could call for it.'

'So wherever they go they've got to take the picture with them now, I suppose?' said Pip. 'A bit of a nuisance, I should think!'

'A *great* nuisance!' said Fatty. 'But unless they can undo the crate, destroy it, take out the picture and hide it somewhere really safe, they've *got* to carry it around!'

'And that's what they've been doing,' said Larry. 'And I bet they've brought it here and hidden it somewhere! I bet they came last night with it!'

'I was coming to that,' said Fatty. 'It does seem to me that if they *were* seen at Maidenhead they would not have come so near their home if they were not making for it for some reason. And the only reasons that are possible are—to hide the picture, and to take Poppet.'

'And they *didn't* take Poppet,' said Bets.

'No they didn't, so we were wrong there,' said Fatty. 'Well, I think perhaps we were silly to think they'd take that little poodle. Once it had disappeared from the Larkins, the police would have been told to keep a watch-out for a couple with a beautiful little poodle—you can't hide a dog if it's with you all the time!'

'They could have dyed it black,' said Bets.

'Oh yes—they would certainly have done that,' said Fatty. 'But it would still be a poodle-and would arouse suspicion, black, white or red, if the police were looking for one accompanying a couple of people in a hotel, or boarding-house or wherever the Lorenzos went.'

'I suppose we come now to last night,' said Pip. 'Ern's the only one who really knows about that.'

'Yes, Ern, relate what you know,' said Fatty. 'We

already know it, but it might clear things a bit, and make us think of something new.'

Ern cleared his throat and stood up as if he were going to recite in class.

'Well—I was asleep in the tree-house and a noise woke me up—sort of humming noise, like an aeroplane or car. Then after a bit I heard splashing and I looked out and saw the swans on the river, sailing on the water. Fine they looked, too. Then I went to sleep—and I woke up again thinking I heard voices not far off—maybe outside the Larkins' cottage—and I heard Poppet barking madly––sort of happy-like. That's all.'

Ern sat down abruptly, blushing red. Everyone felt as if they really ought to clap, but nobody did. Bets gave him an admiring smile and Ern felt proud of himself.

'Now we come to this morning, when we all go off expectantly to the Larkins' cottage, feeling sure that Poppet will be gone—and lo and behold, she is there, as happy as a sand-boy!' said Fatty.

'Which is a bit funny,' said Larry, 'because the Larkins haven't been nice to her, as *we* know!'

'Yes, said Fatty. 'Well-there's our recap, Bets. Now— has anyone any remarks to make, or any good suggestions.'

'I'm sure the Lorenzos were there last night, because Poppet is so happy this morning,' said Pip.

'I thought that too,' said Bets. 'But now 'I'm wondering! If they had come *and gone* last night wouldn't Poppet be down in the dumps again?'

'You've got a point there, Bets,' said Fatty.

'I say! Perhaps they're still there!' said Pip. 'Hiding in the cottage!'

'Yes. Or perhaps in the house,' said Daisy, 'the *big*

house, I mean. They would have keys, wouldn't they?'

'Oh yes,' said Fatty. 'Actually it did cross my mind that the Larkins might be hiding the Lorenzos. It would make the cottage very crowded though—and the Larkins would be scared in case the police came to search. But Poppet is so very happy that I can't help thinking they are still somewhere about. *Mrs.* Lorenzo anyhow!'

'Fatty! Can't we somehow manage to look in the cottage?' said Bets. 'Oh, do think of some way. *It* would be too marvellous if *we* discovered the Lorenzos, after the police have been looking for them for ages!'

'Right. That's a good plan,' said Fatty. 'Does anyone happen to know if the cottage has got electric light? I didn't notice. Very remiss of me!'

'Yes. It has,' said Larry, surprised. 'Fatty! What are you going to do? *I know* you've got a plan. What is it?'

FATTY certainly had a plan. That was quite clear. His eyes shone and he looked excited.

'Yes! I'll tell you what I'll do! I'll dress up as an electricity man, and go to the Larkins' cottage to read the meter!' He looked round at the others with a broad grin.

Larry slapped him on the back. 'Wizard! You can get right in then and it wouldn't take you a minute to see if there was any place for people to hide in that tiny cottage. There can only be three rooms at the most—all downstairs. There's no second storey.'

'It's a pity Mrs. Larkin is ill, or you could have gone today,' said Bets.

'Blow!' said Fatty. 'I forgot that for the moment. I can't very well go blundering into the cottage if she's sick in bed.'

'I'll watch from the tree-house,' said Ern, excited. 'If I see her about I'll nip along and tell you, Fatty. I'll sit up there all the afternoon.'

'Right,' said Fatty. 'Well—anyone else got any suggestions or brain-waves?'

'I was wondering how the Lorenzos arrived last night,' said Daisy. 'If they came by car—which would be rather a silly thing to do, I should think—wouldn't the car be hidden somewhere in the grounds? That's if the Lorenzos themselves are still in hiding there, I mean. Unless, of course, someone drove them there and dropped them. It might have been the car that Ern heard.'

'That's a point, too,' said Fatty. 'We could go up to the grounds this afternoon, and have a look at the drive entrances. If we see recent tracks we'll know a car came last night—and we'll look for it!'

'Another thing,' said Pip, 'can we find out if the big house has been entered by the Lorenzos? They might even have been daring enough to go into it and hide the picture there. The house has been already searched for that—so it might be a jolly good hiding-place.'

'Yes, We can find that out too,' said Fatty. 'I could ring up the Superintendent to ask him if he's had any report about it.'

'Well—we're getting on!' said Pip. 'My mind is certainly a lot clearer since our recap!'

'I don't see that there's anything more we can suggest,' said Larry. 'At the moment we are going on the hope that the Lorenzos came by car last night, hid it in the grounds, got into the big house, hid the picture there, went to the Larkins and woke them up, and persuaded them to let them into the cottage to hide till all the hoo-ha has blown over.'

'Right!' said Fatty. 'You put that very well, Larry. This has been a very good conference-*real* detectives couldn't have had a better one! Now let me see—my first job is to ring up the Superintendent and ask if he knows whether the house was entered last night or not. Next, we must go up this afternoon and examine the drive entrances. Third, I must disguise myself as a meter-reader, and see if I can examine the cottage.'

'Meter-readers carry a kind of card backed by a board with elastic round, don't they?' said Daisy. 'I know ours does. And a peaked cap—and a torch to read the meter. That's all. Ours doesn't have a uniform.'

'I'll find out from our cook,' said Fatty. 'But I don't think it much matters what I wear really, so long as I produce a card and flourish a torch, and announce "Come to read your meter, Mam!" in a loud voice.'

They all laughed. 'You'll get into the cottage all right if you say it like that!' said Bets.

'I say! What about you dressing up in whatever you're going to wear, and coming with us to examine the drive entrances,' said Larry. 'You can put your torch and cap and card into your pocket to use if we find out that Mrs. Larkin is out and about again. Otherwise you'd be sitting at home waiting for Ern to nip down and fetch you as soon as he saw any sign of Mrs. Larkin. And if he *doesn't* see anything of her, you'll be moping at home all alone!'

'Yes. That's an idea,' said Fatty. 'Ern, listen—you can do what you suggested this afternoon, and sit up in the tree-house, with a whistle—and if you see anything of Mrs. Larkin, just whistle three times, because we shall be somewhere snooping the grounds.'

'Whistle *twice* if you want to warn us about anything––Goon or strangers and so on,' said Larry. 'Three times for Mrs. Larkin.'

'And I'll then come up to the cottage and do my meter-reading act,' said Fatty. 'Well––is that all understood?'

'Yes,' said everybody.

'Be here at two-thirty,' said Fatty. 'We'll all go together––except you, of course, Ern. You'll be up in the tree as soon after your dinner as you can, won't you?'

'Yes, Fatty,' said Ern importantly. Then he leapt to his feet with a yell that startled everyone considerably and set Buster barking madly.

'Coo—look at the time! Twenty to one and my Aunt Woosh said I was to be back by half-past twelve. I won't get no dinner at all! So-long, everybody!'

Ern disappeared up the garden path at top speed, Buster running excitedly beside him. Everyone laughed. Good old Ern!

That afternoon at half-past two everyone but Ern was outside Fatty's house with bicycles. Fatty, looking rather peculiar, came out with his, Buster with him.

'Are you going to take Buster?' said Bets, pleased. 'I didn't think you would.'

'Well, I can leave him with you if Ern gives the signal for me to go and do some meter-reading!' said Fatty. 'He does so badly want to come—don't you, Buster?'

'Wuff!' said Buster joyfully. He couldn't bear it when the children went off without him. He ran beside the bicycles as they all rode off. Fatty said the run would take off some of his fat, and it wasn't too far for him to run all the way to the river.

'Wait—we're not *going* to the river-path this time!' said Larry, as they all turned down the river-road. 'We've forgotten—we're going to the drive-gates that open on to the lane that leads out of the main road.'

'So we are!' said Pip, and they all swerved the other way. Bets looked at Fatty and giggled.

'You don't really look respectable enough to come riding with us,' she said. 'Did you *have* to make yourself so untidy, Fatty?'

'No really,' said Fatty, with one of his grins. 'I just let myself go, rather!'

He wore an old suit, too big for him, no collar but a scarf instead, and had brushed his hair over his forehead instead of back. In his pocket was cap with a black shiny peak, a card with figures scribbled on it, backed by a small board, a pencil tied to it with string, and a torch.

'No Electricity Board would employ you as a meter-reader,' said Bets. 'For one thing, you're not only untidy but you don't look old enough.'

'Oh, I'll soon remedy that!' said Fatty, and put his hand into his pocket. He pulled out a silly little moustache and stuck it on his upper lip. At once he looked older. Bets laughed.

'You look really *dreadful*! I'm sure no one would ever let you into their house!'

They turned off the main road and came into the little lane that led to the entrance gates of Tally-Ho. They got off when they came to the big gate-posts.

The big double gates were shut. There were two at each entrance to the long, curving drive. Fatty looked at them.

'Well! Whoever drove in there with a car would have quite a business opening those big gates-they're so heavy. I wonder why they're shut.'

'So that people can't drive in, I suppose,' said Larry. 'Fatty, did you ring up the Chief about the house—to know if by any chance anyone had got into it last night?'

'Yes, I did. And apparently even if the Lorenzos had keys to the back, front and side-doors it wouldn't be any good,' said Fatty. 'All the doors have been bolted inside, except a side-door. The police bolted them all—and got out by the side-door, in which they have had a special lock fitted. So nobody can get in except the police——and that too, only by the side-door! Apparently there are a lot of valuable things in Tally-Ho belonging to its real owner-the one who let the house furnished to the Lorenzos.'

'Oh. Well then we needn't bother about the house,'

said Larry. 'We'll just concentrate on trying to find out if a car came here last night, and is hidden away somewhere.'

Fatty was looking at the ground, which was very frosty that day. 'There are wheel-marks,' he said, 'but I can't tell if they are old or new. Anyway, of course, they might be the marks of any police-car that has been here.'

Pip had gone up to the gates to look through them. He gave a sudden exclamation. 'Look here—no car could came through these gates—they have a wooden bar nailed across them!'

The others went to see. Pip was right. A bar was nailed right across each of the double gates. Obviously the police did not mean anyone to go to the house at the moment!

'Well, that rather rules out the Lorenzos coming by car, and leaving it in the grounds,' said Fatty. 'Let's go to the river-path entrance, and see if Mr. Larkin is anywhere about. He might have something to say for once. You never know!'

They went back, and took the road down to the river-path. They were soon standing outside the wicket-gate.

'Look!' said Bets. 'The swans again. What a pity we haven't any bread for them!'

They stood and watched them, the big swans leading the little cygnets to the bank. A boat came by, the oars splashing in the water with a pleasant noise. The swans swam off out of the boat's way.

'Splash-splash!' said Bets, remembering something. 'Ern said he remembered hearing splashes in the night I wonder now—could he have heard a *boat*?'

'Gosh! I never thought of that!' said Fatty. 'A boat!

Yes, they could have come by boat, of course! Let's look and see if there's one in the boat-house-that's the boat-house belonging to Tally-Ho over there, isn't it?'

It was. It was not locked. The children pushed the little door open and looked inside. A small boat lay there, bobbing gently on the little ripples that ran into the boat-house.

Fatty looked at it. Its name was Tally-Ho, so there was no doubt that it belonged there. He was about to step into it when he stopped. A shrill sound had come to his ears.

'Ern's whistle!' he said. 'My goodness, he must have got hold of a *police*-whistle! What a row! He's whistled three times-that is to say he's seen Mrs. Larkin. I'll go and do my meter-reading. Have a look round the boat-house while I'm gone, you others. I'll join you later!'

FATTY pulled on his cap with the black peak, and smoothed his ridiculous little moustache. He tightened the scarf round his neck, and off he went. The others grinned at one another.

'He'll be reading that meter in two minutes!' said Pip. 'I wish I was with him to see what happens.'

Fatty strode off to the wicket-gate and went through it, whistling loudly. He marched straight up to the door—and then saw Mrs. Larkin outside, with Poppet dancing about.

She looked round at him, startled. She really was a peculiar-looking person with her extraordinary wig, her dead-white face, and dark glasses. She sniffed loudly.

'What is it?' she said hoarsely, and coughed. She took out a dirty handkerchief from behind her dull red shawl, and wiped her nose vigorously. She coughed again and kept her handkerchief over her mouth, as if the cold air was too much for her.

'You've got a bad cold, Mam,' said Fatty politely. 'Sorry to bother you, but I've come to read the meter, if it's convenient.'

The woman nodded. She went to the little clothesline and began to take down some washing. Fatty took his chance and went into the house at once, hoping that Mr. Larkin was not there.

There was no one in the front room. Fatty took a hurried look round, and could see nowhere at all for anyone to hide. He went into a back room—a small bedroom in which the bed took up most of the room. Nobody was there either. Fatty looked under the bed to see if anyone was hiding there. No—there were only cardboard boxes and rubbish of all kinds.

The little dog suddenly ran in and put her tiny paws on his leg. Fatty petted her and she wagged her tail. The woman called her. 'Poppet!' and the poodle rushed out again. Fatty went into the third room, an untidy kitchen, with a miserable little larder. There was not much in it, and it was very dirty.

'What a place!' thought Fatty. 'Certainly the Lorenzos are not being hidden by the Larkins—and anyway they'd never be able to endure hiding in a filthy little hole like this. Pooh—it smells!'

He looked at the ceilings of the three rooms, wondering if there might be an attic or boxroom up above. There was no trap-door, no opening of any kind. The Lorenzos were definitely not there—so that was that, thought Fatty!

The woman appeared at the little front door. 'Ain't you finished yet?' she said, her harsh voice grating unpleasantly on Fatty's ears. She sniffed and pulled her old shawl tightly round her.

'Yes. Just going,' said Fatty briskly, snapping the elastic round the card and the board the carried. 'Bit of a job to find the meter. Well, so-long!'

He stepped out into the little garden. Then he looked back suddenly. 'Can I get into Tally-Ho House to read the meter?' he asked. 'I did hear as the folk had done a bunk. Did you know them?'

'It's none of your business,' said the woman sullenly. She sniffed again and shut the door. Poppet had gone in with her.

'Well—I've learnt something definite—and that is that the Lorenzos are certainly not being hidden in that cottage!' he thought, as he made his way to the wicket-gate.

He found Ern just outside, waiting for him. Ern had done his job of watching and whistling and now wanted to join up with the others again. He stared hard at Fatty.

'Lovaduck! You don't half look queer with that moustache, Fatty,' he said. 'Did you find out anything?'

'Only that the Lorenzos are definitely not there,' said Fatty. 'And we also decided that no car had been to the house last night, Ern, because the gates are nailed together with wooden bars.'

'Oh,' said Ern. 'It couldn't have been a car I heard then.'

'Ern—do you think the splashing noise you heard could have been *oars*?' asked Fatty, as they walked along to the boat-house.

'Oars? Well, yes—they might have been,' said Ern. He watched a boat coming up the river and nodded his head. 'Yes, of course! The noise those oars make is exactly like the splish-splash noise I heard.'

'Good! I didn't think it could be the swans,' said Fatty. "They swim so silently. Well, we think now that perhaps last night's visitors came by *boat*!'

'By boat! Where from?' said Ern, startled.

'We don't know—we haven't thought yet,' said Fatty. He hailed the others as they came up to the boat-house. 'Here's Ern—and he thinks those splashes he heard *were* made by the oars of a boat!'

'Oh—it's you, Fatty!' said Bets, looking out of the boat-house door. 'Any news? You don't look very excited!'

'I'm not,' said Fatty, and went into the boat-house, where the others were waiting with Buster. 'I went to read the meter—which I couldn't find, by the way; and there are only three rooms in the place. There was absolutely no sign of the Lorenzos there. I only saw that awful woman with the wig and the sniffs. I must say she looks jolly ill.'

'Oh. Then we're all wrong again,' said Larry, in disappointment. 'The Lorenzos *aren't* hiding here! Now we've got to think of something else. Do you suppose they just came and went away again—without even taking Poppet?'

'Let's get into the boat and talk,' said Fatty. 'We're nice and private in this boat-house.'

They all got into the little boat and let it bob under them up and down, up and down, as the waves ran in and out.

'What I can't understand now is why the Lorenzos *came* last night—if it was them—talked to the Larkins, and then went away again,' said Fatty. 'And where did they come from, in the boat? They must have taken a boat from the opposite bank—or from somewhere further up or down the river . . .'

'Maidenhead!' said Bets, at once.

'Why yes, of course—*Maidenhead*!' said Fatty, at once. 'What an ass I am! Of *course*—that's why they went to Maidenhead—so that they could come here by river.'

'Jolly long way to row,' said Larry. 'Miles!'

'Did they come by motor-boat?' wondered Fatty—and immediately got a clap on the back from Ern.

'You've got it, Fatty! You've got it! *That* was the noise I heard last night! Not a car—nor an aeroplane—but a motor-boat!'

The boat rocked with Ern's excitement! Fatty sat up straight. 'Yes, Ern! That's what you heard! And the oars you heard splashing were the oars of *this* boat going out in mid-stream to the motor-launch! She couldn't come close in here because the water's much too shallow!'

SOME VERY GOOD IDEAS

'WHO took this boat out to the launch?' said Larry at once. There was a pause as all the children sorted out these new ideas.

'There must be somebody here who took out the rowing-boat and brought one or both of the Lorenzos back in it,' said Pip. 'And then probably took them back to the motor-launch again, as they're not hiding here after all.'

'Then, if that's so, the only thing they could have come for would be to bring the picture here to hide!' said Fatty.

'Yes! And if it was Mrs. Lorenzo, she came to see her little poodle too,' said Bets.

'I think you're right, Bets,' said Fatty. 'Certainly the poodle seems much happier now—and her little tail was wagging like anything. Just as if she had seen her mistress—and her master too, probably—and felt that they hadn't really deserted her.'

'I'm sure we're right,' said Daisy, in excitement. 'We've reasoned it all out jolly well! The Lorenzos went to Maidenhead in order to get here by boat. They came by motor-boat—and old Larkin met them in this rowing-boat. He rowed them back here to the bank—helped them to carry the crated picture to shore—took Mrs. Lorenzo to see her precious dog...'

'Yes! That's when I heard the talking and the barking!' said Ern, almost upsetting the boat in his excitement.

'And then when the picture was put in some safe hiding-place, old Larkin rowed them out to the motor-boat again, rowed himself back here and put the boat in this boat-house—and went to bed,' finished Fatty, triumphantly.

'We've solved the mystery!' said Ern, thrilled. The others laughed.

'Indeed we haven't, Ern,' said Fatty. 'We still don't know the two important things—where the Lorenzos are—and where the picture is!'

'Sright!' said Ern, his excitement fading.

'We really ought to have a JOLLY GOOD LOOK for that hidden picture,' said Pip. 'We *know* it was brought here last night—at least, we're pretty sure—so it must be somewhere in the grounds. A big crate wouldn't easily be hidden. It's in some out-house or somewhere like that. It might even be buried.'

'It's too late to look for it now,' said Fatty, looking at his watch.

'Oh, Fatty—just let's have a *quick* look round,' begged Bets. 'We could easily pop our heads into the green-houses and out-houses.'

'All right,' said Fatty. 'Let's get out of this boat then. Be CAREFUL, Ern—you nearly upset us all, leaping out like that!'

'I say—here's something at the bottom of the boat,' said Bets, 'something bright.' She bent down to get it. 'Oh—it's only a nice new drawing-pin, look!'

Fatty took it and stared at it. 'I bet I know where *that* came from!' he said, in excitement. 'From the crate the picture was in! I bet this was one of the pins that pinned the label to the create—big crates usually have labels fastened on with drawing-pins. This is a good find, Bets—it's certain now that the picture and its crate were in this boat last night.'

'Come on, quickly! Let's find it!' cried Pip, and he too almost upset the boat as he leapt out. Everyone felt suddenly excited again.

'It's a clue!' said Bets, taking the pin from Fatty. 'Isn't it, Fatty? Our first real clue!'

Fatty laughed. 'I hope so. Come on, Buster—keep to heel.' They all left the boat-house and went back to the wicket-gate. They looked to see if the Larkins were anywhere about. There was a light already in the little cottage and the six felt sure that the old man and his wife were safely indoors.

They slipped silently into the grounds. Pip stopped and pointed over to a distant corner. 'What's that?' he said. 'It's a bonfire, isn't it? Let's go and see it. I could do with a bit of warmth!'

They were soon standing round the bonfire, which was roaring up as if it had had paraffin put on it. Bets gave a sudden exclamation, and bent down to pick something up. 'Fatty! Look—another drawing-pin just like the other one. The crate must be somewhere here!'

FATTY looked at the pin and compared it with the first one. Yes—they were exactly the same. Then he looked closely at the roaring flames. He picked up a fallen branch of dead wood and poked the fire, raking out what was in it.

'Look!' he said. 'Here's the crate! It's burning in the fire! It's been chopped up well, and thrown here —and then set alight so that no sign may be left of it!'

The children stared as Fatty pointed out bits of wood that had obviously come from a cheap crate. 'Here's a fragment of a label,' said Larry, pouncing on a burning piece of thick paper. He blew out the flames. Only three letters still showed on the paper.

'n-h-e.' said Larry. 'That's all that's left, I'm afraid.'

'It's enough,' said Fatty, at once. 'It tells us where the crate comes from—where it was last sent to be picked up by the Lorenzos! "n-h-e" are the sixth, seventh and eighth letters of the word Maidenhead! Count and see!'

'Gosh Yes!' said Pip. 'You're jolly sharp, Fatty. Well, I suppose the picture's gone now—burnt with the crate, so that no one can discover it.'

'Don't be an ass,' said Fatty. 'The picture has been *unpacked and hidden*—and the crate has been burnt to destroy all signs of it. It would be easy to hide just a painting. I expect it was cut neatly out of its frame— and then the frame and crate burnt together. There's

some funny golden-looking stuff here and there in the fire
—I bet that's all that is left of the lovely frame.'

The fire was still blazing, for the crate had been quite
big. The children left it, certain that there was nothing
more to be learnt there.

'We're getting warm!' said Fatty, as they walked
away. 'We know now that the picture we have to look
for is no longer in a big crate, nor even in a frame. It's
probably just a rolled-up bit of canvas!'

'Yes. That would be *much* easier to hide!' said Daisy.
'It's probably in the Larkins' house.'

'I don't think so,' said Fatty. 'The Lorenzos wouldn't
give the picture itself into the care of those dirty old
Larkins! They might easily ruin it. No—it's put in a
very safe place—but not in that cottage!'

They went out of the wicket-gate and took their
bicycles. They were just about to walk them down the
path to the river-road when Fatty pulled them back.

'Look out! There's Goon!' he said. And, sure enough,
skulking in the shadows not very far in front of them
was the familiar figure of Mr. Goon!

'What's he doing?' whispered Fatty. 'He's following
someone, isn't he?'

'Yes—there's a man some way ahead of him,
carrying a bag of some kind,' whispered back Larry.
'Who is it?'

'I don't know. But we'll soon find out,' said Fatty
briskly. 'As soon as we get to the road, and can ride
our bikes, get on them and ride right up to Goon, ringing
your bells madly, just to tell him we're here—and then
ride on as fast as you can to see who he's following.
I've no idea who it can be—but we ought to find out if
Goon has got some kind of a Suspect he's trailing!'

They leapt on their bicycles as soon as they reached the road and raced after Mr. Goon, who was still hugging the shadows. It was getting dark now and the children had switched on their lamps. They made quite a bright light on the road. As they overtook Mr. Goon he crouched back into the shadows, not wanting to be seen.

'Jingle-jingle-rrrrr-ing, tinga-linga-long!' went the bells as they raced past him.

'Night, Mr. Goon!' yelled Fatty. 'Pleasant walk to you!'

'Good night, good night, Mr. Goon,' shouted everyone, and Ern boldly yelled, 'Night, Uncle!' as he raced past, almost deafening Goon with his very loud bell.

'Gah!' said Mr. Goon in angry disgust. Now they had warned the man he was trailing—yes, he had shot off into a nearby wood. He'd never find him again! Gah!

The six bicyclists saw the man quite clearly. It was Mr. Larkin, with a shopping bag over his arm, shuffling along, his back bent and his head poked forward. His old cap was down over his nose as usual. He went into a little thicket of trees and disappeared.

'He must have been going shopping,' said Bets. 'Why is Goon trailing him? Perhaps he thinks he may lead him to some Clue!'

'Probably,' said Fatty. 'Well, he'll find it difficult to trail old Larkin now. How I'd love to lead Goon a good old dance if he followed me!'

'Yes! You'd have him panting and puffing!' said Pip. 'You'd better disguise yourself as Larkin, and have some fun with Goon!'

Fatty laughed. 'I've a jolly good mind to! I really have! It would serve Goon right for telling that frightful fib about me to the Superintendent—saying I'd locked him up in the boiler-house—and Johns too. I don't suppose either of them even *heard* the door being locked. I bet they were snoring too loudly.'

'Oh, Fatty—will you *really* dress up as Larkin? When?' asked Bets. 'Please, please show us yourself if you do.'

'All right,' said Fatty, feeling very drawn to the idea of giving Goon a slight punishment for his untruthful tale to the Chief. 'I'll have tea and then I'll have a shot at it. I only hope Goon won't retire to bed for the evening, seeing that he had a late night last night! I'd dearly love to lead him round the town!'

'Don't forget to come and see us first!' called Bets, as they parted at the cross-roads. Fatty grinned to himself as he rode on. Yes—he'd certainly like to have a bit of fun with Goon!

Fatty had a very good tea indeed. He had it by himself because his mother was out, and the cook, who completely spoilt him, piled his tray with all the things he liked best. By the time he had finished Fatty didn't feel very like having a bit of fun with anyone!

'Well—at any rate I'm fat enough to masquerade as the plump Mr. Larkin!' he thought, looking at himself in the long mirror down in his shed. 'Now then—let's sort out a few Larkin-like clothes.'

He went rapidly through his enormous collection of clothes, pulling out drawer after drawer of the big old chest. 'Ah—baggy trousers, stained and messy. Good. Old boots. Frightful old overcoat—my very worst one!'

He pulled out a coat that had long since been

discarded by the last-but-one gardener the Trottevilles had had. Just right!

'Scarf—dirty grey and raggedy. This will do.' He shut his eyes for a moment and pictured old Bob Larkin clearly in his mind. Fatty had a wonderful gift for clear observation, and he could see the old fellow almost as if he were there before him.

'Nasty little unkempt beard—straggly moustache—shaggy eyebrows—glasses with thick lenses—and a horrible cap with a peak pulled sideways over his face. Yes—I can do all that!'

Fatty worked quickly and happily. First of all he made up his face and changed it utterly. Wrinkles appeared, and shaggy eyebrows over eyes almost hidden under thick glasses. A straggly moustache, a tooth gone in front (Fatty blacked one out!) and a beard that he trimmed to resemble Mr. Larkin's—thin and untidy. He glued it to his chin and looked at himself in the glass.

'You horried old fellow!' said Fatty to his reflection. 'You nasty bit of work! Ugh!! I don't like you a bit! Put on your scarf and cap!'

On went the scarf, and then the cap at exactly the right angle. Fatty grinned at himself. He was old Larkin to the life!

'I hope to goodness I don't meet Mother coming in or she'll scream the place down!' said Fatty. 'Now, Buster, I regret to say I can't take you with me tonight-and in any case a self-respecting, well brought-up dog like you wouldn't want to be seen out with an old rogue like me!'

Buster didn't agree. He didn't mind how Fatty looked—he was always his dearly-beloved master!

Fatty shut Buster up and made his way cautiously to the road. It was dark now and no one was about.

Fatty took his bicycle and rode to Pip's. He gave their special whistle and Pip came flying down to the garden.

'Is it you, Fatty? I'm longing to see you. Larry and Daisy are here—and Ern's come along too. I can' see you here, it's too dark—it's quite safe to come up because Mother's got a bridge party on. Don't make a noise, that's all.'

Fatty went up to the playroom. Pip flung the door open and Fatty went in, bent and stooping, shuffling along with a half-limp just like old Larkin.

Bets gave a little scream. 'Oh no—it's not Fatty. It's Mr. Larkin himself. Fatty's sent him in to trick us!'

'Lovaduck!' said Ern, startled.

'Marvellous, Fatty, marvellous!' cried Larry, and clapped him on the back.

Fatty gave a horrible hollow cough, and then cleared his throat as he had heard Larkin do. He spoke in a cracked old voice.

"Ere! Don't you slap the stuffing out of me like that, young feller! I'll have the police on you, straight I will. Yus—I'll call in me old pal, Mr.Goon!'

They all roared with laughter. 'It's the best you've ever done, Fatty, quite the best. Oh, can't we come with you?'

'No,' said Fatty, straightening up and speaking in his own voice. 'For all we know I shan't find Goon wandering about on the watch for me, thinking I'm Larkin—he'll probably be in his armchair, snoozing over a pipe.'

'You'd better go now,' said Pip urgently. 'I can hear Mother bustling about. She's probably coming up here to fetch something. Go, Fatty—and jolly good luck. You look simply FRIGHTFUL!'

Fatty went downstairs cautiously, and crept to the garden door just as Mrs. Hilton came along to go up the stairs. He found the big black cat outside the garden door, waiting to come in, and gave her such a shock that she leapt into the night with a howl!

Fatty mounted his bicycle and rode off to Goon's. He saw a light in Goon's front window and looked in. Yes—Goon was there, looking through some letters. Fatty decided to give him a fright.

He went up the window, and pressed his face against it. Then he coughed his hollow cough. Mr. Goon looked up at once, and gaped when he saw what he thought to be the face of old Larkin at his window.

'Hey, you!' cried Mr. Goon. 'I want to speak to you! Hey!' He grabbed his helmet, put it on and rushed out.

Fatty hurried away, and then began to walk like old Larkin, shuffle-limp, shuffle-limp. Goon saw him in the distance and paused. Oho—so old Larkin had been spying on him through the window, had he? Well, he, Goon, would have another try at stalking him. Where was he going to at this time of night? Goon felt very, very suspicious of Mr. Larkin!

'Peering in at me like that! Must be mad! He knows more than he's said he does,' thought Goon to himself, and set off after the supposed Mr. Larkin, keeping well to the shadows.

Fatty chuckled. 'Come on, Mr. Goon! I'll take you for a lovely walk! Do you good to take off some of your weight. Come along!'

GOON followed Fatty as closely as he dared. Fatty, looking back every now and again, decided to lead Goon to an allotment, where there were a few sheds. He could look into each one and make Goon wonder what he was doing.

He went as quickly as he could, shuffle-limp, shuffle-limp, and Goon marvelled that old Larkin could get along so quickly with his bad leg. Fatty, having a quick look round, also marvelled that big, burly Goon managed to hide himself so well in the dark shadows. Goon was really quite clever sometimes!

He came to the allotments, and Goon took a loud hissing breath! Oho! He was after tools or something, was he? That Larkin! He never had liked him, and now that he was mixed up in this Lorenzo case Goon was even more suspicious of him. He even began to wonder if Larkin knew where the stolen picture was!

Fatty enjoyed himself. He examined sheds and even bent down to pick some grass, which Goon immediately noted. 'Ah—what's he picking now? Brussels sprouts, I'll be bound! The rascal!'

Fatty left the allotments and went into the children's playground not far off. Goon, standing behind a tree, watched him suspiciously. Now what was old Larkin going into the playground for? Something queer, anyway!

To his great astonishment Fatty went to one of the swings and sat down. He began to swing to and fro watching the amazed Goon out of the corner of his eye.

'Look at that!' said the mystified Goon to himself. 'He must be daft—quite daft. Coming here at night to have a swing! Ah—he's off again. I wouldn't be surprised if he's not on the look-out for a little burglary!'

Fatty slipped out of the playground chuckling. He went into the well-lighted main street. There someone stopped him.

'Well, Bob Larkin! Haven't seen you for some time! Come and have a bite with me and my missus!'

Fatty looked at the speaker—a tall thin man with a drooping moustache. He answered in Larkin's quavering old voice.

'I'm not too bad! Can't stop just now, though. Got some business to do!' And off he went, shuffle-limp, shuffle-limp. Goon loomed up out of the shadows. Who was that Larkin had spoken to? Had he come out to meet anyone—someone sent by the Lorenzos, perhaps? Dark suspicions began to form in Mr. Goon's mind. What was old Bob Larkin up to?

Fatty took him back to the playground again and had another swing. By this time Goon didn't know whether to think that Larkin was completely mad, or was waiting about to meet somebody—and filling in his time with a few odd things such a having a swing.

He decided to tackle old Larkin. This wasn't funny any more—hanging about under bushes and trees on a cold January night, watching somebody rush up and down through the town, peep into sheds, swing to and fro... he'd have to find out what he was doing. So he hailed the shuffling fellow in front of him.

'Hey, you! Bob Larkin! I want to speak to you!' But the figure in front only hurried on more quickly, trying to keep under the dark trees. Goon became much more suspicious.

'Why doesn't he stop when he's told to! He knows my voice all right! HEY! BOB LARKIN!'

On went Fatty, grinning to himself. Come on, Goon—a nice long walk will do you all the good in the world. Where shall we go now?

Fatty thought that a really good finish would be to take Goon right back to Larkin's cottage! He could easily disappear somewhere there, and Goon would think that old Larkin had gone into his little house. Fatty chuckled.

Goon soon realized that Larkin was off home, and he began to run. To his enormous surprise, the figure in front began to run too! Gone was the limp, gone was the shuffle! Goon couldn't believe his eyes.

Down to the river—along the river-path—through the little wicket-gate—up the path to Larkin's cottage which stood under the shadow of the tall tree in which was Ern's tree-house.

Goon panted after Fatty. Slam, went the gate and up the path came Goon, full of rage. He'd teach old Larkin to lead him a dance like this, and not answer when he was shouted at!

Fatty hid in a bush, and watched Mr. Goon stride up to the little cottage. He knocked so fiercely on it with his knuckles that he almost scraped the skin off. The door opened cautiously, and Bob Larkin's head appeared in the crack, gazing at Goon's angry face in amazement.

'Now then, you!' said Goon angrily, 'what's the meaning

of all this?'

'All what?' said Larkin.

Goon snorted. It was one of his very best snorts. 'Gah! Don't try and put it across me that you don't know what you've just been doing. Leading me such a dance— swinging in the playground. . .'

Larkin looked more and more amazed. He called back over his shoulder to Mrs. Larkin. 'I haven't set foot out of doors tonight, have I?'

'No,' came back the answer, followed by a sniff and a cough.

'There you are!' said Larkin. 'You've made a silly mistake.' He tried to shut the door but Mr. Goon put his big foot in to prevent him.

'You mean to tell me you haven't been trotting in front of me this last hour?' he panted in rage. 'You mean to tell me you didn't snoop in them allotment sheds to see what you could take—and...'

'You're mad!' said Mr. Larkin, really alarmed now.

'What were you out for tonight?' asked Mr. Goon. 'That's what I want to know. You'll be sorry for this, Larkin. Obstructing the Law, that's what you're doing. And you can be put in prison for that, and well you know it. Where's me notebook?'

He took his foot out of the door for half a moment and quick as lightning. Mr. Larkin crashed it shut. There was the sound of a key turning in the lock.

Fatty began to laugh. He had been bottling it up, but now he couldn't hold it in any longer. Afraid that Mr. Goon would hear him, he made his way to the back of the cottage, his handkerchief over his mouth. He stood there, shaking with mirth, thinking of old Larkin's amazement, and Goon's fury. Oh, what a night!

After a while he quietened down. Where was Goon?

There wasn't a sound of him now. He must have gone home in rage, to write out a report of the night's doings. How queer it would sound!

Fatty decided to wait a minute or two, in case Goon hadn't gone. He sat down on an old box, looking exactly like a poor, tired old man!

Then things began to happen again. The back door suddenly opened, and a beam of light shone right on the surprised Fatty. Mrs. Larkin stood there with some rubbish in her hand to put into the dust-bin, and she saw Fatty clearly. She put her hand up to her mouth, and a look of real terror came over her white face. She rushed screaming indoors.

Fatty got up at once, suddenly sobered. He hadn't meant to frighten anyone—but, of course, Mrs. Larkin must have been completely amazed to see him sitting there.

'She leaves her husband sitting indoors—opens the back door and apparently sees him sitting outside too!' thought Fatty. 'No wonder she screamed. A husband behind her, and a husband in front of her—not too good!'

Fatty crept away to the Woosh's garden, which was very near the back of the Larkins' cottage. He didn't want to risk being seen by Mrs. Larkin again—she would probably faint with fright, poor thing!

He was just squeezing through the hedge into the Woosh's garden, when he heard someone coming out of the Larkins' back door, someone speaking in an urgent whisper, though Fatty could not hear what was said.

He wished he hadn't chosen such a thick piece of the hedge—blow it, he couldn't get through! Then somebody came right up to the hedge, and caught hold of him. Fatty caught the glint of glasses, and saw that it was old Larkin himself. Now what was he to do!

He shook off the man's hand and with one great heave, fell into the garden next door. The voice came urgently again. 'How did you get back? What have you come for?'

But Fatty did not wait to answer. He fled.

He ran to the Woosh's gate and slipped out of it—only to hear a familiar voice say, 'Ah! I *thought* you'd be out and about again, Bob Larkin! You come alonga me!'

Goon was standing in the shelter of some bushes, and he made a grab at Fatty's arm as he passed. Fatty had a terrible shock! He pulled away, and heard his coat ripping. But he was like a hare, with Goon after him. Where now?

The wicket-gate of the Larkins' had been left open—and Fatty dashed back through it. He could easily hide somewhere in the grounds. Goon panted after him—and just then, round the corner of the cottage, attracted by the noise, came Bob Larkin himself, having found it impossible to get through the hedge after Fatty.

Fatty ran full-tilt into him, and they both fell over. Goon came up, and shone his lamp downwards in glee. Ah—now he'd got that fellow all right!

To his enormous astonishment he saw two Mr. Larkins on the ground. Two faces with straggly beards and shaggy eyebrows and thick glasses looked up at him, blinking in the light of the lantern.

'Ow!' said Goon, his hand beginning to shake, "Ere—what's all this? I don't like it! I... I... d-d-don't li...'

Poor Goon couldn't bear it any longer. He turned and ran down the path as if a dozen Mr. Larkins were after him. He made a peculiar moaning sound as he went,

To his enormous astonishment he saw two Mr. Larkins

and if Fatty hadn't had all the wind knocked out of him by the collision with Larkin, he would have laughed loudly.

'Now,' said Mr. Larkin, in a peculiarly unpleasant voice, 'Now, just you . . .'

But Fatty was off again, and away into the darkness. He made for Tally-Ho House. There were many corners there to hide in if Larkin came after him.

But he heard no more sound from Larkin. He stood for a while near the boiler-house, listening, but could hear nothing at all. Fatty gave a little sigh. What an evening! He thought it would be just as well to go home again now—he really felt astonishingly tired!

He cautiously left his hiding-place and made his way round the house. It was very dark there, with high trees all round, overshadowing the house. Fatty didn't dare to put on his torch, for fear of being spotted, so he stepped forward slowly and carefully.

He bumped his head into something hard, and stopped. What was this? He put out his hand and took hold of something. It felt like a long pole of wood, slanting upwards—and wait, there was more—gosh, of course—it was a ladder! A ladder leading up to the balcony. Wheeeew! What was this now?

Fatty went up the ladder! It led to the balcony rails. Fatty cautiously climbed over the rails and felt about for the door. Was someone inside the house?

But the door wouldn't open. It was locked. Fatty remembered what the Superintendent had told him—all doors were bolted on the inside except the garden door, which had had a special lock put on it so that only the police could get in and out.

Who put the ladder there then? An ordinary burglar? Was he still waiting about in the shadows, furious with

Fatty for discovering his ladder?

Fatty was suddenly overcome with panic, and slid down the ladder at top speed. He tore off to the wicket-gate, seeing Goons and Larkins and burglars in every shadow! It wasn't till he was safely in the very middle of a well-lighted road that he calmed down, and felt ashamed of himself—gosh, he didn't often feel scared! Whatever had come over him?

ABOUT half an hour later Fatty sat in a hot bath and thought over the extraordinary evening. It needed a little sorting out!

First of all, should he ring up the Chief and tell him about the ladder? No—he might have to explain his mad idea of disguising himself as Larkin and leading Goon such a dance. Fatty felt that the Chief might not see the funny side of that. He wondered if Goon would make a report on the evening. How would he explain two Larkins?

Then that ladder. Fatty was inclined to think that the thief had been up it, tried the door and given up the idea of getting in when he found it was both locked *and* bolted. In any case it would take a bold burglar to come back again after he had heard all the shouting and scrimmaging that had been going on. Fatty felt sure that if the burglar *had* been anywhere about, he would certainly have gone while the going was good!

He was sorry he had frightened Mrs. Larkin. Then he remembered Goon's face of horror when he shone his lantern down and saw two Mr. Larkins on the ground looking up at him. Two! He must have thought he was seeing double! Fatty grinned, and began to soap himself thoroughly.

He thought about Mr. Larkin. What was it that he had said to Fatty when he first saw him? Fatty frowned and tried to remember. It was something like 'How did you get back? What have you come for?'

It seemed a funny thing to say—unless Larkin imagined he was Lorenzo. He probably couldn't see him properly in the dark. Or more likely Fatty hadn't heard him correctly. Fatty dismissed the incident from his mind and began to worry once more about whether he ought to telephone Superintendent Jenks or not.

'No. I'll leave well alone,' thought Fatty, soaping himself all over again. 'Of course, if Goon telephones him with his tale of chasing two Bob Larkins, and the Chief puts two and two together, and jumps to the fact that one of them was me, then I shall quite likely be all set for trouble—I'll chance it. I don't think Goon *will* send in that report!'

Goon didn't. When at last he got home, in a state of fury, fright and utter bewilderment, he sat down heavily in his armchair, and stared at nothing. He forgot that he had asked the daily woman to come in and cook his dinner for him that night, and when she knocked at his door, he almost leapt from his chair in fright. He gazed at the door, half afraid that another Mr. Larkin would appear round it.

'Who—who is it?' he said, in husky tones.

The woman put her untidy head round the door, surprised at Goon's unusual voice. 'Only me, sir. About your dinner.'

'Ah,' said Goon, in a more ordinary voice. 'Yes. Yes, bring it in.'

The evening's mishaps had not spoilt Goon's appetite. He thought hard as he ate his stew, and gradually recovered from his fright. He jabbed at a bit meat.

'*Two* larkins. Sure as I'm here, there were two. But what will the Chief say if I send in a report and say I saw *two*? "My dear Goon," he'll say, "you must have been seeing double. Hadn't you better buy yourself some glasses?"'

Goon mimicked the Chief's voice, and felt very pleased with his imitation. 'Ho, Chief!' he said. 'Ho! Glasses I need, do I? Let me tell you this—I don't need glasses, and I don't need advice from you—all I want is a spot of promotion, which is more than due to me...'

He jumped at another knock at the door, but it was only the woman again. 'Oooh—I thought you must have someone here,' she said. 'I heard talking.'

'Bring in the pudding,' said Goon loftily. Ha, *he'd* tell the Chief a few things if he had him here this very minute! But no, not about the two Larkins. On the whole it would be better to keep that to himself. Goon began to doubt whether he *had* seen two? Had he? Yes, he had. No, he hadn't. Yes—ah, here was the pudding, steaming hot, too!

Next morning Fatty sent for the others early. He had such a lot to tell them. He had got up very early himself because he had suddenly remembered that he had left his bicycle somewhere near Goon's house, and he didn't want Goon to spot it there. So, before eight o'clock Fatty had shot off to get it, and was very thankful to see that it was still there!

'Fatty! What happened last night? Did Goon see you?' asked Bets, as soon as she saw him.

Fatty nodded. He felt rather pleased with himself now. What a tale he had to tell! He began to tell it, and the others roared with laughter. As for Ern, he rolled over and over on the floor unable to stop—the thought of his fearsome uncle chasing Fatty all over the place, and even watching him on the swings was too much for him.

'Stop, Fatty! Stop a bit, and let me get over this,' begged

poor Ern. 'Oooh, my sides! Fatty, stop!'

The story went on to its thrilling end. Everyone listened with the utmost attention, even Buster. When Fatty came to the bit where he had bumped into the ladder, everyone exclaimed. 'Here's the bump I got on my forehead—see?' said Fatty, displaying quite a satisfactory bump.

'Oh! I *wish* I'd been there to see all this!' said Bets. 'What did you do after you had come down the ladder, Fatty?'

'Oh—I just went home and had a bath,' said Fatty, deciding that he needn't spoil this thrilling tale by relating how he had scuttled back home at top speed!

'A very interesting evening!' said Pip. 'But it doesn't seem to get us much farther, Fatty, does it? Do you plan for us to do anything this morning?'

'Well—I thought we'd go and see if the ladder is still there,' said Fatty. 'We might find footprints or something at the bottom—you never know.'

'I can't think why old Larkin asked you why you had come back, when he saw you,' said Larry. 'He must have thought you were Lorenzo.'

'Yes. That's what *I* thought,' said Fatty. 'If he'd seen me *properly*—looking exactly like himself, of course—he wouldn't have asked such an idiotic question. Mrs. Larkin saw me all right though—that's what gave her such a shock, I expect—leaving old Larkin behind her in the house—and seeing another Larkin outside!'

'Let's go,' said Pip, getting up. 'That was a marvellous tale, Fatty. I wish I dared do the things you do, but I daren't. And if I did they wouldn't have such fine endings as yours. I wonder what old Goon is thinking this morning?'

They all went off on their bicycles, Buster in Fatty's

basket. They decided not to go in at the wicket-gate in case old Bob Larkin was in a temper because of the happenings of the night before.

They went past the gate and came to a place where they could easily get into the grounds. They left their bicycles there and made their way to the big house.

'The ladder was on the other side,' said Fatty, and led the way. But as soon as they turned the corner of the house he saw that the ladder was gone.

'It's not there!' he said. 'Well—I wonder if the burglar got in after I left, then—he must have been about, because he's removed the ladder! Gosh—I wish I'd reported seeing it, now—I might have prevented a burglary! I wonder if he managed to get in. Look—there are the marks made by the foot of the ladder in the ground.'

'Let's walk round the house and peep in at the windows to see if any rooms have been ransacked,' said Daisy. So they walked all round, peeping into every window. Nothing was disturbed at all, as far as they could see.

They came to the last window and peered through it. 'Ah—this is the one with the big bowl of dead flowers,' said Fatty, remembering. 'There they are still—deader than ever! And the chairs are still all in their dust-sheets.'

His eyes slid round, remembering everything—and then he frowned. Something was missing. He was sure it was. Something that had puzzled him. Yes—there had been a little rubber bone on the floor, beside that stool. But it was gone now!

Fatty peered and peered, trying to see the bone. But it had definitely gone! How puzzling!

'There's one thing missing,' said Fatty' 'A little rubber

bone-a dog's plaything. It probably used to belong to Poppet the poodle. I saw it down by that stool!'

'You must be mistaken, Fatty,' said Larry. 'Nobody would steal a dog's rubber bone! Nothing seems to be disturbed at all. I don't think that burglar could have managed to get in.'

'I *did* see a rubber bone,' said Fatty. 'I don't make mistakes about a thing like that. I call that very curious. Very curious indeed.'

They left the house and wandered around a little more. Buster left them and went off by himself, having suddenly had a very good idea. He'd go and play with that nice little poodle!

So he trotted off to the cottage and barked a small and polite bark. Poppet at once leapt up to the window-ledge and looked out.

Bets heard Buster barking and ran to get him. She saw the little poodle at the window—and how Bets stared! Not at Poppet—but at something she held in her mouth! She raced back to Fatty, her face scarlet with excitement.

'Fatty! Listen! Poppet's up at the window, and she's got a rubber bone in her mouth!'

Fatty whistled. They all went cautiously down the path—and sure enough, there was Poppet trying vainly to bark with the little rubber bone between her teeth.

'Yes—that's the one,' said Fatty. 'Buster, come here. Look—let's all go quietly back to our bikes and have a talk. This is important.'

They all went to their bikes, feeling suddenly excited. Fatty's eyes shone. 'It must have been the *Larkins* who went into the house last night! Nobody else would have bothered about a rubber bone. *They* had a dog, so it was an ordinary thing to do to pick it up and take it back to Poppet, and...'

'I don't think it was an ordinary thing for them to do,' said Bets. 'We know they're unkind to Poppet—we've even heard them "lamming" her, as they call it. I don't think they'd even *bother* to take her bone back to her!'

'Yet she's got it,' said Fatty. 'Well, then—who else could have taken it to her?'

'Mrs. Lorenzo might,' said Bets. 'Perhaps it was the Lorenzos who got in last night. Perhaps they were here again.'

'Yes, they might have been,' said Fatty. 'If so, that looks as if Larkin did mistake me for Lorenzo when he saw me last night and asked me why I had come back.'

'Oh—here's Poppet! She must have escaped out of the house to look for Buster!' said Bets. 'Listen—Mrs. Larkin is calling her.'

'Take her back, Bets,' said Fatty, 'and see if you can have a chat with Mrs. Larkin. Go on—you might be able to get something out of her!'

'All right,' said Bets, half-scared, and took little Poppet into her arm. She went up the river-path to the wicket-gate, Buster at her heels, trying his hardest to jump up and lick the little poodle's nose.

Bets went right up to the cottage. She could hear Mrs. Larkin calling 'Poppet! Poppet!' and knew she was looking for her over by the big house. Perhaps Bets would have time just to have a look at that rubber bone so that she could tell Fatty exactly what it was like.

So Bets slipped into the small cottage and looked round for the bone. She couldn't see it, but she saw a few that made her scare!

The kitchen table was piled with tins of food- big, expensive tins! How strange! Bets tiptoed into the bedroom. On the bed, neatly folded, were spotlessly clean blankets and an eiderdown! So it *was* the Larkins then who had put that ladder up-and they *had* got in, and *had* stolen things-food-and warm coverings-and they had picked up Poppet's rubber bone and taken it back to her.

WELL! Fatty must be told this at once!

BEFORE Bets could put Poppet down and run to Fatty, there came the sound of footsteps hurrying to the door. Bets turned. It was Mrs. Larkin, in the same old red shawl, hideous wig and dark glasses.

'Oh—you've got Poppet!' she said. 'I thought she'd fallen into the river.'

She took the little poodle from Bets, and the girl watched Poppet licking the woman's face. 'You're kind to her now,' said Bets. 'You weren't at first.'

The woman put Poppet down at once. 'Now you go,' she said harshly. 'You shouldn't have walked in without permission.'

'I'm going,' said Bets. 'Is that Poppet's basket? Oh —there's her rubber bone!'

She took it out of the basket, but the woman snatched it out of her hand and gave her a rough push. Bets ran out. She was puzzled. She waited till the door was shut then she tiptoed back and peeped in at the window. The woman was putting a mat down under the dog's basket, with Poppet fussing round.

Bets made her way back to the others, still puzzled. Why did Mrs. Larkin treat Poppet differently? Perhaps the little dog was so sweet that nobody could be unkind for long. No—it would need something more than that to make the Larkins kind. Well, perhaps the Lorenzos had promised them a lot of money if Poppet was kept happy. That must be it.

Bets told her tale to the others. 'Big, expensive tins! Nice blankets and rugs! They must have helped themselves well,' she said. 'I didn't get anything much out of the woman, though. She was cross and pushed me out.'

'Look—there's somebody going in at the wicket-gate,' said Pip. 'Oh—it's old Larkin. Been shopping, I suppose. No—he's got no basket—and anyway they're plentifully supplied with tins now. All he's got are some papers.'

Fatty looked ti see. 'Quite a few papers!' he said, surprised. 'I suppose he looks through them all each day to see if there is any news of the Lorenzos. He might read at any moment that they had been caught.'

'What so we do now?' asked Pip. 'Go and telephone to the Chief? Nobody but us knows that things have been taken from the house. It beats me how the Larkins got in, because the police said they hadn't keys. I suppose they *must* have some—and knew that possibly the only door that might not be bolted would be the balcony door. And they were right.'

'Come on,' said Fatty, taking his bicycle. 'We'll telephone.'

'I'm glad that horrid Mrs. Larkin is so much nicer to dear little Poppet,' said Bets. 'Honestly, she might be Mrs. Lorenzo the way she fusses her now. Why, she was even putting a rug down under Poppet's basket when I peeped in at the window!'

Fatty suddenly gave such a terrific wobble on his bicycle that he almost fell off. Bets looked at him in surprise.

'What's up, Fatty?' she said.

'Don't speak to me for a minute,' said Fatty in a peculiar voice. 'I'm going to get off. You ride on, all of you.'

Bets looked at him in alarm. 'Are you ill?'

'No I've just got an idea, that's all. Something you said

rang a bell in my mind. Leave me alone for a minute,' said Fatty urgently. The others, quite mystified, rode on a little way and then got off to wait for Fatty. He was standing frowning by the side of the road, still holding his bicycle, and so lost in thought that he didn't even notice Mr. Goon cycling by.

'Ho! What's the matter with *you*!' said Mr. Goon, surprised.

'Be quiet,' said Fatty. 'I'm working something out.'

Mr. Goon went purple. Telling him to be quiet indeed! 'What you working out?' he said. 'Still worrying about them Lorenzos! They're in America or somewhere by now-so's the picture. You'll see! You just work out how to behave yourself and learn a few manners!'

Buster suddenly appeared out of the nearby hedge and flew at Mr. Goon's ankles barking delightedly. The big policeman hurriedly mounted his bicycle, and rode off, kicking out at Buster as he went.

Not even that disturbed Fatty. Goodness, what *could* he be thinking of?

'The great brain's working overtime,' said Pip. 'What *can* have struck him so suddenly?'

'He'll come along and say he's solved everything in a minute,' said Ern. 'You see if he doesn't. He's a wonder, he is!'

Fatty mounted his bicycle again, and came sailing up, looking extremely happy.

'I've got it,' he said. 'I've solved the whole thing! All tied up neatly, read to lay at the Superintendent's feet! My word, I've been a mutt. So have we all!'

'I told you so!' said Ern triumphantly, looking round at the others. 'I said he was solving everything, didn't I, Bets?'

'But—what have you solved?' said Pip. 'Not everything, surely!'

'I think so. I'm just not quite certain about one thing,'
said Fatty. 'However, we'll soon know!'

'Tell us,' begged Larry. 'It's frightful, not knowing
what you're talking about! Do tell us.'

'No time,' said Fatty, riding fast. 'I must get to a
telephone box immediately. Buck up, all of you!'

Everyone rode behind Fatty in a terrific state of
excitement. Fatty pedalled furiously, as if he was in a
race. Poor old Buster was far behind, and Bets felt very
sorry for him, but not even she felt that she could slow
down and pick him up. Buster was most surprised at
everyone's hard-heartedness!

Fatty leapt off his bicycle at the nearest telephone kiosk.
He dashed in, shut the door, and gave a number. The others
congregated outside in wonder.

An answer came at once. 'Police here.'

'I want to speak to the Superintendent, please,' said
Fatty. 'Tell him it's Frederick Trotteville here, and I've
something urgent to say.'

'Right,' said the voice. In a second or two the
Superintendent's crisp voice came over the wire.

' Yes? What is it, Frederick?'

'Sir, can you possibly come over here at once?' said
Fatty. 'I've got everything tied up nicely for you!'

'What do you mean?' said the Chief. 'You don't
mean the Lorenzo case, surely?'

' Yes, sir. I know everything!' said Fatty exultantly.
'I suddenly tumbled to it this morning. It's too long to
tell you over the phone, sir. Can you come over at once
—before things go wrong?'

'You're talking in riddles, Frederick,' said the Chief.

'But I'd better trust you, I suppose. I'll get the car and come at once. Where shall I find you?'

'Up by the Larkins' Cottage, sir,' said Fatty. 'Do you know where it is?'

'Yes,' said the Chief. 'I'll be there.' He rang off, and Fatty put back the receiver, his face glowing. He rubbed his hands in glee before he stepped out of the kiosk.

'Fatty! You *might* tell us what's up,' said Pip. 'It's too bad—seeing you shouting into that phone and not hearing a word you were saying—and then you rub your hands in glee when you've finished. Whatever has happened so suddenly?'

'Tell you as soon as I can,' said Fatty, wheeling his bicycle into the road. 'Come on—we've got to go back to the wicket-gate leading to the Larkins' cottage. The Chief will be there as soon as possible.'

'Gosh-so that's who you've been ringing up!' said Larry, cycling madly after Fatty. 'Is he really coming over?'

'Yes—at once,' said Fatty. 'Hello—where's Buster?'

'We've left him all behind again,' panted Bets. 'He's so miserable. Oh Fatty, do stop and pick him up.'

Fatty stopped. Buster came up at a valiant trot, his tongue hanging out almost to the ground. Fatty picked him up. 'My Poppet!' he said ridiculously, and put him into his bicycle basket. Buster heaved a great sigh of relief.

They set off again, and came to the river-path, where they had to get off and wheel their bicycles. Ern called to Fatty. 'Can't you tell us now, Fatty?'

'Too many people about,' said Fatty aggravatingly. 'Hallo, who are these?'

Two small girls had just rushed out of a nearby gate

and flung themselves on Ern.

'Ern! Come and play with us! Mum's given us a picnic dinner to eat up in the tree-house.'

'Sorry,' said Ern, shaking them off. 'I've got Important Business to do, Liz and Glad. Er—these are my two cousins, Fatty-Liz, or Elizabeth. And Glad. Glad, what's *your* name short for? I never did know.'

'Gladys!' said Glad, with a giggle. 'Ern, we kept watch up in the tree-house as usual this morning, but we only saw Mr. Larkin once—he's just come in-and Mrs. Larkin once. She hung an old rug out on the line, and she's beating it.'

'All right, all right,' said Ern, while all the others looked on, amused. 'They sit up in the tree-house for me and keep their eyes open,' he explained to Fatty. He turned back to Liz and Glad.

'You go back,' he said. 'I *might* come and have dinner with you in the tree-house. Buzz off, now! I'm busy.'

They buzzed off, two skinny little things, delighted that Ern was going to have dinner with them.

'Better not gather round the wicket-gate all in a bunch,' said Fatty, in a low voice, when they got there. 'Let's go up the river-path a little way. Hallo, who's this coming?'

It was Mr. Goon, on his way to tell Mr. Larkin what he thought of him for leading him such a dance the night before. Goon had decided that he hadn't really seen two Mr. Larkins—he was so tired he must have seen double—that was what it was—and Mr. Larkin was going to hear what he thought of old men who went on the swings in the playground at dark of night. Ho!

Goon saw the children further up the path and scowled.

'You clear orf!' he called to them. 'And keep hold of that there dog! What you doing here, crowding up the pathway?'

'We're waiting for someone,' said Fatty calmly.

'Ho yes!' said Mr. Goon rudely. 'And who may you be waiting for, I'd like to know? Your friend the Superintendent perhaps? You just clear orf!'

'Actually yes, we *are* waiting for him,' said Fatty. 'That was a clever guess of yours, Goon.'

'Now don't you try to stuff me up with your Superintendent Jenks!' said Goon, most sarcastically. 'He's miles from here. That I do know, for he telephoned me himself this morning.'

'Well, *you* don't need to wait and see him,' said Fatty. 'He's coming to see *us*, actually!'

Mr. Goon went slowly purple. 'Telling me fairy-tales like that!' he said. 'You clear orf, I say.'

There came the sound of a car in the distance. It stopped. A car door slammed.

'Here he is,' said Fatty to Goon, as quick footsteps came up the river-path. Goon swung round—and his mouth fell open.

It *was* Superintendent Jenks, tall and broad-shouldered as ever, followed by another man. He grinned at Fatty. 'Well.' he said, 'here I am!'

'GOOD morning, sir' said Fatty. Goon was quite tongue-tied, and couldn't say a word. The Chief nodded to Fatty and then to Goon.

'Good morning, Frederick. Well, Goon—you here too? I didn't expect to see you as well.'

'He came along by accident,' said Fatty. 'All the others are here too, sir.'

The Chief saluted all of them solemnly and they saluted back. Ern even clicked his heels together.

'Well, now, let's get down to business,' said the Chief. 'You telephoned to say you'd got this Lorenzo business nicely tied up. Do you mean you know where the Lorenzos are?'

'Yes, sir,' said Fatty, at once, and Goon's eyes nearly fell out of his head. He stared at Fatty and swallowed hard. That boy! That Toad of a Boy. How could *he* know where the Lorenzos were?

The Chief laughed. 'Don't tell me you know where the picture is as well' he said.

'I think I do,' said Fatty, 'but if I don't you can easily make the Lorenzos tell you.'

The Chief turned to Goon. 'I suppose you're in on this too?' he said.

Goon shook his head. He didn't dare to trust himself to speak. The Chief turned back to Fatty. 'Well, where are the Lorenzos?' he said. 'As you've brought me over here, I imagine they're hiding in this district.'

'Yes, sir,' said Fatty. "They're hiding in the Larkins' cottage.'

"That they're not!' burst out Goon. 'Begging your pardon, sir, but I've gone through that cottage three times-there's no one there but the two Larkins. I'm ready to swear to that.'

'Well, the Lorenzos *are* there,' said Fatty. 'Come along, Chief—I'll show you.'

He led the way, the others following in wonder.

What kind of hiding-place were the Lorenzos in? It must be a very small one! Goon went along too, angry and disbelieving.

Fatty rapped at the Larkins' door. It was opened by old Larkin himself, cap on head as usual, and dirty old scarf round his throat. He peered through his thick glasses at Fatty.

'What you want?' he said. Then he saw the rest of the children and the tall Superintendent of police, and made as if to shut the door quickly. But Fatty put his foot in at once.

'We're coming in,' he said. The man that the Chief had brought with him held open the door and everyone filed in, even Buster. Mrs. Larkin was not in the room. They could hear her out in the little kitchen, rattling pans and crockery.

'What's all this?' said Larkin gruffly, in his old man's voice. 'I ain't done nuffin'.'

The little room was very crowded with so many people in it. Larkin shrank back.

'Here's *one* of the Lorenzos,' said Fatty and suddenly snatched off old Larkin's cap. Then, with a quick twist, he stripped off the man's beard, and grabbed off his shaggy eyebrows! Off came the thick glasses too! At once Larkin became a much younger man, an angry man, and a frightened one.

The Chief saluted solemnly and they saluted back

'Wheeeew!' whistled the Superintendent astounded. '*Bill Lorenzo*! Well, you may be a fourth-rate film-actor, but you're a first-class fraud! Masquerading as old Larkin! I saw you myself at the beginning of this case—and I could have sworn you were old Bob Larkin.'

'He wasn't Bob Larkin at *first*,' said Fatty. 'Not for some time. The real Mr. and Mrs. Larkin were here at first. Oh—here comes the other one!'

Mrs. Larkin, hearing voices, had opened the kitchen door, and stood there, staring in fright, with little Poppet in her arms. Before she could shut the door Fatty had stepped behind her.

'And here's *Mrs. Lorenzo*!' he said, and twitched off the extraordinary wig. Underneath it was pale golden hair, wavy and thick. She took off her dark glasses and looked defiantly at the surprised Chief.

'All right! I'm Gloria Lorenzo—and glad to get out of that filthy old wig of Mrs. Larkin's.' She turned to her husband. 'Bill—the game's up.'

The man nodded. It was surprising how the years fell off both of them once they had their glasses off, their own hair exposed, and stood up straight, instead of stooping. How could anyone have thought they were old and ugly?

'A marvellous disguise!' said Fatty in great admiration. 'And you both got away with it, too. Nobody had any suspicions at all that *you* were here instead of the Larkins.'

'Where are the Larkins?' inquired the Chief, looking all round as if they were there too.

'Bob Larkin was about last night,' said Goon. 'I saw him—*and* this fellow too.'

'What—*both together*?' said the Chief in astonishment.

'Why didn't you do something about it? Surely it must have struck you as rather odd that there should be two Bob Larkins?'

'One of them was *me*,' said Fatty smoothly. 'I disguised myself like old Larkin too. Sorry I led you such a dance last night, Goon—still, I had a nice swing!'

Goon almost passed out. He staggered back against the wall and put his hand in front of his eyes. So he'd been chasing *Fatty* last night not Bob Larkin-and even the other Larkin he had seen wasn't the real one. Goon began to feel extremely muddled.

'What happened to the *real* Larkins?' said the Chief. 'I really do want to know. Are they all right?'

'Well, sir, the real Larkins were left here in charge of Poppet, as you know,' said Fatty, 'and they were not kind to her at all. Then one night the Lorenzos hired a motor-launch at Maidenhead, and took it down the river. It stopped in mid-stream opposite the boat-house here...'

'How do you know all this?' asked Bill Lorenzo angrily. 'Has anyone split on us?'

'No,' said Fatty. He turned to the Chief. 'Ern heard noises in the night, sir, and we put two and two together, you see—about the motor-launch, I mean. Well, the *real* Bob Larkin had been warned somehow—I don't know how—to be ready that night with the rowing-boat from the boat-house. So out he went to the launch, and came back with the two Lorenzos.'

'Go on.' said the Superintendent, listening intently.

'Well, my guess is that the Lorenzos and the Larkins changed clothes,' said Fatty. 'The Lorenzos stayed behind in the cottage, and the Larkins went back to the launch, and were whisked off somewhere safe—probably paid quite a bit of money, too!'

'I see, I see it all,' said the Chief, glancing at the two sullen Lorenzos. 'A very astute idea—to come back into the heart of things, where nobody would possibly be looking for them.'

'Yes—very smart, sir,' said Fatty. 'And as they are both actors, and used to making themselves up and acting all kinds of characters, it was easy to imitate the old Larkins. Er-as I have already told you, I myself imitated Larkin so successfully last night that Mr. Goon chased me all over the place!'

'It was *you* I saw here yesterday evening then!' said Bill Lorenzo. 'I thought it was old Bob Larkin himself come back again, and I couldn't understand it!'

'I know—and it was your words to me that partly helped me to understand everything.' said Fatty.

'You said—"*How did you get back? What have you come for?*" And that seemed a pretty queer thing to say to someone masquerading as *yourself!* It could only mean one thing—that you were not Bob Larkin—and therefore thought the other fellow was. But he was me.'

The listening Goon gave a groan. He simply couldn't follow all this. But the others could. Bets gave a little scream. 'Oh, Fatty—of course! That's why he asked you such queer questions—I never thought of that!'

'What made you *really* stumble on the whole thing?' asked the Chief. 'You'd have telephoned me last night if you had guessed then.'

'Yes, I would,' said Fatty. 'Well, lots of things gave me hints, sir. For instance, someone broke into the big house last night—and the only thing that appeared to be taken was that rubber bone on the floor there. And why should anyone *take that*? Only because they had a dog they wanted to give it to! And Bets saw tins of food on the table, and rugs and blankets on the bed-things that the Larkins wouldn't have thought of.'

'*I told* you not to take that bone' said Bill Lorenzo angrily to his wife.

'And then we noticed that whereas at first Mrs. Larkin was very unkind to the poodle, after a bit she wasn't-and the dog ran about happily all the time. That seemed queer too. And then Bets said something that rang a bell in my mind—and everything was as plain as daylight!'

'Whatever did I say?' said Bets, in wonder.

'You said—"*I'm glad that that horrid Mrs. Larkin is so much nicer to dear little Poppet. She might be Mrs. Lorenzo the way she fusses her now!*" And immediately I saw it all—of course, the supposed Mrs. Larking was Mrs. Lorenzo—hence the fuss She made of Poppet, the taking of the tins, and the blankets for warmth--and, of course, the curious taking of such a thing as a rubber bone. It was all easy after that,' said Fatty modestly.

'Well, I'm blessed!' said the Chief. 'You've solved some things in your time, Frederick—but this beats the lot—it really does! What do you say, Goon?'

Goon said absolutely nothing at all. He was in a complete fog. He wished he was the rubber bone on the floor. He wished he was anywhere but where he was!

'You've done a remarkably fine piece of detection, Frederick,' said the Chief warmly. 'I congratulate you. What about the stolen picture? Any idea where it is? You said you weren't sure.'

The Lorenzos both stiffened, and looked quickly at Fatty.

"The Lorenzos hope *I don't* know,' said Fatty.

They don't mind going to prison if they can hope to sell the hidden picture and get plenty of money for it when they come out! I'm not certain about the picture, sir—it's not in the crate any longer, I can tell you that. It was brought here in the boat that night, when the Lorenzos changed over with the Larkins. It was still in the crate then.'

'What happened to it?' asked the Chief.

"The picture was taken out, and the crate and frame were burnt,' said Fatty.

Bill Lorenzo gave a loud exclamation. 'How do you know all this, boy?'

'Brains, just brains,' said Fatty. He turned to the Chief. 'Now, sir, Bets happened to look in at the window here this morning, and saw Mrs. Larkin putting a rug under the poodle's basket—putting it down very carefully too. Quite a nice rug it was, too good to put under a dog's basket—and I think probably the picture has been sewn inside that rug. It's probably backed with hessian, or something—and you'll find the picture between rug and lining.'

'There's no rug under the dog's basket now!' said Bets, looking.

'Lovaduck! *I* know where it is!' said Ern. 'Liz and Glad told us, don't you remember?'

The Chief looked puzzled. So did everyone else. 'They're my twin cousins, sir,' said Ern. 'They've been Keeping an Eye on the Larkins for me. Well, they came rushing out to us this morning and said that they'd seen Mrs. Lorenzo hang a rug on the line, sir. I bet that's it! Nobody would ever bother to examine a rug on the line, sir! It would be a fine hiding—place—right out in the open, too! Nobody would think anything of a rug on the washing-line!'

Fatty glanced at the Lorenzos. A look of utter dismay had come over their faces. The Chief turned to his man. 'Get that rug,' he said.

They all went out of the cottage, and watched the sergeant take a rug from the washing-line. Goon stood near to Mrs. Lorenzo, and the Chief was beside Bill Lorenzo—just in case!

The rug was slit open—and inside, just as Fatty had said, was the picture, packed flat in grease-proof paper, quite unharmed.

'Phew! Fifty thousand pounds' worth of picture sewn inside a rug!' said the Chief. 'It makes me feel quite ill. Take it to the car, Sergeant.'

The Lorenzos were also taken to the car too, carefully escorted by a rather green-faced and very silent Goon, and the big Sergeant. Poppet barked a good-bye to Buster, who had been held tightly in Bets' arms all the time.

'Dear little Poppet,' said Bets, almost in tears. 'She oughtn't to belong to horrible people like that.'

'Cheer up,' said the Chief, swinging her up into the air. 'You haven't grown much, Bets! Frederick, I think this last remarkable—yes, truly remarkable feat of yours deserves a celebration! You've surpassed yourself, my boy. My word, how I shall enjoy myself when you come to work for me!'

'Thank you, sir,' said Fatty modestly. 'May I suggest, sir, that as it's rather cold, we all go to my shed and celebrate there? I know our cook's making mince-pies today, sir, and I've got a few things I'd like to show you— —a new set of false teeth, sir, and a gadget to make large ears, and...'

The Chief roared. 'Large ears! Why don't you invent

something in the way of large brains, Frederick—and hand a few out to poor old Goon?'

'That's an idea, sir!' said Fatty grinning, and off they all went, Ern too. What a morning!

We can't follow them, alas! The shed door is shut and there is a fine smell of mince-pies on the air. Hey, Fatty, don't wait too long for another mystery, will you!

Enid Blyton

THE MYSTERY OF THE BURNT COTTAGE

This is the first of Enid Blyton's thrilling mystery books. Fatty, Larry, Daisy, Pip, Bets-and Buster the dog—turn detectives when a mysterious fire destroys a thatched cottage in their village. Calling themselves the 'Five Find-Outers and Dog' they set out to solve the mystery and discover the culprit. The final solution, however, surprises the Five Find-Outers almost as much as Mr. Goon the village policeman. They can hardly wait for the next mystery to come along!

Enid Blyton

THE MYSTERY OF THE DISAPPEARING CAT

The second book in the popular *Mystery* series in which the Find—
Outers—Larry, Fatty, Daisy, Pip, Bets and Buster the dog—turn
detectives again to solve a very puzzling mystery.

A valuable Siamese cat is stolen from next door and suspicion falls on the
children's friend, Luke the gardener's boy. How can they find the real
thief and clear Luke of blame, especially with Mr Goon the policeman
interfering as usual? The Find-Outers are plunged into the middle of a
first class mystery with only the strangest of clues to work on.

Enid Blyton

THE MYSTERY OF THE SECRET ROOM

This is the third book in the *Mystery* series.

It is the Christmas holidays, and the Five are looking for mysteries. Then out of the blue Pip discovers a room, fully furnished, at the top of an empty house. Whose room is it? What is it used for? This is the problem that must be solved in *The Mystery of the Secret Room*. With the help of their friend Inspector Jenks, the Five Find-Outers eventually reach a solution in this most entertaining book.

Enid Blyton

THE MYSTERY OF THE SPITEFUL LETTERS

This is the fourth in the amusing adventures of the Find-Outers, and Dog. Fatty, Larry, Daisy, Pip and Bets are together once more for the Easter Holidays and quickly become involved in a very peculiar situation, trying to solve the mystery of the spiteful letters that arrive unsigned, for various people in Peterswood.

Mr. Goon, the policeman, tries to solve the mystery too, and comes up against Fatty, who in various disguises, manages to mystify the poor old policeman completely.

Enid Blyton

THE MYSTERY OF THE MISSING NECKLACE

The fifth book of the popular *Mystery* series, in which Fatty, Larry, Daisy, Pip, Bets—and Buster the dog, all play their parts as Find-Outers.

There are a great many clever burglaries going on and it is suspected that members of the gang have their meeting place somewhere in Peterswood. The children naturally determine to solve the mystery, and they tumble into other mysteries, too, in the process. Who is the old man on the seat? Who is Number Three? Where is the missing necklace? For once Mr. Goon, the policeman, defeats Fatty one strange night at the Waxworks Hall! But it all ends up most unexpectedly and amusingly with the children finally triumphant.

Enid Blyton

THE MYSTERY OF THE HIDDEN HOUSE

The sixth adventure in the popular *Mystery* series about Larry, Fatty, Daisy, Pip, Bets and Buster-the Five Find-outers and Dog.

When P.C. Goon's nephew, Ern, comes to Peterswood full of ideas of detecting, the Find-Outers think up a first-class mystery, complete with clues, and send both Ern and Mr. Goon off on a wild-goose chase to Christmas Hill. But Ern loses his way and suddenly stumbles into what the Find-Outers are sure is a real mystery. Once again they are on the trail of a really thrilling mystery, but Fatty's love of disguises lands both him and Ern in a very tricky situation.

Enid Blyton

THE MYSTERY OF HOLLY LANE

Who stole the money that the old man in Holly Lane had so carefully hidden in his cottage and where is it now? Why did his furniture disappear in the middle of the night?

Fatty and the other Find-Outers have a long list of suspects, and a few clues, but this latest mystery just won't be solved! Mr. Goon, the policeman, is hot on the scent too and he is sure that he has the answer when the others are still utterly confused. But who will solve the mystery first?

The eleventh book in the *Mystery series*.

Enid Blyton

THE MYSTERY OF THE MISSING MAN

The Five-Outers think their holiday will be ruined when Fatty is ordered to look after the dreadful Eunice. However, a fair and a conference of beetle-lovers bring an escaped convict and a peculiar mystery to the village which Bets, Pip, Daisy, Larry, Fatty and Buster the dog determine to solve.

When they get more than they bargained for, it is Eunice who comes up trumps and together they outwit Mr. Goon, the local policeman, to solve the case.

The thirteenth book in the *Mystery series*.

Enid Blyton

THE ENCHANTED WOOD

"Up the Faraway Tree, Jo, Bessie and me!"

Jo, bessie and Fanny move to the country and find an Enchanted Wood right on their doorstep! And in the wood stands the magic Faraway Tree where the Saucepan Man, Moon-Face and Silky the elf live. Together they visit the strange lands which lie at the top of the tree and have the most exciting adventures-and narrow escapes!

More magical stories can be found in *The Magic Faraway Tree and The Folk of the Faraway Tree.*

Enid Blyton's

THE MYSTERY

OF THE SPITEFUL LETTERS

Enid Blyton's

MYSTERY
THE
OF THE SPITEFUL LETTERS

MAMMOTH

CONTENTS

1 THE EXTRAORDINARY TELEGRAM

BETS and Pip were waiting impatiently for Larry, Daisy and Fatty to come. Bets was on the window-seat of the play-room looking anxiously out of the window.

'I wish they'd buck up,' she said. 'After all, they came home from boarding-school yesterday, and they've had plenty of time to come along. I do want to know if Fatty's got any more disguises and things.'

'I suppose you think there'll be another first-class mystery for us to solve these hols,' said Pip.

'Golly, that was a wizard one we had in the Christmas hols, wasn't it?'

'Yes,' said Bets. 'A bit too wizard. I wouldn't really mind not having a mystery these hols.'

'*Bets!* And I thought you were such a keen detective!' said Pip. 'Don't you want to be a Find-Outer any more ?'

'Of course I do. Don't be silly !' said Bets.

'I know you don't think I'm much use, because I'm the youngest and only nine, and you're all in your teens now— but I did help an awful lot last time, when we solved the mystery of the secret room.'

Pip was just about to say something squashing to his little sister when she gave a yell. 'Here they are ! At least—here are Larry and Daisy. Let's go down and meet them.'

They tore downstairs and out into the drive. Bets flung herself on the boy and girl in delight, and Pip stood by and grinned.

'Hallo, Larry ! Hallo, Daisy ! Seen Fatty at all ?'

'No,' said Larry. 'Isn't he here ? Blow ! Let's go to the gate and watch for him. Won't it be fun to see old Buster again too, wagging his tail and trotting along on his short Scottie legs !'

The four children went to the front gate and looked out. There was no sign of Fatty and Buster. The baker's cart drove by. Then came a woman on a bicycle. Then up the lane plodded a most familiar figure.

It was Mr. Goon the policeman, or old Clear-Orf as the children called him. He was going round on his beat, and was not at all pleased to see the four children at Pip's gate, watching him. Mr. Goon did not like the children, and they certainly did not like him. There had been three mysteries to solve in their village of Peterswood in the last year, and each time the children had solved them before Mr. Goon.

'Good morning,' said Larry politely, as Mr. Goon came by, panting a little for he was plump. His frog-eyes glared at them.

'So you're back again, like bad pennies,' he said. 'Ho ! Poking your noses into things again, I suppose !'

'I expect so,' said Pip cheerfully. Mr. Goon was just about to make another crushing remark when there came a wild ringing of bicycle bells and a boy came round the corner at top speed on a bicycle.

'Telegraph-boy,' said Pip. 'Look out, Mr. Goon, look out !'

THE EXTRAORDINARY TELEGRAM

The telegraph-boy had swerved right over to the police-man, and it looked as if he was going straight into him. Mr. Goon gave a yelp and skipped like a lamb out of the way.

'Now then, what you riding like that for ? A public danger, that's what you boys are !' exploded Mr. Goon.

'Sorry, sir, my bicycle sort of swerved over,' said the boy. 'Did I hurt you, sir ? I'm down-right sorry !'

Mr. Goon's temper cooled down at the boy's politeness. 'What house are you wanting ?' he asked.

'I've got a telegram for Master Philip Hilton,' said the telegraph-boy, looking at the name and address on the orange envelope in his hand.

'Oh ! Here's Pip !' said Bets. 'Oooh, Pip—a telegram for you !'

'The boy propped his bicycle by the side of the pavement, its pedal catching the kerb. Bur he didn't balance it very firmly and it fell over with a clatter, the handle-bar catching Mr. Goon on the shin.

He let out such a yell that all the children jumped. He hopped round, trying to hold his ankle and keep his balance too. Bets gave a sudden giggle.

'Oh, sir, I'm sorry !' cried the boy. 'That dratted bike ! It's always falling over. Don't you be angry with me, sir. Don't you report me, will you ? I'm that sorry !'

Mr. Goon's red face was redder than ever. He glared at the telegraph-boy, and rubbed his ankle again. 'You deliver your telegram and clear-orf,' he said. 'Wasting the time of the post-office, that's what you're doing !'

'Yes, sir,' said the boy meekly, and gave Pip the orange envelope. Pip tore it open, full of curiosity. He had never had a telegram sent to him before.

He read it out loud. It was from Fatty.

'SORRY NOT TO SEE YOU THESE HOLS. HAVE GOT A MYSTERY TO SOLVE IN TIPPY-LOOLOO, AND AM LEAVING BY AEROPLANE TO-DAY. ALL THE BEST ! FATTY.'

The children crowded round to see the telegram. They couldn't believe their ears. What an extraordinary telegram ! Mr. Goon could hardly believe his ears either.

'You let me see that,' he said, and took it out of Pip's hand. He read it out loud to himself.

'This is from that boy Frederick Trotteville, isn't it ?' he said. 'Fatty, you call him, don't you ? What does it mean ? Leaving by aeroplane for Tippy-Tippy-whatever it is. Never heard of the place in my life !'

'It's in South China,' said the telegraph-boy unexpectedly. 'I got an uncle out there, that's how I know.'

'But—but—why should Fatty go—why should he solve a mystery out there—why, why . . .' began the four children, absolutely taken aback.

'We shan't see him these hols,' suddenly wailed Bets, who was extremely fond of Fatty, and had looked forward very much to seeing him.

'And a good thing too,' said Mr. Goon, giving the telegram back to Pip. 'That's what I say. A jolly good thing too. He's a tiresome nuisance that boy is, pretending to play at being a detective—and using disguises to deceive the Law—and poking his nose in where it's not wanted. Perhaps we'll have a little peace these holidays if that interfering boy has gone to Tippy—Tippy—whatever it is.'

'Tippylooloo,' said the telegraph-boy, who seemed as much interested as any one else. 'I say, sir—is that telegram from that clever chap, Mr. Trotteville? I've heard about him.'

'*Mr.* Trotteville!' echoed Mr. Goon, indignantly. 'Why, he's no more than a kid. *Mr.* Trotteville! Mr. Interfering Fatty, that's what *I* call him!'

Bets gave a sudden giggle again. Mr. Goon had gone purple. He always did when he was annoyed.

'Sorry, sir. Didn't mean to make you all hot and bothered, sir,' said the telegraph-boy, who seemed very good indeed at apologizing for everything. 'But of course we've all heard of that boy, sir. Very very clever chap, he seems to be. Didn't he get on to some big plot last hols, sir, before the police did?'

Mr. Goon was not at all pleased to hear that Fatty's fame was apparently spread abroad like this. He did one of his snorts.

'You got better things to do at the post-office than listen to fairy-tales like that!' he said to the eager telegraph-boy. 'That boy Fatty's just an interfering little nuisance and always was, and he leads these kids here into trouble too. I reckon their parents'll be pretty glad that boy's gone to Tippy—Tippy—er...'

'Tippylooloo,' said the telegraph-boy obligingly. 'Fancy him being asked out there to solve a mystery, sir. Coo, he must be clever!'

The four children were delighted to hear all this. They knew how the policeman must hate it.

'You get along now,' said Mr. Goon, feeling that the telegraph-boy was a real nuisance. 'Clear-orf! You've wasted enough time.'

'Yes sir; certainly, sir,' said the polite boy. 'Fancy that fellow going off to Tippylooloo—by aeroplane too. Coo! I must write to my uncle out there and get him to tell me what Mr. Trotteville's doing. Coo!'

'Clear-orf!' said Mr. Goon. The boy winked at the others and took hold of his bicycle handles. The children couldn't help liking him. He had red hair, freckles all over his face, red eyebrows and a funny twisty mouth.

'He got on his bicycle, did a dangerous swerve towards Mr. Goon, and was off down the road ringing the two bells he had as loudly as ever he could.

'There's a boy that's civil and respectful to the Law,' said Mr. Goon to the others. 'And he's an example to follow, see!'

But the other children were no longer paying attention to the fat policeman. Instead they were looking at the telegram again. How surprising it was! Fatty *was* surprising, of course—but to go off by plane to China!

'Mother would never let *me* do a thing like that,' said Pip. 'After all, Fatty's only thirteen. I can't believe it!'

Bets burst into tears. 'I did so want him to come back for the hols and find another mystery!' she wailed. 'I did, I did!'

'Shut up, Bets, and don't be a baby,' said Pip. 'We can solve mysteries without Fatty, can't we?'

But privately each of them knew that without Fatty they

couldn't do much. Fatty was the real leader, the one who dared to do all kinds of things, the real brain of the Find-Outers.

'Without Fatty we're like rabbit-pie without any rabbit in it,' said Daisy dolefully. That sounded funny, but nobody laughed. They all knew what Daisy meant. Things weren't nearly so exciting and interesting without Fatty.

'I just can't get over it,' said Larry, walking up the drive with the others. 'Fatty off to South China! And what *can* be the mystery he's solving there ? I do think he might have found time to come and tell us.'

'That telegraph-boy thought an awful lot of Fatty, didn't he ?' said Bets. 'Fancy! Fatty must be getting quite famous!'

'Yes. Old Clear-Orf didn't like him praising up Fatty, did he !' chuckled Larry. 'I liked that boy. He sort of reminded me of some one, but I can't think who.'

'I say—what's going to happen to Buster?' suddenly said Bets, stopping still in the drive. 'Fatty wouldn't be allowed to take his dog with him—and Buster would break his heart left alone. What do you suppose is happening to him ? Couldn't *we* have him?'

'I bet Fatty would like us to have him,' said Pip. 'Let's go up to Fatty's house and ask his mother about Buster. Come on. We'll go now.'

They all turned and went back down the drive. Bets felt a little comforted. It would be some thing to have Fatty's dog, even if they couldn't have Fatty. Dear old Buster! He was such a darling, and had shared all their adventures.

They came to Fatty's house and went into the drive. Fatty's

mother was picking some daffodils for her vases, and she smiled at the children.

'Back for the holidays?' she said. 'Well, I hope you'll all have a nice time. You're looking very solemn. Is anything the matter?'

'Well—we just came to see if we could have Buster for the hols,' said Latty. 'Oh, there he is! Buster, Buster old fellow! Come here!'

2   FATTY REALLY IS SURPRISING

BUSTER came tearing up to the children, barking madly, his tail wagging nineteen to the dozen. He flung himself on them and tried to lick and bark at the same time.

'Good old Buster!' said Pip. 'I bet you'll miss Fatty!'

'It was a great surprise to hear that Fatty has gone to China,' said Daisy to Mrs. Trotteville. Fatty's mother looked surprised.

'In an aeroplane too!' said Larry. 'You'll miss him, won't you, Mrs. Trotteville?'

'What exactly do you mean?' asked Mrs. Trotteville, looking as if she thought the children had gone mad all of a sudden.

'Gracious—Fatty can't have told her!' said Bets, in a loud whisper.

'Told me *what*?' said Mrs. Trotteville, getting impatient. 'What's the mystery? What's Fatty been up to?'

'But—but—don't you know?' stammered Larry. 'He's

gone to Tippylooloo, and...'

'Tippylooloo! What's all this nonsense?' said Mrs. Trotteville. She raised her voice. 'Frederick! Come here a minute!'

The children turned breathlessly to the house —and out of the front door, stepping lazily, came Fatty! Yes, it really was Fatty, as large as life, grinning all over his plump face. Bets gave a loud shriek and ran to him. She hugged him.

'Oh, I thought you'd gone to Tippylooloo! Didn't you go? Oh, Fatty, I'm so glad you're here!'

The others stared. They were puzzled. 'Did you send us that telegram?' said Daisy suddenly. Was it a joke on your part, Fatty?'

'What telegram?' asked Fatty innocently. 'I was just about to come down and see you all.'

'This telegram!' said Pip, and pushed it into Fatty's hand. He read it and looked astonished.

'Somebody's been playing a joke on you,' he said. he said. 'Silly sort of joke. And anyway, fancy you all believing I was off to Tippylooloo! Gosh!'

'You and your jokes!' said Mrs. Trotteville. 'As if I should let Frederick go to China, or whatever that ridiculous Tippylooloo place is. Now, if you want to go and talk to Frederick, either go indoors or go for a walk.'

They went indoors. They still felt very puzzled. Buster danced round, barking in delight. He was overjoyed because the whole company of Find Outers was together again.

'Who delivered this telegram?' asked Fatty.

'The telegraph-boy,' said Pip. 'A red-haired chap with freckles and a cheeky kind of voice. He let his bike-handle catch old Clear-Orf on the shin ! You should have seen him dance round!'

'Hm,' said Fatty. 'There's something strange about that telegraph-boy, *I* think! Delivering a telegram I didn't send! Let's go out and look for him and ask him a few questions !'

They went out, and walked down the lane together, Buster at their heels. 'You go that way, Larry and Daisy, and you go the opposite way, Pip and Bets,' said Fatty. 'I'll take this third way. We'll scour the village properly for that boy, and meet at the corner by the church in half an hour's time.'

'I want to go with *you,* Fatty,' said Bets.

'No, you go with Pip,' said Fatty, unexpectedly hard-hearted. He usually let Bets have her own way in every-thing. Bets said nothing but walked off with Pip, feeling rather hurt.

Larry and Daisy saw no telegraph-boy at all, and were waiting by the church corner in twenty-five minutes' time. Then Pip and Bets came up. They hadn't seen him either. They looked up and down for Fatty and Buster.

Round the corner came a bicycle, and on it was—the red-headed telegraph-boy, whistling loudly. Larry gave a yell.

'Oy! Come over here a minute!'

The telegraph-boy wobbled over, and balanced himself by the kerb. His red hair fell in a big lock over his forehead, and his uniform cap was well on one side.

'What's up, mate?' he said.

'It's about that telegram,' said Larry. 'It's all nonsense! Our friend Frederick Trotteville hasn't gone to China—he's here!'

'Where?' said the boy, looking all round.

FATTY REALLY IS SURPRISING

'I mean he's in the village somewhere,' said Larry. 'He'll be along in a minute.'

'Coo!' said the boy. 'I wouldn't half like to see him! He's a wonder, he is! I wonder the police don't take him on, and get him to help them with their problems.'

'Well, we *all* helped to solve the mysteries you know,' said Pip, beginning to feel that it was time he and the others got a bit of praise too.

'No, did you really?' said the boy. 'I thought it was Mr. Trotteville that was the brains of the party. Coo, I'd like to meet him! Do you think he'd give me his autograph?'

The children started at him, thinking that Fatty must indeed be famous if telegraph-boys wanted his autograph.

'That was a dud telegram you brought,' said Larry. 'A fake, a joke. Did *you* fake it?'

'Me fake it! Coo, I'd lose my job!' said the telegraph-boy. 'Look here, when's this famous friend of yours coming? I want to meet him, but I can't wait here all day. I've got to get back to the P.O.'

'Well, the post-office can wait a minute or two, I should think', said Pip, who felt that none of them had got very much information out of the telegraph-boy, and was hoping that perhaps Fatty might.

A small dog rounded the corner, and Bets gave a yell. 'Buster! come on, Buster! Where's Fatty? Tell him to hurry.'

Every one thought that Fatty would come round the corner too, but he didn't Buster trotted on towards them alone. He didn't growl at the telegraph-boy. He gave him a lick and then sat down beside him on the kerb, turning adoring eyes up to him.

Bets was most astonished. She had never seen Buster adoring any one but Fatty in that way. She stared at the little black dog, surprised. What should make him like the telegraph-boy so much?

Then she gave a loud squeal and pounced on the telegraph-boy so suddenly that he jumped.

'Fatty!' she said. 'Oh, Fatty! What idiots we are! FATTY!'

Pip's mouth fell open. Daisy stared as if she couldn't believe her eyes. Larry exploded and banged the telegraphy-boy on the back.

'You wretch! You absolute wretch! You took us all in properly—and you took old Clear-Orf in too. Fatty, you're a marvel. How do you do it?'

Fatty grinned at them all. He removed his red eyebrows with a pull. He rubbed off his freckles with a wetted hanky. He shifted his red wig a little so that the others could see his sleek black hair beneath.

'Fatty! It's the most wonderful disguise!' said Pip enviously. 'But how do you manage to twist up your mouth to make it different and screw up your eyes to make them smaller and all that kind of thing?'

'Oh, that's just good acting,' said Fatty, swelling a little with pride. 'I've told you before, haven't I, that I always take the chief part in our school plays, and this last term I...'

But the children didn't want to hear about Fatty's wonderful doings at school. They had heard about those too often. Larry interrupted him.

'Golly! Now I know why the telegraph-boy praised you up so! Idiot! Calling yourself *Mr.* Trotteville and waiting for your own autograph! Honestly, Fatty, you're the limit!'

FATTY REALLY IS SURPRISING

They all went to Pip's house and were soon settled in the playroom, examining Fatty's cap and wig and everything.

'It's a new disguise I got,' explained Fatty. 'I wanted to try it out, of course. Fine wig, isn't it? It cost an awful lot of money. I daren't tell Mother. I could hardly wait to play that joke on you. I'm getting awfully good at disguises and acting.'

'You are, Fatty,' said Bets generously. 'I would never have known it was you if I hadn't noticed Buster sitting down looking up at you with that sort of adoring look he keeps for you, Fatty.'

'So that's how you guessed, you clever girl!' said Fatty. 'I call that pretty good, Bets. Honestly, I sometimes think you notice even more than the others!'

Bets glowed, but Pip did not look too pleased. He always thought of Bets as his baby sister, and thought she ought to be kept under, and not made conceited about herself.

'She'll get a swelled head,' he growled. 'Any of us could have spotted Buster's goofy look at you.'

'Ah, but you didn't, said Fatty. 'I say—isn't it great that old Clear-Orf thinks I've gone to Tippylooloo! That *was* a bit of luck, his happening to be with you when I cycled up this morning. Didn't he jump when I let my bike fall on his shin!'

They all stared at Fatty in admiration. The things he did! The things he thought of! Bets giggled.

'Won't he be surprised when you turn up!' she said. 'He'll think you've come back from Tippylooloo already!'

'What a name!' said Daisy. 'How in the world did you

think of it?'

'Oh, things like that are easy,' said Fatty modestly. 'Poor old Clear-Orf! He just swallowed that telegram whole!'

'Are you going to use that disguise when we solve our next mystery?' asked Bets, eagerly.

'What's our next mystery?' said Pip. 'We haven't got one! It would be too much to expect one these hols.'

'Well, you never know,' said Fatty. 'You simply never know! I bet a mystery will turn up again—and I jolly well hope we'll be on to it before old Clear-Orf is. Do you remember how I locked him up in the coal-hole in our last mystery?'

Every one laughed. They remembered how poor old Mr. Goon had staggered up out of the coal-hole, black with coal-dust, his helmet lost, and with a most terrible sneezing cold.

'And we sent him some carbolic soap and found his helmet for him,' remembered Daisy. 'And he wasn't a bit grateful, and never even thanked us. And Pip's mother said it was rather an insult to send him soap and was cross with us.'

'I'd like another mystery to solve,' said Pip. 'We'll all keep our ears and eyes open. The hols have begun well, with you in your new disguise, Fatty—taking old Goon in as well as us!'

'I must go,' said Fatty, getting up. 'I've got to slip back and change out of this telegraph-boy's suit. I'll just put on my wig and eyebrows again in case I meet Clear-Orf. Well—so long!'

3   OH, FOR A MYSTERY!

A WHOLE week went by. The weather was rather dull and rainy, and the children got tired of it. It wasn't much fun going for walks and getting soaked. On the other hand they could't stay indoors all day.

The five of them and Buster met at Pip's each day, because Pip had a fine big playroom. They made rather a noise sometimes, and then Mrs. Hilton would come in, looking cross.

'There's no need to behave as if you were a hurricane and an earthquake rolled into one!' she said, one day. Then she looked in surprise at Pip. 'Pip, what on earth are you doing?'

'Nothing, Mother,' said Pip, unwinding himself hurriedly from some weird purple garment. 'Just being a Roman emperor, that's all, and telling my slaves what I think of them.'

'Where did you get that purple thing,' asked his mother. 'Oh, *Pip*— surely you haven't taken Mrs. Moon's bed-spread to act about in?'

'Well, she's out,' said Pip. 'I didn't think it would matter, Mother.'

Mrs. Moon was the cook-housekeeper, and had been with the Hiltons only a few months. The last cook was in hospital ill. Mrs. Moon was a really wonderful cook, but she had a very bad temper. Mrs. Hilton was tired of hearing her grumble about the children.

'You just put that bed-spread back *at once!*' she said. 'Mrs. Moon will be most annoyed if she thinks you've been into

her bedroom and taken her bed-covering. That was wrong
of you, Pip. And will you all please remember to wipe your
feet when you come in at the garden-door this wet weather?
Mrs. Moon says she is always washing your muddy foot-
marks away.'

'She's a spiteful old tell-tale,' said Pip sulkily.

'I won't have you talking like that, Pip,' said Mrs. Hilton.
'She's a very good cook and does her work extremely well.
It's no wonder she complains when you make her so much
extra cleaning—and, by the way, she says things sometimes
disappear from the larder and she feels sure it's you children
taking them. I hope that's not so.'

Pip looked uncomfortable. "Well, Mother,' he began, 'it's
only that we're most awfully hungry sometimes, and you
see . . .'

'No, I don't see at all, said Mrs Hilton. 'Mrs. Moon is in
charge of the larder, and you are not to take things without
either my permission or hers. Now take back that bed-spread,
for goodness sake, and spread it out neatly. Daisy, go with
Pip and see that he puts it back properly.'

Daisy went off meekly with Pip. Mrs. Hilton could be
very strict, and all five children were in awe of her, and of
Mr. Hilton too. They would not stand any nonsense at all,
either from their own children or from other people's! Yet
they all liked Mrs. Hilton very much, and Pip and Bets
thought the world of her.

Daisy and Pip returned to the playroom. Mrs.Hilton had
gone. Pip looked at the others and grinned.

'We put it back.' he said. 'We pulled it this way and that,
we patted it down, we draped it just right, we . . .'

'Oh, shut up!' said Larry. 'I don't like Mrs. Moon. She may be a good cook—and I must say she makes marvellous cakes—but she's a tell-tale.'

'I bet poor old Gladys is scared of her,' said Daisy. Gladys was the housemaid, a timid, quite little thing, ready with shy smiles and very willing to do anything for the children.

'I like Mrs. Cockles the best,' said Bets. 'She's got a lovely name, I think. She's the char-woman. She comes to help Mrs. Moon and Gladys twice a week. She tells me all kinds of things.'

'Good old Cockles!' said Pip. 'She always hands us out some of Mrs. Moon's jam-tarts on baking day, if we slip down to the kitchen.'

Larry yawned and looked out of the window. 'This disgusting weather!' he said. 'Raining again! It's jolly boring. I wish to goodness we'd got something to do—a mystery to solve, for instance.'

'There doesn't seem to be a single thing,' said Daisy. 'No robberies—not even a bicycle stolen in the village. Nothing.'

'I bet old Clear-Orf will be pleased if we don't get a mystery this time,' said Fatty.

'Has he seen you yet?' asked Bets. Fatty shook his head.

'No. I expect he still thinks I'm away at Tippylooloo,' he said a grin. 'He'll be surprised when I turn up.'

'Let's go out, even if its *is* raining,' said Pip. 'Let's go and snoop about. Don't you remember how last hols I snooped round an empty house and found that secret room at the top of it? Well, let's go and snoop again. We might hit on *something*!'

So they all put on macks and sou'-westers and went for a snoop. 'we might find some clues,' said Bets hopefully.

'Clues to *what*!' said Pip scornfully. 'You have to have a mystery before you can find clues, silly!'

They snooped round a few empty houses, but there didn't seem anything extraordinary about them at all. They peered into an empty shed, and were scared almost out of their wits when a tall tramp rose up from the dark corners and yelled at them.

They tramped over a deserted allotment and examined a tumble-down cottage at one end very thoroughly. But there was absolutely nothing odd or strange or mysterious to find.

'It's tea-time,' said Fatty. 'We'd better go home. I've got an aunt coming. See you tomorrow!'

Larry and Daisy drifted off home too. Pip and Bets splashed their way down their wet lane and went gloomily indoors.

'Dull and boring!' said Pip, flinging his mack down on the hall-cupboard floor. 'Nothing but rain! Nothing to do!'

'You'll get into a row if you leave your wet mack on the ground,' said Bets, hanging hers up.

'Pick it up then,' said Pip, in a bad tamper. He hadn't even an exciting book to read. His mother had gone out to tea. He and Bets were alone in the house with Gladys.

'Let's ask Gladys to come up to the playroom and play cards,' said Pip. 'She loves a game. Mrs. Moon isn't in to say No.'

Gladys was only too delighted to come and play. She was about nineteen, a pretty, dark-haired girl, timid in her ways, and easily pleased. She enjoyed the game of Happy

Families as much as the two children did. She laughed at all their jokes, and they had a very happy time together.

'It's your bed-time now, Miss Bets,' she said at last. 'And I've got to go and see to the dinner. Do you want me to run your bath-water for you, Miss?'

'No, thank you. I like doing it myself,' said Bets. 'Goodbye, Gladys. I like you!'

Gladys went downstairs. Bets went to run the bath-water. Pip went off whistling to change into a clean suit. His parents would not let him sit up to dinner unless he was clean and tidy.

'Perhaps it will be fine and sunny to-morrow,' thought Pip, looking out of the window at the darkening western sky. 'It doesn't look so bad to-night. We might be able to get a few bike-rides and picnics in if only the weather clears.'

It *was* fine and sunny the next day. Larry, Daisy, Fatty and Buster arrived at Pip's early, full of a good plan.

'Let's take our lunch with us and go to Burnham Beeches,' said Larry. 'We'll have grand fun there. You should just see some of the beeches, Bets—enormous old giants all gnarled and knotted, and some of them really seem to have faces in their knotted old trunks!'

'Oooh—I'd like to go,' said Bets. 'I'm big enough to ride all the way with you this year. Mummy wouldn't let me last year.'

'What's up with your Gladys?' said Fatty, scratching Buster on the tummy, as he lay upside down by his chair.

'Gladys? Nothing!' said Pip. 'Why?'

'Well, she looked as if she'd been crying when I saw her in the hall this morning,' said Fatty. 'I came in at the garden door as usual, and bumped into her in the hall. Her eyes looked as red as anything.

'Well, she was quite all right last night,' said Pip, remembering the lively game they had had 'Perhaps, the got into a row with Mrs. Moon.'

'Shouldn't think so,' said Fatty. 'Mrs. Moon called out something to her quite friendly as I passed. Perhaps she's had bad news.'

Bets felt upset. She went to find Gladys. The girl was sweeping the bedroom floors. Yes, her eyes were very red!

'Gladys, have you been crying?' asked Bets. 'What's the matter? Has somebody been scolding you?'

'No,' said Gladys, trying to smile. 'Nothing's the matter, Miss Bets. I'm all right. Right as rain.'

Bets looked at her doubtfully. She didn't look at all happy. What could have happened between last night and now?

'Have you had bad news?' said Bets, looking very sympathetic.

'Now just you heed what I say,' said Gladys. 'There is nothing the matter. You run off to the others.'

There was nothing to do but go back. 'She *has* been crying,' said Bets, 'but she won't tell me why.'

'Well, leave her alone,' said Larry, who didn't like crying females. 'Why should we pry into her private affairs? Come on, let's go and ask about this picnic.'

Mrs. Hilton was only too glad to say that the children could go off for the day. It was tiring having them in the house all day long, especially as Pip's playroom was the general meeting-room.

'I was going to suggest that you went off for the day

myself,' she said. 'You can take your lunch *and* your tea, if you like! I'll get it ready for you, whilst Fatty and the others go back to get theirs.

It was soon ready. Mrs. Hilton gave them the packets of sandwiches and cake. 'Now just keep out for the whole day and don't come tearing back because you're bored,' she said firmly. I don't want to see any of you till after tea. I've got important things to do to-day.'

'What are they, Mother?' asked Pip, hoping he was not going to miss anything exciting.

'Never you mind,'said his mother. 'Now, off you go and have a lovely day!'

They rode off on their bicycles. 'Mother seemed to want to get rid of us to-day, didn't she?' said Pip. 'I mean—she almost *pushed* us out. I wonder why? And what's so impor- tant to-day? She didn't tell us about any Meeting or any- thing.'

'You're trying to make it out to be quite a mystery!' said Bets. 'I expect she's going to turn out cupboards or some- thing. Mothers always seem to think things like that are very important. Hurrah, Pip—there are the others! Come on!'

With a jangling of bicycle bells the little party rode off. Buster sat solemnly in Fatty's basket. He loved a picnic. A picnic meant woods or fields, and woods or fields meant one thing and one thing only to Buster—rabbits!

4   MR. GOON'S GLOVE

THE children had a lovely day. It was warm and sunny, there were primroses everywhere, and the little bright mauve dog-voilets made a carpet with the wind-flowers.

'This is glorious,' said Daisy. 'Thank goodness the weather's changed at last. Let's lay out our macks and sit on them.'

Buster went off happily. The children watched him go. 'Off to solve the great Rabbit Mystery!' said Fatty. 'Where is the rabbit-hole that is big enough to take a dog like Buster's always hoping to solve.'

Every one laughed. 'I wish we had a great problem to solve,' said Daisy. 'I've sort of got used to having something for my brains to chew on each hols. It seems odd not to have anything really to think about.'

The day passed quickly. It was soon time to go home again, and the five mounted their bicycles. Buster had with difficulty been removed from halfway down a rather big rabbit-hole. He had been very angry at being hauled out, and now sat sulkily in Fatty's basket, his ears down. Just as he had almost reached that rabbit! Another minute and he'd have got him!

'Buster's sulking,' said Pip, and laughed. 'Oy, Buster! Cheer up!'

'I wonder if Mother's done all the important things she said she had to do,' said Bets to Pip. 'Anyway she can't say she's been much bothered with us to-day!'

They all parted at the church corner to go their different ways. 'We'll meet at Larry's to-morrow!' said Fatty. 'In the garden if it's fine. Cheerio!'

Pip and Bets biked down their lane and into their drive.
'I'm jolly thirsty,' said Pip. 'I wonder if Gladys would give
us some ice out of the frig to put into a jug of water. I feel
like a drink of iced water, I'm so hot.'

'Well, don't ask Mrs. Moon,' said Bets. 'She's sure to
say no!'

They went to find Gladys. She wasn't in the kitchen, for
they peeped in at the window to see. She wasn't upstairs
either, for they went up and called her. Their mother heard
them and came out of the study to greet them as they ran
downstairs again.

'Did you have a lovely day?' she said. 'I was pleased it
was so fine for you.

'Yes, a super day,' said Pip. 'Mother, can we have a drink
of iced water? We're melting!'

'Yes, if you like,' Mrs.Hilton said. They shot off to the
kitchen. They peeped in. Mrs. Moon was there knitting.

'What do you want?' she said, looking unexpectedly
amiable.

'Just some iced water, please,' said Pip. 'But we weren't
going to ask you for it, Mrs. Moon. We were going to ask
Gladys. We didn't want to bother you.'

'No bother,' said Mrs. Moon, getting up. 'I'll get it.'

'Is Gladys out?' asked Bets.

'Yes,' said Mrs. Moon shortly. 'Now, take these ice-cubes
quick, and slip them into a jug. That's right.'

'But it isn't Glady's day out, is it?' said Pip, surprised.
'She went the day before yesterday.'

'There now—you've dropped an ice-cube!' said Mrs.

Moon. 'Well, I'm no good at chasing ice-cubes round the kitchen floor, so you must get it yourselves.'

Bets giggled as Pip tried to get the cold slippery ice-cube off the floor. He rinsed it under the tap and popped it into the jug.

'Thanks, Mrs. Moon,' he said and carried the jug and two glasses up to the playroom.

'Mrs. Moon didn't seem to want to talk about Gladys, did she?' said Pip. 'Funny.'

'Pip—you don't think Gladys has left, do you?' suddenly said Bets. "I do hope she hasn't. I did like her.'

'Well—we can easily find out,' said Pip. 'Let's go and peep in her bedroom. If her things are there we'll know she's just out for a while and is coming back.'

They went along the landing to the little room that Gladys had. They opened the door and peeped in. They stared in dismay.

Every single thing that had belonged to Gladys had gone! Her brush and comb, her tooth-brush, and the little blue night-dress case she had embroidered at school for herself. There was nothing at all to show that the girl had been there for a month or two.

'Yes—she *has* gone!' said Bets. 'Well, why didn't Mother tell us? Or Mrs. Moon? What's all the mystery?'

'It's jolly funny,' said Pip. 'Do you think she stole any-thing? She seemed so nice. I liked her.'

'Let's go and ask Mother,' said Bets. So they went down to the study. But their mother was not there. They were just turning to go out when Pip's sharp eyes caught sight of something lying under a chair. He picked it up.

It was a large black woollen glove. He stared at it, trying to remember who wore black woollen gloves.

'Whose is it?' asked Bets. 'Look—isn't that a name inside?'

Pip looked—and the name he saw there made him stare hard. On a little tab was printed in marking ink, five letters: 'T. GOON.'

'T. GOON! Theophilus Goon!' said Pip, in surprise. 'Golly! What was old Clear-Orf here for today? He came here and sat in this study, and left a glove behind. No wonder Mother said she had important things to do if she had old Clear-Orf coming for a meeting! But why did he come?'

Bets burst into a loud wail. 'He's taken Gladys to prison! I know he has! Gladys has gone to prison, and I did like her so much.'

'Shut up, idiot!' said Pip. 'Mother will hear you.'

Mrs. Hilton came quickly into the study, thinking that Bets must surely have hurt herself. 'What's the matter dear?' she asked.

'Mother! Mr. Goon's taken Gladys to prison, hasn't he?' wept Bets. 'But I'm sure she didn't steal or anything. I'm sure she didn't. She was n-n-nice!'

'Bets, don't be silly,' said her mother. 'Of *course* Mr. Goon hasn't done anything of the sort.'

'Well, why was he here then?' demanded Pip.

'How do you know he was?' said his mother.

'Because of this,' said Pip, and he held out the large woollen glove. 'That's Mr. Goon's glove. So we know he has been here in the study—and as Gladys is gone we feel

pretty certain Mr. Goon's had something to do with her going.'

'Well, he hasn't,' said Mrs. Hilton. 'She was very upset
about something to-day and I let her go home to her aunt.'

'Oh,' said Pip. 'Then why did Mr. Goon come to see
you, Mother?'

'Really, Pip, it's no business of yours,' said his mother,
quite crossly. 'I don't want you prying into it either. I know
you all fancy yourselves as detectives, but this is nothing
whatever to do with you, and I'm not going to have you
mixed up in any of your so-called mysteries again.'

'Oh—is there a mystery then?' said Bets. 'And is old
Clear-Orf trying to solve it? Oh Mother, you might tell us,
you might!'

'It's nothing whatever to do with you,' said Mrs. Hilton
firmly. 'Your father and I have discussed something with
Mr. Goon, that's all.'

'Has he been complaining about us?' asked Pip.

'No, for a wonder he hasn't,' said his mother. 'Stop howling, Bets. There's nothing to wail about.'

Bets dried her eyes. 'Why did Gladys go?' she said. 'I
want her to come back.'

'Well, maybe she will,' said her mother. 'I can't
tell you why she went, except that whe was upset
about something, that's all. It's her own private
business.'

Mrs. Hilton went out of the room. Pip looked at Bets,
and slipped his hand into the enormous black glove. 'Golly,
what a gaint of a hand old Clear-Orf must have,' he said. 'I
do wonder why he was here, Bets. It was something to do

with Gladys, I'm certain.

'Let's go up and tell Fatty,' said Bets. 'He'll know what to do. Why is everything being kept such a secret? And oh, I do hate to think of Clear-Orf sitting here talking with Mother, and grinning to think we were not to know anything about it!'

They couldn't go up to Fatty's that evening, because Mrs. Hilton suddenly decided she wanted to wash their hair. 'But mine's quite clean,' protested Pip.

'It looks absolutely black,' said his mother. 'What *have* you been doing to it to-day, Pip? Standing on your head in a heap of soot, or something?'

'Can't we have our heads washed to-morrow night?' said Bets. But it wasn't a bit of good. It had to be then and there. So it wasn't until the next day that Pip and Bets were able to see Fatty. He was at Larry's, of course, because they had all arranged to meet there.

'I say,' began Pip, 'a funny thing's happened at our house. Old Clear-Orf went there yesterday to see my father and mother about something so mysterious that nobody will tell us what it was! And Gladys, our nice housemaid, has gone home, and we can't find out exactly why. And look—here's a glove Goon left behind.'

Every one examined it. 'It might be a valuable clue,' said Bets.

'Idiot!' said Pip. 'I keep telling you you can't have clues before you've got a mystery to solve. Besides, how could Goon's glove be a clue! You're a baby.'

'Well—it *was* a clue to his presence there in your study yesterday,' said Fatty, seeing Bets, eyes fill with tears. 'But I say—it's all a bit funny, isn't it? Do you think Goon is on to some mystery we haven't heard about, but which your mother and father know of, Pip, and don't want us to be mixed up in? I know that your parents weren't very pleased at that adventure we had in the Christmas hols. I wouldn't be a bit surprised if there isn't something going on that we children are to be kept out of!

There was a silence. Put like that it seemed extremely likely. What a shame to be kept out of a mystery when they were such very good detectives!

'What's more, I think the mystery's got something to do with Glady's,' said Fatty. 'Fancy! To think there may have been something going on under our very noses and we didn't know it! There we were snooping about in barns and sheds and all the time there was a mystery in Pip's own house!

'Well—we'll jolly well find out what it is!' said Larry. 'And what's more if Goon is on to it, we'll be on to it too, and we'll get to the bottom of things before *he* does! I bet he'd like to do us down just once, so that Inspector Jenks would pat him on the back, and not us, for a change.'

'How are we going to find out anything?' asked Daisy. 'We can't possibly ask Mrs. Hilton. She'd just shut us up.'

'I'll go down and tackle Goon,' said Fatty, much to every one's admiration. 'I'll take his glove back, and pretend to know lots more that I do—and maybe he'll let out something.'

'Yes—you go,' said Pip. 'But wait a bit—he thinks you're

in China!'

'Oh, I've come back now after solving the case there very quickly!' laughed Fatty. 'Give me the glove, Pip. I'll go along now. Come with me, Buster. Goon isn't likely to lose his temper with me quite so violently if you're there!'

5   THE 'NONNIMUS' LETTER

FATTY rode off on his bicycle, Buster in the basket. He came to Mr. Goon's house, and went to knock at the door. It was opened by Mrs. Cockles, who cleaned for Mr. Goon, and for the Hiltons as well. She knew Fatty and liked him.

'Is Mr. Goon in?' asked Fatty. 'Oh good. I'll come in and see him then. I've got some property to return to him.'

He sat down in the small, hot parlour. Mrs. Cockles went to fetch the policeman. He was mending a puncture in his bicycle, out in his backyard. He put his coat on and came to see who wanted him.

His eyes nearly fell out of his head when he saw Fatty. 'Lawks!' he said. 'I thought you was in foreign parts!'

'Oh—I solved that little mystery out there,' said Fatty. 'Didn't take me long! Just a matter of an emerald necklace or so. Pity you didn't come out with me to Tippylooloo, Mr. Goon. You'd have enjoyed eating rice with chop-sticks.'

Mr. Goon was sure he would have enjoyed no such thing. 'Pity you didn't stay away longer,' he grumbled. 'Where you are, there's trouble. I know that by now. What you want this morning?'

'Well—er—Mr. Goon, you remember that little matter you went to see Mr. and Mrs. Hilton about yesterday?'said Fatty, pretending to know a great deal more than he actually did. Mr. Goon looked surprised.

'Now look-ere,' he said. 'Who's been telling you about that? You wasn't to know anything, any of you, see?'

'You can't keep things like that secret,' said Fatty.

'Things like what?' asked Mr. Goon, pretending he didn't know what Fatty was talking about.

'Well—things like you-know-what,' said Fatty, going all mysterious. I know you're going to set to work on that little matter, Mr. Goon, and I wish you luck. I hope, for poor Gladys's sake, you'll soon get to the bottom of the matter.'

This was quite a shot in the dark, but it seemed to surprise Mr. Goon very much. He blinked at Fatty out of his bulging frog-eyes.

'Who told you about that there letter?' he suddenly said.

'Oho,' thought Fatty, 'so it's something to do with a letter!' He spoke aloud.

'Ah, I have ways and means of finding out these things, Mr, Goon. We'd like to help you if we can.'

Mr. Goon suddenly lost his temper,and his face went brick-red. 'I don't want none of your help!' he shouted. 'I've had enough of it! Help? Interference is what I call it! Can't I manage a case on my own without all you children butting in? You keep out of it! Mrs. Hilton, she promised me she wouldn't say nothing to any of you, nor, show you that letter either. She didn't want you poking your noses in no more than I did. Anyway, this is a case for the police not for little busy-bodies like you! Clear-Orf now, and don't let me see you messing about any more.'

'I thought perhaps you would like your glove, Mr. Goon,' said Fatty politely, and he held out the policeman's big glove. 'You left it behind you yesterday.'

Mr. Goon snatched at it angrily. Buster growled. 'You and that dog of yours!' muttered Mr. Goon. 'Tired to death of both of you I am. Clear-Orf!'

Fatty cleared off. He was pleased with the result of his interview with Mr. Goon, but very puzzled. Mr. Goon had given a few things away—about that letter, for instance. But what letter? What could have been in a letter to cause this mystery? Was it something to do with Gladys? Was it *her* letter?

Puzzling out all these things Fatty cycled back to the others. He soon told them what he had learnt.

'I think possibly Mrs. Moon may know something,' he said. 'Bets, couldn't you ask her? If you just sort of prattled to her, she might tell you something.'

'I don't prattle,' said Bets indignantly. 'And I don't expect she'd tell me anything at all. I'm sure she's in this business of keeping everything secret from us. She wouldn't even tell us yesterday that Gladys had gone.'

'Well, anyway, see what you can do,' said Fatty. 'She's fond of knitting, isn't she? Well, haven't you got a bit of tangled up knitting you could take down to her and ask her to undo for you—pick up the stitches or whatever you call it? Then you could sort of prat . . . er—talk to her about Gladya and Goon and so on.'

'I'll try,' said Bets 'I'll go downstairs to her this afternoon when she's sitting down resting. She doesn't like me messing about in the morning.'

So that afternoon Bets went down to the kitchen with some very muddled knitting indeed. She had been planning earnestly what to say to Mrs. Moon, but she felt very nervous. Mrs. Moon could be very snappy if she wanted to.

There was no one in the kitchen. Bets sat down in the rocking-chair there. She always liked that old chair. She rocked herself to and fro.

From the back-yard came two voices. One was Mrs. Moon's and the other was Mrs. Cockles's. Bets hardly listened—but then she suddenly sat up.

'Well, what I say is, if a girl gets a nasty letter telling her things she wants to forget, and no name at the bottom of the letter, it's enough to give any one a horrid shock!' came Mrs. Moon's voice. 'And a nasty, yes right-down nasty thing it is to do! Writing letters and putting no name at the bottom.'

'Yes, that's a coward's trick all right,' said Mrs. Cockles's cheerful voice. 'You mark my words, Mrs. Moon, there'll be more of those nonnimus letters, or whatever they calls them—those sort of letter-writer don't just stop at the one person. No they've got too much spite to use up on one person, they'll write more and more. Why, *you* might get one next!'

'Poor Gladys was right-down upset,' said Mrs. Moon. 'Cried and cried, she did. I made her show me the letter. All in capital letters it was, not proper writing. And I said to her, I said, "Now look here, my girl, you go straight off to your mistress and tell her about this. She'll do her best for you, she will." And I pushed her off to Mrs. Hilton.'

'Did she give her her notice?' asked Mrs. Cockles.

'No,' said Mrs. Moon. 'She showed Mr. Hilton the letter, and he rang up Mr. Goon. That silly, fussing fellow! What do they want to bring *him* in for!'

'Oh, he's not so bad,' sais Mrs. Cockles's cheerful voice. 'Just hand me that broom, will you? Thanks. He's all right if he's treated rough. I don't stand no nonsense from him, I don't. I've cleaned for him now for years, and he's never had a harsh word for me. But my, how he hates those children!'

'Ah, that's another thing,' said Mrs. Moon. 'When Mr. Hilton told him about this here letter, he was that pleased to think those kids knew nothing about it—and he made Master and Mistress promise they'd not let those five interfere. And they promised. I was there, holding up poor Gladys, and I heard every word. "Mrs. Hilton," he said, "Mrs. Hilton, madam, this is not a case for children to interfere in and I must request you, in the name of the law, to keep this affair to yourselves."

'Lawks!' said Mrs. Cockles. 'He can talk grand when he likes, can't he? I reckon, Mrs. Moon maybe there's been more of these letters than we know. Well, well—so poor Gladys went home, all upset-like. And who's going to come in her place, I wonder? Or will she be coming back?'

'Well, it's my belief she'd better keep away from this village now,' said Mrs.Moon. 'Tongues will wag, you know. I've got a niece who can come next week, so it won't matter much if she keeps away.'

'What about a cup of tea?' said Mrs. Cockles. 'I'm that thirsty with all this cleaning. These rugs look a fair treat now, Mrs. Moon.'

THE MYSTERY OF THE SPITEFUL LETTERS

Bets fled as soon as she heard footsteps coming in at the scullery door. Her knitting almost tripped her up as she went. She ran up the stairs and into the playroom, painting. Pip was there, reading and waiting for her.

'Pip! I've found out everything, simply everything!' cried Bets. 'And there *is* a mystery to solve—a kind we haven't had before.'

Sounds of laughter floated up from the drive. It was the others coming. 'Wait a bit,' said Pip, excited. 'Wait till the others come up. Then you can tell the whole lot. Golly, you must have done well, Bets!'

The others saw at once from Bets' face that she had news for them. 'Good old Bets!' said Fatty. 'Go on, Betsy. spill the beans!'

Bets told them everything. 'Somebody wrote a nonnimus letter to Gladys,' she said. 'What *is* a nonnimus letter, Fatty?'

Fatty grinned. 'You mean an *anonymous* letter, Bets,' he said.'A letter sent without the name of the sender at the bottom—usually a beastly cowardly sort of letter, saying things that the writer wouldn't dare to say to any one's face. So poor Gladys got an anonymous letter, did she?'

'Yes,' said Bets. 'I don't know what it said though. It upset her. Mrs. Moon got out of her what it was and made her go and see Mother and Daddy about it. And they rang up Mr. Goon.'

'And he came popping along, his eyes bulging with delight because he'd got a mystery to solve that we didn't know about !' said Fatty. 'So there's an anonymous letter-writer somewhere here, is there? A nasty, cowardly letter-writer—well, here's our mystery, Find-Outers ! WHO is the writer of the "nonnimus" letters ?'

'We shall never be able to find that out,' said Dasiy. ' How on earth could we ?'

We must make plans,' said Fatty. 'We must search for clues!' Bets' face lighted up at once. She loved hunting for clues. 'We must make a list of suspects—people who could do it and would. We must...'

'We haven't got to work with Goon, have we ?' said Pip. 'We don't need to let him know we know, do we?'

'Well—he already thinks we know most of this,' said Fatty. 'I don't see why we shouldn't tell him we know as much as he does, and not tell him how we've found out, and make him think we know a lot more than we do. That'll make him sit up a bit!'

So, the next time that the Five Find-Outers met the policeman, they stopped to speak to him.

'How are you getting on with this difficult case ?' asked Fatty gravely. It—er—it abounds with such strange clues, doesn't it ?'

Mr. Goon hadn't discovered a single clue, and he was astonished and annoyed to hear that there were apparently things the children knew and he didn't. He stared at them.

'You tell me your clues you've found,' he said at last. ' We'll swap clues. It beats me how you know about this affairs. You wasn't to know a thing, not a thing.'

'We know much more than you think,' said Fatty solemnly. 'A very difficult and—er—enthralling case.'

'You tell me your clues,' said Mr. Goon again. 'We'd better swap clues, like I said. Better help one another than hinder, I always say.'

'Now, where did I put those clues?' said Fatty, diving into his capacious pockets. He brought out a live white rat and stared at it. 'Was this a clue or not?' he asked the others. 'I can't remember.'

It was impossible not to giggle. Bets went off into a delighted explosion. Mr. Goon glared.

'You clear-off,' he said majestically. 'Making a joke of everything ! Call yourself a detective ! Gah!'

'What a lovely word !' said Bets, as they all walked off, giggling. 'Gah! Gah, Pip ! Gah, Fatty!'

Fatty brought out a live white rat

6 THE FIND-OUTERS MAKE THEIR FIRST PLANS

EVERY one went to tea at Fatty's that day. Mrs. Trotteville was out, so the five children had tea in Fatty's crowded little den. It was more crowded than ever now that Fatty had got various disguises and wigs. The children exclaimed in delight over a blue-and-white striped butcher-boy's apron and a lift-boy's suit complete with peaked cap.

'But, Fatty, whenever could you disguise your self as a lift-boy?' asked Larry.

'You never know,' said Fatty. 'You see, I can only get disguises that do for a boy. If I were a grown-up I could get dozens and dozens—a sailor's suit, a postman's even a policeman's. But I'm a bit limited, being a boy.'

Fatty also had a bookcase crammed full of detective stories. He read every one he could find. 'I pick up quite a lot of hints that way,' he said. 'I think Sherlock Holmes was one of the best detectives. Golly, he had some fine mysteries to solve. I don't believe even I could have solved all of them!'

'You're a conceited creature,' said Larry, trying on the red wig. He looked very startling in it. 'How do you put those freckles on that you had with this?' he asked.

'Grease-paint,' said Fatty. 'There are my grease-paints over there—what actors use for make-up, you know. One day I'm going to make myself up as a monster and give you all a fright.'

'Oh—do give old Clear-Orf a scare too!' begged Bets.

'Let me try on that wig, Larry; do let me.'

'We really ought to be making our plans to tackle this mystery,' said Fatty, taking a beautiful gold pencil out of his pocket. Pip stared.

'I say! Is that gold ?'

'Yes.' said Fatty airily. 'I won it last term for the best essay. Didn't I tell you ? It was a marvellous essay, all about...'

'All right, all right,' said Larry and Pip together. 'We'll take your word for it, Fatty!'

'I had a marvellous report again,' said Fatty. 'Did you, Pip?'

'You know I didn't,' said Pip. 'You heard my mother say so. Shut up, Fatty.'

'Let's talk about out new mystery,' said Daisy, seeing that a quarrel was about to flare up. 'Write down some notes, Fatty. Let's get going.'

'I was just about to,' said Fatty, rather pompously. He printed in beautiful small letters a heading to the page in the lovely leather notebopok he held. The others looked to see what he had printed:

MYSTERY NO. 4.   BEGUN APRIL 5TH.

'Ooh—that looks fine,' said Bets.

'CLUES' was the next thing printed by Fatty, over the page.

'But we haven't got any,' said Pip.

'We soon shall have,' said Fatty. He turned over the page. 'SUSPECTS' was what he printed there.

'We don't know any of those yet either,' said Daisy. 'And I'm sure I don't know how we're going to find any.'

THE MYSTERY OF THE SPITEFUL LETTERS

'Leave it to me,' said Fatty. 'We'll soon have something to work on.'

'Yes, but what?' said Pip. 'I mean, it's no use looking for footprints or cigarette-ends or dropped hankies or anything like that. There's just nothing at all we can find for clues.'

'There's one very important thing,' said Fatty.

'What's that?' said every one.

'That anonymous letter,' said Fatty. 'It's most important we should get a glimpse of it. Most important!'

'Who's got it?' asked Larry.

'My mother might have it,' said Pip.

'More likely Gladys has got it, said Fatty. 'That's the first thing we must do. Go and see Gladys, and ask her if she knows or guesses who could have written her that letter. We must also find out what's in it.'

'Let's go now,' said Pip, who always liked to rush off as soon as anything had been decided.

'Right. You take us,' said Fatty. Pip looked rather blank.

'But I don't know where Gladys lives,' he said.

'Ha, I thought you didn't', said Fatty. 'Well, Pip, you must find out. That's the first thing we've got to do—find out where Gladys lives.'

'I could ask Mother,' said Pip doubtfully.

'Now don't be such a prize idiot,' said Fatty at once. 'Use your brains! You know jolly well your parents don't want us mixed up in this mystery, and we've got to keep it dark that we're finding out things. Don't on any account ask your mother anything—or Mrs. Moon either.'

'Well, but how am I to find out then?' said Pip, looking bewildered.

THE FIND-OUTERS MAKE THEIR FIRST PLANS

'I know a way, I know a way!' sang out Bets suddenly. 'Gladys lent me a book once and I didn't have time to give it her back before she left. I could go to Mrs. Moon and tell her, and ask her for Gladys's address so that I sould send the book on to her.'

'Clever girl!' said Fatty. 'You're coming on well, you are, Bets! Perhaps you'd better handle this, and not Pip'

'I've got an idea too now,' said Pip, rather sulkily.

'What?' said Bets.

'Well—if I got a bit of paper and stuck it in an envelope, and wrote Gladys's name and our address on it and posted it—Mother would re-address it and I could hang about and see what it was, when, she puts the letter on the hall-stand to be posted,' said Pip.

'Yes, that's a very fine idea too,' said Fatty. 'Couldn't have thought of a much better one myself. Go to the top of the class, Pip.'

Pip grinned. 'Well—both Bets and I will carry out our ideas,' he said, 'and surely one of us will get Gladys's address!'

'Here's a bit of paper and an envelope,' said Fatty. 'But disguise your writing, Pip.'

'Why?' said Pip, surprised.

'Well—seeing that yout mother gets a letter from you every single week when you're away at boarding-school, it's likely she *might* recognize your writing and wonder why on earth you were writing to Gladys when she was gone!' said Fatty, in a very patient, but rather tired voice.

'Fatty thinks of everything!' said Daisy admiringly. Pip saw the point at once, but doubted very much if he could disguise his writing properly.

'Here—give it to me. I'll do it,' said Fatty, who was apparently able to disguise his writing as easily as he could disguise his appearance and his voice. He took the envelope, and, to the children's enormous admiration, wrote Gladys's name and Pip's address in small, extremely grown-up handwriting, quite unlike his own.

'There you are,' he said. 'Elementary, my dear Pip!'

'Marvellous, Mr. Sherlock Holmes!' said Pip. 'Honestly, Fatty, you're a wonder. How many different writings can you do?'

'Any amount,' said Fatty. 'What to see the writing of a poor old charwoman? Here it is !'

He wrote a few words in a scrawling, untidy writing. 'Oh, it's just like Mrs. Cockles's writing!' cried Bets in delight. 'Sometimes she puts out a notice for the milkman—"TWO PINTS' or something like that—and her writing is just like that!'

'Now write like old Clear-Orf,' said Larry. 'Go on! What does *he* write like?'

'Well, I've seen his writing, so I know what it's like,' said Fatty, 'but if I hadn't seen it I'd know too—he'd be bound to write like this. . . .'

He wrote a sentence or two in a large, flourishing hand with loops and tails to the letters—an untidy, would-be impressive hand—yes, just like Mr.Goon's writing.

'Fatty, you're always doing something surprising,' said Bets, with a sigh. 'There's nothing you can't do. I wish I was like you.'

'You be like yourself. You couldn't be nicer,' said Fatty,

giving the little girl a squeeze. Bets was pleased. She liked and admired Fatty very much indeed.

'You know, once last term I thought I'd try out a new handwriting on my form-master,' said Fatty. 'So I made up a marvellous handwriting, very small and neat and pointed, with most of the letters leaning backwards—and old Tubbs wouldn't pass it—said I'd got some one to do that prep for me, and made me do it all again.'

'Poor Fatty,' said Bets.

'Well, the next time I gave my prep in, it was written in old Tubbs, own handwriting,' said Fatty, with a grin. 'Golly, it gave him a start to see a prep all done in his own writing!'

'What *did* he say?' asked Pip.

'He said, "And who's done this prep for you this time, Trotteville?" And I said, " My goodness, sir, it looks as if *you* have!"' said Fatty. The others roared with laughter. Whether Fatty's school tales were true or not, they were always funny.

Pip slipped the blank piece of paper into the envelope that Fatty had addressed and stuck it down. He took the stamp that Fatty offered him and put it on.

'There!' he said. 'I'll post it on my way home to-night. It'll catch the half-past six post and it will be there to-morrow morning. Then if I don't manage to spot the re-addressed letter my name isn't Pip.'

'Well, it isn't,' said Bets. 'It's Philip.'

'Very funny!' said Pip. 'I don't think!'

'Now don't squabble, you two,' said Fatty. 'Well, we've done all we can for the moment. Let's have a game. I'll teach you Woo-hoo-colly-wobbles.'

'Gracious! Whatever's that?' said Bets.

It was a game involving much woo-hoo-ing and groaning and rolling over and over. Soon all the children were reduced to tears of mirth. Mrs. Trotteville sent up to say that if anybody was ill they were to go down and tell her, but if they were just playing, would they please go out into the garden, down to the very bottom.

'Oooh. I didn't know your mother was back,' said Pip, who had really let himself go. 'We'd better stop. What an awful game this is, Fatty.'

'I say—it's almost half-past six!' said Larry. 'If you're going to post that letter, you'd better go, young Pip. Brush yourself down, for goodness sake. You look awful.'

'Gah!' said Pip, remembering Mr. Goon's last exclamation. He brushed himself down, and re-tied his tie. 'Come on, Bets,' he said. 'Well, so long, you others—we'll tell you Gladys's address to-morrow, and then we'll go and see her and examine our first clue—the "nonnimus" letter!'

He ran down the path with Bets. Fatty leaned out of the window of his den and yelled, 'Oy! You're a fine detective! You've forgotten the letter!'

'So I have!' said Pip and tore back for it. Fatty dropped it down. Pip caught it and ran off again. He and Bets tore to the pillar-box at the corner and were just in time to catch the postman emptying the letters from the inside.

'One more!' said Pip. 'Thanks, postman! Come on, Bets. We'll try out your book-idea as soon as we get home.'

7   DISAPPOINTMENT FOR PIP AND BETS

BETS flew to find the book that Gladys had lent her, as soom as she got home. She found it at once. It was an old school prize, called *The Little Saint*. Bets had been rather bored with it. 'The Little Saint' had been a girl much too good to be true. Bets preferred to read about naughty, lively children.

She wrapped the book up carefully, and then went down to say good-night to her mother. Mrs. Hilton was reading in the drawing-room.

'Come to say good-night, Bets?' she said, looking at the clock. 'Did you have a nice time at Fatty's?'

'Yes! We played his new game, Woo-hoo-colly-wobbles,' said Bets. 'It was fun.'

'I expect it was noisy and ridiculous if it was anything to do with Frederick,' said her mother. 'What's that you've got, Bets?'

'Oh Mother, it's a book that Gladys lent me,' said Bets. 'I was going to ask Mrs. Moon her address so that I could send it to her. Could I have a stamp, Mother?'

'You don't need to ask Mrs. Moon,' said her mother. 'I'll see that Gladys gets it.'

'Oh,' said Bets. 'Well—I'll just put her address on it. I've written her name. What's her address, Mother ?'

'I'll write it,' said Mrs. Hilton. 'Now don't stand there putting off time, Bets. Go up to bed. Leave the parcel here.'

'Oh, do let me just write the address,' said poor Bets, feeling that her wonderful idea was coming to nothing, and that it wasn't fair. 'I feel like writing, Mother.'

'Well, it must be for the first time in your life then!' said Mrs.Hilton. 'You've always said how much you hate writing before. Go up to bed, Bets, now.'

Bets had to go. She left the book on the table by her mother, feeling rather doleful. But perhaps Pip would see the address later on in the evening, if her mother wrote it on the parcel.

Pip said he'd keep an eye open. Anyway, what did it matter? His own letter would come in the morning and they'd soon find out the right address.

He saw the book on the table when he went down ready for dinner, cleaned and brushed. He read the name on the wrapping-paper... but there was no address there yet.

'Shall I write Gladys's address for you, Mother?' he asked politely. 'Just to save you time.'

'I can't imagine why you and Bets are so anxious to do a little writing to-night!' said Mrs. Hilton, looking up from her book. 'No, Pip. I can't remember it off-hand. Leave it.'

So it had to be left. Pip was glad to think his letter was coming in the morning. He was sure that had been a better idea than Bets'!

Pip was down early next morning, waiting for the postman. He took all the letters out of the box and put them by his mother's plate. His own was there, addressed in Fatty's disguised handwriting.

'There's a letter for Gladys, Mother,' said Pip, at breakfast-time. 'We'll have to re-address it.'

'My dear boy, you don't need to tell me that!' said Mrs. Hilton.

'Did you put the address on my parcel?' asked Bets, attacking her boiled egg hungrily.

'No. I couldn't remember it last night,' said Mrs. Hilton, reading her letters.

'Shall Pip and I take the letters and the parcel to the post for you this morning?' asked Bets, thinking this was really a very good idea.

'If you like,' said Mrs.Hilton. Bets winked at Pip. Now things would be easy! They could both see the address they wanted.

A telephone call came for Mrs. Hilton after breakfast, whilst the children were hanging about waiting to take the letters. Mrs. Moon answered it. She went in to Mrs. Hilton.

'There's a call for you, Mam,' she said.

'Who is it?' asked Mrs. Hilton. Pip and Bets were most astonished to see Mrs. Moon winking and nodding mysteriously to their mother, but not saying any name. However, Mrs. Hilton seemed to understand all right.She got up and went to the telephone, shutting the door behind her so that the children could not follow without being noticed.

'Well—who's on the phone that Mother doesn't want us to know about?' said Pip, annoyed. 'Did you see how mysterious Mrs. Moon was, Bets?'

'Yes,' said Bets. 'Can't we just open the door a bit and listen, Pip?'

'No,' said Pip, 'We really can't. Not if Mother doesn't want us to hear.'

Their mother came back after a minute or two. She didn't say who had telephoned to her and the children didn't dare to ask.

'Shall we go to the post-office now?' said Pip, at last.

'We're ready.'

'Yes. There are the letters over there,' said Mrs. Hilton.

'What about my parcel for Gladys?' said Bets.

'Oh, that doesn't need to go—nor the letter for her,' said Mrs. Hilton. 'Somebody's going to see her to-day and he will take them. That will save putting a stamp on the parcel.'

'Who's going to see Gladys?' asked Pip. 'Can we go too? I'd like to see Gladys again.'

'Well, you can't,' said Mrs. Hilton. 'And please don't start trying to find out things, Pip, because, as I've already told you, this is nothing whatever to do with you. You can take the other letters to the post for me. Go now and you will catch the ten o'clock post.'

Pip and Bets went off rather sulkily. Bets was near tears. 'It's too bad, Pip,' she said, when they got out-of-doors, 'we had such good ideas—and now they're no use at all!'

'We'll post the letters and then go up and see Fatty,' said Pip gloomily. 'I expect he'll think we ought to have done better. He always thinks he can do things so marvellously.'

'Well, so he can,' said Bets loyally. 'Let *me* post the letters, Pip. Here's the post office.'

'Here you are then. What a baby you are to like posing letters still!' said Pip. Bets slipped them into the letter-box and they turned to go up to Fatty's house. He was at home, reading a new detective book.

'Our ideas weren't any good,' said Pip. He told Fatty what had happened. Fatty was unexpectedly sympathetic.'

'That was hard luck,' he said. 'You both had jolly fine ideas, and it was only a bit of bad luck that stopped them having their reward. Now—who is it that is going to see

Gladys to-day?'

'Mother said it was a "he," said Pip. 'She said, "Somebody's going to see Gladys to-day, and *he* will take them!"'

'That's easy then,' said Fatty briskly. '*He* can only mean one person—and that's old Clear-Orf! Well, now we know what to do.'

'*I* don't know,' said Pip, still gloomy. 'You always seem to know everything, Fatty.'

'Brains, my dear fellow, brains!' said Fatty. 'We'll, look here—if it's Goon that's going to see Gladys, we can wait about and follow him, can't we? He'll go on his bike, I expect—well, we can go on ours! Easy!'

Pip and Bets cheered up. The idea of stalking old Clear-Orf was a pleasing one. They would have the fun of doing that, and would find out too where Gladys lived. Yes, to-day looked much more exciting now.

'You go and tell Larry and Daisy,' said Fatty. 'We shall have to keep a watch on old Goon's house so that we know when he leaves. I vote we ask our mothers for food again, so that we can go off at any time and come back when we like.'

'I'm going to buy Gladys some sweets,' said Bets. 'I like her.'

'It would be a good idea if we all took her some little present,' said Fatty thoughtfully. ' Sort of show we were sorry for her and were on her side, so that she'll be more willing to talk.'

'Well, I'll go and tell Larry and Daisy to get out their bikes and bring food along,' said Pip. 'I'd better hurry in case old Clear- Orf goes this morning. Bets, you'd better come back home with me too, and get your bike, because we'll both need them. Then we'll go to Larry's and then we'll buy some little things for Gladys.'

'I'll go and keep a watch on Goon's house in case he starts off before you're back,' said Fatty. 'I'll just get some sandwiches first. See you round the corner from Goon's!'

In about half an hour's time Larry, Daisy, Bets, and Pip were all with Fatty, round the corner near Clear-Orf's house, complete with sandwiches and little presents for Gladys. There had been no sign of Goon.

But in about ten minutes' time, Larry, who was on guard, gave a whistle. That was the signal to say that Goon was departing somewhere. He was on his bicycle, a portly, clumsy figure with short legs ending in enormous boots that rested on pedals looking absurdly small.

He set off down the road that led to the river. 'May be going across in the ferry!' panted Fatty, pedalling furiously. 'Come on! Don't all tear round the corners together in case he spots us. I'll always go first.'

But unfortunately all that Mr. Goon had gone to do down the river-lane was to leave a message with the farmer there. He was the farmer in the field and called out the message to him, then quickly turned his bicycle round and cycled back up the lane again. He came round the corner very quickly and found himself wobbing in the middle of the Five Find-Outers!

He came off with a crash. The children jumped off and Fatty tried to help him up, whilst Buster, jumping delightedly out of Fatty's basket, yelped in delight.

'Hurt yourself, Mr.Goon?' asked Fatty politely. 'Here,

let me give you a heave up.'

'You let me alone!' said Mr. Goon angirly. 'Riding five abreast like that in a narrow lane! What do you mean by it!'

'So sorry, Mr. Goon,' said Fatty. Pip gave a giggle. Old Clear-Orf looked so funny, trying to disentangle himself form his bicycle.'

Yes, you laugh at me, you cheeky little toad!' roared Mr.Goon. 'I'll tell of you, you see if I don't. I'll be seeing your Ma this morning and I'll put in a complaint. I'm going right along there now.'

Fatty brushed Mr. Goon down so smartly that the policeman jumped aside. 'You're all dusty, Mr. Goon,' said Fatty anxiously. 'You can't go to Mrs. Hilton's in this state. Just a few more whacks and you'll be all right!'

'Wait till you get the whacks *you* want!' said Mr. Goon, putting his helmet on firmly. 'Never knew such children in me life! Nothing but trouble round every corner where you are! Gah!'

He rode off, leaving the children standing in the lane with their bicycles. 'Well, that was a bit of a nuisance bumping into him like that,' said Fatty. 'I didn't particularly want him to see any of us to-day. I don't want him to suspect we're on his track. Now let me see—he's off to collect those things of Gladys from your mother, Pip. There's no doubt about that. So all we've got to do now is to lie in wait for him somewhere and then follow him very carefully.'

'Let's go to the church corner,' said Pip. 'He's sure to pass there, wherever he goes. Come on!'

So off they went, and hid behind some trees, waiting for old Clear-Orf to show them the way to where Gladys lived.

8   A TALK WITH POOR GLADYS

IN about half an hour Mr. Goon came cycling along, and went right by the hidden children without seeing them

'Now listen!' said Fatty. 'It's no use us all tearing after him in a bunch because we'd be so easy to spot. I'll go first and keep a long way ahead. You follow, see? If I have to take a turning you may not know I'll tear a sheet out of my notebook and drop it the way I go.'

'It's windy to-day. Better hop off your bike and chalk one of those arrows on the road that gypsies always seem to make,' said Pip. 'Your bit of paper might blow away. Got any chalk, Fatty?'

'Of course!' said Fatty and took a piece out of his capacious pockets. 'Yes, that's a better idea. Good for you, Pip! Well, I'll get along in front of you now. Look, there goes old Clear-Orf panting up the hill in the distance. Looks as if he's going to take the main road.'

Fatty rode off, whistling. The others waited a little while and then rode after him. It was easy to see him in the distance in the open country. But soon they came to where the road forked, and Fatty seemed nowhere in sight.

'Here you are! Here's his chalk arrow!' said Daisy, her sharp eyes spotting it at once, marked on the path at the side of one of the roads. 'This is the way!'

They rode on again. They rarely saw Fatty now, for he and Mr. Goon had left the main raod and were cycling down narrow, winding lanes. But at every doubtful fork or corner they saw his chalk mark.

'This is fun,' said Bets, who liked looking for the little

arrows. 'But oh dear—I hope it's not much farther!'

'Looks as if Gladys lives at Haycock Heath,'said Larry. 'This road leads there. My, here's a steep hill. Up we go! I bet old Fatty found it heavy going here, with Buster in his basket. Buster seems to weigh an awful lot when he's in a bicycle basket.'

At the top of the hill, just at a bend, Fatty was waiting for them. He looked excited.

'He's gone into the very last cottage of all!' he said. 'And isn't it good luck—it's got a notice with "Minerals" printed on it, in the window. That means lemonade or ginger-beer is sold there. We've got a fine excuse for going in, once Clear-Orf has gone.'

'Better get back into this other little lane here, hadn't we?' said Larry. 'I mean—if old Clear-Orf suddenly comes out, he'll find us!'

So they all wheeled their bicycles into a crooked, narrow little lane, whose trees met overhead and made a green tunnel. 'Must give old Buster a run,' said Fatty and lifted him out of the basket. But unfortunately a cat strolled down the lane, appearing suddenly from the hedge, and Buster immediately gave chase, barking joyfully. Cats and rabbits were his great delight.

The cat gave one look at Buster and decided to move quickly. She shot down the lane, and took a flying leap over the little wall surrounding the back-garden of the cottage into which Mr. Goon had disappeared. Buster tried to leap over too, and couldn't—but, using his brains as a Buster should, he decided that there must be another way in, and went to look for the front gate.

Then there was such a hurricane of barks and yowls, mixed with the terrified clucking of hens, that the children stood perrified. Out came Mr. Goon, with a sharp-nosed woman—and Gladys!

'You clear-orf!' yelled Mr. Goon to Buster. 'Bad dog, you! Clear-orf!'

With a bark of joy Buster flung himself at the policeman's ankles, and snapped happily at them.Mr. Goon kicked at him and let out a yell.

'It's that boy's dog! Get away, you! Now what's he doing here? Has that boy Frederick Trotteville been messing about up here, now?'

'Nobody's been here this morning but you,' said Gladys. 'Oh, Mr. Goon, don't kick at the dog like that. He wasn't doing much harm.'

It was quite plain that Buster meant to get a nip if he could. Fatty, feeling most annoyed at having to show himself, was forced to cycle out and yell to Buster.

'Hey, Buster! Come here, sir!'

Mr. Goon turned and gave Fatty a look that might have cowed a lion if Fatty had been a lion. But, being Fatty, he didn't turn a hair.

'Why, Mr. Goon!' he said, taking off his cap in a most aggravatingly polite manner, 'fancy seeing *you* here! Come for a little bike-ride too? Lovely day, isn't it?'

Mr. Goon almost exploded. 'Now what are *you* a-doing of here?' he demanded. 'You tell me that, see?'

'All I'm a-doing of at the moment is having a nice bike-ride,' answered Fatty cheerfully. 'What are *you* a-doing of, Mr. Goon? Having a ginger-beer? I see there's a card in the window. I think I'll have something to drink myself. It's a jolly hot day.'

And, to the other children's delight, and Mr. Goon's annoyance, Fatty strolled up the little front path and entered the door. Inside was a small table at which people could sit down to have their lemonade. Fatty sat down.

'You clear-orf out of here,' ordered Mr. Goon. 'I'm here on business, see? And I'm not having busy-bodies like you interfering. *I* know what you've come here for—snooping around—trying to find clues, and making nuisances of yourselves.'

'Oh, that reminds me,' said Fatty, beginning to feel in his pockets with a serious look, 'didn't we say we'd swap clues, Mr. Goon? Now where did I put that. . .'

'If you bring out that there white rat again I'll skin you alive!' boomed Mr. Goon, whose fingers were itching to box Fatty's ears.

'That white rat wasn't a clue after all,' said Fatty gravely. 'I made a mistake. That must have been a clue in another case I'm working on. Wait a bit—ah, this may be a clue!'

He fished a clothes-peg out of his pocket and looked at it solemnly. Mr. Goon, quite beside himself with rage, snatched at it, threw it down on the floor, and jumped on it! Then, looking as if he was going to burst, he took his bicycle by the handle-bars, and turned to Gladys and the other woman.

'Now don't you forget what I've said. And you let me hear as soon as anything else happens. Don't talk to nobody at all about this here case—them's my strict orders!'

He rode off, trying to look dignified, but unfortunately Buster flew after him, jumping up at his pedalling feet, so that poor Mr. Goon wobbled dreadfully. As soon as he had gone the children crowded up to Fatty, laughing.

'Oh, Fatty! How can you! One of these days old Clear-Orf will kill you!'

Gladys and her aunt had been listening and watching in surprise. Bets ran to Gladys and took her hand.

'Gladys! I *was* sorry you left! Do come back soon! Look, I've brought you something!'

The sharp-nosed aunt made an impatient noise. 'I'll never get to the shops this morning!' she said. 'I'm going right away now, Gladys. See and get the dinner on in good time— and mind you heed what the policeman said.'

Much to the children's relief, she put on an old hat and scarf, and disappeared down the lane, walking quickly. They were glad to see her go, for she looked rather bad-tempered. They crowded round Gladys, who smiled and seemed very pleased to see them.

'Gladys! We know something made you unhappy,' said little Bets and pressed a bag of sweets in the girl's hand. 'We've come to say we're sorry and we've brought a few little things for you. And please, please come back!'

Gladys seemed rather overcome. She took them all into the little front-room and poured out some glasses of ginger-beer for them.

'It's right down kind of you,' she said, in a tearful voice. 'Things aren't too easy— and my aunt isn't too pleased to have me back. But I couldn't go on living in Peterswood when I knew that—that––that . . . '

'That what?' asked Fatty gently.

'I'm not supposed to talk about it,' said Gladys.

'Well—we're only children. It can't matter talking to *us*,' said Bets. 'We all like you, Gladys. You tell us. Why, you never know, we might be able to help you!'

'There's nobody can help me,' said Galdys, and a tear ran down her cheek. She began to undo the little things the children had brought her—sweets, chocolate, a little brooch with G on, and two small hankies. She seemed very touched.

'It's kind of you,' she said. 'Goodness knows I want a bit of kindness now.'

'Why?' asked Daisy. 'What's happened? You tell us, Gladys. It will do you good to tell some one.'

'Well—it's like this,' said Gladys. 'There's something wrong I once did that I'm ashamed of now, see? And I had to go into a Home, and I liked it and I said I'd never do wrong again. Well, I left there and I got a job—with your mother, Master Pip and wasn't I happy working away there, and every-body treating me nice, and me forgetting all about the bad days!'

'Yes?' said Fatty, as Gladys paused. 'Go on, Gladys. Don't stop.'

'Then—then...' began Gladys again, and burst into tears. 'Somebody sent me a letter, and said, "We know you're a wrong-un, and you didn't ought to be in a good place with decent people. Clear out or we'll tell on you!"'

'What a shame!' said Fatty. 'Who sent the letter?'

'I don't know that,' said Gladys. 'It was all in printed letters. Well, I was that upset I broke down in front of Mrs. Moon, and she took the letter from me and read it, and said I should ought to go to your mother, Master Pip, and tell her—but I didn't want to because I knew I'd lose my place. But

she said, yes go, Mrs. Hilton would put things right for me.
So I went, but I was that upset I couldn't speak a word.'

'Poor old Gladys!' said Daisy. 'But I'm sure Pip's mother
was kind to you.'

'Oh yes—and shocked at the cruel letter,' said Gladys,
wiping her eyes. 'And she said I could have two or three
days off and go to my aunt to pull myself together, like—
and she'd make inquiries and find out who wrote that letter—and stop them talking about me, so's I could have a
chance. But my aunt wasn't too pleased to see me!'

'Why didn't you go to your father and mother, Gladys?'
asked little Bets, who thought that surely they would have
been the best friends for any girl of theirs who was unhappy.

'I couldn't,' said Gladys, and looked so sad that the
children felt quite scared.

'Why—are they—are they—dead?' asked Bets.

'No. They're—they're in prison!' said poor Gladys and
wept again. 'You see—they've always been dishonest folk—
stealing and that—and they taught me to steal too. And the
police got them, and when they found I was going into shops
with my mother and taking things I didn't ought, they took
me away and put me into a Home. I didn't know it was so
wrong, you see—but now I do !'

The children were horrified that any one should have such
bad parents. They stared at Gladys and tears ran down Bets'
cheeks. She took Gladys's hand.

'You're good now, Gladys, aren't you?' said the little girl.
'You don't look bad. You're good now.'

'Yes—I've not done nothing wrong ever since,' said poor
Gladys. 'Nor I never would now. They were so kind to me at

the Home—you can't think! And I promised the Matron there I'd always do my best wherever I was, and I was so glad when they sent me to your mother's, Miss Bets. But there—they say your sins will always find you out! I guess I'll never be able to keep a good job for long. Somebody will always put it round that I was a thief once, and that my parents are still in prison.'

'Gladys—the person who wrote that letter and threatens to tell about you, is far, far wickeder than you've *ever* been!' said Fatty earnestly. 'It's a shame!'

'There was another girl in the Home with me,' said Gladys. 'She's with old Miss Garnet at Lacky Cottage in Peterswood. Well, she's had one of them letters too—without any name at the bottom. But she doesn't mind as much as I do. She didn't give way like I did. But she met me and told me, that's how I know. She didn't tell nobody but me. And she don't know either who wrote the letters.

'Did you tell Mr. Goon that?' asked Fatty.

'Oh yes,' said Gladys. 'And he went to see Molly straightaway. He says he'll soon get to the bottom of it, and find out the mischief-maker. But it seems to me that the mischief is done now. I'll never be able to face people in Peterswood again. I'll always be afraid they know about me.'

'Gladys, where is that letter?' said Fatty.'Wll you show it to me? It might be a most important clue.'

Gladys rummaged in her bag. Then she looked up. 'No good me looking for it!' she said. 'I've given it to Mr. Goon, of course! He came to fetch it this morning. He's got Molly's letter too. He reckons he'll be able to tell quite a lot from the writing and all!'

THE MYSTERY OF THE SPITEFUL LETTERS

'Blow!' said Fatty, in deep disappointment. 'There's our one and only clue gone!'

THE children sat and talked to Gladys for a little while longer. They were so disappointed about the letter being given to Mr. Goon that she felt quite sorry for them.'

'I'll get it back from him, and Molly's letter too,' she promised. 'And I'll show you them both. I'll be going down to see Molly this evening, when it's dark and no one will see me—and I'll pop into Mr. Goon's, say I want to borrow the letters, and I'll lend them to you for a little while.'

'Oh thanks!' said Fatty, cheering up. 'That'll be splendid. Well, now we'd better be going. We've got our lunch with us and it's getting a bit late-ish. You haven't put that dinner on yet Gladys, either?'

'Oh lawks, nor I have!' said Gladys, and began to look very flustered. 'I've been that upset I can't think of a thing!'

'You'll be passing my door on your way to Molly's to-night,' said Fatty. 'Could you pop the letters in at my letter-box, and call for them on your way back?'

'Yes, I'll do that,' said Gladys. 'Thank you for all your kindness. You've made me feel better already.'

The children went off. 'A nice girl, but not very bright,' said Fatty, as they cycled away. 'What a mean trick to play on her—trying to make her lose her job and get all upset like that! I wonder who in the world it is? I bet it's some one who knows the Home Gladys went to, and has heard about her there. My goodness, I'm hungry!'

'We've had quite and exciting morning,' said Larry. 'It's a pity we couldn't see that letter though.'

'Never mind—we'll see it is this evening—if old Clear-Orf will let Gladys have it!' said Fatty. 'Which I very much doubt. He'll suspect she's going to show it to us!'

'We'll all come round to you after tea,' said Larry. 'And we'll wait for the letters to come. I think you'd better wait about by the front gate, Fatty—just in case somebody else takes them out of the letter-box instead of you.'

So, when it was dark, Fatty skulked about by the front gate, scaring his mother considerably when she came home from an outing.

'Good gracious, Fatty! Must you hide in the shadows there?' she said. 'You gave me an awful fright. Go in at once.'

'Sorry, Mother,' said Fatty, and went meekly in at the front door with his mother—and straight out of the garden door, back to the front gate at once! Just in time too, for a shadowy figure leaned over the gate and said breathlessly: 'Is that Master Frederick? Here's the letters. Mr. Goon was out, so I went in and waited. He didn't come, so I took them, and here they are.'

Gladys pushed a packet into Fatty's hands and hurried off. Fatty gave a low whistle. Gladys hadn't waited for permission to take the letters! She had reckoned they were hers and Molly's and had just taken them, What would Mr. Goon say to that? He wouldn't be at all pleased with Gladys—especially when he knew she had

Gladys pushed the letter into Fatty's hand

handed them to him, Fatty! Fatty knew perfectly well that Mr. Goon would get it all out of poor Gladys.

He slipped indoors and told the others what had happened. 'Think I'd better try and put the letters back without old Clear-Orf knowing they've gone,' he said. 'If I don't Gladys will get into trouble. But first of all, we'll examine them!'

'I suppose it's all right to?' said Larry doubtfully.

'Well—I don't see that it matters, seeing that Gladys had given us her permission,' said Fatty. He looked at the little package.

'Golly!' he said. 'There are more than two letters here! Look—here's a post-card—an anonymous one to Mr. Lucas, Gardener, Acacia Lodge, Peterswood—and do you know what it says?'

'What?' cried every one.

'Why, it says: "WHO LOST HIS JOB THROUGH SELLING HIS MASTER'S FRUIT?" said Fatty, in disgust. 'Gracious! Fancy sending a *card* with that on—to poor old Lucas too, who must be over seventy!'

'So other people have had these beastly things as well as Gladys and Molly!' said Larry. 'Let's squint at the writing, Fatty.'

'It's all the same,' said Fatty. 'All done in capital letters, look—and all to people in Peterswood. There are five of them—four letters and a card. How disgusting!'

Larry was examining the envelopes. They were all the same, square and white, and the paper used was cheap. 'Look,' said Larry, 'they've all been sent from Sheepsale—that little market-town we've sometimes been to. Does the mean it's somebody who lives there?'

'Not necessarily,' said Fatty. 'No, I reckon it's some-body who lives in Peterswood all right, because only a Peterswood person would know the people written to. What exactly does the post-mark say?'

'It says, "Sheepsale, 11.45 .am. April 3rd," said Daisy.

'That was Monday,' said Fatty. 'What do the other post-marks say?'

'They're all different dates,' said Daisy. 'All of them except Gladys's one are posted in March—but all from Sheepsale.'

Fatty made a note of the dates and then took a small pocket calendar out. He looked up the dates and whistled.

'Here's a funny thing,' he said. 'They're all a Mon-day! See—that one's a Monday—and so is that—and that—and that. Whoever posted them must have writ-ten them on the Sunday, and posted them on Monday. Now—if the person lives in Peterswood, how can he get to Sheepsale to post them in time for the morning post on a Monday? There's no railway to Sheepsale. Only a bus that doesn't go very often.'

'It's market-day on Mondays at Sheepsale,' said Pip, remembering. 'There's an early bus that goes then, to catch the market. Wait a bit—we can look it up. Where's a bus time-table?'

As usual, Fatty had one in his pocket. He looked up the Sheepsale bus.

'Yes—here we are,' he said. 'There's a bus that goes to Sheepsale from Peterswood each Monday—at a quar-ter-past ten—reaching there at one minute past eleven. There you are—I bet our letter-writing friend leaves

Peterswood with a nasty letter in his pocket, catches the bus, gets out at Sheepsale, posts the letter—and then gets on with whatever business he has to do there!'

It all sounded extremely likely, but somehow Larry thought it was *too* likely. 'Couldn't the person go on a bike?' he said.

'Well—he *could*—but think of that awful hill up to Sheepsale,' said Fatty. 'Nobody in their senses would bike there when a bus goes.'

'No—I suppose not,' said Larry. 'Well—I don't see that all this gets us much farther, Fatty. All we've found out is that more people than Gladys and Molly have had there letters—and that they all come from Sheepsale and posted at or before 11.45—and that possibly the letter-writer may catch the 10.15 bus from Peterswood.'

'*All* we've found out!' said Fatty. 'Gosh, I think we've discovered an enormous lot. Don't you realize that we're really on the track now—the track of this beastly letter-writer. Why, if we want to, we can go and see him—or her—on Monday morning!'

The others stared at Fatty, puzzled.

'We've only got to catch that 10.15 bus!' said Fatty. "See? The letter-writer is sure to be on it. Can't we discover who it is just by looking at their faces? I bet *I* can!'

'Oh, Fatty!' said Bets, full of admiration . 'Of course—we'll catch that bus. But, oh dear, *I* should never be able to tell the right person, never. Will you really be able to spot who it is?'

'Well, I'll have a jolly good try,' said Fatty. 'And now I'd better take these letters back, I think. But first of all I want to make a tracing of some of these sentences—especially words like "PETERSWOOD" that occur in each address—in case I come across somebody who prints their words in just that way.'

'People don't print words, though—they write them,' said Daisy. But Fatty took no notice. He carefully traced a few of the words, one of them being 'PETERS-WOOD'. He put the slip into his wallet. Then he snapped the bit of elastic round the package and stood up.

'How are you going to get the letters back without being seen?' asked Larry.

'Don't know yet,' said Fatty, with a grin. 'Just chance my luck, I think. Wait about for Gladys, will you, and tell her I didn't approve of her taking the letters like that in case Mr. Goon was angry with her—amd tell her I'm returning him the letters, and hope he won't know she took them at all.'

'Right,' said Larry. Fatty was about to go when he turned and came back. 'I've an idea I'd better pop on my telegraph-boy's uniform,' he said. 'Just in case old Goon spots me. I don't want him to know *I'm* returning his letters!'

It wasn't long before Fatty was wearing his disguise, complete with freckles, red eyebrows and hair. He set this telegraph-boy's cap on his head.

'So long!' he said, and disappeared. He padded off to Mr. Goon's, and soon saw, by the darkness of his parlour, that he was not yet back. So he waited about, until he remembered that there was a darts match at the local inn, and guessed Mr. Goon would be there, throwing a dart or two.

His guess was right. Mr. Goon walked out of the inn in about ten minutes' time, feeling delighted with himself because he had come out second in the match. Fatty padded behind him for a little way, then ran across the road, got in front of Mr. Goon, came across again at a corner, walked towards the policeman and bumped violently into him.

'Hey!' said the policeman, all his breath knocked out of him. 'Hey! Look where you're going now.' He flashed his torch and saw the red-handed telegraph-boy.

'Sorry, sir, I do beg your pardon,' said Fatty earnestly. 'Have I hurt you? Always seem to be damaging you, don't I, sir? Sorry, sir.'

Mr. Goon set his helmet straight. Fatty's apologies soothed him. 'All right, my boy, all right,' he said.

'Good-night, sir, thank you, sir,' said Fatty and disappeared. But he hadn't gone more than three steps before he came running back again, holding out a package.

'Oh, Mr. Goon, Sir, did you drop these, sir? Or has somebody else dropped them?'

Mr. Goon stared at the package and his eyes bulged. 'Them letters!' he said. 'I didn't take them out with me, that I do know!'

'I expect they belong to somebody else then,' said Fatty. 'I'll inquire.'

'Hey, no you don't!' said Mr. Goon, making a grab at the package. 'They're my property. I must have brought them out unbeknowing-like. Dropped them when you bumped into me, shouldn't wonder. Good thing you found them, young man. They're valuable evidence, they are. Property of the Law.'

'I hope you won't drop them again, then, sir,' said Fatty earnestly. 'Good-night, sir.'

He vanished. Mr. Goon went home in a thoughtful frame of mind, pondering how he could possibly have taken out the package of letters and dropped them. He felt sure he *hadn't* taken them out—but if not, how could he have dropped them?

'Me memory's going,' he said mournfully. 'It's a mercy one of them kids didn't pick them letters up. I won't let that there Frederick Trotteville set eyes on them. Not if I know it!'

10   ON THE BUS TO SHEEPSALE

THERE was nothing more to be done until Monday morning, The children felt impatient, but they couldn't hurry the coming of Monday, or of the bus either.

Fatty had entered a few notes under his heading of Clues. He had put down all about the anonymous letters, and the post-marks, and had also pinned to the page the tracings he had made of the printing capital letters.

'I will now write up the case as far as we've gone with it,' he said. 'That's what the police do—and all good detectives too, as far as I can see. Sort of clears your mind, you see. Sometimes you get awfully, good ideas when you read what you've written.

Every one read what Fatty wrote, and they thought it was excellent. But infortunately nobody had any good ideas after reading it. Still, the bus passengers to Sheepsale might provide further clues.

The five children couldn't help feeling rather excited on Monday morning. Larry and Daisy got rather a shock when their mother said she wanted them to go shopping for her—but when she heard that they were going to Sheepsale market she said they could buy the things for her there. So that was all right.

They met at the bus stopping-place ten minutes before the bus went, in case Fatty had any last-minute instructions for them. He had !

'Look and see where the passengers are sitting when the bus comes up,' he said. 'And each of you sit beside one if you can, and begin to talk to him or her. You can find out a lot that way.'

Bets looked alarmed. 'But I shan't know what to say !' she said.

'Don't be silly,' said Pip. 'You can always open the conversation by saying, "Isn't that a remarkably clever-looking boy over there?" and point to Fatty. That's enough to get any one talking.'

They all laughed. 'It's all right, Bets,' said Fatty. 'You can always say something simple, like "Can you tell me the time, please?" Or, "What is this village we're passing now?" It's easy to make people talk if you ask them to *tell* you something.'

'Any other instructions, Sherlock Holmes?' said Pip.

'Yes—and this is most important,' said Fatty. 'We must watch carefully whether anybody posts a letter in Sheepsale—because if only one of the passengers does, that's a pretty good pointer, isn't it ? The post-office is by the bus-stop there, so we can easily spot if any one catches the 11.45 post. We can hang around and see if any of the bus passengers posts a letter before that time, supposing they don't go to the letter-box immediately. That's a most important point.'

'Here comes the bus,' said Bets in excitement. 'And look—there are quite a lot of people in it !'

'Five !' said Larry. 'One for each of us. Oh gosh ! One of them is old Clear-Orf ! '

'Blow !' said Fatty. 'So it is. Now whatever is he doing on the bus this morning? Has he got the same idea as we have, I wonder? If so, he's brainier than I thought. Daisy, you sit by him. He'll have a blue fit if I do and I know Buster will try to nibble his ankles all the time.'

Daisy was not at all anxious to sit by Mr. Goon, but there was no time to argue. The bus stopped. The five children and Buster got in. Buster gave a yelp of joy when he smelt the policeman. Mr. Goon looked round in astonishment and annoyance.

'Gah !' he said, in tones of deep disgust. 'You again ! Now, what you doing on this bus to-day ! Everywhere I go there's you children traipsing along !'

'We're going to Sheepsale markert, Mr. Goon,' said Daisy politely, sitting beside him. 'I hope you don't mind. Are you going there too?'

'That's *my* business,' said Mr. Goon, keeping a watchful eye on Buster, who was trying to reach his ankles, straining at his lead. 'What the Law does is no concern of yours.'

Daisy wondered for a wild moment if Mr. Goon could possibly be the anonymous letter-writer. After all, he knew the histories of every one in the village. It was his business to. Then she knew it was mad idea. But what a nuisance if Mr. Goon was on the same track as they were—sizing up the people in the bus, and going to watch for the one who posted the letter to catch the 11.45 post.

Daisy glanced round at the other people in the bus. A Find-Outer was by each. Daisy knew two of the people there. One was Miss Trimble who was companion to Lady Candling, Pip's next-door neighbour. Larry was sitting by her. Daisy felt certain Miss Trimble—or Tremble as the children called her, could have nothing to do with the case. She was far too timid and nervous.

Then there was fat little Mrs. Jolly from the sweet-shop, kindness itself. No, it couldn't possibly be her ! Why, every one loved her, and she was exactly like her name. She was kind and generous to every one, and she nodded and smiled at Daisy as she caught her eye. Daisy was certain that before the trip was ended she would be handing sweets out to all the children !

Well, that was three out of the five passengers ! That only left two possible ones. One was a thin, dark, sour-faced man, huddled up over a newspaper, with a pasty complexion, and a curious habit of twitching his nose like a rabbit every now and again. This fascinated Bets, who kept watching him.

The other possible person was a yound girl about eighteen, carrying sketching things. She had a sweet, open face, and very pretty curly hair. Daisy felt abso-lutely certain that she knew nothing what-ever about the letters.

'It must be that sour-faced man with the twitching nose,'

said Daisy to herself. She had nothing much to do because it was no use tackling Mr. Goon and talking to him. It was plain that he could not be the writer of the letters. So she watched the others getting to work, and listened with much interest, though the rattling of the bus made her miss a little of the conversation.

'Good morning, Miss Trimble,' Daisy heard Larry say politely. 'I haven't seen you for some time. Are you going to the market too? We thought we'd like to go to-day.'

'Oh, it's a pretty sight,' said Miss Trimble, setting her glasses firmly on her nose. They were always falling off, for they were pince-nez, with no side-pieces to hold them behind her ears. Bets loved to count how many times they fell off. What with watching the man with the twitching nose and Miss Timble's glasses, Bets quite forgot to talk to Mrs. Jolly, who was taking up most of the seat she and Bets was sitting on.

'Have you often been to Sheepsale market?' asked Larry.

'No, not very often,' said Miss Trimble. 'How is your dear mother, Laurence?'

'She's quite well,' said Larry. 'Er—how is *your* mother, Miss Tremble? I remember seeing her once next door.'

'Ah, my dear mother isn't too well,' said Miss Trimble. 'And if you don't mind, Laurence dear, my name is *Trimble,* not Tremble. I think I have told you that before,'

'Sorry. I keep forgetting,' said Larry. 'Er—does your mother live at Sheepsale, Miss Trem—er Trimble? Do you often go and see her?'

'She lives just outside Sheepsale,' said Miss Trimble, pleased at Larry's interest in her mother. 'Dear Lady Candling lets me go every Monday to see her, you know—such a help. I do all the old lady's shopping for the week then.'

'Do you always catch this bus?' asked Larry, wondering if by any conceivable chance Miss Trimble could be the wicked letter-writer.

'If I can,' said Miss Trimble. 'The next one is not till after lunch you know.'

Larry turned and winked at Fatty.. He didn't think that Miss Trimble was the guilty person, but at any rate she must be down as a suspect. But her next words made him change his mind completely.

'It was such a nuisance,' said Miss Trimble. 'I lost the bus last week, and wasted half my day!'

Well! That put Miss Trimble right out of the question, because certainly the letter-writer had posted the letter to poor Gladys the Monday before—and if Miss Trimble had missed the bus, she couldn't have been in Sheepsale at the right time for posting!

Larry decided that he couldn't get any more out of Miss Trimble that would be any use and looked out of the window. Bets seemed to be getting on well with Mrs. Jolly now. He couldn't hear what she was saying, but he could see that she was busy chattering.

Bets was getting on like a house on fire! Mrs Jolly greeted her warmly and asked after her mother and father, and how the garden was, and had they still got that kitchen cat that was such a good hunter. And Bets answered all her questions, keeping an interested eye on Miss Trimble's glasses and on the sour-faced man's twitching nose.

It was not until she saw how earnestly Fatty was trying to make the sour-faced man talk to him that she suddenly realized that she too ought to find out a few things from Mrs. Jolly. Whether, for instance, she always caught this bus!

'Are you going to the market, Mrs. Jolly?' she asked.

'Yes, that I am!' said Mrs. Jolly. 'I always but my butter and eggs from my sister there. You should go to her stall too, Miss Bets, and tell her you know me. She'll give you over-weight in butter then and maybe a brown egg for yourself!'

'She sounds awfully kind—just like you' said Bets.

Mrs. Jolly was pleased and laughed her hearty laugh. 'Oh, you've got a soft tongue, haven't you?' she said. Bets was surprised. She thought all tongues must surely be soft.

She looked at Mrs. Jolly, and decided not to ask her any more questions about going to Sheepsale every Monday because nobody, nobody with such kind eyes, such a lovely smile, such a nice apple-cheeked face could possibly write an unkind letter! Bets felt absolutely certain of it. Mrs. Jolly began to fumble in her bag.

'Now where did I put those humbugs?' she said. 'Ah, here they are? Do you like humbugs, Miss Bets? Well, you help yourself, and we'll pass them over to the others as well.'

Pip was sitting by the young girl. He found it easy to talk to her..

'What are you going to paint?' he asked.

'I'm painting Sheepsale market,' she answered. 'I go every Monday. It's such a jolly market—small and friendly and very picturesque, set on the top of the hill, with that lovely country all round. I love it.'

'Do you always catch the same bus?' asked Pip.

'I have to,' she said. 'The market's in the morning, you know. I know it by heart now—where the hens and ducks are, and the sheep, and the butter-stalls and the eggs and everything!'

'I bet you don't know where the post-office is!' said Pip quickly.

The girl laughed and thought. 'Well, no, I don't!' she said. 'I've never had to go there and so I've never noticed. But if you want it, any one would tell you. There can't be much of a post-office at Sheepsale though. It's only a small place. Just a market really.'

Pip felt pleased. If this girl didn't know where the post-office was, she could never have posted a letter there. Good. That ruled her out. Pip felt very clever. Anyway, he was certain that such a nice girl wouldn't write horrid letters.

He looked round at the others, feeling that his task was done. He felt sorry for Daisy, sitting next to the surly Mr. Goon. He wondered how Fatty was getting on.

He wasn't getting on at all well! Poor Fatty—he had chosen a very difficult passenger to talk to.

THE sour-faced man appeared to be very deep indeed in his paper, which seemed to Fatty to be all about horses and dogs.

Buster sniffed at the man's ankles and didn't seem to like the smell of them at all. He gave a disgusted snort and strained away towards where Mr. Goon sat, a few seats in fornt.

'Er—I hope my dog doesn't worry you, sir,' said Fatty.

The man took no notice. 'Must be deaf,' thought Fatty and raised his voice considerably.

'I hope my DOG doesn't WORRY you, sir,' he said. The man looked up and scowled.

'Don't shout at me. I'm not deaf,' he said.

Fatty didn't like to ask again if Buster worried him. He cast about for something interesting to say.

'Er—horses and dogs are very interesting aren't they?' he said. The man took no notice. Fatty debated whether to raise his voice or not. He decided not.

'I said, horses and dogs are very interesting, aren't they?' he repeated.

Depends,' said the man, and went on reading.

That wasn't much help in a conversation, Fatty thought gloomily. The others were jolly lucky to have got such easy people to tackle. But still—of all the passengers in the bus, this man looked by far the most likely

THE MYSTERY OF THE SPITEFUL LETTERS

to be the letter-writer—sour-faced, scowling, cruel-mouthed! Fatty racked his brains and tried again.

'Er—could you tell me the time?' he said, rather feebly. There was no reply. This was getting boring! Fatty couldn't help feeling annoyed too. There was no need to be so rude, he thought!

'Could you tell me the time?' he repeated.

'I could, but I'm not going to, seeing that you've got a wrist-watch yourself,' said the man. Fatty could have kicked himself.

'You're not being much of a detective this morning!' he told himself. 'Buck up, Frederick Algernon Trotteville, and look sharp about it!'

'Oh—look at that aeroplane!' said Fatty, seeing a plane swoop down rather low. 'Do you know what it is, sir?'

'Flying Fortress,' said the man, without even looking up. As the aeroplane had only two engines and not four, this was quite wrong and Fatty knew it. He looked at his fellow passenger in despair. How could he ever get anything out of him?'

'I'm going to Sheepsale market,' he said. 'Are you, sir?'

There was no answer. Fatty wished Buster would bite the man's ankles. 'Do you know if this is Buckle Village we're passing?' asked Fatty, as they passed through a pretty little village. The man put down his paper and glared at Fatty angrily.

'I'm a stranger here,' he said. 'I know nothing about Buckle or Sheepsale or its market! I'm just going there to be picked up by my brother, to go on some where else—and all I can say is that the further I get away form chatterboxes like you, the better I shall like it!'

As this was all said very loudly, most of the people in the bus heard it. Mr. Goon chuckled heartily.

'Ah, I've had some of him too!' he called. 'Proper pest, I reckon he is.'

'Go and sit somewhere else and take your smelly dog with you,' said the sour-faced man, pleased to find that somebody else agreed with his opinion of poor Fatty.

So Fatty, red in the face, and certain that he would not be able to get anything more out of the annoyed man, got up and went right to the front of the bus, where nobody was sitting. Bets was sorry for him and she left Mrs. Jolly and joined him.

Larry, Pip and Daisy came across too, and they talked together in low voices.

'I can't see that it can be any one here,' said Fatty, when he had heard all that the others had to say. 'It's obviously not old Clear-Orf—and we can rule out Miss Tremble and Mrs. Jolly surely. And I agree with Pip that the artist girl isn't very likely either, especially as she doesn't even know where the post-office is. And my man said he was a stranger here, so it doesn't look as if he could be the one. A stranger wouldn't know any of the Peterswood people.'

'Does he come on this bus every Monday?' asked Pip, in a low voice.

'I didn't get as far as asking him that,' said Fatty gloomily. 'Either he wouldn't answer, or he just snapped. He was hopeless. It doesn't look really as if any of the people here could have posted those letters.'

'Look—there's somebody waiting at the next bus-stop!' said Bets suddenly. 'At least—it isn't a bus-stop—it's just somebody waving to the bus to stop it for himself. That must be the person we want, if there's nobody else.'

'Perhaps it is,' said Fatty hopefully, and they all waited to see who came in.

But it was the vicar of Buckle! The children knew him quite well because he sometimes came to talk to them in their own church at Peterswood. He was a jolly, burly man and they liked him.

'Can't be him!' said Fatty, disappointed. 'Can't possibly. Blow! We're not a bit further on.'

'Never mind—perhaps one of them will post a letter when they get out of the bus,' said Pip. 'We'll hope for that. Maybe your sour-faced man will, Fatty. He looks the most likely of the lot. He may be telling lies when he says he is a stranger.'

The vicar talked to every one in the bus in his cheerful booming voice. The thin huddled man took no notice, and as the Vicar did not greet him, the children felt sure that he did not know him. So perhaps he *was* a stranger after all?

'Soon be at Sheepsale now,' said Fatty. Golly, isn't this a steep pull-up? They say it wanted eight horses to pull the coach up in the old days before motor-buses.'

The bus stopped under some big trees in Sheepsale. A babel of baaing, mooing, clucking and quacking came to every one's ears. The market was in full swing!

'Quick—hop out first!' said Fatty to the others. 'Stand by the post-office—and keep a close watch.'

The children hurried off. Miss Trimble nodded to

them and walked away down a little lane. The Find-Outers spotted the post-office at once and went over to it. Fatty produced a letter, and began to stamp it carefully.

'Don't want Goon to wonder why we're all standing about here,' he murmured to the others. 'May as well post this letter.'

Mrs. Jolly went off to the market to find her sister. The children watched her go.

'Well, neither Miss Trimble nor Mrs. Jolly have posted letters,' said Fatty. 'That lets those two out. Ah—here comes the artist girl.'

The girl smiled at them and went on. Then she suddenly turned back. 'I see you've found the post-office!' she called. 'I'm so glad! How silly of me never to have noticed it when I pass it every single Monday. But that's just like me!'

'She's not the one, either,' said Pip, as she disappeared in the direction of the market. 'I didn't think she was. She was too nice.'

The vicar disappeared too, without coming in their direction at all. Now only Mr. Goon and the sour-faced man were left. Mr. Goon stared at Fatty, and Fatty raised his eyebrows and smiled sweetly.

'Anything I can do for you, Mr. Goon?'

'What you hanging about here for?' said the policeman. 'Funny thing I can't seem to get rid of you children. Always hanging on my tail, you are.'

'We were thinking the same thing about you too,' said Fatty. He watched the sour-faced man, who was standing nearby at the kerb, still reading his paper about dogs and horses. Fatty wondered if he wanted to post a letter, but was waiting till the children and Mr. Goon had gone. Or was he *really* waiting for his brother, as he had said?

'There's the sweet-shop over the road,' said Fatty, in a low voice, popping his letter into the post-box. 'Let's go over there and buy something. We can keep a watch on the post-box all the time. Then if dear old Clear-Orf or the sour-faced fellow are bursting to post letters, they can do it without feeling that we are watching!'

So they all crossed to the sweet-shop and went in. Larry and Daisy started an argument about whether to buy peppermints or toffees, and Fatty watched the post-office carefully through the glass door. He could see, but could not be seen, for it was dark in the little shop.

The sour-faced man folded up his paper and looked up and down the village street. Mr. Goon disappeared into a tobacco shop. Fatty watched breathlessly. There was no one about in the street now—would that man quickly slip a letter into the post-box?

A car drove up. The driver called out a greeting, and the sour-faced man replied. He opened the door and got in beside the driver. Then they drove off quickly. Fatty gave such a heavy sigh that the others looked round.

'He didn't post a letter,' said Fatty. 'He was telling the truth. Somebody picked him up in a car. Blow! Bother! Dash!'

'Well, even if he *had* posted a letter, I don't see that we could have collared him,' said Pip. 'We didn't know his name or anything about him. But I say—it's pretty peculiar, isn't it—not a single one of the passengers posted a letter—and yet one is always posted every single

Monday!'

'Well—we'll just wait till 11.45 when the postman comes to collet the letters,' said Fatty. 'In case one of the passengers come back. Ah, there goes Goon, off to the market. I suppose he's buying butter and cream to make himself a bit fatter!'

The children waited patiently by the post-office till the postman came and took out the letters. Nobody came to post any. It was most disappointing.

'We're just where we were!' said Fatty gloomily. 'Sickening, isn't it? I don't think we're such good detectives as we hoped we were! You go off to the market. I want to have a good think. I may get a much better idea soon!'

So off to Sheepsale market went the others, leaving poor Fatty behind, looking extremely gloomy.

12   A LOVELY DAY

THE children had a really lovely time at the market. They loved every minute of it. It was such a noisy, lively, friendly place, the birds and animals were so excited, the market-folk so good-humoured and talkative.

They found Mrs. Jolly's sister, and she insisted on giving each of them a large brown egg, and a small pat of her golden home-made butter for their breakfast. Bets was simply delighted. She always loved an unexpected present more than any other.

'Oh *thank* you!' she said. 'You *are* kind—just exactly

like Mrs. Jolly. She gives us sweets. Is your name Jolly, too?'

'No. I'm Mrs. Bunn,' said Mrs. Jolly's sister and Bets very nearly said, 'Oh, that's *just* the right name for you!' but stopped herself in time. For Mrs. Bunn was exactly like her name—big and round, and soft and warm, with eyes like black-currants.

'Let's go and find Fatty and tell him to come and see the market,' said Bets. 'I don't like to think of him glooming by himself. We're stuck over this case, and I don't believe even Fatty can unstick us.'

'There's the artist girl, look!' said Pip. And there she was, in the middle of the market, painting hard, gazing at all the animals and birds around her in delight. The children went and looked at her picture and thought it was very good indeed.

Bets went to find Fatty. He was sitting on a bench in the village street, lost in thought. Bets looked at him in admiration. She could quite will imagine him grown-up, solving deep mysteries that nobody else could. She went up to him and made him jump.

'Oh, Fatty, sorry! Did I make you jump? Do come and see the market. It's marvellous.'

'I haven't quite finished my pondering yet,' said Fatty. Perhaps if I talk to you , Bets, I might see things a little more clearly.

Bets was thrilled and proud. 'Oh yes, *do* talk to me Flatty. I'll listen and not say a word.'

'Oh, you can talk too,' said Fatty. 'You're a very sensible little person, I think. I haven't forgotten how you guessed that telegraph-boy was me, just because you happened to see Buster staring up at me adoringly.'

Buster looked up at the mention of his name. He was looking gloomy, because he was still on the lead. He badly wanted to go off to the market, because the smells that came from it were too exciting for words. He wagged his tail feebly.

'Buster looks as if he's pondering too,' said Bets. Fatty took no notice. He was looking off into the distance, deep in thought. Bets decided not to disturb him. He could talk to her when he wanted to. She began to practise twitching her nose just as she had seen the sour-faced man do. Buster watched her.

Fatty suddenly noticed it too and stared. 'Whatever's the matter with your nose?' he said.

'I'm only just twitching it like that man did,' said Bets. 'Talk to me, Fatty.'

'Well, I'm trying to work out what's best to do next,' said Fatty. 'Now—every Monday for some weeks past somebody has posted a letter to catch the 11.45 post here in Sheepsale—and each of those letters has gone to people in Peterswood. Well, if you remember, I said that that looked as if somebody living in Peterswood, who knew those people and possibly their histories, must have posted them.'

'Yes, that's right,' said Bets.

'And we worked out that the letter-writer probably caught that bus on a Monday and posted the letter on getting out,' said Fatty. 'So we caught the same bus, but we haven't found any one we could *really* suspect— though mind you every one of those bus passengers must go down on out list of Suspects—and we didn't catch any one posting a letter either.'

'You're not going to put Clear-Orf or the vicar down on the list, are you?' said Bets, astonished.

'Every single person is being put there,' said Fatty firmly. 'We can easily cross them out if we think we should—but they've all got to go down.'

'I dare say Clear-Orf has put *us* all down on *his* list of Suspects too then,' said Bets unexpectedly. 'I expect he was on that bus for the same reason as we were—to have a look at the passengers and watch who posted a letter.'

Fatty stared at Bets. Then he burst out into such a hearty laugh that Bets was startled. 'Have I said something funny?' she asked.

'No, Bets. But don't you realize which of the passengers posted a letter?' said Fatty, grinning.

'Nobody did,' said Bets. 'Well—expect you, of course!'

'Yes—me!' said Fatty. 'And it's going to make old Goon scratch his head hard when he thinks that of all his precious Suspects only one posted a letter—and that was his pet aversion, Frederick Trotteville!'

Bets laughed too. 'That's funny!' she said. 'But, Fatty, nobody could possibly think *you* would write horrid letters like that!'

'Old Clear-Orf would believe I'd stolen the Crown Jewels, if there was any suspicion of it,' He'd think me capable of anything. Golly—he must be in a state, wondering who's going to get that letter to-morrow morning!'

'And nobody *will* get a letter!' said Bets. 'Because one hasn't been posted. It will be the first Monday that is missed for six weeks. I wonder why?'

'So do I,' said Fatty. 'Of course—if one *does* arrive—it will mean that the writer lives in Sheepsale after all, and has just posted the letter any time this morning, before the bus came up. Then we shall be properly stuck. We can't watch all the inhabitants of Sheepsale posting letters!'

'Perhaps whoever comes up on the bus to post the letters each Monday didn't come to-day for some reason,' said Bets.

'That's an idea,' said Fatty. 'When we go back on the bus we'll ask the conductor if he always has his regular passengers each Monday, and see if any didn't go this morning. We could make inquiries about them too—see if they've got any spite against Gladys or Molly or the others, and so on.'

'When's the next bus back?' asked Bets. 'I wish we could stay here for the day, Fatty. You'd love the market. But we haven't got our lunch with us.'

'We could have it in that little shop over there,' said Fatty, pointing. 'Look—it says, 'Light Lunches.' That probably means eggs and bread, and butter and cake. How would you like that?'

'Oh, it would be *lovely*,' said Bets. 'I wish we could stay here for the day, Fatty. You'd love the market. But Mother would be anxious if we didn't come back.'

'I'll do a spot of phoning,' said Fatty, who never minded doing things of that sort. Bets thought how like a grown-up he was, always deciding things, and, what was more, always seeming to have plenty of money to pay for everything!

Fatty disappeared into the post-office and went into the telephone box. He made three calls very quickly and came out.

'It's all right,' he said. 'I phoned up your mother and Larry's mother and mine—and they all said, 'Good riddance to you for the day!'

'They didn't, Fatty!' said Bets, who simply couldn't imagine her mother saying any such thing.

'Well—not exactly those words,' grinned Fatty. 'But I could tell they weren't sorry to be rid of us for the day. I don't think my mother, for instance, liked that new game of ours very much.'

'I shouldn't think she did, really,' said Bets, remembering the yowling and groaning and rolling over and over that went with Fatty's new game. 'Let's go and tell the others we can stay here for lunch. Won't they be thrilled!'

They were. 'Good old Fatty!' said Larry. 'It's a treat to be up here on a day like this, among all the forming folk and their creatures. What's the time? I'm getting jolly hungry.'

'It's a quarter to one,' said Fatty. 'I vote we go and have some lunch now. Come on. It looks a nice little place like a dairy and cake shop mixed.'

It *was* a nice little place—shining and spotless, with a plump woman in a vast white apron to serve them and beam at them.

Yes, she could do two boiled eggs a piece and some plates of bread and butter, and some of her own bottled gooseberries if they liked, with a jug of cream. And she'd made some new buns, would they like some?

'This is just the kind of meal I like,' said Bets, as the eggs arrived, all brown and smooth and warm. 'I like it much better than meat. Oh—is that strawberry jam, how lovely!'

'I thought you might like some with the bread and butter, after you've had your eggs,' said the plump woman, smiling at them all. 'They're my own growing, the strawberries.'

'I think,' said Daisy, battering with her spoon at her egg, 'I think that there can't be any thing nicer than to keep your own hens and ducks, and grow your own fruit and vegetables, and do your own bottling, and pickling, and jamming. When I'm grown-up I'm not going to get a job in an office and write dreary letters, or things like that —I'm going to keep a little house and have my own birds and animals and make all kinds of delicious food like this!'

'In that case,' said Larry, 'I shall come and live with you, Daisy—especially if you make jam like this!'

'I'll come too,' said both Fatty and Pip at once.

'Oh—wouldn't it be lovely if we could *all* live together, and have lovely meals like this, and solve mysteries for the rest of our lives!' said Bets fervently.

Everybody laughed. Bets always took things they said so seriously.

'Well, I can't say we've made much headway at solving *this* one!' said Fatty, beginning his second egg. 'All right, Buster, old fellow, we'll get you a meal too when we've finished. Be patient!'

Fatty paid the smiling woman for the meal when they

had finished. The others wanted to pay their share, but hadn't enough money. 'We'll take it out of our money-boxes when we get home,' said Larry. 'And give it to you, Fatty.'

'That's all right,' said Fatty. 'Now let's go and watch them clearing up the market. Then we'd better inquire about our bus.'

They spent a lovely time watching the market folk packing up their unsold goods, taking away the birds and animals bought and sold, talking, laughing, and clapping one another on the back. Mrs. Jolly was there, talking to her sister, and she called to them.

'Don't you miss that bus back now! There's only two more to-day, and the last one goes too late for you!'

'Golly! We forgot to look up the bus-time,' said Fatty, and ran to a bus time-table to look. 'We've only got three minutes!' he said. 'Come on, we must run for it!'

They caught the bus with about half a minute to spare. But to Fatty's deep disappointment the driver and conductor were different. Apparently the morning and afternoon buses were manned by different men.

'Blow!' said Fatty, sitting down at the front. 'I call this a real waste of a day!'

'Oh *Fatty*—how can you say that?' said Daisy, who had enjoyed every single minute of it. 'Why, it's been the nicest day we've had these hols!'

'I daresay,' said Fatty. 'But of you remember, we came up here to try and get a bit further forward in our Mystery—and all we've done is to have a jolly good time, and not find out anything at all. A good day for five children—but a poor day for the Find-Outers–and Dog!'

NEXT day the children felt rather full after their exciting time at the market. They met in Pip's playroom, and Fatty seemed rather gloomy.

'I wish we could find out if any one has had an anonymous letter *this* Tuesday,' he said. 'But I don't see how we can. Old Clear-Orf is in a much better position than we are—such a thing would probably be reported to him at once !'

'Well—never mind about the letters to-day,' said Pip. 'My mother's out—so if you want to play that woo-hoo-colly-wobbles game, we can.'

'Won't Mrs. Moon object ?' asked Fatty.

'I shouldn't think she'd hear, away down in the kitchen,' said Pip. 'Anyway, we don't need to bother about her!'

They were just beginning their extremely hilarious game, when a knock came at the playroom door and Mrs. Moon stuck her head in. The children looked at her, expecting a complaint.

But she hadn't come to complain. 'Master Philip, I've got to run down to the shops,' she said. 'The butcher hasn't sent me my kidneys this morning. Will you answer the telephone whilst I'm gone, and listen for the milkman ?'

'But isn't Mrs. Cockles here ?' asked Pip. She always

comes on Tuesdays, doesn't she?'

'She does, usually,' said Mrs. Moon. 'But she hasn't turned up yet, so I'm all on me own. I won't be above ten minutes gone—but I must get my kidneys.'

She disappeared. The children giggled. 'I hope the butcher hands her her kidneys all right,' said Larry. 'I shouldn't like to be without mine!'

'Idiot!' said Daisy. 'Come on now—we can really let ourselves go, now the house is empty!'

In the middle of all the hullabaloo, Pip heard a noise. He sat up, trying to push Fatty off him. 'Listen—is that the telephone?' he asked.

It was. Goodness knows how long the bell had been ringing! 'I'll go, if you like,' said Fatty, who knew that Pip hated answering the telephone. 'It's probably from the butcher to say he's sending Mrs. Moon's kidneys!'

He ran downstairs. He lifted the telephone receiver and spoke into it. 'Hallo!'

' 'Allo!' said a voice. 'Can I speak to Mrs. Hilton, please?'

'She's out,' said Fatty.

'Oh, Well, is Mrs. Moon there?' said the voice. 'It's Mrs. Cockles speaking.'

'Oh, Mrs. Cockles, this is Frederick Trotteville here, answering the phone for Philip Hilton,' said Fatty. 'Mrs. Moon has just gone down to—er—fetch her kidneys. Can I give her a message when she comes back?'

'Oh yes, Master Frederick, please,' said Mrs. Cockles. 'Tell her, I'm that sorry I can't come to-day— but my sister's upset and I've had to go round to her. Tell Mrs. Moon she's had one of them there letters. She'll know what I mean.'

Fatty at once pricked up his ears. 'One of them there letters !' That could only mean one thing surely—that the wicked letter-writer had been busy again as usual, and had sent a letter to somebody else—Mrs. Cockles's sister this time. His brain worked quickly.

'Mrs. Cockles, I'm so sorry to hear that,' he said in a rather pompous, grown-up tone. 'Very sorry indeed. So upsetting, those anonymous letters, aren't they ?'

'Oh—you've heard about them then,' said Mrs. Cockles. 'Yes, right down wicked they are. Upset folks properly they do. And to think as my pore innocent sister should have had one of them. Mrs. Moon will be sorry to hear that—not that she ever had much time for my pore sister, they never did get on, but Mrs. Moon she knows how it upsets people to get one of these here nonminus letters, and she'll understand why I've got to be with my pore sister this day instead of coming to help as I usually do. . . .'

This was all said without Mrs. Cockles taking a single breath, and Fatty felt slightly dazed. He felt that if he didn't interrupt, Mrs. Cockles might quite well go on for another ten minutes.

'Mrs. Cockles, do you think you sister would let me see the letter ?' he asked. 'I'm—er—very interested in these things—and, as you perhaps know, I am quite good at solving mysteries, and . . .'

'Yes, I've heard how you found Lady Candling's cat for her, and found the real guilty person too, said Mrs. Cockles. 'You come round to my sister's if you like, and she'll show you the letter. She lives at 9, Willow Lane. I'll be there. And give my regrets to Mrs. Moon and say I'll be along on Thursday for sure.'

Fatty replaced the receiver and rushed upstairs in the greatest excitement. He burst into the play-room and stood dramatically in the doorway.

'What do you *think*!' he said. 'There's been another of those beastly letters—sent to Mrs. Cockles's sister! She got it this morning and is all upset and that's why Mrs. Cockles didn't turn up to help Mrs. Moon! And Mrs. Cockles said if I go round to her sister's, she'll show me the letter. I simply *must* find out where it was posted and when.'

'Golly!' said every one.

'Let me come too,' said Pip.

'No. Best for only one of us to go,' said Fatty. 'Give Mrs. Moon this message when she comes back, Pip— say that Mrs. Cockles rang up and said she had to go to her sister, who was upset because she'd had a nasty letter. Don't let on that you know any more than that.'

'Right,' said Pip. 'Well, you hop off now, Fatty, before old Goon gets going on the job. He'll be round at Mrs. Cockle's sister in no time, as soon as he hears about the letter.'

Fatty shot off. He knew where Willow Lane was. He found number 9 and went to the little front door. It was a dirty, untidy little plac. He rapped on the wooden door.

'Come in!' called Mrs. Cockles's voice. 'Oh, it's you, Master Frederick. Well, my sister says she won't show you the letter. She says what's in it isn't for any one to read but me and the police. And I won't say but what she's right, now I've read the letter properly.'

Fatty was most bitterly disappointed. 'Oh, I say !' he said. 'You might just let me have a squint. I've seen all the others. Go on, be a sport and let me see it.'

Mrs. Cockles's sister was a fat, undity woman, who breathed very loudly through her mouth and talked through her nose.

''Taint fit for a child to read,' she said. 'It's a right down spiteful letter, and not a word of truth in it, neither!'

'I'm not a child !' said Fatty, making himself as tall as he could. You can trust me to read the letter and not say a word to anyone. I'm—er—I'm investigating the case, you see.'

Mrs. Cockles was very much impressed. But she still agreed with her sister that the letter was not one for him to read. Fatty, of course, was not in the least curious about its content—but he did badly want to see the printing and, of course, the envelope.

'Well—could I just see the envelope ? he asked. 'That would do quite well.'

Neither Mrs. Cockles nor Mrs. Lamb, her sister, could see any reason why he should not see the envelope. They handed it to him. Fatty looked at it eagerly to make out the post-mark.

But there was none ! There was no stamp, no post-mark ! Fatty stared in surprise.

'But—it didn't come by post !' he said.

'I never said it did,' said Mrs. Lamb. 'It come this morning, very early—about half-past six, I reckon. I heard something being pushed under the door, but I was too sleepy to get up. So I didn't get it till about half-past eight—and then I was that upset, I sent for Mrs. Cockles here. And you come at once, didn't you, Kate ?'

'Course I did,' said Mrs. Cockles. 'Only stopped to have a word with Mr. Goon about it. He'll be along soon to have a look at the letter too.'

Fatty felt slightly alarmed. He didn't want to bump into Clear-Orf at the moment. He stared hard at the envelope once more. The name and address were printed in capital letters again, and the square envelope was the same as the others that had been used. Fatty took his note-book out of his pocket and looked at the page headed CLUES.

He compared the tracing of the word PETERS-WOOD with the same word on the envelope. Yes there was no doubt at all, but that the same hand wrote both words. They were exactly alike.

Fatty handed the envelope back to Mrs. Lamb. He had got from it all he wanted. He didn't want to see the letter inside. He could imagine it—a few sentences of spite and hurtfulness, with perhaps a little truth in them. He had enough to puzzle himself with—here was the usual letter, received on a Tuesday morning—but this time not through the post, and not from Sheepsale. Funny !

'Well, I'll be going,' said Fatty. 'Thanks for showing me the envelope, Mrs. Lamb I'm so sorry you had one of these beastly letters. I shan't rest till I find out who is the writer of them.'

'Mr. Goon, he's on to them to,' said Mrs. Cockles. 'Says he's got a very good idea who it is, too.'

Fatty doubted that. He was sure that Mr. Goon was as puzzled as he was. He said good-bye and went out of the dirty little room.

ANOTHER OF THOSE LETTERS

But coming in at the front gate was the burly figure of Mr. Goon ! Fatty was annoyed. He tried to get out of the gate before Mr. Goon came in, but the policeman, surprised and exasperated at seeing Fatty there, caught hold of his arm. He pulled the boy inside the cottage.

'Has this boy been interfering with the Workings of the Law ?' he demanded, in an angry voce. 'What's he doing here, that's what I want to know ?'

Mrs. Lamb was afraid of Mrs. Goon, but Mrs. Cockles was not.

'He's not been interfering,' she said. 'Only taking a friendly interest like.'

'How did he know that Mrs. Lamb had received one of these here letters ?' inquired Mrs. Goon, still in a furious voice.

'Well, I had to ring up Mrs. Moon to tell her as how I wouldn't be along this morning, because my sister had had a letter,' said Mrs. Cockles. 'And Master Frederick, he happened to be there, and he took the message. And he said he knew all about the letters and would like to see this one, and I knew he wasn't half-bad at snooping out things, so . . .'

'Mrs. Lamb, you didn't show this interfering boy that letter before you showed it to me, did you ?' thundered Mr. Goon.

'Well—well, sir—he did say as he's seen them all,' stammered poor Mrs. Lamb, frightened out of her life. 'So I thought there wouldn't be much harm. I only showed him the envelope though, Mr. Goon, sir.'

Mr. Goon turned his frog-like gaze on to Fatty. 'What's that mean—that you've seen *all* the letters ?' he demanded.

Mr. Goon caught hold of Fatty's arm

ANOTHER OF THOSE LETTERS

'They've been in my possesssion—never out of it for a minute. What you mean—you've seen them *all*?'

'I must have been dreaming,' answered Fatty, in an amiable voice. This was the voice that drove poor Mr. Goon to fury. He snorted.

'You're telling untruths,' he said. 'Yes, you know you are. Them letters haven't been out of my possession, not for one minute!'

'Haven't they really?' said Fatty. 'Well, I couldn't have seen them then.'

'Unless you know more about them than you make out!' said Mr. Goon, darkly and mysteriously, suddenly remembering how he had seen Fatty post a letter at Sheepsale the morning before. 'Ho, you're a deep one, you are—never know what your game is, I don't! I wouldn't put anything past you, Master Frederick Trotteville!'

'Thank you, Mr. Theophilus Goon,' said Fatty, and grinned. Mr. Goon longed to box his ears. Then he suddenly remembered that those letters *had* been out of his possession once—that time when he had apparently dropped them in the road, after colliding with the red-haired telegraph-boy. He stared suspiciously at Fatty.

'That telegraph-boy your friend?' he asked suddenly. Fatty looked mildly surprised.

'What telegraph-boy?' he asked.

'That red-haired fellow with the freckles,' said Mr. Goon.

'I'm afraid I've no red-haired, freckled telegraph-boy for a friend, much as I would like one,' said Fatty. 'But why all these questions about a telegraph-boy?'

Mr. Goon wasn't going to tell him. But he made a mental

note to get hold of that telegraph-boy and ask him a few questions. Perhaps he and Fatty were in league together!

'Well, I'll go now,' said Fatty politely, 'unless you've got any more questions to ask me about telegraph-boys, Mr. Goon? Oh—and would you like another clue? Wait a bit, I'll see if I've got one about me!'

To Mr. Goon's rage he felt in his pockets and produced a doll's straw hat. 'Now was that a clue?' murmured Fatty, but, seeing Mr. Goon gradually turning a familiar purple, he moved swiftly through the door.

'If you don't clear-orf,' said Mr. Goon, between his teeth, 'if you don't clear-orf . . .I'll . . .I'll . . .'

But Fatty had cleared-orf. He sprinted back to Pip's. The mystery of the letters was warming up again!

14   THREE MORE SUSPECTS

HE was soon back in the playroom, relating everything to the other. How they roared when they heard about Mr. Goon coming in and hearing that Fatty had seen all the letters!

'That must have given him a shock!' said Pip. 'He'll wonder for hours how you've seen them. I bet he'll go about looking for that telegraph-boy now—he knows he's the one who handed him the letters he was supposed to have dropped.'

'Well, he'll be lucky if he finds the telegraph-boy, even if he goes up to the post-office to look for him!' said Fatty. 'But I say—*now* we know why none of the bus passengers posted the letter! It was delivered by hand instead ! No wonder we didn't see any one popping the letter into Sheepsale post-box !'

'It must be some one who didn't catch the bus yesterday for some reason,' said Daisy thoughtfuly. 'We really must find out if any one who regularly catches that bus, didn't take it yesterday. If we can find out the person who didn't go as usual, we *may* have discovered who the letter-writer *is* !'

'Yes—you're right, Daisy,' said Larry. 'Shall one of us catch the 10.15 bus to-morrow, Fatty and ask the conductor a few questions ?'

'Perhaps we'd better not,' said Fatty. 'He might think it a bit funny, or think us cheeky, or something. I've got a better idea than that.'

'What ?' asked the others.

'Well, what about going in to see Miss Tremble this morning ?' said Fatty. 'We know she usually takes the Monday morning bus. We could get from her the names of all the people who always catch it at Peterswood. After all, it starts off by the church, and that's where she gets in. She must know everyone who takes it on Mondays.'

'Yes. Lets go and see her now,' aid Bets. 'Mrs. Moon is back with her kidneys, Fatty. She wasn't long. Pip gave her the message, and she said, 'Well, well, she wasn't surprised to hear that Mrs. Lamb had got one of those letters, she was the dirtiest, laziest woman in the village !'

'Well, I must say her cottage was jolly smelly,' said Fatty. 'Come on—let's go in next door. We'll ask Miss Trimble if she's seen your cat, Pip.'

'But Whiskers is here,' said Pip in surprise, pointing to the big black cat.

'Yes, idiot. But Miss Trimble's not to know that,' said Fatty. 'We've got to have *some* excuse for going in. She'll probably be picking flowers in the garden, or taking the dog for an airing. Let's look over the wall first.'

Their luck was in. Miss Trimble was in the garden, talking to Miss Harmer who looked after Lady Candling's valuable Siamese cats for her.

'Come on. We'll go up the front drive and round to where she's talking,' said Fatty. 'I'll lead the conversation round to the bus.'

They set off, and soon found Miss Trimble. Miss Harmer was pleased to see them too. She showed them all the blue-eyed cats.

'And you really must come and see the daffodils in the orchard,' said Miss Trimble, setting her glasses firmly on her nose. Bets gazed at them, hoping they would fall off.

They all trooped after her. Fatty walked politely beside her, holding back any tree-branches that might catch at her hair. She thought what a very well-mannered boy he was.

'I hope you found your mother well on Monday,' said Fatty.

'Not so very well,' said Miss Trimble. 'She's got a bad heart, you know, poor old lady. She's always so glad to see me on Mondays.'

'And you must quite enjoy Mondays too,' said Fatty. 'Such a nice trip up to Sheepsale, isn't it, and such a fine little market !'

Miss Trimble's glasses fell off, and dangled on the

end of their little gold chain. She put them on again, and smiled at Fatty.

'Oh yes, I always enjoy my Mondays,' she said.

'I expect you know all the people who go in the bus!' said Daisy, feeling that it was her turn to say something now.

'Well, I do, unless there are strangers, and we don't get many of those,' said Miss Trimble. 'Mrs. Jolly always goes, of course—such a nice person. And that artist-girl goes too—I don't know her name—but she's always so sweet and polite.'

'Yes, we liked her too,' said Fatty. 'Did you see the man I sat by, Miss Trimble ? Such a surly fellow.'

'Yes. I've never seen him before,' said Miss Trimble. 'The vicar often gets on the bus at Buckle, and I usually have such a nice talk with him. Mr. Goon sometimes goes up on that bus too, to have a word with the policeman in charge of Sheepsale. But I'm always glad when he's not there, somehow.'

'I suppose one or two of the regular Monday bus-people weren't there yesterday, were they?' said Fatty innocently. 'I thought the bus would be much more crowded than it was.'

'Well, let me see now—yes, there *are* usually more people,' said Miss Trimble, her glasses falling off again. The children held their breath. Now they would perhaps hear the name of the wicked letter-writer !

'Anyone *we* know ?' asked Fatty.

'Well, I don't know if you know Miss Tittle, do you?' said Miss Trimble. 'She *always* goes up on a Monday, but she didn't yesterday. She's a dressmaker, you know, and goes up to Sheepsale House to sew all day Mondays.'

'Really ?' said Fatty. 'Is she a special friend of yours, Miss Trimble ?'

'Well, no,' said Miss Trimble. 'I can't say she is. She's like a lot of dressmarkers, you know—full of gossip and scandal—a bit spiteful, and I don't like that. It's not Christian, I say. She pulls people to pieces too much for my liking. Knows a bit too much about everybody !

The children immediately felt absolutely certain that Miss Tittle was the writer of those spiteful letters. She sounded exactly like them !

'Aren't the daffodils simply lovely ?' said Miss Trimble, as they came to the orchard.

'Glorious !' said Daisy. 'Let's sit down and enjoy them.'

They all sat down. Miss Trimble looked anxiously at the children and went rather red.

'I don't think I should have said that about Miss Tittle,' she said. 'I wasn't thinking. She sometimes comes here to sew for Lady Candling, you know, and I do find it very difficult not to be drawn into gossip with her—she asks me such questions ! She's coming here this week, I believe, to make up the new summer curtains—and I'm not looking forward to it. I can't bear all this nasty spitefulness.'

'No, I should think not,' said Bets, taking her turn at making a remark. 'You're not a bit like that.'

Miss Trimble was so pleased with this remark of Bets that she smiled, wrinkled her nose, and her glasssses fell off.

'That's three times,' said Bets. Miss Trimble put back her glasses and did not look quite so pleased. She couldn't bear Bets to count like that.

'We'd better be going,' said Fatty. Then a thought struck him. 'I suppose there aren't any other Monday regulars on that bus, Miss Tremble—Trimble, I mean ?'

'You seem very interested in that bus !' said Miss Trimble. 'Well, let me think. There's always old Nosey, of course. I don't know why he didn't go yesterday. He always goes up to the market.'

'Old Nosey ? Whoever is he ?' asked Fatty.

'Oh, he's the old fellow who lives with his wife in the caravan at the end of Rectory Field,' said Miss Trimble. 'Maybe you've never seen him.'

'Oh yes, I have ! Now I remember !' said Fatty. 'He's a little stooping fellow, with a hooked nose and a droopy little moustache, who goes about muttering to himself.

'He's called Nosey because he's so curious about everyone,' said Miss Trimble. 'The things he wants to know! How old my mother is—and how old I am too—and what Lady Candling does with her old clothes—and how much the gardener gets in wages. I don't wonder people call him Old Nosey.'

Fatty looked round at the others. It sounded as if old Nosey, too, might be the letter-writer. He might be a bit daft and write the letters in a sort of spiteful fun. Fatty remembered a boy at his school who had loved to find out the weak spots in the others, and tease them about them. It was quite likely that Old Nosey was the letter-writer !

'And then, of course, there's always Mrs. Moon, your cook, Pip,' said Miss Trimble, rather surprisingly. 'She always had Mondays off to go and see to her old mother, just like me—and I usually see her every single Monday. But I didn't see her yesterday.'

'Well, you see, our housemaid, Gladys, has gone away for a few days,' explained Pip. 'And so I suppose Mother couldn't let Mrs. Moon off for the day. Yes– now I think of it—Mrs. Moon does go off on Mondays.'

'Any one else a regular passenger on the bus?' asked Larry.

'No, nobody,' said Miss Trimble. 'You *do* seem interested in that bus. But I'm sure you didn't come in here to ask me about that Monday morning bus, now did you! What did you come to ask?'

The children had forgotten what reason they were going to give! Bets remembered just in time.

'Oh—we were going to ask if you'd seen our cat!' she said.

'So that's what you came in for!' said Miss Trimble. 'No—I'm afraid I haven't seen your cat. It's that big black one, isn't it? I shouldn't think you need to worry about *him*! He can look after himself all right.'

'I've no doubt he's indoors sitting by the fire this very minute,' said Pip, quite truthfully. 'Well, we must go, Miss Tremble.'

'Trimble, dear boy, not Tremble,' said Miss Trimble, her glasses falling off again. 'I simply cannot imagine why you keep making that mistake. Any one would think I was like an aspen leaf, all of a tremble!'

The children laughed politely at this small joke, said good-bye and went. They said nothing at all till they were safely in Pip's playroom with the door shut. Then they looked at one another in excitement.

'Well! Three more really fine Suspects!' said Fatty,

opening his notebook. 'Would you believe it ? I think there's no doubt that one of them is the letter-writer.'

'Not Mrs. Moon,' said Bets. 'She was so kind to Gladys. Gladys said so. She couldn't be mean to her and kind to her as well.'

'I suppose not,' said Fatty. 'But all the same she's going down on our list. Now then—Miss TittleTattle.'

The others laughed. 'Miss Tittle, not Tittle-Tattle !' said Pip.

'I know, idiot,' said Fatty. 'But I think Tittle-Tattle suits her jolly well. Miss Tittle—old Nosey—and Mrs. Moon. We're getting on. Now we'll have plenty more inquiries to make.'

'What inquiries ?' asked Pip.

'Well—we must try and find out if Old Nosey, Miss Tittle, and Mrs. Moon were out early this morning,' said Fatty. 'That letter was pushed under Mrs. Lamb's door at about half-past six. It was only just getting light then. If we can find out that any of those three were out early, we've got the right one !'

'However are you going to find *that* out ?' said Larry. 'I shouldn't have thought even you were clever enough for that, Fatty !'

'Well, I am !' said Fatty. 'And what's more I'll go and do it now—and come back and tell you all about it in an hour's time !'

15   FATTY MAKES A FEW ENQUIRIES

FATTY went off, whistling. The others watched him from the window. 'I suppose he's going to interview Old Nosey, Miss Tittle, and Mrs. Moon !' said Pip. 'He's a wonder ! Never turns a hair, no matter what he's got to do.'

'All the same, he won't find Mrs. Moon an easy one to interview,' said Larry. 'She doesn't seem to me to be in a very good temper to-day—because Mrs. Cockles hasn't turned up, I suppose.'

An hour went by. It was a quarter to one. The children went to the window and watched for Fatty. He came cycling up the drive—but dear me, how different he looked ! He had put on his red wig again, but with black eyebrows this time, and had reddened his face till it looked weather-beaten. He wore a dirty old suit and a butcher-boy apron round his waist !

But the children knew it was Fatty all right, by his whistle ! He stopped under their window. 'Any one about ?' he said. 'Shall I come up ?'

'It's safe,' said Pip, leaning out of the window. 'Mrs. Moon's in the back-yard.'

Fatty came up, looking a real, proper butcher-boy. It was amazing how he could alter even his expression when he was supposed to be somebody else. He took off his apron and wig, and looked a bit better.

'Well—what have you found out ?' said Larry eagerly. 'And why ever are you dressed like that ?'

'I've found out a lot,' said Fatty. 'But I don't know that I'm any further forward really ! I'll tell you everything. I'm dressed like this because it's natural for a butcher-boy to hang about and gossip.'

He opened his notebook, and turned to the pages headed 'SUSPECTS.'

'Old Nosey,' he began. 'Old Nosey was up and about before half-past six this morning, with his dog, Lurcher. He left his caravan and went down Willow Lane, and into the village. He was back at eight o'clock.'

He turned over another page.

'Miss Tittle,' he said. 'Miss Tittle was about with her dog at half-past six, as she is every single morning. She lives in a turning off Willow Street. She always wears an old red shawl in the mornings.'

'Mrs. Moon,' went on Fatty, turning over a page again. 'Mrs. Moon was out this morning, early and was seen talking to Old Nosey. Well, there you are, Find-Outers. What do you make of that? Every one of our three Suspects could have popped that letter under the door!'

'But, Fatty—however did you find out all this?' said Bets, in great admiration. 'You really are a most marvellous Find-Outer.'

'Elementary, my dear Bets!' said Fatty, putting his notebook down. 'You know the field opposite Willow Lane? Well, old Dick the shepherd lives there in a little hut. I noticed him this morning. So all I had to do was to go and engage him in conversation, and ask him a few innocent questions—and out it all came! Old Dick was wide awake at five o'clock—always is—and he takes a great interest in the people that pass up and down by his field. They're about all he has to see, except his sheep. He says Nosey's always up and about at unearthly hours—a poacher most likely. He's a gypsy anyway. And apparently Miss Tittle always takes her dog for a trot early in the morning. So there's nothing unusual about that. He says he saw Mrs. Moon quite distinctly, and heard her voice too, talking to Old Nosey.'

'I'm sure it's Mrs. Moon!' said Larry. 'She *never* goes out so early, surely. I've heard your mother say she gets up too late, Pip.'

'Sh! Here she comes, to say our lunch is ready,' said Pip warningly. Sure enough, it was Mrs. Moon.

She put her head in at the door. 'Will you come now, Master Philip?' she said, 'I've put your lunch and Miss Bets in the dining-room.'

'Thank you, Mrs. Moon,' said Pip. Then, on a sudden impulse, he called out.

'I say, Mrs. Moon—isn't it queer, the old shepherd told Fatty that he saw you out at half past six this morning! He must be dreaming, mustn't he!'

There was a sudden pause. Mrs. Moon looked startled and surprised.

'Well there now,' she said at last. 'Who would have thought any one'd be peeping out at that time of day. Yes, it's quite right. I *was* out early this morning. You see, I usually go up to see my old mother at Sheepsale on a Monday, and I couldn't let her know in time that I wasn't coming yesterday. I knew she'd be worrying, and I remembered that Old Nosey, the gypsy fellow, might be going up to-day, so I got out early and gave him a note for my mother, and a packet of food in case she hasn't been able to get some one to buy any for her. He'd be taking the 10.15 bus.'

'Oh,' said the children, really quite relieved at this explanation.

'So that's it !' said Pip, without thinking.

'That's what ?' asked Mrs. Moon sharply.

'Nothing,' said Pip hastily, feeling a nudge from Fatty. 'Nothing at all !'

Mrs. Moon looked at the children curiously. Fatty got up. He didn't want to make Mrs. Moon suspicious about anything.

'Time I went,' he said. 'Your lunch will get cold, Pip and Bets if you don't go and have it. See you later.'

'Here's your notebook, Fatty !' Bets called after him, as he went downstairs. 'Your precious notebook with all its Clues and Suspects ! Fatty, are you going to write up the case again ? You've got some more to put down now, haven't you ?'

'Chuck the book down to me,' said Fatty. 'Yes, I'll write up the case as far as it's gone. I bet old Goon would like to see my notes !'

He went out of the garden-door with Larry and Daisy. Fatty did not put on his wig or apron agin. He stuffed them into his bicycle basket. 'Good thing I'd taken them off before Mrs. Moon came in,' he said. 'She'd have wondered why you were hobnobbing with the butcher-boy !'

'Fatty, who do you think is the letter-writer ?' said Daisy, who was burning with curiosity. 'I think it's Mrs. Moon. I do really.'

'I do too,' said Larry. 'But I don't see how we are to get any proof.'

'Yes, it certainly *might* be Mrs. Moon,' said Fatty thoughtfully. 'You remember that Pip told us she wanted her niece to come here ? She might have got Gladys out of the way for that. And yet—there are all the other letters too. Whoever wrote them must be a bit mad, I think.'

'What do we do next ?' asked Larry.

'I think we'll try and find out a bit more about Mrs. Moon,' said Fatty. 'We'll meet at Pip's at half-past two.'

When they arrived back at Pip's, they found him and Bets in a great state of excitement.

'What do you think ! Old Clear-Orf is here and he's been going for Mrs. Moon like anything !' cried Pip. 'We heard a lot of it, because the kitchen window's open and it's just under our playroom !'

'What's he been going at her for ?' asked Fatty.

'Well, apparently she used to live near the Home where Gladys was,' said Pip. 'And once she was working there as cook, and she got the sack because the girls complained of her bad temper. Maybe Gladys was one of those that complained ! Old Clear-Orf has been making inquiries himself, I suppose, and when he found out that Mrs. Moon actually knew the Home Gladys had been in, I suppose he came over all suspicious. He shouted at her like anything—and she shouted back !'

A noise of voices arose again. The children leaned out of the window.

'And what right have you got to come here and talk to an innocent woman like you have !' shouted Mrs. Moon. 'I'll have the law on you !'

'I *am* the Law,' came Mr. Goon's ponderous voice.

FATTY MAKES A FEW ENQUIRIES

'I'm not accusing you of anything, Mrs. Moon, please understand that. I'm just asking you a few questions in the ordinary way of business, that's all. Routine questions is what we call them. Checking up on people, and finding out about them. Clearing them if they're innocent—as I've no doubt you are. You didn't ought to go on like this just because the Law asks you a few civil questions!'

'There's others you could well ask questions of,' said Mrs. Moon darkly. 'Yes, others I could tell you of.'

I've got a list of people I'm asking questions of,' said Mr. Goon. 'And all I hope is they'll be more civil than you've been. You don't make a good impression, Mrs. Moon, you don't, and that's flat.'

Whereupon Mr. Goon took his departure, and cycled slowly and heavily up the drive, the back of his neck looking bright red with rage.

'Old Goon's a bit brighter than we think,' said Fatty. 'He seems to have got his list of Suspects just as we have—and Mrs. Moon is down on his too!'

'I thought when he saw you posting that letter yesterday at Sheepsale he'd suspect *you* !' said Larry.

'Oh, I think he's sure I'm "messing about" somehow, as he puts it,' said Fatty. 'He's probably expecting some one to get a stupid letter from *me*, as well as from the real letter-writer. Well—I've a jolly good mind to let him have one !'

'Oh no, Fatty !' said Daisy.

Fatty grinned. 'No, I didn't mean it. Well, let's go out into the garden, shall we ? We'll go up to that old summer-house. I'll write up my notes there, whilst you all read or do something. It's too hot to stay indoors.'

They all went up to the summer-house. It backed on to the next-door garden, and was a nice, secluded little place, well away from the house. The children pulled some early radishes from the garden and washed them, meaning to nibble them all the afternnon.

They all talked hard about their mystery. They discussed everything and everybody. They read out loud what Fatty had written. It sounded very good indeed. He had even written up the interview between Mr. Goon and Mrs. Moon that afternoon. It began :

> 'Said Mr. Goon
> To Mrs. Moon'

and went on in such a funny strain that the children roared.

Then, quite suddenly, they heard voices very near them. They stopped their talk, startled. Who could be so near ?

They peeped out of the summer-house. They saw Mrs. Moon, with some lettuces in her hand, talking to a stranger over the wall, almost within touch of their summer-house.

'Well, that's what I always say, Miss Tittle,' they heard Mrs. Moon say. 'If a thing's too tight, it's not worth wearing!'

'You're quite right,' said the little, neat woman looking over the wall. 'But people will have their things made so tight. Well, do come in and see me about that dress of yours, Mrs. Moon, sometime. I'd enjoy a good talk with you.'

'I bet she would,' whispered Daisy. 'The two of them together would just about pull every one in Peterswood to pieces !'

'Miss Tittle didn't look a very nice person,' said Bets, watching Mrs. Moon go down the path with her lettuces.

She had obviously just been up the kitchen garden nearby to pull them.

'I suppose you realize that we've been talking very loudly, and that both Miss Tittle and Mrs. Moon could have heard every word, if they'd been listening ?' said Fatty, with a groan. 'I never thought of any one coming up here. Miss Tittle must have been just the other side of the wall, and Mrs. Moon must have come up to get the lettuces. They grow quite near the summer-house. Now both will be on their guard, if they've heard what we've been saying !'

'They won't have heard !' said Pip.

'They may quite well have done,' said Fatty. 'What idiots we are. Really ! Giving all our clues and facts away at the tops of our voices. And Bets reading out loud from my notes !'

'Why didn't Buster bark ?' said Bets.

'Well, he knows Mrs. Moon all right and wouldn't bark if she came by,' said Fatty. 'And I don't expect he bothers about any one in the next garden. Do you, Buster, old fellow ?'

'Woof,' said Buster lazily. He was lying in a patch of sun and it was pleasantly warm on him. He cocked his ears up, hoping to hear the magic word 'Walk.'

He soon heard it. 'I vote we go for a walk,' said Larry. 'It's getting stuffy here. let's go down to the river and watch the swans. We'll take some bread.'

Pip asked Mrs. Moon for some bread. She seemed sulky and upset. 'No wonder,' thought Pip, 'after having Mr. Goon bellowing at her !'

They had a lovely time by the river. they sauntered

back to tea, but parted at Pip's, because each had to get back home for tea that afternoon.

'See you to-morrow,' said Fatty. 'We seem to be rather stuck again, don't we ? This mystery wants oiling a bit ! Well—maybe something will happen to-morrow!'

Fatty was quite right. Plenty happened—and it was very exciting too !

16   MR. GOON IS PUZZLED

FATTY thought he would wear his butcher-boy disguise the next morning, in case he had to go and do a bit more snooping or interviewing. It was a simple disguise, and very effective. He put on his red wig, with no cap. He adjusted the black eyebrows and made his face red. Then, with his striped apron tied round his middle, he set off to Pip's.

Mrs. Hilton saw him as he flashed by the window. 'Ah, the butcher-boy,' she thought. 'Now Mrs. Moon won't have to go and fetch the meat again.'

The others greeted Fatty with delight. They were always thrilled when he disguised himself. He pulled off his wig, eyebrows, and apron when he got up into the playroom in case Mrs. Hilton should come in and see him.

He had no sooner done this than a great commotion began downstairs. The children listened, quite startled. They heard wails and groans, and somebody speaking sharply, then more wails.

They went to the head of the stairs and listened. It's Mrs. Moon—and Mother,' said Pip' 'What-ever is happening ? Mrs. Moon is crying and howling like anything and Mother is trying to make her stop. Gracious, what can be the matter ?'

'Perhaps Mother's discovered that Mrs. Moon is the bad letter-writer !' suggested Bets, looking rather scared.

'I'll go down and see what's up,' said Fatty, rising to the occasion as usual. He went down-stairs quietly. He heard Mrs. Hilton's stern voice.

'Now Mrs. Moon, you are not to go on like this. I won't have it ! Pull yourself together at once !'

'Oh Mam, to think I'd get one of those nasty letters!' wailed Mrs. Moon's voice. 'And such a spiteful one too ! Look here what it says.

'I don't want to see, Mrs. Moon. Pay no attention to it,' said Mrs. Hilton. 'You know quite well it is only something written out of somebody's spiteful imagination. Let Mr. Goon see it, and then forget all about it.'

'That Mr. Goon !' wailed Mrs. Moon. 'Didn't he come here yesterday and tell me I might be one of them he suspects could have written the letters-me, a law-abiding, peaceful woman that never did no one no harm. Ooooooo-o-oh !'

'Pull yourself together at once,' said Mrs. Hilton sharply !' You're getting hysterical and I won't have it! When did the letter come ?'

'Just this minute as ever was !' wailed Mrs. Moon. 'Somebody pushed it in at the kitchen door, and I picked it up and opened it—and there was that nasty spiteful message—oh, to think somebody could write to me like that, me that hasn't an enemy in the world.'

'Somebody pushed it in just *now*?' said Mrs. Hilton thoughtfully.'Well now—I saw the butcher-boy coming by my window a minute ago'.

'He never came to my back door!' declared Mrs. Moon. 'Never left any meat or nothing.'

'Strange,' said Mrs. Moon. 'Could it possibly have been that boy who delivered the note—for somebody else? Well, we can easily make inquiries at the butcher's.'

Fatty wished heartily that he hadn't put on his butcher-boy disguise. He must hide it well away when he went upstairs.

'I'll go and telephone to Mr. Goon now,' said Mrs. Hilton. 'Make yourself a cup of tea, Mrs. Moon, and try and be sensible.'

Fatty shot upstairs as Mrs. Hilton came out into the hall to telephone. The others clutched him.

'What's the row about?' they asked. 'Quick, tell us!'.

'What do you think!' said Fatty. Mrs. Moon's had one of those letters—delivered by hand a few minutes ago. We might any of us have seen who it was that left it here—but we didn't. But your mother spotted me in my butcher-boy disguise, Pip, and that's a pity, because she thinks *I'm* the one that delivered the letter!'

'Mrs. *Moon's* had a letter!' said Larry, and gave a low whistle. '

Well, that rules her out then. That leaves only Nosey and Miss Tittle'.

'Let's watch for Mr. Goon,' said Bets. So they

watched. He came cycling up the drive and dismounted by the front door. Mrs. Hilton let him in. The children stood at the top of the stairs, but Mrs. Hilton, worried and puzzled, did not even see them.

'I sent for you to say that Mrs. Moon has now had one of those unpleasant letters,' said Mrs. Hilton 'She is naturally very upset.'

'Well, Madam, I may tell you that I've had one too, this morning !' said Mr.Goon. 'It's getting beyond a joke, this is. I found mine in the letter-box this morning. Course, it may have been delivered in the dark of night, probably was. Making fun of the Law like that. Things have come to a pretty pass if the Law can be treated like that !'.

'It's very worrying,' said Mrs. Hilton. 'I can't imagine anyone wanting to send *you* that kind of letter, Mr. Goon.'

'Ah, no doubt the wrong-doer knows I'm on their track,' said Mr.Goon. 'Thinks to put me off, no doubt ! Tells me I'm a meddler and a muddler ! Ah, wait till I get me hands on them !'

'Well——come and see Mrs. Moon,' said Mrs. Hilton.'Please handle her carefully, Mr. Goon. She's almost hysterical.'

Obviously Mr. Goon couldn't handle a hysterical person, judging by the angry voices soon to be heard from the kitchen. The door opened again at last and Mr. Goon came out into the hall, looking extremely flustered, to find Mrs. Hilton, who had retired to the drawing-room.

'And that'll teach you to come pestering and accusing a poor, innocent woman !' Mrs. Moon's voice came from the kitchen. 'Pestering me yesterday like you do—and me struck all of a heap to-day!'.

Mr.Goon heard next about the red-headed butcher-boy, who had so mysteriously ridden up and left no meat, and had apparently departed without being seen.

Mr. Goon immediately thought of the red-headed telegraph-boy. 'Funny goings-on !' he said to himself. 'Them dropped letters now—and that telegraph-boy picking them up—and now this red-headed butcher-boy, without his meat—and maybe delivering that letter to Mrs. Moon. This wants looking into.'

'The five children are upstairs,' said Mrs. Hilton. 'I don't know if you want to ask them if they saw the butcher-boy. They may give you a few more details.'

'I'll see them,' said Mr. Goon, and went upstairs to the playroom. When he got there the children were apparently playing a game of snap. They looked up as Mr. Goon walked heavily into the room.

'Good morning,' he said. 'Did any of you see a red-headed butcher-boy coming along here this morning ?'

'Yes, I saw him,' said Pip with a grin.

'Ho, you did ! What did he do ? asked Mr. Goon.

'Just rode up the drive,' said Pip.

'And rode down again at once, I suppose,' said Mr.Goon.

'No. I didn't see him ride down,' said Pip. Nobody had apparently. Mr. Goon began to feel that this mysterious red-headed boy must be somewhere about the premises.

'He a friend of yours ? he said.

Pip hesitated. Fatty *was* his friend—and yet to say that

the butcher-boy was his friend would lead him into difficulties. Fatty saw him hesitate and came to the rescue.

'We've got no butcher-boy friends,' he said. 'And no telegraph-boy friends either. You remember you asked me that one too ?'

'I'm not speaking to you,' said Mr. Goon, with a scowl. 'I'm speaking to Master Philip here. I'd like to get hold of them two red-headed lads ! And I will too, if I have to go to the post-office and speak to the postmaster, and ask at every butcher's in the town !'

'There are only two butchers.' said Pip.

'Mr. Goon, I'm so sorry to hear you've had one of those horrid letters too,' said Fatty earnestly. 'I can't think now anyone could have the nerve—er, I mean—the heart to write to you like that'.

'Like what ? said Mr. Goon sharply.'What do you know about any letters I've had ? I suppose you'll tell me next you've seen the letter and know what's in it hey ?'

'Well, I can more or less guess,' said Fatty modestly.

'You tell me what was in that letter then,' said Mr. Goon, growing angry.

'Oh I couldn't,' said Fatty. 'Not with all the others here.' He didn't know of course, what was in the letter at all, beyond that Goon was a meddler and a muddler, but it was amusing to make the policeman think he did.

'Well, it wouldn't surprise me at all if *you* didn't write that there letter to me !' said Mr.Goon.

'It might not be the letter-writter at all—it might just be you !'

'Oh, you *couldn't* think that of me !' said Fatty,

looking pained. Larry and Daisy, rather alarmed, looked at him. They remembered how he had said he would love to write a letter to Mr. Goon. Surely he *hadn't*?

Mr. Goon departed, determined to run the red-headed butcher-boy, and the equally red-headed telegraph-boy to earth. Larry turned to Fatty.

'I say! You didn't really write to him did you, Fatty?'

'Of course not, silly! As if I'd send an anonymous letter to any one, even for fun!' said Fatty. But my word, fancy somebody delivering a letter right into the lion's mouth! To Goon himself. I can't see Miss Tittle doing that—or even Old Nosey the gypsy.'

'And now Mrs. Moon's ruled out,' said Larry. 'Gracious—it seems more of a muddle than ever, really it does. Got any ideas as to what to do next, Fatty?'.

'One or two,' said Fatty. I think it would be rather helpful to get specimens of Miss Tittle's writing and old Nosey's. Just to compare them with my tracing. That might tell us something.'

'But how in the world can you do that? said Daisy. 'I wouldn't be able to get Old Nosey's writing if I thought for a month!'

'Easy!' said Fatty. 'You wait and see!'

THE next day both Mr. Goon and Fatty were very busy. Fatty was trying to get specimens of Nosey's writing and Miss Tittle's and Mr. Goon was trying to trace the two red-headed boys.

Fatty pondered whether to disguise himself or not, and then decided that he would put on the red wig, red eyebrows, and freckles, and a round messenger-boy's hat. It was essential that people should think he was a delivery boy of some sort, in order for him to get specimens of their writing—or so Fatty worked it out.

He set off on his bicycle to the Rectory Field, where Old Nosey, the gypsy, lived in a dirty caravan with his wife. In this basket he carried a parcel, in which he had packed two of his father's old pipes, and a tin of tobacco he had bought. Larry met him as he cycled furiously down the village street, keeping a sharp look-out for Goon.

'Fatty!' said Larry, and then clapped his hand over his mouth, hoping that no passer-by had heard.

'Fathead !' said Fatty, stopping by Larry. 'Don't yell my name out when I'm in disguise ! Yell out Bert, or Alf, or Sid—anything you like, but not Fatty'.

'Sorry ! I did it without thinking,' said Larry. 'I don't think any one heard. What are you going to do, Fatty—er, I mean Sid ?'

'I'm going to deliver a parcel to Old Nosey,' said Fatty. From an Unknown friend ! And he's got to sign a receipt for it. See ?'

'Golly, you're clever,' said Larry, filled with admiration. 'Of course—you can easily get him to sign his name—and address too, I suppose by delivering a parcel to him and asking for a receipt ! I'd never have thought of that. Never.'

'I've put a couple of old pipes and some tobacco in,' said Fatty, with a grin. 'Nice surprise for Old Nosey ! I'm delivering a parcel to Miss Tittle too—and one to Mrs. Moon later. I've a feeling that if we've got specimens of all three in the way of hand-writing, we shall soon be able to spot the real letter-writer ! I'm going to ask them to give me a receipt in capital letters, of course.'

'Good for you,' said Larry. 'I'll tell Pip and Bets to look out for you later—delivering something to Mrs. Moon!'

Fatty rode off, whistling. He soon came to Rectory Field. He saw the caravan standing at the end, its little tin chimney smoking. Mrs. Nosey was outside, cooking something over a fire, and Nosey was sitting beside it, sucking at an empty pipe. Fatty rode over the field-path and jumped off his bicycle when he came to Nosey.

'Good morning,' he said. 'Parcel for you ! Special delivery !'

He handed the parcel to the surprised Old Nosey. The gypsy took it and turned it round and round, trying to feel what was inside. 'Anythink to pay ? asked Mrs. Nosey.

'Good Morning. Parcel for you'

'No. But I must have a receipt, please,' said Fatty, briskly, and whipped out a notebook, in which was printed in capital letters :

RECEIVED, ONE PARCEL,

by . . . .

'Will you sign your name and address there, please, in capital letters ?' he asked, showing Nosey where he meant.

'I'm not signing nothing,' said Nosey, not looking at Fatty.

'Well, if you want the parcel, you'll have to sign for it,' said Fatty. Always get a receipt, you know. It's the only thing I've got, to show I've delivered the parcel. See ?'

'*I'll* sign it,' said Mrs. Nosey, and held out her hand for the pencil.

'No,' said Fatty. 'The parcel is for your husband. I'm afraid he must sign it, Madam.'

'You let me,' said Mrs. Nosey. 'Go on—you give it to me to sign. It don't matter which of us does it.'

Fatty was almost in despair. Also he thought it a very suspicious sign that Nosey didn't seem to want to sign his name and address in capital letters. It rather looked as if he was afraid of doing so.

'I shall have to take the parcel back if your husband doesn't give me a proper receipt fot it.' he said, in as stern a voice as he could manage. 'Got to be business-like over these things, you know. Pity—it smells like tobacco.'

'Yes, it do,' said Old Nosey, and sniffed the parcel eagerly. 'Go on, wife, you sign for it.'

'I tell you,' began Fatty. But Nosey's wife pulled at his elbow. She spoke to him in a hoarse whisper.

'Don't you go bothering 'im. 'E can't write nor read !'

'Oh,' said Fatty blankly, and let Mrs. Nosey sign a receipt without further objection. He could hardly read what she wrote, for she put half the letters backwards, and could not even spell Peterswood.

Fatty cycled off, thinking. So Old Nosey couldn't write. Well, he was ruled out too, then. That really only left Miss Tittle—because Mrs. Moon had had one of the letters and could be crossed off the List of Suspects.

He went home and fetched a cardboard box into which he had packed a piece of stuff he had bought from the draper's that morning. He was just in time to catch Miss Tittle setting out to go for the day to Lady Candling's again.

'Parcel for you,' said Fatty briskly. 'Special delivery. Will you please sign for it—here—in capital letters for clearness—name *and* address, please'.

Miss Tittle was rather surprised to receive a parcel by special delivery, when she was not expecting one, but she supposed it was something urgent sent to be altered by one of her customers. So she signed for it in extremely neat capital letters, small and beautiful like her stitches.

'There you are,' she said. 'You only just caught me ! Good morning.'

'That was easy !' thought Fatty, as he rode away. 'Now—I wonder if it's really necessary to get Mrs. Moon's writing ? Better, I suppose, as she's been one of the Suspects. Well, here goes!'

He rode up the drive of Pip's house. Pip and the

others were lying in wait for him, and they called out in low voices as he went past.

'Ho there, Sid !'

'Hallo, Bert !'

'Wotcher, Alf !'

Fatty grinned and went to the back door. He had a small and neat parcel this time, beautifully wrapped up and tied with string and sealed. It really looked a very exciting parcel.

Mrs. Moon came to the kitchen door, 'Parcel for you,' said Fatty, presenting it to her. 'Special delivery. Sign for it here, please, in capital letters for clearness, name and address'.

'Me hands are all over flour,' said Mrs. Moon. 'You just sign it for me, young man. Now who can that parcel be from, I wonder !'

''Fraid you'll have to sign it yourself,' said Fatty. Mrs. Moon made an exasperated noise and snatched the pencil from Fatty's hand. She went and sat down at the table and most laboriously pencilled her name and address. But she mixed up small letters and capital letters in a curious way. The receipt said :

RECEIVED, ONE PARCEL

by. . . . .

WInnIe MOOn,

ReDhoUSe

peTeRSWOOD

'Thank you,' said Fatty, looking at it closely. 'But you've mixed up small letters and capital ones, Mrs. Moon ! Why did you do that ?'

'I'm no writer !' said Mrs. Moon, annoyed. 'You take that receipt and be off. Schooling in my days wasn't what it is now, when even a five-year-old knows his letters.'

Fatty went off. If Mrs. Moon didn't very well know the difference between small and capital letters, he didn't see how she could have printed all those spiteful anonymous letters. Anyway, he didn't really suspect her. He thought about things as he rode down the drive and back through the village. Nosey couldn't write. Rule him out. Mrs. Moon couldn't have done it either. Rule her out. That only left Miss Tittle—and the difference between her small and beautiful printing and the untidy, laboured scrawl of the nasty letters was amazing.

'I can't think it can be *her* writing, in those letters,' thought Fatty. 'Well, really, this case is getting more and more puzzling. We keep getting very good ideas and clues-and then one by one they all fizzle out. Not one of our Suspects really seems possible now—though I suppose Miss Tittle is the likeliest.'

He was so deep in thought that he didn't look where he was going, and he almost ran over a dog. It yelped so loudly with fright that Fatty, much concerned, got off his bicycle to comfort it.

'What you doing to make that dog yelp like that ?' said a harsh voice suddenly, and Fatty looked up, started, to see Mr. Goon standing over him.

'Nothing, sir,' stammered Fatty, pretending to be scared of the policeman. A curious look came into Mr. Goon's eyes—so curious that Fatty began to feel *really* scared.

Mr. Goon was gazing at Fatty's red wig. He looked at Fatty's messenger-boy hat. He looked very hard indeed. Another red-headed boy ! Why, the village seemed full of them.

'You come-alonga me !' he said suddenly, and clutched hold of Fatty's arm. 'I want to ask you a few questions, see ? You just come-alonga me !'

'I've done nothing,' said Fatty, pretending to be a frightened messenger-boy. 'You let me go, sir. I ain't done nothing.'

'Then you don't need to be scared,' said Mr. Goon. He took firm hold of Fatty's arm and led him down the street to his own small house. He pushed him inside, and took him upstairs to a small box-room, littered with rubbish of all kinds.

'I've been looking for red-headed boys all morning !' said Mr. Goon grimly. 'And I haven't found the ones I want. But maybe *you*'ll do instead ! Now you just sit here, and wait for me to come up and question you. I'm tired of reheaded boys, I am—butting in and out— picking up letters and delivering letters and parcels— and disappearing into thin air. Ho yes, I'm getting a bit tired of these here red-headed boys !'

He went out, shut the door and locked it. He clumped downstairs, and Fatty heard him using the telephone though he couldn't hear what he said.

Fatty looked round quickly. It was no use trying to get out of the window, for it looked on to the High Street and heaps of people would see him trying to escape that way and give the alarm.

No—he must escape out of the locked door, as he had done once before when an enemy had locked him in. Ah, Fatty know how to get out of a locked room ! He felt in his pocket and found a folded newspaper there. It was really amazing what Fatty kept in his pocket ! He opened the newspaper, smoothed it out quite flat, and pushed it quietly under the crack at the bottom of the door.

Then he took a small roll of wire from his pocket, and straightened one end of it. He inserted the end carefully into the lock. On the other side, of course, was the key that Mr. Goon had turned to lock the door.

Fatty jiggled about with the piece of wire, pushing and moving the key a little. Suddenly, with a soft thud, it fell to the floor outside the door, on to the sheet of newspaper that Fatty had pushed underneath to the other side. He grinned.

He had left a corner of the newspaper on his side, and this he now pulled at very gently. The whole of the newspaper sheet came under the door bringing the key with it ! Such a clever trick and so simple, thought Fatty.

It took him just a moment to put the key into the lock his side, turn it and open the door. He took the key, stepped out softly, locked the door behind him and left the key in.

Then he stood at the top of the little stairway and listened. Mr. Goon was evidently in the middle of a long routine telephone call, which he made every morning about this time.

There was a small bathroom nearby. Fatty went into it and carefully washed all the freckles off his face. He removed his eyebrows and wig and stuffed them into his pocket. He took off his rather loud tie and put another one on, also out of his pocket.

Now he looked completely different. He grinned at himself in the glass. 'Disappearance of another red-headed boy,' he said, and crept downstairs as quietly as he could. Mr. Goon was still in his parlour, telephoning.

Fatty slipped into the small empty kitchen. Mrs. Cockles was not there to-day.

He went out of the back door, down the garden and into the lane at the end. He had to leave his bike behind —but never mind, he'd think of some way of getting it back! Off he went, whistling, thinking of the delight of the Find-Outers when he told them of his adventurous morning!

18   THE MYSTERY OF THE RED-HEADED BOYS

MR. GOON finished his telephoning and went clumping upstairs to give that boy What-For, and to Properly-Put-Him-Through-It. Mr. Goon was sick and tired of chasing after red-headed boys that nobody seemed to have heard of. Now that he had got one really under his thumb, he meant to keep him there and find out a great many things he was bursting to know.

He stood and listened outside the door. There wasn't a sound to be heard. That boy was properly scared. That's how boys should feel, Mr. Goon thought. He'd no time for boys—cheeky, don't care, whistling creatures! He cleared his throat and pulled himself up majestically to his full height. He was the Law, he was !

The key was in the lock. The door was locked all right. He turned the key and flung open the door. He trod heavily into the room, a pompous look on his red face.

There was nobody there. Mr. Goon stared all round the

room, breathing heavily. But there simply wasn't anybody there. There was nowhere to hide at all—no cupboard, no chest. The window was still shut and fastened. No boy had got out that way.

Mr. Goon couldn't believe his eyes. He swallowed hard. He'd been after two red-headed boys that morning, and nobody seemed to have heard of either of them—and now here was the third one gone. Disappeared. Vanished. Vamoosed. But WHERE? And HOW?

Nobody could walk through a locked door. And the door *had* been locked, and the key his side too. But that boy had walked clean through that locked door. Mr. Goon began to feel he was dealing with some kind of Magic.

He walked round the room just to make sure that the boy hadn't squeezed into a tin or a box. But he had been such a plump boy! Mr. Goon felt most bewildered. He wondered if he had got a touch of the sun. He had just reported over the telephone his capture of a red-headed boy, for questioning—and how was he to explain his complete disappearance? He didn't feel that his superior officer would believe a boy could walk out of a locked door.

Poor Mr. Goon! He had indeed had a trying morning—a real wild-goose chase, as he put it to himself.

He had first af all gone to the post-office to ask the post-master to let him talk to the red-headed telegraph-boy.

But when the telegraph-boy had come, he wasn't red-headed! He was mousey-brown, and was a thin, under-sized little thing, plainly very frightened indeed to hear that Mr. Goon wanted to speak to him.

'This isn't the lad,' said Mr. Goon to the post master. 'Where's your other boy? The red-headed one?'.

'We've only got the one boy,' said the post-master, puzzled. 'This is the one. We've never had a red-headed fellow, as far as I can remember. We've had James here for about fourteen months now'.

Mr. Goon was dumbfounded. No red-headed telegraph-boy? Never had one! Well then, where did that fellow come from? Telegraph-boys were only attached to post-offices, surely.

'Sorry I can't help you,' said the post-master. 'But I do assure you we've got no red-headed boys at all here. But we've got a red-headed girl here – now would you like to see *her*?'

'No,' said Mr.Goon, 'This was a boy all right, and one of the civilest I ever spoke to—too civil by a long way. I see now! Pah! I'm fed up with this.

He went out of the post-office, feeling very angry, knowing that the post-master was thinking him slightly mad. He made his way to one of the butcher's, frowning. Just let him get hold of that there red-headed butcher-boy, delivering letters for the anonymous letter-writer. Ho, just let him! He'd soon worm everything out of him!

Mr. Veale, the butcher, was surprised to see Mr. Goon. 'Bit of nice tender meat, sir, for you to-day?' he asked, sharpening his knife.

'No thanks,' said Mr. Goon. 'I want to know if you've got a red-headed boy here, delivering your meat'.

'I've got no boy,' said Mr. Veale. 'Only old Sam, the fellow I've had for fifteen years. Thought you knew that'.

'Oh, I know old Sam,' said Mr.Goon. 'But I thought maybe you had a new boy as well. I expect it's the other butcher's delivery-boy I want.'

He went off to the other shop. This was a bigger establishment altogether. Mr. Cook, the owner, was there, cutting up meat with his two assistants.

'You got a boy here, delivering your meat for you ?' asked Mr. Goon.

'Yes, two,' said Mr. Cook. 'Dear me. I hope they haven't either of them got into trouble, Mr. Goon. They're good boys, both of them.'

'One of them isn't,' said Mr. Goon grimly. 'Where are they ? You let me see them.'

'They're out in the yard at the back packing their baskets with meat-deliveries,' said Mr. Cook. 'I'll come with you. Dear me. I do hope it's nothing serious.'

He took Mr.Goon out to the back. The policeman saw two boys. One was fair-haired with blue eyes and the other was black-haired dark as a gypsy.

'Well, there they are, Mr. Goon,' said Mr. Cook. 'Which of them is the rascal?'

The boys looked up, surprised. Mr. Goon took one look and scowled. 'They're neither of them the boy I want,' he said. 'I want a red-headed fellow.'

'There aren't any red-headed delivery-boys here, sir,' said the fair-haired lad. 'I know them all.'

Mr. Goon snorted and went back into the shop.

'Well, I'm glad it wasn't one of my boys,' said Mr. Cook. 'The fair-haired one is really a very clever fellow—he...'

But Mr. Goon didn't want to hear about any clever fair-haired boys. He wanted to see a red-headed one—and the more he tried to, the less likely it seemed he would ever find one.

He clumped out of the shop, disgusted. Who was the telegraph-boy ? Hadn't he seen him delivering a telegram to those children some time back—and again at night when he had bumped into him ? And what about that red-headed butcher-boy that Mrs. Hilton and Philip Hilton both said they had seen ? Who were these red-headed fellows flying around Peterswood, and not, apparently, living anywhere, or being known by any one?

Mr. Goon began to feel that he had red-headed boys on the brain, so, when he suddenly heard the loud yelping of a frightened dog, and looked up to see, actually to see a red-headed messenger-boy within reach of him, it was no wonder that he reached out and clutched that boy hard !

That was when Fatty had been trying to comfort the dog he had nearly run into. Mr. Goon had felt that it was a miracle to find a red-headed boy, even if he wasn't a telegraph-boy or a butcher-boy. He was red-headed, and that was enough!

And now he had lost that boy too. He had just walked out of a locked room and disappeared into thin air. Hey presto, he was there, and hey presto, he wasn't.

Mr.Goon forgot all about the boy's bicycle in his worry. It had been left out in the little front garden when he had pushed the boy into his house. The Policeman didn't even notice it there when he went out to get his mid-day paper.

Nor did he notice Larry waiting about at the corner.

But Larry had been posted there by Fatty to watch what Mr. Goon did with his bike. Fatty was afraid that Mr. Goon might make inquiries and find out who the right owner was, and he didn't want the policeman to know that.

Larry saw Mr. Goon come out. He imagined that having found that Fatty was gone, he would at least lock up his bicycle, and take a delight in doing it. He didn't realize poor Mr. Goon's stupefied state of mind. The puzzled man had sat down in his chair to think things out, but had got into such a muddle that he had decided to go out, get his paper and have a drink. Maybe he would feel better then.

Mr. Goon went out of his little front garden as if he was walking in a dream. He saw neither Larry nor the bicycle. He drifted on towards the paper-shop.

Larry gaped. Wasn't old Goon going to lock up the bicycle? Surely he ought to do that? Could he possibly have overlooked it? It really did seem as if he had.

Mr. Goon went into the paper-shop. Larry acted like lightning! He shot across the road, went into the little garden, took Fatty's bike out, mounted it and rode off at top speed. Nobody even saw him!

Mr. Goon got his paper, and had a little talk with the owner of the shop. As he went out again, he suddenly remembered the bicycle.

"Lawks! I ought to have locked it up at once!' thought Mr.Goon, and began to hurry back to his house. 'How did I come to forget it? I was that mazed.'

He hurried into his front garden—and then stopped short in dismay. The bicycle was gone! It was now of course, half-way to Pip's house, ridden furiously by Larry, who was absolutely longing to know the whole of Fatty's story. But Mr. Goon didn't know that.

He gulped. This was getting too much for him. Three red-headed boys all vanishing into thin air—and now a completely solid bicycle doing the same thing. He supposed that red-headed fellow must have taken it somehow without his seeing-but how ?

'Gah !' said Mr. Goon, wiping his hot forehead. 'What with these here letters—and hysterical women— and red-headed disappearing fellows—and that cheeky toad, Frederick Trotteville—my life in Peterswood ain't worth living ! First one thing and then another. I'd like to talk to that Frederick Trotteville. I wouldn't put it past him to write me that cheeky anonymous letter. It's him that done that—I'd lay a million dollars it was. Gah !'

19   CLUES, REAL CLUES AT LAST !

THE Five-Find-Outers and Buster met in the little summer-house at the top of Pip's garden that afternoon. It was warm and sunny there, and they wanted to be quite alone and hear again and again of all that Fatty had done that morning—especially of his neat escape from Mr. Goon's boxroom.

'I simply can't *imagine* what he said when he unlocked the door and found you gone, Fatty' said Bets. 'I'd have loved to be there !'

Fatty showed them the two specimens of hand-writing he had taken from Miss Tittle and Mrs. Moon. He told them that Nosey couldn't write, so that ruled him out completely. 'And if you look at this receipt, which Mrs. Nosey signed, you'll see she could never have written those letters either, even if Nosey had told her what to put into them,' said Fatty.

'It's a funny thing,' said Daisy, 'we've had plenty of Suspects—but one by one we've had to rule them out. There honestly doesn't seem to be a single real Suspect left, Fatty.'

'And except for seeing the letters, we've got no real Clues either,' said Larry, 'I call this a most disappointing Mystery. The letter-writer went a bit mad this week, didn't he—or she—sending letters to Mrs. Lamb—and Mrs. Moon and Mr. Goon. Before that, as far as we know, only one a week was sent.'

'Isn't old Clear-Orf funny when I keep pretending I've got a new Clue ? said Fatty, grinning. 'Do you remember his face when I pulled old Waffles, the white rat, out of my pocket ? I just happened to have him there that day.'

Poor old Clear-Orf doesn't believe anything we say any more,' said Pip. 'I do wonder if he really suspects somebody of writing those letters—some one we don't know about ?'

'He may have some clues or ideas we haven't been able to get,' said Fatty. 'I shouldn't be surprised if he solves this Mystery after all—and not us'.

'Oh, *Fatty* !' cried every one in dismay.

'How *can* you say that ? said Bets. 'Wouldn't it be dreadful if he did—so that Inspector Jenks was pleased with him, and not with us.

Inspector Jenks was their very good friend, and had

always been very pleased with them because they had managed to solve some curious mysteries in Peterswood before. They had not seen him since the Christmas holidays.

'Let's get out of this summer-house,' said Larry. 'It's absolutely melting in here ! Fatty, don't forget to take your red-haired wig and things back with you to-night. This summer-house isn't an awfully safe hiding-place for them. Pip's mother might easily walk in and see them stuffed under the seat.'

'I'll remember,' said Fatty, yawning. 'Golly, it was funny going into Goon's house this morning as a red-headed messenger-boy-and coming out just myself, and nobody spotting me ! Come-on let's go for a walk by the river. It'll be cool there. I shall fall asleep in this heat !'

As they went down the drive they met Mr. Goon cycling up. They wondered which of the household he was going to see. He stopped and got off his bike.

'You know that there telegraph-boy, that brought you that telegram some time back ?' he said. 'Well, I happen to know he's fake, see ? There's no telegraph-boy like that. And I'm making strict inquiries into the matter, I am-yes and into fake telegrams too, see ? And I warn you all, if you hob-nob with red-heads, you'll get into Serious Trouble. Very Serious Trouble'.

'You do frighten me,' said Fatty, making his eyes go big.

'And I'll have None of your Sauce !' said Mr. Goon majestically. 'I know more than what you think, and I advise you all to be careful. Call that dog orf !'

'Come here, Buster,' said Fatty, in such a mild voice that Buster took no notice at all. He went on prancing round Mr. Goon's ankles.

'I said, call him *orf*!' repeated Mr. Goon, doing little prances too, to avoid sudden rushes by Buster.

'Come here, Buster.' said Fatty again, in an extremely polite voice. Buster ignored him completely.

'That's not calling him orf !' shouted Mr. Goon, beginning to lose his temper. 'Yell at him, go on ! Nuisance of a dog !'

Fatty winked at the others, and with one accord they all opened their mouths and yelled at the top of their voices. 'COME HERE, BUSTER !'

Mr. Goon jumped violently at the noise. He glared. Buster also jumped. He went to Fatty.

'Not pleased even now, Mr. Goon ?' said Fatty sweetly. 'Oh dear-there's no pleasing you at all, I'm afraid. Wait a minute—I believe I've got a really good clue to hand you—ah, here it is !'

He took out a match-box and gave it to the policeman. Mr. Goon opened it supiciously. It was a trick match-box, and, as Mr. Goon opened it, he released a powerful spring inside which sprang up and shot the match-box high in the air. Mr. Goon got quite a shock.

He went purple, and his eyes bulged.

'So sorry, so sorry,' said Fatty hastily. 'It must have been the wrong match-box. Wait a bit-I've got another....?'

If Buster had not been there with his ready teeth Mr. Goon might quite well have boxed Fatty's ears. He looked ready to burst. Fearing that he might say something he ought not to, poor Mr. Goon hurriedly mounted his bicycle and rode up the drive, breathing so heavily that he could be heard all the way to the kitchen-door.

'He's gone to talk to Mrs. Moon again,' said Pip. 'I expect they'll come to blows! Let's get on. Oh, Fatty, I thought I should burst when that trick match-box went up in the air. Goon's face !'

They strolled down the lane to the river. It was pleasant there, for a breeze blew across the water. The children found a sunny place beside a bigbush and lay down lazily. A swan came swimming by, and two moor-hens chugged across the water, their heads bobbing like clock-work.

'Let's forget all about the Mystery for a bit.' said Daisy. 'It's so nice here. I keep on thinking and thinking about those letters, and who could be writing them— but the more I think the less I know'.

'Same here,' said Pip. 'So many Suspects-and not one of them could apparently have Done the Deed. A most mysterious mystery'.

'One that even the great detective, Mr. Frederick Sherlock Holmes Trotteville can't solve either !' said Larry.

'Correct !' said Fatty, with a sigh. I almost—but not quite—give it up !'

Larry's hat blew away and he got up to go and get it. 'Blow !' he said. 'There's old Clear-Orf again—cycling over the field-path. He's seen me too. Hope he doesn't come and make a row again. He'd like to eat you alive, Fatty, you're aggravating'.

'Sit down quickly, in case he hasn't seen you,' said Daisy. 'We don't want him here.'

Larry sat down. They all watched the blue water flowing smoothly by . The moor-hens came back again, and a fish jumped at a fly. A very early swallow dipped down to the water. It was all very peaceful indeed.

'I should think old Clear-Orf didn't see me after all.' said Larry. 'Thanks goodness. I think I'am going to sleep. There's something very soothing about the gurgling of the water—a lovely, peaceful afternoon.

Heavy breathing disturbed the peace, and clumsy footsteps came over the grass towards their bush. Mr. Goon appeared, his face a familiar purple. He carried a small sack in his hand, and looked extremely angry. He flung the tittle sack down fiercely.

'More Clues, I suppose !' he sneered. 'More of your silly, childish jokes ! White rats and match boxes ! Huh ! Gah ! What a set of chiildren ! And now these Clues— hidden nicely under a bush for me to find, I suppose ? What do you think I am ? A nitwit ?'

The children were astonished at this outburst, and Bets was really alarmed. Fatty put out a quick hand on Buster's collar, for the little Scottie had got his hackles up and was growling fiercely, showing all his teeth.

'What's up, Goon ? said Fatty, in a sharp, rather grown-up voice.

'You know as well as I do !' said the policeman. 'More Clues ! I suppose you'll tell me next that you don't know anything about that sack of Clues ! Gah !'

'What sack ? What clues ?' said Fatty, really puzzled. 'No—I really don't know what you're talking about,

Mr. Goon.'

'You don't know—ho no, you don't know !' said Mr. Goon, and he laughed a nasty laugh. 'You don't know anything about red wigs, either, I suppose ? Or writing rude letters to the Law ? Well, I know a lot ! Oho, don't I ? I'll teach you to lay clues about for me to find. Think I'm a real hignoramus, don't you.

'Shut up, Buster,' said Fatty, for Buster was now snarling very loudly indeed. 'Mr. Goon, please go. You're frightening little Bets, and I don't think I can hold Buster in much longer. I don't know *what* you're talking about—and certainly I've never seen the sack before.'

Buster gave such a fearfully loud snarl that Mr. Goon thought it would be best to do as Fatty said and go. He went, leaving the little sack on the ground, and stepped heavily away looking as majestic as he could.

'Well, what an unpleasant fellow,' said Fatty, slipping his arm round Bets, who was in tears. 'Don't bother about him, Bets. We know the blustering, roaring old fellow by now. You need never he scared of *him* !'

'I don't like p-p-people to shout like that,' sobbed Bets. 'And oh Fatty, he said about your red wig! Has he found it?'

'I wondered about that to,' said Fatty. 'We'll look when we go back. I left it in the summer house, didn't I ? Wish I hadn't now.'

'What's this sack of clues that old Clear-Orf kept yammering about ?' said Larry. He pulled it towards him. 'Some old collection of rubbish some tramp had left behind him under a bush, I suppose—and Mr. Goon found it and thought it was some more of your false clues, Fatty, planted for him to find.'

Larry undid the neck of the little sack. It was not much bigger than a three-pound flour bag. Inside, half-wrapped in brown paper, were some curious things.

There was a small school dictionary—and when he saw it Pip sat up in surprise. 'Golly ! That's my dicky. I do declare!' he said. The one I lost last hols. Isn't it, Bets ? Gracious, how did it get into this sack ?'

This made every one sit up and take notice at once. Fatty reached out his arm and took the sack. He ran his fingers quickly throgh the dictionary, and noted that several words were underlined. One of them was 'thief'. Another was 'fruit'. Fatty found others, all underlined.

Pip's name was in the front of the dictionary. There was no doubt at all but that it was his lost book. Fatty put his hand into the sack to see what else there was there.

He drew out—an alphabet book. 'A is for Apple, so rosy and red !' he chanted, 'B is for Baby who's just off to bed.' My goodness, no wonder old Clear-Orf thought we'd planted these things for him—a dictionary—and an alphabet book. Most peculiar !'

The next thing was a child's copy-book with some of the pages filled in, not very neatly. Larry laughed.

'This is some village kid's little treasure-store, I should think,'he said. 'Though goodness knows how the kid got hold of Pip's dictionary.'

Fatty dipped his hand in again. His eyes were suddenly very bright indeed. He pulled out an old bus time-table. He looked at it and then flipped it. It fell

Fatty dipped his hand in again

open at one much-thumbed page—and on that page there was a mark.

'Do you know what is marked ?' said Fatty. 'The 10.15 bus to Sheepsale ! What do you think of that ?'

The others stared at him. They were all very puzzled now. Fatty spoke excitedly.

'These are *real* Clues ! Don't you understand, you donkeys ? Goon thought they were silly, false ones put there by us to deceive him—but they're *real* ones, ones that may help us to put our hand on the letter-writer this very day.'

Now it was the turn of the others to get excited. 'Oooh,' said Bets. 'How silly of Mr. Goon to give them all to *us*.'

Fatty put his hand in once again and drew out a little, torn scrap of paper with some untidy writing on it. There were only two or three words to be made out. One was 'spoonful'. another was 'stir,' and another was 'oven'. Fatty read them and nodded. He was evidently very pleased indeed with this find.

'Poor old Goon !' he said. 'He makes the one glorious find in this Mystery—and throws it down at our feet. Won't he kick himself when he knows? What a bit of luck, oh what a bit of luck !'

THE other four tried in vain to make Fatty tell them more. But he wouldn't. 'You can look at all these clues as much as you like,' he said, 'and if you use your brains they will tell you exactly what they tell me. Exactly. I could tell you everything in two minutes—but I do really think you should try to find out what I have found out.'

'But that silly alphabet book !' said Daisy. 'It doesn't tell me a thing !'

'And all that time-table tells me is that there's a bus to Sheepsale at 10.15, and it's the bus the letter-writer probably took—but it doesn't tell me anything else,' said Pip. 'As to my dictonary—well that beats me !'

'Come on—let's get back home,' said Fatty. 'I've got to think this all out. It's not a scrap of good going to Goon about it. He won't believe a word. In fact I think he's got it firmly in his head that I'm mixed up in all this letter-writing. I'm sure he thinks I wrote the letter to him !'

'Well—who are we going to, then ? asked Bets. 'Inspector Jenks? I'd like that !'

'I thought perhaps we'd better tell your mother first,' said Fatty. 'I don't somehow feel as if I want to bring Inspector Jenks down here for an affair like this-and go right over Goon's head with the clues that Goon himself presented us with. Doesn't seem quite fair somehow'.

'It seems quite fair to *me* !' said Bets, who disliked

Mr. Goon more than any of the others did. 'Oh, Fatty—tell us all you know from these clues, do, do, do !'

'Now, Bets, if you like to think hard and study these clues, you would know as much as I do,' said Fatty. 'Come on—let's go home and on the way you can all think hard and if nobody can find out what these clues mean, or who they're pointing to, then I'll tell you myself. But give your brains a chance, do!'

In silence except for Buster's occasional yaps at a stray cat, they went home to Pip's. When they got into the drive they saw a big black car there.

'Whose is that ?' said Bets, in wonder.

'And there's Mr. Goon's bike,' said Daisy, pointing to where it stood by the front door. 'He's here too.'

Mrs. Hilton suddenly opened the front door and stood there, waiting for them, looking pale and worried.

'Come in this way,' she said. 'I'm glad you've come. Mr. Goon is here—saying most peculiar things—and he's got Inspector Jenks over too !'

'Oh! Is *he* here ?' cried Bets in delight, and rushed into the drawing-room. The big Inspector sat there, his eyes twinkling as he saw Bets. He was very fond of her.

She flung herself on him. 'I haven't seen you since the Christmas holidays ! You're bigger than ever ! Oh—there's Mr. Goon !'

So there was, sitting upright in a corner, looking curiously pleased with himself.

The other four came in more quietly, and shook hands with the big Inspector. They knew him well, for he had come to their help very often, when they were solving other problems. Buster capered round his ankles in delight, awaiting for the pat he knew would come.

Mrs. Hilton waited till the greetings were over, and then spoke in a worried voice.

'Children! Mr. Goon brought Inspector Jenks over here to-day, when he was visiting Peterswood, because he had a serious complaint to make of your behaviour, especially one of you, and he thought that it would be a good thing if the Inspector reprimanded you himself. But I cannot imagine what you have been doing-unless you have been interfering in this anonymous letter business—and I said you were not to.'

Nobody said anything. Fatty looked politely and inquiringly at the Inspector.

'Suppose you hold forth, Goon,' said the Inspector, in his pleasant, courteous voice. 'You have quite a lot to say, I believe.'

'Well, sir,' began Mr. Goon, in a righteous sort of voice, 'I know your opinion of these here children has always been high—but I've always known more of them than you have, if you'll pardon me saying so, sir—and they've bin getting above themselves, sir-meddling in things that don't concern them, and hindering me in my business, sir—and one of them—this here boy by name of Frederick Trotteville, sir, I regret to inform you that he has meddled in this anonynmous writing, and sent me a most rude and incivil letter, sir—and what's more he goes about pretending to be what he's not, sir—and deceiving me proper-like,....'

'Exactly what do you mean by that, Goon? asked the Inspector mildly. 'Going about pretending to be what he's not?'

'Well, sir, he's a whole lot of red-headed boys, sir,' said Mr. Goon, to the great mystification of the Inspector and Mrs. Hilton. 'Took me in proper he did. First he was a red-headed telegraph-boy, sir—then he was a butcher-boy—and a messenger-boy, sir—tearing round on his bike, a public danger, sir, and a nuisance. But as soon as I found the red wig, sir......'

'Who told you where it was ?' asked Fatty.

'Mrs. Moon showed me,' said Mr. Goon. 'Yes, and she told me, too, all the things you've been saying about me, Master Frederick—you and the others—and how she overheard you planning to write that there cheeky letter to me !'

'Really ?' said Fatty his eys gleaming curiously. 'Perhaps she told you also, who is the writer of those other anonymous letters ?'

'Well, no, she didn't,' admitted Mr. Goon. 'Unless it was some one she's Got Her Eye On. But she wasn't mentioning any names just yet.'

Frederick, this is all very disturbing,' said Mrs. Hilton., 'I cannot imagine what you have been doing ! And surely, surely you did not write that letter to Mr. Goon !'

'No, Mrs. Hilton, of course I didn't,' said Fatty. 'As for the disguises—well, I mean to be a famous detective when I grow up—and I'm just practising, that's all. I *have* been looking into the mystery of the anonymous letter-writing—and by great good luck I've had a whole lot of clues thrust upon me. As a matter of fact we were going to tell you the whole thing as soon as we got back.'

'Ho yes !' said Mr. Goon disbelievingly.

'That will do, Goon,' said the Inspector. 'What are these clues, Frederick, that you've had thrust upon you?'

Fatty went into the hall and came back with the little sack. He placed it on the table. Mr. Goon stared at it and his eyes bulged.

'Those clues!' he said, scornfully. 'Those clues you planted for me to find! Ho! Copybooks and alphabet books! White rats and match-boxes that jump! Clothing pegs and doll's hats!'

The Inspector looked most astonished at this long list of things. Fatty looked a little uncomfortable.

'Just my little joke,' he murmured.

'Well, your little jokes have landed you into Serious Trouble,' said Mr. Goon. 'Just like I said they would. It was lucky the Inspector was in Peterswood to-day. Soon as I told him about everything, along he came.'

'Very kind of him,' said Fatty. 'In fact, as far as we are concerned, he has come at exactly the right moment. We were just discussing whether or not we should telephone him and ask him to come over. Now he's here!'

'And what did you want to see me about?' asked the Inspector.

'About this anonymous letter-writing business, sir,' said Fatty. 'You see, we couldn't let a mystery like that happen under our very noses, so to speak, without going into it a bit. And we were all sorry for Gladys.'

'Quite so,' said the Inspector. 'Another case for the Five Find-outers-and Dog!'

'Yes, sir,' said Fatty. 'A very difficult affair too, sir, We got on a lot of wrong trails.'

'We found out that the letter-writer caught the 10.15 bus to Sheepsale,' said Bets. 'And we went on it on Monday, to see who the passengers were. but nobody posted a letter there!'

'Except Master Frederick!' shot out Mr. Goon. 'There—I told you Mr. Goon would put you down on his List of Suspects if he saw you posting that letter!' said Bets.

'I rather hoped he would!' said Fatty, with a grin. Mr. Goon scowled. This interview wasn't coming off quite as he had hoped it would. That wretched boy, Fatty! He always seemed to get away with anything. And the Inspector didn't seem to be taking the matter very seriously, either. It was too bad.

'I expect Mr. Goon has told you about the bus to Sheepsale, though Sir, and how, the letters were always posted there by the 11.45 post,' said Fatty. 'And how nobody posted any that day—except me !—and I expect, like us, he made inquiries to see if any of the regular bus passengers failed to go on the bus that day for some reason or other-and got his Suspects narrowed down to Old Nosey, Miss Tittle, and Mrs. Moon'.

'Yes. He did tell me,' said the Inspector. 'And I think, if I may say so, that it was pretty smart work on the part of you children to work all that out !'

This was too much for Mr. Goon. 'Smart work! Interfering with the Law, that's what I call it,' he said. I suppose he'll tell you next that he knows who that letter-writer is !'

'Yes. I was going to come to that,' said Fatty quietly. 'I *do* know who the letter-writer is !'

Every one gaped at Fatty. Even the Inspector sat up

straight at once. As for Goon, his mouth fell open and he goggled at Fatty in disbelief.

'Who is it ?' he said.

'Mrs. Hilton—may I ring the bell ?' said Fatty. She nodded. He went over to the wall and rang the bell hard. Every one waited.

21   WELL DONE, FATTY !

THE bell sounded loudly. The door opened in the kitchen and footsteps came up the hall. Mrs. Moon appeared in the drawing-room. She looked surprised and rather scared when she saw so many people sitting quietly there.

'Did you ring, Madam?' she asked, and her voice shook a little.

'I rang.' said Fatty. He turned to the Inspector. 'This is the anonymous letter-writer,' he said. 'Mrs. Moon!'

Mrs. Hilton gasped. Mr. Goon snorted loudly. All the children drew in their breath sharply. Only the Inspector seemed unperturbed.

Mrs. Moon went pale. She stared at Fatty. 'What do you mean ?' she said fiercely. 'How dare you say things like that to a respectable law—abiding woman ?'

'Hardly law-abiding, Mrs.Moon,' said the Inspector's stern voice. 'It is against the law to send spiteful and untrue letters through the post anonymously. But Frederick—please explain. I have enough faith in your intelligence to know that you are making no mistake, if I may say so—but I want to know all about it.'

Mrs. Moon began to cry. 'Sit down and keep quiet,' commanded Inspector Jenks.

'I won't be treated like this, I won't !' wailed Mrs. Moon. An innocent woman like me! Why, I've even had one of them awful letters meself !'

'Yes-you nearly took me in over that' said Fatty. 'I thought that ruled you out-but it was just a bit of artfulness on your part. I see that now.'

'You bad, wicked boy!' moaned Mrs. Moon.

'Silence !' said the Inspector, in such a fierce voice that Bets jumped. 'Speak when you're spoken to, Mrs. Moon, and not unless. If you are innocent you will be given plenty of chance to prove it. We will hear what you have to say when Master Frederick has told his story. Frederick, begin.'

Fatty began, and the other childeren leaned forward, knowing most of the story well, but longing to hear what the end of it was. Only Fatty knew that.

'Well, sir, you know already that we worked out that as the letters were posted in Sheepsale each Monday to catch the 11.45 post there, that it was probable the guilty person was some one who took the 10.15 bus from Peterswood to Sheepsale.' said Fatty.

'Quite so.' said the Inspector.

'Well, we found that none of the bus-passengers last Monday could be the letter-writer,' said Fatty, 'and certainly none of them posted a letter. So then we decided to find out if any regular Monday passenger was *not* on the bus that Monday, and make inquiries about them. And as you know, we found that three regular passengers didn't travel that day—Miss Tittle, Old Nosey, and Mrs. Moon.'

'Mr. Goon also worked on the same lines,' said the Inspector. A sound from Goon made every one look up.

'How did you get to see them letters, and see the post-mark ?' demanded Mr. Goon. That's what I want to know.'

'Oh, that's not an important detail,' said Fatty, anxious not to give away Gladys' part in that affair. 'Well, to continue, sir—we found out next that another letter had been sent that Monday— but not from Sheepsale—it had been delivered by hand. So that definitely pointed to somebody in Peterswood, and possibly one of our three Suspects— Old Nosey, Miss Tittle, or Mrs.Moon.'

'Quite.' said the Inspector, deeply interested. I must say that your powers of deduction are good, Frederick.'

'Well, the letter was delivered very early in the morning,' said Fatty, 'so I had to find out which of the three Suspects was up early that Tuesday. And I found that all of them were !'

'Very puzzling,' said the Inspector. 'I don't think Mr. Goon got quite as far as that, did you, Mr. Goon ? Go on, Frederick.'

'That rather shook me,' said Fatty, 'and the only thing I could think of next was getting specimens of the handwriting of each of the three—to compare with the printed letters, you see.'

'A good idea,' said Inspector Jenks, 'but surely a little difficult ?'

'Not very,' said Fatty modestly. 'You see, I put on a disguise—a red-headed delivery-boy I was.' There was a snort from Mr. Goon at this. 'And,' went on Fatty, 'I just delivered parcels to all three, and got them to sign receipts in capital letters—so that I could compare them with the capital letters in the anonymous notes!'

'Most ingenious, if I may say so,' said the Inspector. He turned to Mr. Goon, whose eyes were bulging at hearing about all this detective work on Fatty's part. 'I am sure you agree with me ?' said the Inspector. Mr. Goon did not agree with him at all, but couldn't very well say so.

'Well, I found that Nosey couldn't write at all,' said Fatty. 'So that ruled him out. Then I saw that Miss Tittle's printing, very small and neat and beautiful, wasn't anything at all like the printing of the letters in the anonymous notes-and that rather ruled *her* out too-and to my surprise Mrs.Moon's printing was such a mixture of big and small letters that I couldn't think she could be the culprit either.'

'And I'm not!' said Mrs. Moon, rocking herself to and fro. 'No, I'm not.'

'Here's a specimen of her writing—or rather, printing sir,' said Fatty, opening his notebook and showing the Insector Mrs. Moon's curious printing, big and small letters mixed. 'When I asked her about it, she gave me to understand that she couldn't help it—it appeared to me, sir, that she was muddled in her mind as to which were big and which were small letters.'

'Quite,' said Inspector Jenks. So you ruled her out too, as the messages and the addresses on the anonymous letters were apparently printed quite correctly in capitals, with no small letters at all ?'

'Yes, sir,' said Fatty.'And I almost gave up the case. Couldn't see any light anywhere—and had n't got any real clues, either. I didn't think at the time, either, that Mrs. Moon would write an anonymous letter to herself—though I *should* have thought of that, of course. . . .'

'And what about that letter to *me* ?'said Mr.Goon, suddenly. 'That was you, wasn't it, Master Frederick ? Come on, you own up now—that was you, calling me a meddler and a muddler and cheeking me like you always do !'

'No—I certainly didn't write you that letter,' said Fatty. And I think if you compare it with the others, Mr. Goon, you'll see it's just like them.'

'Well, Frederick—how did you come to know in the end that it *was* Mrs. Moon and nobody else ?' inquired the Inspector.

'I tell you it wasn't, it wasn't,' moaned Mrs. Moon.

'That was a sheer bit of luck, sir,' said Fatty, modestly. 'Can't give myself any marks for that ! It was Mr. Goon who put me right on the track !'

'Gah !' said Mr. Goon disbelievingly.

'Yes—he suddenly gave us a whole sack of clues— that sack of things on the table !' said Fatty. 'And, as soon as I saw them I was able to piece things together and know who had written those disgusting, spiteful letters!'

The Inspector picked up the things one by one and looked at them with interest. 'Exactly what did these things tell you?' he said curiously.

'There's a dictionary, sir—with Pip's name in,' said Fatty. 'That told me that it probably came from this house and was used by somebody living here. Then I noticed that various words had been looked up for the spelling, and had been underlined—and every one of those words, sir, has been used in the anonymous letters !'

Mr. Goon's face went redder than ever. To think that boy had got all that out of the things in that sack !

'The next thing, sir, was the alphabet book,' said Fatty. 'And, as I daresay you've noticed, the alphabet letters in such a book are always in capitals. A is for Apple, and so on . So I guessed that book had been bought as a kind of reference book for capital letters, by somebody who wasn't quite sure of the difference in shape of big and small letters. The capital letter G, for instance, is quite different from the small letter g. Naturally the anonymous letter-writer didn't want to give away the fact that she hadn't had enough education to know the difference.'

'Well worked out, Frederick, well worked out,' said the Inspector, most interested. 'What about this ?' He held up the copybook.

'That's easy, sir,' said Fatty. 'Even Bets could read *that* clue now !'

'Yes, I can !' called Bets. 'That's a copybook Mrs. Moon must have bought to practise writing capital letters in. There's lots of capitals printed there in pencil.'

'I expect if you ask at the stationer's, Inspector, you'll find that Mrs. Moon did buy a copybook there some weeks ago !'

'Make inquiries, Goon,' said the Inspector. Goon hurriedly made a note in his notebook.

'The bus time-table was an easy clue,' said Fatty. 'I

guessed I'd find that 10.15 bus marked. And this bit of torn paper, sir—used as a bookmark in the dictionary, I should think—must have been torn from a recipe of some sort. I knew that as soon as I read the words— 'spoonful'—'stir'—'oven'. I except you will find that they are in Mrs. Moon's ordinary handwriting, and torn from her kitchen recipe-book.'

'A most ingenious reading of rather peculiar clues !' said the Inspector, looking really pleased. 'What a pity, Mr. Goon you didn't take the trouble to look carefully through the clues yourself and deduct from them all that Frederick has done.'

'Thought they was all false clues,' muttered Mr. Goon. 'Made me angry, they did.'

'It's a mistake to let anger cloud your thinking, Goon.' said the Inspector. 'If you had only examined these clues carefully, you might have arrived at the same conclusions as Frederick here—but again, you might not !'

It was apparent that the Inspector believed that Goon would certainly not have made such good use of the clues as Fatty had !

Mrs. Moon suddenly threw her apron over her head and wailed loudly. She rocked to and fro again, and Bets watched her in dismay. She didn't like people who shouted and howled.

'You're all against me, you are !' wailed Mrs. Moon. 'Not a friend have I got in the world ! You're all against me !'

'You have only yourself to blame, my good woman,' said Inspector Jenks sharply. ' 'You yourself are apparently filled with spite against a great many people-and you cannot be surprised if you have no friends. I'm afraid you must come with me for further questioning. Mrs. Hilton, I fear that Mrs. Moon will not be returning to you.'

'I don't want her,' said Mrs. Hilton, with a shudder. 'A cruel, underhand, spiteful woman like that in my house ! No, never. Poor Gladys. I'll fetch her back at once. I'm horrified and disgusted, Mrs. Moon. You have caused a great deal of pain and grief to many people, and I hope you will be well punished'.

'You don't mind us having investigated the case now, Mother, do you ? said Pip, thinking this was a good opportunity to get his mother to agree.

'Well—I didn't want you mixed up in such an un-pleasant business,' said Mrs. Hilton. 'And I must say that I thought Mr. Goon could manage it himself. But I do think you worked out things very cleverly—especially Fatty, of course.'

'Oh, all the Find-Outers did their bit,' said Fatty loyally. 'I couldn't have done without them. And,' he said, with a glance at Mr. Goon, 'we did have a lot of fun at times-didn't we, Pip ?'

'We did !' said all the others, and grinned at poor Mr. Goon, who did one of his snorts, and scowled heavily at them.

The Inspector got up. 'Get your outdoor things, Mrs. Moon,' he said. 'You must come with me. Goon, I want you too. But perhaps, when I have finished my work here, at about four o'clock this afternoon, Mrs. Hilton, the children could come over to Nutting, where I'm going then,

and have tea with me in the big hotel there? I feel I would like to have a little chat with the Five Find-Outers-and Dog–
–again!'

'Oooh!' said Bets, delighted.

'Woof,' said Buster, pleased.

'Oh thanks!' said the others.

Mrs. Moon went out, weeping. The Inspector shook hands with Mrs. Hilton and went out to his car. 'See you this afternoon!' he said, to the delighted children.

Mrs. Hilton went out to see that Mrs. Moon did what she was told. The children followed the Inspector to his black car. Mr. Goon was left behind in the drawing-room, looking gloomily at the carpet. He was alone with his thoughts.

No—he wasn't alone! Buster was there too, regarding his old enemy with a bright eye. No one was there to say, 'Come here, Buster!' What a chance!

With a joyful yelp he flung himself at Mr. Goon's ankles, and pulled at his blue trousers. Mr. Goon rose up in alarm.

'Clear-orf!'

The children heard the shouting and laughed at the familiar words. 'Poor old Clear-Orf,' said Bets. 'Always in trouble. Fatty, go and rescue him'.

Fatty went. Mr. Goon came out, frowning, trying to see if his trouser-ankles had been torn. Buster struggled in Fatty's arms.

'Get in, Goon, whilst you're safe,' said the Inspector, opening the door of the car. 'Ah, here is Mrs. Moon. The other side, please, Mrs. Moon. Goodbye, children—

and thanks for your help once more. I must say I'm pleased with the Five Find-Outers and Dog !'

'Oh well—I suppose we ought to thank Mr. Goon for all those clues !' said Fatty. He winked at the others, and they all opened their mouths together at once and chanted :

'THANKS, MR. GOON !'

And what did Mr. Goon reply ? Exactly what you would expect.

'GAH!'

Also available in the Mystery Series

THE MYSTERY OF THE BURNT COTTAGE

This is the first of Enid Blyton's thrilling mystery books. Fatty, Larry, Daisy, Pip, Bets–and Buster the dog–turn detectives when a mysterious fire destroys a thatched cottage in their village. Calling themselves the 'Five Find-Outers and Dog' they set out to solve the mystery and discover the culprit. The final solution, however, surprises the Five Find-Outers almost as much as Mr. Goon, the village policeman. They can hardly wait for the next mystery to come along!

THE MYSTERY OF THE DISAPPEARING CAT

The second book in the popular Mystery series in which the Find-Outers–Larry, Fatty, Daisy, Pip, Bets and Buster the dog–turn detectives again to solve a very puzzling mystery.

A valuable Siamese cat is stolen from next door and suspicion falls on the children's friend, Luke the gardener's boy. How can they find the real thief and clear Luke of blame, especially with Mr. Goon the policeman interfering as usual ? The Find-Outers are plunged into the middle of a first class mystery with only the strangest of clues to work on.

THE MYSTERY OF THE SECRET ROOM

This is the third book in the Mystery series.

It is the Christmas holidays, and the Five are looking for mysteries. Then out of the blue Pip discovers a room, fully furnished, at the top of an empty house. Whose room is it ? What is it used for ? This is the problem that must be solved in *The Mystery of the Secret Room*. With the help of their friend Inspector Jenks, the Five Find-Outers eventually reach a solution in this most entertaining book.

THE MYSTERY OF THE MISSING NECKLACE

The fifth book of the popular Mystery series, in which Fatty, Larry, Daisy, Pip, Bets–and Buster the dog, all play their parts as Find-Outers.

There are a great many clever burglaries going on and it is suspected that members of the gang have their meeting place, somewhere in Peterswood. The children naturally determine to solve the mystery, and they tumble into other mysteries, too, in the process. Who is the old man on the seat ? Who is Number Three ? Where is the missing necklace ? For once Mr. Goon, the policeman, defeats Fatty one strange night at the Waxworks Hall ! But it all ends up most unexpectedly and amusingly with the children finally triumphant.

THE MYSTERY OF THE HIDDEN HOUSE

The sixth adventure in the popular Mystery series about Larry, Fatty, Daisy, Pip, Bets and Buster–the Five Find-Outers and Dog.

When P.C. Goon's nephew, Ern, comes to Peterswood full of ideas of detecting, the Find-Outers think up a first-class mystery, complete with clues, and send both Ern and Mr Goon off on a wild-goose chase to Christmas Hill. But Ern loses his way and suddenly stumbles into what the Find-Outers are sure is a real mystery. Once again they are on the trail of a really thirlling mystery, but Fatty's love of disguises lands both him and Ern in a very tricky situation.